The Edge of Sanity

Chris Thomas

For Mum and Dad

Chapter 1

Sometime in early 2018

The Smart Man stared, cold and emotionless, at the wretched figure rocking back and forth on the scummy brown armchair in the middle of the room. As the single shadeless bulb hanging from the ceiling flickered, an old analogue clock on the wall ticked and a slow leak dripped from the roof onto the hard, bare concrete floor. Every few seconds, their dissonance became briefly synchronised into a single beat, before separating again into randomness.

Eventually, he spoke. "I'm waiting, Stephen."

The young man on the armchair shook his head, his claw-like fingers quivered as he raked them through his thick matted blond hair. He stared at the small packet of blue powder on the coffee table in front of the armchair, sweat pouring down his face, and he chewed on one of his filthy brown fingernails.

"You agreed, Stephen."

It had been two days since this man had forced his way into the dingy bedsit that Stephen shared with his equally drug-addled girlfriend Cherry. He had pointed a gun at Cherry's head as she lay in a semi-conscious stupor and very calmly told Stephen, "In this bag I'm holding is the latest batch of our new recreation enhancement, working title 'Drone Strike'. Personally, I don't like the name. I would have preferred something more light-hearted like 'Brainfood' or… 'Blue Candy Floss' or… 'Pointless scum-of-society brain-fucker'. But, hey, my organisation went with their name and so be it. It's just like the regular mephedrone-based crap that you two pump into your veins on a daily basis, except it's purer, almost super-charged if you will. One for the connoisseurs I'd say, which once it hits the streets would be way out of reach of the regular gutter-crawlers like you. But you, my friend, you have been chosen to be the lucky recipient of the very first bag."

*

Stephen stared at the man. His dark grey single breast suit, crisp blue shirt and yellow stripy tie, he looked more like an estate agent than a drug-pusher. Which messed with Stephen's brain. Usually at this point in his come-down, his ability to talk endless amounts of bullshit was legendary, but on this occasion his brain struggled to muster any sort of coherent response. Other than to stand up and make a break for the door. But the echoing click of a gun being cocked stopped him and, once he saw the black hole at the end of the barrel pointing straight at his face, he quickly changed his mind.

"Stephen," the man said, taking him aback somewhat since he had no idea how this man knew his name, "I would happily kill you. Then kill her. Then walk out of here leaving you both to rot in your own filth. So I suggest you sit back down, make yourself comfortable and we get to know each other a little better."

Stephen stood firm, one hand on the door, the other subconsciously raised in surrender. As he held his arm out, he subtly tried to lower the handle as slowly as he could manage.

The Smart Man sighed and replaced the barrel of the gun to the side of Cherry's exposed neck. He simply shrugged, enough for Stephen to release his grip on the door and go back and sit down.

"Why… why us?" Stephen stammered, his teeth grinding between every other word. "Why can't you just leave us alone? We've got nothing; we just sit here all day not bothering no one."

"Spare me," replied the Smart Man. "I'll attempt to keep this as simple as I can for you. We know that you buy copious amounts of mephedrone so we figured that you would be the perfect candidate to try our new deluxe version. In a couple of days, you will take it, I'll watch what happens, and then I'll walk out of your life and you will never see me again. Sorry, does that sound a little melodramatic?"

"What if I don't?"

"Then you die. And so does she."

Stephen sobbed quietly. He rubbed his hands over his face and through his hair, wishing he could make more sense of the situation than the final strains of his hit two hours earlier would allow. He was starting to wish he had snorted the whole lot in two massive lines. Instead he chose to dab it to make it last. At least he would still be vaguely buzzing when confronted with this nutter, rather than his current predicament of drowning into one huge paranoid shit-heap.

"So, okay," he said, snorting a huge lump of phlegm down the back of his throat. "Look, dude, it sounds fun, right? Just, you know, don't hurt me or Cherry. Okay? Dude?"

The Smart Man released the pistol and unbuttoned his jacket. Stephen caught sight of the very expensive-looking maroon satin lining as he replaced it in the inside pocket.

"Good boy. I'm glad that you have seen sense," the Smart Man said, making his way over to the armchair. He stood in front of Stephen, pulling his black leather gloves tighter onto his hands before swiftly bending down and grabbing Stephen by the throat. "And let's get one thing straight. If you call me 'dude' one more time, I will rip your throat out and stuff it down that tart's gob."

Stephen choked as the pressure caused the almost constant supply of mucus — the result of relentless daily snorting — to climb back up in his throat and he gasped for air.

After a few seconds, he was released and inhaled violently as he rubbed the skin on his neck which had already come up in a bruise.

The Smart Man stood up straight, clapped his hands and walked over towards the corner of the room to the small sink unit and filled up the kettle. "Don't know about you, Stephen, but I'm parched."

Stephen silently shook his head. "I won't last two days without a hit of something. I'll go fucking ape-shit. And Cherry, when Cherry comes round, she's always got the—"

But his sentence was cut off by a loud slam of the fridge door followed by a teacup smashing against the opposite wall. "Fucking actual hell!"

Stephen turned, startled, his heart which was already beating in the high nineties somewhere, suddenly went into overdrive.

"What is it with your type?" shouted the Smart Man. "I get that you turds of society have nothing better to do than fill yourselves full of whatever shit you can stick in a syringe and shove down your Jap's eye, but is it really beyond the scope of all human comprehension that you might, just might, have some fucking milk in the fridge?"

"S… s… sorry. There might be some vodka kicking around somewhere."

"Vodka? In tea? What kind of hideous shit are you taking, Stephen?"

"No," he said, his nervousness heightened by his over-the-top heartbeat. "I meant instead of tea. Not in it. I don't think we have any teabags either."

"I brought my own. We'll have to get rid of any alcohol. The drug must be taken sober and I don't want you sneaking some when I'm not looking. It'll be hard enough keeping you off the drugs for two days."

"I can't do nothing, not for that long. I said I'll go fucking mental."

"Yes, I vaguely remember you mentioning that a moment ago," said the Smart Man as he squeezed the teabag between his thumb and forefinger before discarding it on the floor. "Those are the rules I'm afraid. Our buyers are very particular during the testing phase that the pigs, sorry I mean guinea pigs, meaning you, aren't contaminated by any other, how shall we say, 'inferior product'."

The Smart Man stood back next to the sofa on which Cherry lay, quickly checked his watch and then retrieved the gun from inside his jacket which he pointed downwards at the girl's head as he took sips from the mug in his other hand.

"What now?" Stephen asked.

"We," replied the man between sips, "sit here and do nothing until precisely forty-seven hours and fifty-eight minutes from now."

*

And so it had been for the last two days. The three of them sat, or stood, in the same ten-foot square area of a fag-burnt, piss-stained rug. Cherry had experienced some mildly excitable delusions, one too many in fact, that the Smart Man had needed to deal with. Instead of lying on the sofa, she was sitting on the floor, legs bent and arms tied underneath her knees, and wrapped in as much electrical flex as the Smart Man could find. The filthy rag stuffed in her mouth at least gave some small respite from the, at times, incessant wailing.

Despite his relative freedom, Stephen felt little better. He had taken his last lot barely a couple of hours before this man had entered their life. Even with the reduced effects he experienced, hardened from years of prolonged usage, the massive speed-like buzz and euphoria of those magical couple of hours made every single one of the following hours feel like an entire week. But what bothered Stephen the most was how this man could stand up for two whole days, barely batting an eyelid and subsisting on nothing but tea, and still manage to be as scary as shit.

"You agreed, Stephen."

As he rocked back and forth in his armchair, he looked at Cherry sitting wide-eyed and vacant. Not that she was much help at any time, but he really wished that she could have done something to get them out of this mess. His whole body ached. And itched. His hair itched, his skin itched, even his blood itched. He knew that whatever that blue powder was in the bag, his ability to stop himself caning the lot was diminishing by the second.

He bent over the coffee table and tipped the blue powder out over the glass cover. Using a rust-specked double-edge razor blade, he chopped through the granules and separated it out into two even lines. Taking the rolled up fifty-pound note graciously handed to him by the Smart Man, Stephen snorted the two lines, one up each nostril, and slumped back into the armchair, squeezing and sniffing on both sides.

The Smart Man smiled, removed a stopwatch from his pocket, set it running and filmed Stephen on his iPhone. Stephen made the perfect candidate for the new product, his resistance was good, and other than Cherry there was probably no one in the world who gave the slightest shit about him. It would make for an interesting demonstration of the potential once the new drug hit the streets. If it did *him* in, the effects on the general casual drug taking community would be beautiful.

The back of his throat felt awful, as though someone had thrust steel wool up each nostril and pulled it back out of his mouth. On the plus side, the buzz was instantaneous.

"Mate, this is seriously fucking good. What is it again? Where can I get some? I tell you who would bloody love this. Cherry, that's who. Where is she anyway? Oh, she's over there. Hey, Cherry, you want to try some of this stuff, it's amazing. Dude, I fucking love your suit. Do you work out? I can't imagine you do living off nothing but tea. How much is this? Come on, dude, chill out, have a dab."

The Smart Man carried on filming and looked at the stopwatch. Stephen stood up from the armchair and stomped his way around the bedsit, every now and again a shoulder barging into the wall while the Smart Man side-stepped out of his way whenever he got close.

"Let's put some tunes on, bro. I could really do with some munchies. Have you got any crisps? It's quite hot in here."

As Stephen took off his top, the Smart Man leant down and whispered in Cherry's ear, "According to my stopwatch, in precisely ninety seconds, our little chemical alteration is going to kick in and then the real fun will begin."

After another minute and a half of Stephen practically running from one side of the room to the other, he suddenly slowed, bent double and clutched his head. It felt like a million fire ants running all over his body, and he scratched at his torso and head in a desperate attempt to rid his skin of the imaginary irritant.

"Bingo," said the Smart Man to Cherry. "You might want to brace yourself for this, it may sting a little."

*

Cherry rubbed her wrists as he untied the electrical flex and groaned as she stretched her arms and legs for the first time in many hours. She gazed up, groggily, to ask the Smart Man precisely what he was talking about, and as she stood up realised that he had simply vanished. Was this some sort of withdrawal side effect, was she imagining the whole thing? She rubbed her eyes again and glanced in all directions around the room.

Stephen's breathing became heavier, deeper and wheezy. Saliva flew from his mouth with every exhalation and he slowed down the scratching to reveal lines of blood running down from a chequerboard of deep red welts scattered across his ribs and chest. Cherry fixed on him, her scrambled brain incapable of coherent thought. His eyes burned into hers, not even the slightest hint of recognition.

Something in the corner of the room caught her eye, just over Stephen's shoulder, but before she had the time to process it, he leapt at her. The first she saw was the brown and blood-stained fingertips fast approaching her throat, and then behind them the empty, demonic eyes that had once belonged to the one person in the world that she cared about. Instinctively she clamped her eyes shut, only to be stunned back into alertness as her head thudded against the floor. The room spun and the blurry, double-edged form of her boyfriend darted across her field of vision. And then the pain kicked in.

The clawing at her skin, her face, her throat. She screamed for him to stop, as sharp stabs and scratches covered her entire body. He had seemingly acquired a super-human level of strength and her futile attempts to block his attack only drained her energy even quicker.

The last thing she saw was the empty black hole of Stephen's mouth and the blackened, chipped teeth about to encase her eye.

*

Out of the corner of the room, the small light emerged as the Smart Man stepped from the dark shadow, his phone still recording the events unfolding in front of him. At least half the noise in the room had disappeared and was replaced by the sound of lions around a deer carcass. He approached slowly, pausing to collect the razor blade from the coffee table and carefully held it by the edges between his gloved fore finger and thumb.

Stephen was oblivious to everything else in the room while Cherry had slipped into the blessing that was unconsciousness. The Smart Man slid up alongside them, before kneeling down and deftly slicing the razor blade through Stephen's right wrist. Stephen roused from his feasting, grasped his wrist and the arterial pressure sent blood arching halfway across the room.

As Stephen fell sideways off Cherry's mutilated body, the Smart Man knelt down once more, dodging the spray still coming from Stephen's wrist. He grabbed Stephen's wrists and carefully made another slice, followed by another and another, all running parallel up his arm.

As he jumped back out of the way, the Smart Man watched as Stephen writhed on the floor, the arcs of blood diminishing with each pulse until eventually there was silence. The Smart Man gave Stephen a kick on the foot to make sure, before standing over Cherry's body and panning the phone across her body, concentrating mainly on the grotesque injuries to her face.

Calmly, he pressed 'Stop' on the phone screen and dialled a number.

"It's me," he said. "That egghead of yours is a fucking genius. The merch worked an absolute treat. Get him to make as much of this stuff as humanly possible. We'll demo it on the next Members' Club. Let our clients see it in action. Then we'll rape them for every fucking penny they've got."

And with that he slid out of the door, closing it quietly behind him.

Chapter 2

Six months later

The low evening sun dazzled in the rear view mirror, forcing Smith to reach into the door pocket for his aviators. A scrap of paper flapped around the air vents in the middle of the dashboard, the crudely drawn map his only indication of where he was headed. This really was the arse-end of nowhere, even the satnav had stopped bothering to provide sensible directions a couple of miles back. As the countryside flashed past in a blur of green, the wind rushing in through the open sunroof drowned out the sound of 'Here I Go' from the *Dad Rocks!* CD playing in the car stereo. Detective Chief Inspector, or more precisely the former Detective Chief Inspector, Robert Smith had a score to settle.

It had been nine months since he had 'resigned' from the Metropolitan Police's Cyber Crime Unit. He had cited various official reasons for his departure, each one pulled straight from the Office Manager's Handbook of Buzzwords – 'work/life balance', 'experiencing a paradigm shift in his priorities', 'moving towards a more family-centric lifestyle'. All of which was utter bollocks. His position had become untenable. The Brotherhood of the Righteous had seen to it that not only was it a bad idea for him to make any attempt to bring them to justice, but that he had also lost his edge. The constant fear of being outed, the looks from his subordinates, but mainly the constant wondering of which one was watching his every move. His sharpness of mind had weakened, and he had begun to doubt his own ability. Not the best state to be in when you are trying to catch lowlifes, who by their very nature are experts at staying two steps ahead of the authorities. By resigning he had given himself at least the slightest chance of redemption. Redemption in his own eyes, closure perhaps. But almost certainly, revenge.

Eventually he came across a sign by the side of the road, a wooden placard hanging from a metal pole, swinging on its chains in the wind. He slowed to read the name carved and painted black then double-checked the crude map on his scrap of paper. One single long line the length of the piece with an arrow coming out to the left and the words 'Black Hollow Farm'. Despite the shittest map ever, this was finally it.

He turned into the driveway, nothing more than two shallow furrows about wheel-width apart periodically booby-trapped with potholes that would test the suspension of his Prius to breaking point.

After about two hundred metres of relentless bone shaking, the track mercifully turned into a smooth concrete courtyard. He scanned around the yard at the line-up of brand new cars; a couple of blacked-out Land Rovers, two blacked-out BMW 7 series saloons, a sparkling silver McLaren 650S spider, a bright pink Fiat 500. The physical manifestation of easily half a million pounds of very carefully laundered drug money. He pulled the car to stop somewhere near an empty barn.

Reaching into the glove compartment, he pulled out an envelope. He removed the small piece of card, double-checked the details and replaced it, before sealing the envelope properly. Despite going over it a million times in his head, he still needed some convincing that he was doing the right thing. Smith took a deep breath, it was shit-or-bust time. But no matter, soon he would be gone, beyond the reach of the Brotherhood and beyond the reach of the man he was about to meet.

Out of the main farmhouse strode a huge man, followed by another. Smith stepped out of the car and walked towards the men, wondering why a farm in the middle of nowhere needed two nightclub bouncers guarding the door. Just as he got within ten feet, they stood to the side as a third man came from the doorway. He was shorter by a clear foot, but very solidly built.

Out of the three, he was the one it would be least sensible to mess with. The scar running from his right eye to the base of his jaw, the carefully coiffured blond hair, the spider web tattoo on his neck, the Ramones T-shirt and sweatpants; none of his features seemed to fit belonging to one single person. But it was intimidating enough to make Smith stop dead.

"Nice bins, Maverick," said the man, his voice heavy with broad estuary English. "Welcome to my humble abode. I trust you found us with no problems, even in that shit heap?"

Smith removed his sunglasses, slightly embarrassed, disappointed with himself for letting this man get in the first swipe. He was already playing at a hostile away ground and could have done without taking a couple of put-downs early on.

He gathered his composure and approached the man with his hand outstretched. "Mr Slater. Thank you for seeing me. I know you're a busy man," he said in the best businessman-like and unflustered manner he could muster. "Plus, I found you fine, thanks. These two fat bastards seemingly have their own postcodes, so the satnav found its way no problem."

His attempt at a return of banter had failed miserably. The three men simply stared at him, faces as straight as someone who had just been told that their kitten had been run over by a tractor. Smith's heart pounded with the embarrassment as Slater withdrew his hand before Smith could shake it and his nervous attempt at posturing manifested in talking himself into an even deeper hole.

"So, it's a bit bumpy as you come in, isn't it? What did you do, pay a pissed up Irish pikey in a donkey jacket to lay you a new drive and that's what you got?"

"My grandma's Irish," replied Slater, stony-faced.

"Oh lovely. North or s… s…?" Smith began but then thought better of it. He swallowed hard as Slater and his mates continued their stare-down.

He decided it would simply be a wise move to not say anything at all, or at least stop trying to sound like a wise-guy. Not only was he alone, on Curtis Slater's very isolated farm, but he had just insulted his grandmother. Curtis Slater; a man who thought nothing of smashing in a person's kneecaps if they so much as accidentally nudged him slightly in a crowded pub. A man whose previous employee, Cramer McAllister, Smith had watched be tortured and murdered on The Red Room. But more importantly, who Smith had seen be called out, by name, by the Brotherhood as a future guest. Even though the Brotherhood had slipped away in the depths since the raid on the farmhouse, Smith knew that Slater was edgy. No one, not one single person, in their right mind had ever challenged Slater and lived to tell the tale. Somehow Slater had found out about it and was eager to make a pre-emptive strike in revenge for anyone daring to voice even the most flippant of threats. That was about as far as the two men had in common. Smith had spent the best part of half a decade trying to put men like Slater, and at times even Slater himself, away. But now he saw him as nothing more than a means to an end. Not in a 'if you can't beat them, join them' kind of way. More 'this guy's got tonnes of cash and I'll happily whore myself to lay my hands on some of it, rather than rely on the pitiful police pension' kind of way.

"Anyway, enough of the pleasantries," continued Slater, breaking the slightly awkward silence, and gesturing for Smith to follow him inside. "I believe you have something for me?"

Smith followed, trying to avoid any intimidating eye contact with the bouncers who parted, forcing him to walk between the barely large enough gap they had made. He walked after Slater, periodically ducking to avoid the low wooden beams in what was presumably the oldest part of the farmhouse.

"For crying out loud, will you put some proper fucking clothes on, woman? You are not, I repeat not, going out like that!" Slater shouted into one of the rooms as they passed it. "I don't know, kids these days. They reach eighteen and think they rule the fucking world."

Smith peered into the room as he reached the doorway to see a young girl lying on a leather sofa wearing tiny denim hot pants and a tight white crop top, tapping away on her tablet. He just caught the end of a middle finger salute as she lowered her hand and carried on swiping away at the screen on her lap.

"That explains the pink car," said Smith. "I thought it belonged to one of these guys."

Slater stopped, paused for a minute, before turning round in the corridor and squaring up to Smith. "Will you stop trying to be funny? Because you're not. I'm not in the fucking mood for bent coppers trying to be my mate, and the next hilarious quip that comes out your mouth may well be your last. Got it?"

Smith nodded silently.

"Good boy."

Slater carried on down the hallway as Smith paused briefly to gather his thoughts before a sharp shove in his back prompted him to move. At the end of the hallway, Slater arrived at a set of double doors, pressed some numbers on the keypad and went inside. Smith followed and gazed around the office more befitting the CEO of an investment bank than that of a criminal. The immense oak desk with green leather writing surface, the huge padded maroon leather chair, a bank of three computer monitors, a row of photo frames. On the walls were numerous photographs of Slater with celebrities. B-list celebrities though: soap stars, boxers, lower league footballers, that kind of thing. Clearly, Slater saw himself as some sort of celebrity gangster, enjoying the limelight with the types of famous people who would show up to the opening of a book.

Slater sat down behind the desk and motioned for Smith to sit. He assumed that they had planned for his visit by finding the flimsiest, wobbliest, plastic chair they could on the whole farm. The comfort of this particular guest clearly not high on their agenda. In fact, the more uncomfortable they could make him the better. Despite this, Smith sat as upright as he could, although it was difficult not to feel like a schoolboy waiting patiently for his punishment from the headmaster.

Slater's face glowed, reflecting the light from the monitors as his PC came to life. He slid the mouse across the desk, click a few screens, and begun reading some emails. Smith waited patiently.

Just get the money, and then disappear. He could deal with Slater's mind games. It wasn't as if he was the only low-life criminal Smith had ever had to deal with in the past, probably not even the worst. He would indulge him his little power play.

"For fuck's sake, the useless wankers!" shouted Slater, grabbing the cordless handset from his ludicrously large phone cradle sitting next to the monitor. Presumably the person at the other end of the line knew precisely who was calling, since Slater felt no need to introduce himself and just got on with the job of bollocking. "How the hell have they lost another one…? Right… uh-huh… uh-huh… I couldn't give a fuck. If they didn't use these cheap Eastern European lorry drivers, they wouldn't get stuck at customs so much. Fuck me, have I got to do all the bloody thinking around here…? Yeah? Well, you tell Davros or Stavros, or whatever the hell his name is, from me, that if another one of my shipments ends up being incinerated, he'll end up with a metal rod rammed up his arse, rotating very slowly on the spit at the local Abra-Kebabra. And so will his kids."

The phone almost shattered as he slammed the handset down. Smith had always known that the legitimate shipping company of which Slater was the managing director was just a front for his drug trafficking business. But he ran it so well that it had always been impossible to pin anything on him. Even when his supply chain was interrupted, as it appeared to have just been, no one in their right mind was going to shop him to the authorities, especially when said lorry had enough legitimate pallets of cuddly toys and Chinese plastic tat all addressed to Slater's business to make the front seem water-tight. After a minute or so of silence punctuated by Slater's breathing slowly calming down, Smith decided it was time.

"Problems, Mr Slater?"

"Sorry, Detective Chief Inspector. I forgot you were here. Nothing I can't handle."

"Of course. I doubt there's very much that you can't handle."

"Spare me the brown-nosing, Smith," Slater said as he turned away from the monitors, put the mouse in its charging base, and stared Smith square in the eyes. "Now, tell me what you know about this Brotherhood of the Righteous."

Smith shifted in his chair as though making himself comfortable before commencing a lengthy anecdote about his holiday. "I don't know much about them."

"Bollocks."

"It's true. Certainly I have no idea who they actually are. What I do know is that they have an inhuman amount of financial resources. If you're going to be scared of anything, it should be that."

"I'm not exactly short of money. And why the hell should I be scared of a bunch of computer geeks?"

"They had ex-Secret Service personnel on their payroll, the most sophisticated technology and they had balls the size of Big Ben. You don't get away with an operation like theirs, for as long as they did, without having something. Look what they did to McAllister — your go-to thug, terroriser of drug-dealers — and they not only took him without anyone, you for instance, noticing, but they humiliated him online and submitted him to the type of punishment even he would be scared of dishing out. I would have said that the very fact they called you out as a possible guest should make you scared. Very. Fucking. Scared."

Slater pressed his index fingers in a steeple shape against his lips as he contemplated what he was listening to. Smith reckoned that he had never had to consider being scared of anyone.

"So why should I pay you for anything? If you don't know who they are then you are next to useless as far as I am concerned," he said, reaching for the mouse. Perhaps some more interesting emails had come in.

"Hang on," Smith said, leaning forward with a hand outstretched. "Like I say, I don't know precisely who they are. They contacted me and offered me a lot of money to be a silent part of their group. Their 'man on the inside' so to speak. To be honest, I thought that what they were doing was good. One of the worst things about being a copper, when you still give a shit that is, is watching the criminals you fought so hard to bring down laugh at you as they're handed a six month stretch in an open prison, and then complain that they don't have a fast enough internet to play their PlayStation games online. It was quite satisfying to watch their work. Then for some reason they got a bit twitchy. So in order to nail me to the floor, they tricked me into installing some files on my computer."

"Files?"

"Yep. I'm sure you can guess the type. It pretty much meant that if I didn't work to cover their activities, I could be exposed. I knew they had someone else in there, closer to them than I was, watching me. I investigated everyone in my team and there was only one person who I thought it could be, but whatever background checks I did they always came up blank. They had covered every track. In the end, covering up the final episode was the last straw and I needed an excuse to get out of there."

"So you came to see me?"

"I figured we could be of mutual benefit to each other."

"Yeah, I'm still struggling to see that myself. I understand how one part of the transaction works — I pay you a quarter of a mil. But I don't see the benefit coming back in my direction."

"I've got an address. It won't give you them directly, but I'm sure that with your very persuasive methods, it will lead you to them."

"For two hundred and fifty grand?"

"I could always wait for them to contact me and tell them where you live, if they don't already know."

"Are you threatening me?" asked Slater, his voice more menacing than usual.

"No, of course not," replied Smith, quickly, suddenly not wanting to push his luck. "Okay, call it two hundred. That's nothing to a man of your means, I'll be long gone, and you can deal with the problem at your leisure."

Slater sat back in his chair, swivelling from side-to-side. After a short while he picked up the mouse and turned to the monitors. "Okay, Smith, deal. Where am I paying this to?"

Smith allowed himself a small sigh of relief and pulled a piece of paper from his back pocket. "I've set up an escrow account for you to transfer the funds into. That way it's harder for either of us to be traced."

"Thanks. I know how moving money works, Smith."

"Of course, how silly of me. There's the website to put your details into. It's already linked to the escrow. Then you ring that phone number there, give them the authorisation code next to it, and then they'll want to speak to me. I provide my code and they'll give you a one-time password that you put back into the website. Then you hit the 'go' button and we're done."

Slater took the piece of paper and typed the overly long URL into his browser. "Surprised you didn't want Bitcoins," he said without moving his eyes from the screen, prompting an ironic snigger from Smith.

"I've got the number in my phone," said Smith, leaning over to pass his phone to Slater.

"No fucking chance. We use my line. It's dedicated. No one traces this." He dialled the number into the keypad and picking up the handset. "Hello, sweetheart. I would like to authorise a wire transfer please… Two hundred and fifty thousand pounds please…"

"Really? Thank you, Mr Slater," said Smith, suddenly acting like a kid being given an extra scoop of ice cream.

"You've been a good boy… No, sorry, not you, sweetheart… The authorisation code is 5C9G089X311… Yes, he's here." Slater passed the handset to Smith.

"Hello, sir?"

"Yes."

"If I could just take your authorisation code, please, sir."

"Certainly. It's 1S6J5D8UF235. Thank you."

He handed the phone back to Slater who listened and typed on the keyboard as the passcode was read out. "Thank you very much, sweetheart."

He hung up the phone and pressed the 'enter' key emphatically. Smith leant forward to try to see what had happened. "Is that it? Did it go through?"

But Slater had already stood up and was walking back around the front of the desk. "Of course, all done. What are you going to spend your two fifty k on then, Smithy boy?"

Smith found Slater's arm on his shoulder in some sort of bizarrely reassuring man hug.

"Oh, er, great thanks. I don't know, probably a nice little place in Spain, maybe even further away like South America," he replied, standing to his feet and placing an equally friendly arm around Slater's waist.

"That's great. I know a lot of people in South America. And Spain for that matter. And if I find out that you have stiffed me with this information, you had better hope that you have spent your money wisely enough to keep you hidden from even your own mother. Because I will come and find you and I will kill you. Oh, we nearly forgot. The address please."

Smith took the envelope from his jacket pocket and handed it to Slater before walking out of the room. "We're done, I think."

*

Slater followed Smith through the house and out into the courtyard and watched him climb into his car. As he stood by the front door, he felt an arm around his own shoulders as his daughter rested her head on his shoulder.

"Do you have to keep having me pretend to be banks? It's doing my head in."

"Come on, sweetheart, you're so bloody good at it."

"Did he fall for it?"

"Like a charm. They can never resist you can they?"

"Speaking of which. Can I borrow the McLaren? I've got to go get my hair done."

"Ha, no fucking chance. Don't think you can start taking liberties with me young lady."

With a huff and general teenage strop, the girl let go of her dad and stormed inside. Slater looked at the envelope before opening it. He pulled out the piece of paper inside. *Pete Harris, The Lookout Guest House, Ventnor, Isle of Wight.*

He folded it up and put it back in the envelope.

"Any use, boss?" asked one of the large associates as Slater went back into the house.

"Very. Must be my lucky day today. Not only do I get Smith handing me the Brotherhood on a plate, but I finally receive my invitation to the biggest party in town."

He took a small cardboard box from the sideboard and opened it up. Inside, resting regally on the velvet interior was a solid silver piece of metal, no bigger than a credit card. Engraved on it were the words *Your invitation to the Members' Area. We look forward to seeing you at Majestic Road. Yours, The Majestic 12.*

"This is the big time, my friend. They don't just hand these out to anybody. It was easier getting my membership to the Wisley. Conveniently, there is a Members' Area on tonight. I think it's time to see what all the fuss is about."

*

Smith pulled out onto the main road and sped off down the winding lane. His mind buzzed with thoughts of his new life. Every now and again doubts sprung in. Did Slater actually make the payment? Was he being traced? No point worrying about it. Just get as far away from here as possible. Hide up somewhere and sort all his affairs, his new wealth. Then just stick a pin in a map of the world and see where it takes him.

As his mind wandered, he didn't realise his own speed. A bend rushed towards him. As the car seemed as though it was going to flip, he saw the oncoming delivery lorry. He pressed down hard on the brake pedal. Nothing. He panicked and pressed his foot again. As the lorry bore down on him, his stamping on the pedal became frantic. The loud air horn of the lorry disoriented him further and he swung the steering wheel to avoid it. This time the car did flip and careered through the hedge, rolling several times down the steep bank the other side.

Eventually it rolled to a stop at the bottom of a small ditch before exploding into flames.

The driver of the lorry had stopped and climbed down the ditch. He could hear Smith's cries and saw him reaching out of the window in a desperate attempt for help. Pulling out his mobile, the lorry driver dialled, all the time watching Smith.

"It's done," the man said before placing the phone back in his pocket and walking away, the sound of Smith's screams cutting through the air.

Chapter 3

The reception bell rang at The Lookout guest house, rousing Pete Harris from his attempted afternoon siesta. He rubbed his eyes, as the bell continued its single, lengthy, stuck-in-its-housing chime. As he made his way from the back room to the reception, he was greeted by his guests even before he saw them.

"Hello?" shouted a broad American accent, Deep South by the sound of it, cutting through the relaxed tranquil of the quiet guest house. "Where in the goddamn hell is everyone?"

"Calm down, honey," came the equally broad, but slightly gentler voice of his female companion. "I'm sure someone will be along shortly."

"Shortly? I've already been waiting here nearly a whole goddamn minute. What is it with these people?"

"Good afternoon, sir," said Pete quickly as he slid in behind the reception. "My apologies, that bell does have a tendency to get stuck."

"It's not stuck, I'm—" replied the man, finally removing his finger from the button, but being cut off before he was able to finish his rather predictable reply.

"You must be Mr Babcock," interrupted Pete. "Welcome to The Lookout. We're always delighted to welcome our Atlantic cousins. Especially when we can assist in emergencies such as yours."

"That's right. Randy Babcock. This is my wife, Petunia. Don't think we're here out of choice. We originally booked at the Seaview down the road. Turns out the old biddy who owns it has been dead for at least a month and this was the only place on the island with any room. All I can say is from what I've seen of the

Island of Wight so far, this had better be the best goddamn motel I've ever stayed in. Wouldn't have chosen it myself. In fact I can't say I've seen anything that makes me want to stay here longer than a night. What's with that boat? Fifty minutes to get across the English Ocean? Why I could piss from one side to the other. And that rental car they gave me? I could fit the whole goddamn thing in the trunk of my car back home. We barely fit all our cases in the back."

"Okay, Mr Babcock. I will do my very best to make your stay in our particular corner of the *Isle* of Wight a pleasant one. If I could take a photocopy of your passports please, just for our records."

The man handed his passports over to Pete, who took them out the back to photocopy. As he waited for the printer to make the copies, he overheard the couple speaking.

"Jeez, honey, please give them a chance. You can't expect everything to be as good as it is back home."

"Here we go, Mr Babcock. They're very new, only issued a couple of weeks ago. Is this your first time away from the States?"

"Sure is. I'm already wishing I hadn't left. This was all her idea."

"I wanted to see the giant garlic farm," she said longingly.

"What is it with you Brits and garlic? And fish and chips. They don't even look like chips, more like fries."

Pete stifled a laugh. It was rare for his guest house to receive any visitors from the United States, but secretly he hoped that any future ones would be as funny as these two.

"Madam, the giant garlic farm is something to behold. Here are your keys. You are in room sixteen. Go down the hallway, turn left up the stairs and it's just on the left."

Mr Babcock grabbed the keys from the desk. "Right, bring me up a bourbon with ice in five minutes. She'll have a Malibu and coke, no ice. We'll take our evening dinner at nineteen hundred hours and if you could have a copy of the Washington Post or USA Today left outside the door in the morning."

Pete took a deep breath and nodded. As the couple collected their suitcases and turned to leave, Pete shouted out to them, "Just so you know, sir, we don't do Waldorf salad."

"Why in the hell would I want a Waldorf salad?" asked Mr Babcock.

"Oh, no reason. Just letting you know in case."

"Ok, right," replied Mr Babcock. "C'mon dear, let's get the hell out of here."

Pete waited until he heard the footsteps clear the top of the stairs and let out the pent up laughter. He continued chuckling to himself as he sat, head down, filling out the paperwork for his latest visitors. This place had been his home for the last year, the sea air, the quiet close-knit community, being his own boss. It was a million miles away from the seedy, violent, disturbing world that he used to be part of in his work at the Cyber Crimes Unit in London.

Nowadays, the only person he had to answer to was himself. And his eleven-year-old daughter Olivia. It was quiet, dull, and frankly tedious. Perfect for bringing her up, away from the city and the people who inhabited it. He often wondered how many people on the island still didn't have a mobile phone, let alone the Internet. He was fairly certain that none of them had ever heard of the dark web. Except him. And he liked to 'keep his eye in' as he called it.

As he copied the details from his new guests' passports onto his guest form, the quiet was again shattered by the bell. "Yes, Mr Babcock?"

"Do I look like Mr Babcock?"

Pete glanced up. The gentle, familiar voice shaking him instantly from his still half-asleep daydreaming.

"Hello, stranger," said Grace Brooks as he stood up and ran around the front of the desk faster than she could say any more.

"Grace, I didn't know you were coming," he said in flustered mixture of surprise and excitement as the two embraced in a hug of friends who had not seen each other for months. "I didn't see your name on the reservation system. Did you book with one of those online travel brokers again? I'm not sure I've got any rooms left."

*

Grace had missed Pete's sarcasm and overwhelming sense of his own importance. "Of course you've got room. No one ever stays here do they? Apart from those charming Americans that came in before. They were lucky to get a room were they?"

"Okay, fine," said Pete, finally releasing the hug. "True, it's not going great. But truth be told, I prefer it when there are no guests."

"So I can stay then?"

"I suppose so. Just don't annoy the Yanks, they seem quite temperamental."

Chapter 4

One by one, the video feeds came online, illuminating the huge bank of monitors in the server room like a newsroom control desk. An array of dials, pipes, gauges sat on the wall behind, echoes from the past and long since defunct. The only colour breaking through the monotony of grey was a few valve wheels, still with flecks of red paint. Each screen showed the crackly, silhouetted figures of the viewers, their forms obscured by the filtering software. This was the assurance granted to the very privileged clientele that privacy and discretion was of the utmost importance, while still maintaining an air of face-to-face courtesy.

Swivelling impatiently in a large leather executive chair at the control desk, the Smart Man watched intently as the twelve guest 'slots' on the master screen filled with names.

"Five minutes, sir," came the voice behind him.

"Yes, I know," he replied, continuing to stare at the main screen. Eight names filled up. Nine. Ten. "Come on, you fuckers." Eleven.

The assistant watched silently, waiting. The Smart Man had a habit of 'over-reacting', to put it mildly, especially as this was his special invite that they were waiting on. The seasoned veterans were all there. The Velasquez Cartel from Columbia, the Gaffer Crew from Johannesburg, the Chamorro Contratistas from Nicaragua. The Smart Man knew them all. He liked to consider that they came for the vast array of narcotics on offer, but they stayed for the entertainment. They were special and they knew it. The Smart Man cared not for their ideals, their reputations, or their notoriety. What he did care for was their influence, their power and most of all, their cold hard cash. The reach of this project was truly global. The path to enlightenment had begun.

*

"Get that fucking thing logged on!" shouted Slater. "Now!"

Curtis Slater marched up and down his office, stopping briefly at his drinks cabinet to refill his glass.

"It's your Internet connection," said the figure sat at his desk frantically hammering the keyboard for any signs of life. "You're so far out in the sticks, even dedicated fibre can be a little temperamental. Just be patient, please. I'm doing my best."

Slater cupped his glass in one hand, pointing his finger at the large flat circular bottle in his other. "Do you know what this is?"

"Haven't got a clue."

"It is a Remy Martin Louis XIII cognac, one of the finest cognacs ever produced. This bottle is a jeroboam, or three litres to an imbecile like you. Every time I pour a shot into this glass, it costs me precisely three hundred and fifty pounds. I've drunk almost a grand's worth of the finest French alcopop in the time it's taken you to fart around logging on to what is currently my single greatest opportunity to become untouchable on a massive scale. And do you know how I came to afford such exquisite pleasures as this?"

"I'm fairly certain I know exactly—"

"By not putting up with shit from the likes of mouthy little nerd wankers like you, that's how! It just makes me sick how much honest, hard-grafting, proper, yes proper businessmen like me have to rely on geeks like you just to stay up to date. I mean, let's be honest here, you were the sort of bloke who, when I was at school, I would spend most lunchtimes shoving their head down the bog and flushing it, before making you pay me money as a thank you. And now you lot rule the world. Yet why is it that when I buy a book for my dear old dad on World War Two history on Amazon, I then get an email where their 'special recommendation' for me is a book called *Collectible Spoons of the Third Reich*. Collectible fucking spoons, I mean what the… And this guy's like the richest man in the world now and he can't even recommend me a decent product. Then here I am working my arse off, giving people exactly what they want and yet still I get hounded by the Inland Revenue. I'm paying you a fuck tonne of money to not be shit at something I was told you are the best at, but all I can see from here is that you—"

"Are you quite finished?"

"No I'm fucking not. Wait… what? Why?"

"We're in."

Slater ran around the other side of his desk, grabbed the man by the arm and pulled him violently out of the chair. He took a hundred-pound gulp of cognac from one hand, his other slamming the mouse around the desk as he tried to focus on which of the four monitors the cursor was.

"It's not encrypted," said Slater. "What the fuck are you trying to do to me, boy?"

"I was just about to do that when you politely asked me to move," came the reply as he picked himself up off the floor. "Just click on the webcam icon on the task bar, it's already configured with the software."

Slater sunk back into the huge leather armchair and rested his glass on the arm. "This is it. The world won't know what's fucking hit it when I'm done."

With that, he clicked on the large flashing sign in the middle of the screen.

Welcome to Majestic Road. Enlightenment Awaits.

*

The final guest slot on the main screen suddenly filled up.

CS Associates

"About bloody time," said the Smart Man. "Call the Professor." He stood up from the chair, handing control of the monitors to his assistant. He grabbed his suit jacket and swept it around his back like a superhero cape, before buttoning it up the front and walking out of the control room.

The metallic echoes of the Smart Man's footsteps quietened as he made his way down the service ramp. Once he was gone, the assistant picked up a walkie-talkie from the desk. "Professor, our guests are ready for you. Cameras are rolling. Showtime in ninety seconds."

Just before he arrived at the entrance to the set, the Smart Man stopped and turned into a small room, previously the office belonging to a supervisor of some sort. A figure stood at the end of the room, dressed in a heavy black ankle-length tunic with a faint green tinge. Two thick black rubber gloves carefully placed a wide-brimmed waxed leather hat over a white mask, and he stood adjusting it in a cracked shard of mirror hanging from the wall.

The Smart Man always found this man fascinating, albeit his choice of garment for the demonstrations a little creepy. An exquisite mind in the rather niche field of designer narcotics coupled with a downright brutal psychoticism. The archetypal evil genius, he would have made Shirō Ishii quake with fear. Together their mutual interests had found a perfect harmony.

"Professor?" he asked respectfully. "It's time to begin."

The Professor turned sharply to face him, the long beak-like protrusion of his plague doctor mask hiding all facial features.

He clapped his hands together in an overly flamboyant demonstration of excitement, the heavy rubber dampening any sound. "Oh such levity awaits, my friend. Such levity. I've unlocked the very essence of our primordial being. The human race is in for one big surprise. This is going to be quite simply… majestic!"

As the Professor walked out of the room, the Smart Man stood to one side letting him pass, catching his own reflection in the small disc of glass covering the eye hole. Past it, he saw the bright blue iris surrounded by streaks of blood shot, and he wondered just what trace of humanity remained behind it. The less the better, he hoped.

"Come, my friend, the pigs are waiting," he called back over his shoulder.

*

Finally, the black screen on Slater's monitor filled with colour and the psychedelic synthesiser music blasted out of the speakers.

"What the hell is this?" shouted Slater, slamming his glass down on the desk, and fumbling for the volume control on the speaker.

"I think it's Baba O'Reilly," replied Terence, the heavy set bouncer-type associate who had replaced the rather nervous I.T. technician who was glad to leave Slater's presence.

"I know what fucking song it is," replied Slater as he relaxed back in his chair. "This is supposed to be a business site, not some jaunty Disney shit. It is a classic though. I think we need to go bigger."

He pressed a button on the screen and turned his chair to face the enormous LCD television mounted on the chimney breast at the side of the room. With it, the surround sound kicked in and the whole room shook like it was heavy metal night at the local Bier Keller. He switched the webcam to the television-mounted one, collected his tablet that played the website and moved into the leather recliner directly in front.

As the first guitar power-chord rang through the room, the light in the studio came up and stood in the middle of a round spotlight was the Professor. Terence shifted uneasily in his seat as the Professor spoke to the camera.

> "As you can see on your screen here, your Professor does appear.
> When to the guinea pigs he's called, who have society appalled.
> My hat, my cloak of fashion old, are made of oilcloth, harsh and cold.
> My mask with glasses is designed, its bill with antidote all lined,
> That foulsome air may do no harm, or cause this doctor man alarm.
> This powder blue in syringe does show, my genius wherever I go."

Slater and Terence sat opened mouthed as they watched the spectacle unfolding on the screen. The amount of work taken to arrive here had exhausted Slater. He wasn't used to being forced to play by other people's rules. When he heard about the opportunities that existed in this very exclusive playground, he would, just once, accept being the underdog. Follow someone else's instructions. And if it hadn't been for the exceptionally gifted computer geek whose family he had threatened to have burned alive in their beds should he fail to crack the code, would probably still be on the outside begging to come inside.

But this he was not expecting. His usual business associates in the world of lifestyle supplements looked like him, dressed like him, spoke like him. There was no pantomime, no theatrics. You went in, got the job done, and got out as quickly as possible. Maybe that wasn't entirely true. There was an inhuman amount of posturing, testosterone-laden displays of manliness and endless care taken to avoid 'disrespecting' the opposite party. But a crazy, squeaky-voiced character, dressed as a plague doctor and talking in rhymes was quite frankly beyond a joke as far as Slater was concerned. And taking liberties with his time. The weeks of hard graft to get to this point were slowly beginning to seem like an utter waste of time.

"This is a fucking joke!" shouted Slater, pointing the controller at the screen. "They've already wasted two weeks of my life, I'm not about to let them waste more."

"Boss, wait!" replied Terence. "Look, something else is happening."

Slater rested the remote on the arm of his chair and watched as the screen filled with light. In front of the Professor were two figures strapped to large wooden chairs. Behind him, a white screen appeared behind which another figure sat, silhouetted as the bright light shone on it.

"My friends," came the voice from behind the screen, "welcome… to Majestic Road. Once again, we have gathered the cream of the supply chain industry to do business. All around the world our merchandise finds its way onto the street thanks to you. And what better way to prove to you the effectiveness of what you are buying, than to demonstrate it. Our way of thanking you once again for your custom. Our seal of approval, a quality assurance stamp if you will. Tonight's product is an absolute belter. I had the pleasure of seeing it in action with my own eyes. Tonight, the esteemed Professor and I will talk you through its development and you will bear witness to its utterly unbelievable effects."

Chapter 5

Slater relaxed back in the chair to watch and took a sip of cognac. "This is still bullshit. I'd rather just find out what they're selling, buy it, and fuck off. I don't trust this Internet streaming. Don't trust it at all."

"I'm sure it's fine, boss. Your boy seemed more than at home on the deep web. Plus, it's very much in his interests to make sure that no one traces us. And these people's. They're not exactly conspicuous. This level of showmanship is bound to attract a shit load of attention unless they know what they're doing. See what they do, might be interesting. Entertaining, if nothing else."

"Okay, ladies and gentlemen. Tonight's chair-bound pigs are fresh from the Chapman Road doss house in Nottingham town centre. It's boyfriend and girlfriend, Brian and Martha," continued the Smart Man.

The camera panned across the warehouse to two sturdy wooden chairs bolted to the floor. Strapped in each sat a blindfolded figure straining against the thick leather straps around their wrists and ankles. They wore filthy, baggy clothes, their long greasy hair clinging to their sweat-sticky faces. As the young man clenched both fists and teeth, he fought in vain against the restraints, while she simply sat, her shoulders rising and falling as the fear clearly sent her breathing into overdrive. Pristine white vests and shorts accentuated the black filth that clung to their skin and nails.

"What we have for you tonight is the very latest advancement in the mephedrone family of lifestyle accessories. Our resident genius over there has not only managed to basically send serotonin levels through the roof, but spectacularly mess with the dopamine pathways as well. In addition, *in addition* you heard me correctly, he has done it in such a way that the full-scale effect that we are all looking at kicks in at precisely the same time with each dose. Ladies and gentlemen, Professor Black and I are proud to introduce for your viewing pleasure – Brainfood."

Black went over to a small table to the side of the two chairs and removed a large cloth covering various metal dishes. The camera zoomed in on the first one as he held it up, and poked his finger around to show the bright blue sand-like substance it contained. He then pulled up a large glass syringe from a lower shelf and placed it on the table next to the bowls.

"As a chemist of such international renown said, a spoonful of water helps the Brainfood go down."

He poured a scoop of the blue powder into a bowl and added some water. The mixture fizzed gently as he stirred it using a glass stirrer.

"From metal to glass, the journey begins.

Then into the veins of our guinea pig twins."

He pulled the metal plunger of the syringe slowly, carefully filling the glass vial to precisely 80ml before giving it a few small flicks. An arc of liquid shot from the opening, adding to the theatrics, as he walked around to the side of Brian. A very neat, very cleanly dressed cannula dangled to the side of his arm.

"So what the Professor is going to do now is administer a standard dose of Brainfood, 20ml, into our pig Brian. The drug works very much in the same vein, if you'll pardon the pun, to mephedrone. You people will probably know it better as M-Cat or Bath Salts. But our product is a much cleaner recipe. It takes all the good stuff from that wonderful plant Khat, mixes it with a little dichloromethane and then some methyl-ethyl-something-or-other. Then the Professor combines the lot with his very own secret recipe of ten herbs and spices to create this wonderful product that you see before you. It'll mess with the dopamine pathways, the serotonin re-uptakers, and a whole bunch of other good stuff."

Just then a message appeared along the bottom banner on Slater's screen.

Just get on with it, hombre

"Ha, couldn't have put it better myself," said Slater. "Couldn't give the slightest flying fuck why or how it does whatever it does."

"Okay, Mr Velasquez," said the Smart Man. "My apologies. Of course, you don't want a chemistry lesson. You just want to see what it does. Professor?"

Black had already begun administering the syringe into the cannula. Very slowly, carefully watching from close up to make sure that the precise 20ml dose went in before pulling the blindfold off Brian's head.

Brian's body became noticeably limper as if all the tension in his muscles released. He put his head back against the hard wooden chair, tracking the coldness of the drug as it washed up his arm and into his shoulder.

"For the sake of scientific accuracy, it is important that we compare across the genders so if you would…"

Martha shuddered as the cold rubber glove rested on her wrist. She shook in the chair as much as the restraints would allow, a vain attempt to fight against what was about to happen.

The Professor took hold of the cannula and again injected a very carefully measured dose into Martha's arm. She screamed and shook her head violently before slumping forward and she sobbed uncontrollably.

"For the record," continued the Smart Man, "these two have been CT for the last seventy-two hours, and they have a well-established history of using many different drugs. As far as demonstrations go, we couldn't have picked two better candidates. The early stages from what we would classify as a 'regular dose' will be very enjoyable to these two wasters. See."

The camera centred on Brian who was laughing uncontrollably and talking crap.

"Martha, Martha," he shouted. "Oi, Martha open your fucking ears. Have you tried this stuff? It's amazing. We've hit the big time here, sexy. No going back to that cheap shit we usually have. I'm going to have to tell Pierre about this, he'll love it. I'll get him to get you some as well if you like. Oi, mate, got any more of this? It's wicked, Martha. If it weren't for this belts, I'd come over there and give you a bloody good seeing to."

"Brian, what's happening," responded Martha in a drowsy drool. "I feel like I'm floating on a sea of a million marshmallows. Do you think Pierre could get us some of this? It's making me want to take all my clothes off and run around playing hopscotch. Excuse me, mister, I want some more."

"Ah more," interrupted the Smart Man. "That's what makes this drug so utterly brilliant. It's just so very moreish, a bit like Pringles. To the pointless dregs of society, like these two, they can't get enough. And the beauty of it is it's almost instant."

Another message on the screen.

Seems just like any other drug we sell day in day out.
"Well, it isn't," snapped the Smart Man at his screen. "Professor, if you could."
The Professor administered another 20ml dose into the two cannulas.
"Tweedledum and Tweedledee, they don't need their eyes to see. My 'Brainfood' helps their minds expand, and very soon they'll understand.
That deep within the human soul, lies a primeval black hole.
Primitive urges buried deep, instincts until now asleep.
Says Tweedledee to Tweedledum, I want to see what we'll become.
Professor Black, please wait no longer, let your Brainfood make us stronger.
In case our viewers are suspicious, this Brainfood really is delicious.
But here's what you have paid to see, the cleansing of society.
As we set free their inner beast, upon the human flesh to feast.
I hope you do enjoy the show. Time is up, pigs. Let 'em go."

"Time to undo the restraints, I think, Professor. And bring in our special guest."

The Professor released the leather straps from around their wrists and ankles. He stood back and folded his arms, watching from a few yards away as his creation took hold. As he did so, a large metal cage, easily four metres square, lowered down from the ceiling, covering the two chairs.

From off stage, two masked assistants dragged a man, his arms bound by gaffer tape at the wrists, across the set floor. The Professor opened a door in the side of the cage. As the assistants went to throw the man into the cage, the Professor put out his hand, stopping the man in the chest, and raised his index finger.

"Such levity awaits, my dear man. Such levity."

With that, he ripped the gaffer tape off the man's mouth and sliced through the wrist bindings with a Swiss army knife. Before the man could respond or attempt to escape, he was shoved with a jolt into the cage, where he fell to the floor, turning just in time to see the door slam shut behind him and a large chain and padlock secure it.

"Our special guest tonight comes courtesy of Mr Velasquez. He won the honours at our previous episode with an immense order for five million pounds' worth of Professor Black's super-saturated LSD product that is currently freaking out his clientele in sunny Bogota. It's Mr Velasquez's former favourite enforcer, Hernando Rodriguez. For anyone who is interested, Hernando here not only tried to turn Velasquez over to the local police chief, but he also informed all of Velasquez's business secrets to his rival gang, the Grupo Garcia. You'd think he would have realised that the police chief was Mr Velasquez's brother-in-law's cousin, the dickhead. But he didn't and now he is here. Enjoy the show, Mr Velasquez."

Rodriguez gripped the bars of the cage, shaking for all his worth. He kicked the padlock in an attempt to break the chain, but it was no use.

After a few minutes of filming Brian and Martha talking mindless gibberish to their guest, seemingly oblivious to their new enclosure, Slater and the rest of the viewers watched as their demeanours changed. Jovial, excited, boisterous was morphing into a more subdued thousand-yard stare, snorting air in through their nose and out through gritted teeth. Rodriguez noticed too, and his attempt to break free of the cage became ever more frantic. Their fists clenched and toes turned up, muscles rigid as though in cramp. Still sat down, their faces reddened and their hands clawed over their bodies, scratching chunks of skin under their nails, and pulling out handfuls of hair in large clumps.

"Everyone ready?" asked the Smart Man, knowing he had everyone's attention behind their screens. "Any. Second... Now."

Almost on cue, Brian and Martha stood up from their chairs at exactly the same time and marched in Rodriguez's direction. He turned inwards to the cage, his back pressing against the bars and slid sideways along the walls, desperately looking for a way out. Before long, he was pinned against the side of the cage, his face briefly being sprayed with bloody saliva as Brian grabbed the other man's head before slamming his own mouth around Rodriguez's eye.

Slater watched, entranced, as Rodriguez's body convulsed. A big man, he was powerless to resist Brian's new strength upgrade, and his arms flailed wildly before he slumped down the side of the cage and onto the floor. Brian and Martha crouched down by Rodriguez's head, feverishly tearing at his face and throat with their mouths before finally Rodriguez's arm fell limp through the cage bars and rested on the floor. Brian then grabbed Martha by the throat and slammed her hard against the cold concrete floor, dazing her enough for him to straddle her and plunge his teeth deep into her neck. The screams of chimpanzees feeding off a colobus monkey echoed around the empty expanse of warehouse, before finally a loud gun shot rang out. And then there was silence.

Chapter 6

"So, any questions?"

The Smart Man's voice broke the silence in Slater's office, practically snapping him back into the real world, into an epiphany the likes of which he never believed was possible.

"Yeah, I've got a question," Slater mumbled, before leaping up from the armchair. "Where… the fuck… have you been all my life? Terence, this place is the stuff of dreams. Do you realise what this means?"

"That there's someone out there more mental than you?"

The questions appeared on the monitor like Saturday afternoon football scores.

-Amazing, Professor. How much do we have to purchase?
-We make it in carefully controlled batches to ensure the recipe is followed precisely. Minimum buy-in is 1000g powder – about 50,000 doses @ 20mg. After that, you can order in 100g increments.
-Professor mixed into a solution. Can it be taken in the powder form? Most of my customers won't bother with the mixing.
-Of course. The first field trial involved powder and produced almost identical effects. See video about to start.

In the top corner of the screen, the shaky mobile phone footage played. The dimly lit squat, Stephen snorting the drug up both nostrils, the silence broken by the calm, slow breathing of the cameraman. Then a fast forward to the important part. The viewer emerging from the dark corner as though they were actually there. The sound of breathing becoming over-taken by the sound of Stephen tearing into his girlfriend's face.

-Okay. We see. What's the lead time for shipment?
-A week or so.
-How will you pack it?
-Usual way. There's no discernible odour so sniffer dog proof. Drop off will be as per previous.
-Price?
-Always the first to ask that, aren't you, Mr Velasquez? 1000g batch is 85BTC.

"Look at the list of viewers on the leader board," replied Slater, ignoring the earlier dig. "There are twelve names, presumably other like-minded business people such as myself. But they're all around the world. And who's the only one in the UK? Me. At first I assumed that it was just a coincidence. All that stuff with that pissed bloke in the pub a couple of weeks back, it seemed too good to be true. But now I see it for what it was. They chose me. They want me to be some sort of sole distributor in the UK for this shit."

"Why the hell would you want to sell this shit at all? Surely if all your customers end up killing each other then—"

"Yes I know," he interrupted impatiently, "there's not much repeat business involved. But, let me think about this. To begin with, those two loved the stuff. So in small doses, it's okay. If we control the market for it, we can control the supply batches and perhaps, with a bit of word spreading, issue a sort of warning. Let's see what they have to say about it."

-Very nice effect. But what is the point if the users all kill each other?
-That's up to you. Control the supply, and you control the addiction. In its small dose, they can't get enough. Unless you give it to them. Drip feed, Mr Slater. I'm sure a man of your reputation enjoyed its 'potential'…

"You could do like the fag companies do," said Terence, "and put a picture of that poor sod with his windpipe hanging out of his throat on the packet."

"Quite. Not that people will pay any attention to it," replied Slater. "But he's got a point. The best part is that any time we want to, *any* time that we want to create havoc we just do. There'll always be people to buy this stuff and there's no such thing as bad publicity. If anything, bad publicity is what we want."

The video on the screen stopped and the camera focused on the Smart Man behind the screen.

"Ladies and gentlemen," the Smart Man said, sounding like a school teacher. "Forgive me for going all formal on you but it's time to get down to the serious matter of purchase orders. As usual, we need to establish your financial credentials. Not that we don't trust any of you, of course, we're all honourable people here I'm sure. We need you to transfer the minimum single batch payment to the escrow and then once that's all done, you can really start showing us the colour of your money."

Slater walked around to the other side of his desk and pulled a document out of the drawer. He had put a lot of faith in his new employee's insistence that he buy a whole load of Bitcoins. But in the two weeks since this geek dumped a sizeable quantity in his virtual wallet, their value had already accrued a profit in the region of fifty thousand pounds. For an old school devotee like Slater, who had turned money laundering into an art form, this virtual currency, practically untraceable, was a revelation. No longer did he have to go through the usual rigmarole of injecting his drug money into his legitimate business, hide it in legal transactions then have his accountant somehow cook the books so he could remove it. This was simply ace as far as he was concerned. And it wasn't even like he was spending real money. Once it had been converted into a series of numbers and letters, it might as well have been Monopoly money.

He punched the wallet details into the transaction box that conveniently appeared on the screen and transferred the eighty-five Bitcoins into the escrow account. And waited. He noticed the CS Associates name on the leader board turn from red to green along with a couple of others.

"So how much is that eighty-five Bitcoins worth, boss?" asked Terence.

Slater sat back down in his armchair and took a large sip of Cognac. He stared with a serious intent at the screen, his eyes not moving from the leader board. "At this precise moment in time? About half a mil."

Terence spat out half his whiskey and choked on the other half. "How fucking much? Half a mil? For a kilo of gear?"

"Yeah, ish. It's probably about as close to half a mil in whole Bitcoins as they could get. But when you consider that I reckon we can easily push 20mg bags of this shit for thirty notes. Even if we get twenty a wrap we're doubling our money. But I've got bigger fish to fry than simply the drugs. If what I have heard during my investigations about this place since we started is true, and indeed tonight's event seems to be backing it up so far, we could be in for one giant double whammy. That quarter mil is just the start."

"Okay, that's nearly everyone," said the Smart Man. "Just waiting for the Sicilians, they're always a bit slow when it comes to technology."

A message appeared on the screen.

- We out. Want no part of this. Too much risk, not enough reward. We leave it to our family in NY.

"Oh, okay," said the Smart Man. The Sicilians were usually one of the largest purchasers of their products. Although they were very traditional in their choice, preferring to stick to what they know. Their name disappeared from the leader board. "So, we have a new opening. After the sales auction, the nominating privilege will pass to the winner."

"This just gets better," whispered Slater.

"Right, everyone's in who's going to be in so let's get down to business. Gentlemen, start your orders."

The names on the leader board flashed as the purchases increased. 1100g. 1200g. Slater bided his time. 2000g.

"Nice one, Gaffer Crew," said the Smart Man. "I have a feeling our Brainfood will go down an absolute storm in Jo-burg!"

2100g. 2200g. Then a few seconds with nothing. Slater typed a few numbers on the tablet on his lap, paused briefly to allow his racing heart to calm down, and then hit the large send button.

The screen flashed up: CS Associates 4000g, sending his name from the bottom of the list straight to the top. He sat back in the chair and swallowed the last half a glass of Cognac in one celebratory swig. "Your two-million-pound Amazon Prime order has been confirmed!"

"Boss, I hope you know what you are doing," said Terence. "That's one massive fuck tonne of drugs you've just bought."

"A means to an end, my friend, a means to an end."

Chapter 7

Grace cradled her huge glass of Rioja as she stood staring out of the expansive French windows, the pristine striped lawn stretching out into the distance, framed by the waves breaking against the rocky coastline. Pete watched from across the bar, her shoulders going up and down as she tried to laugh quietly at his attempts to placate his rather belligerent guests.

"I'm really sorry, Mr Babcock, but as far as we are concerned, a ten-ounce is a fairly large steak. At this time of night, it is wholly unlikely to find any butcher who is even open, let alone one who is willing to cut you a thirty-ounce flat iron," he said, not really believing that the words were actually coming out of his mouth.

"What kind of tin-pot little piss hole is this country? Come on, honey, I'm going to bed." Mr Babcock then stormed out of the room, slamming his tumbler down on the bar as he left.

Pete poured himself a small shot of ginger ale topped up with a glass full of whisky, a couple of ice cubes, and joined Grace by the window.

"It's beautiful here," she said, her gaze fixed on the sea. "Being able to look out to this, you must be thankful every day since you left the force."

"You're right, it is beautiful," he replied. "It's a shame that Mum passed away so soon after we arrived. It hit Olivia for six really. Not only the upheaval, but then to lose her grandmother, only made it worse. But she's a fighter. For eleven, she's incredibly mature, takes no shit from anyone."

Grace sidled closer to Pete and put her arm around him. "Where is she, by the way?"

"On a school trip, residential, so she won't be back until the weekend," he replied, rather awkwardly moving away to plump some cushions on the chaise-longue as an excuse to break the hug. "So, what's happening back at the unit? How are Danny and Smith?"

"Did you not hear?" replied Grace, turning back to face out of the window. "Smith left. Retired apparently, but he was only in his fifties. Danny, no idea. He left a couple of months ago. Just said he had a contract with some rich businessman handling all of his Internet stuff. He left rather abruptly and I've not heard from him since."

Pete sat down on the chaise-longue and parked his glass on the arm. He pulled the footstool closer and sat back to enjoy the view.

"You know, this is just about my favourite position. Sitting here, drink in hand, staring out to sea. It makes the fact that I've got no money, no guests, and a failing business disappear into oblivion."

Grace sat down next to him and put her feet on the footstool next to his. "So come back. This isn't you. This isn't what you do. There are people back home who miss you."

"Like who?"

"Me," she said, taking his hand in hers. "Pete, my life's been pretty empty since I've not had your stupid sarcasm, crap jokes, and general big-headedness rammed down my neck on a daily basis. But since you've not been there, I feel lost."

Pete stared at the ice-cubes drifting around their small space of amber liquid. "I miss you too, Grace. It's just that I have to think of—"

But he was cut off as Grace reached around and grabbed his cheek, pulled his head towards her and planted a big kiss on his lips. "I know, you need to think of Olivia. I understand that. But you need a life too. You deserve it, with everything that you've been through. Anyway, I would rather take it slowly than not at all."

He gazed past her face at nothing in particular before looking her in the eye and smiling the broad smile that Grace had missed for months. Again they kissed, more passionately. "You're right," replied Pete eventually. "I do deserve it."

Grace pushed him away playfully before grabbing his hand and leading him upstairs.

Chapter 8

The leader board changed colour, with all the names locking in white with their final purchase totals alongside. Sitting at the top by a clear margin was Slater.

"It would appear that our newest member is looking to make a name for himself rather quickly. We will begin the production of everybody's order as soon as possible and get them to the usual drop-offs. Notification will be sent out to you all in the usual way confirming the storage container address and number as soon as the drops have been made. We're going to end transmission now. CS Associates, I will shortly open up a secure private line for us to further discuss our new partnership. The Professor and I wish to thank you for your business, and we look forward to you joining us next time."

The screen changed to a holding picture stating 'This hidden site had been seized' and pictures of various US law enforcement agencies' logos. The regular website for Majestic Road had long since been shut-down by these agencies, more interested in stopping the tide of small quantity drug transactions that were taking place in their hundreds of thousands at their peak. But really, it made a perfectly passable home page and allowed the Smart Man to more or less hide in plain sight. Accessible to no one but the elite of drug-dealing crews from around the world.

Slater had not only joined this elite group, that three weeks earlier he didn't even know existed, but had slammed his cards firmly down on the table in his usual style of not-to-be-fucked-with bravado on the first meeting. He was fully versed in the ways of dealing with real-life people on the surface, but was finding the depths of the dark web a piece of piss. It would appear that people, wherever they chose to hide out, wherever they chose to do their business, usually end up bowing to Slater.

Just then, the screen on the wall changed again, a small window opened up in the bottom corner and the familiar silhouette of the Smart Man, still hidden by a sheet of white, appeared. "Good evening, Mr Slater. It's nice to properly make your acquaintance in private."

"Is it? It fucking shouldn't be. We're not exactly making acquaintances here, are we? I'm hugely grateful and all that you have made the very excellent decision to allow me into your little parade. I think we can make very good use of each other's skill. But, and be under no illusions that this is a very big but, I expect to receive equal measures as everyone else, if not more so. I mean, who the fuck are you anyway? Why don't you show your face?"

"That would be bad for business," replied the Smart Man instantly. "But I can see that you are maybe still a tad pumped from our little demonstration and indeed your own flexing of muscles, so why don't we just calm down and agree to be civil so that we can talk, like grown-ups, about the next part of the transaction."

"I just paid you two million quid. I can talk to you however I fucking please," replied Slater.

"Mr Slater, I realise that you consider yourself an alpha male, a Curtis-big-bollocks amongst similarly deluded Curtis-big-bollocks clones. And you have just come to probably the best business decision you've made for a long time."

Slater snorted in contempt. Who was this 'man' to tell him whether he made a good decision or not. He would humour him. For a while at least.

"But we need to get one thing clarified," said the Smart Man, adopting a more measured, sinister tone. "In this shop, I make the rules not you. From now on, you will refer to me as sir and I will refer to you as Mr Slater. How does that sound?"

"Ha, okay, *sirrrr*," replied Slater, with as much sarcasm as he could muster, holding up his tumbler to the side as Terence poured in another large slug.

"Marvellous," interrupted the Smart Man. "Now, given that you managed to successfully solve the little trial that we set you, I am going to credit you with a reasonable amount of intelligence."

"Yes, I did think it particularly brilliant of me that I managed to—"

"Find someone actually capable of negotiating our series of tests," interrupted the Smart Man. "And by 'find' of course I mean, largely kidnap under the pretence of paying them a huge amount of money while simultaneously videoing his family in their own home just so he knew who he was dealing with."

"Like I say, a stroke of genius. Anyway, I find it slightly amusing that someone who has just demonstrated their new drug by watching two junkie wasters rip each other apart with their mouths has the front to, what's the word…"

"Pontificate!" shouted Terence from across the room.

"Pontificate? What the fuck does that mean? No, I mean has the front to sit there all high and mighty and judge me for my actions."

"I withdraw my earlier statement," said the Smart Man.

"Hang on a minute," asked Slater. "How exactly do you know all this?"

"Like I said," replied the Smart Man. "My shop, my rules. We can be of some very large mutual benefit to each other, Mr Slater. But I need you to know your position."

Slater gripped his tumbler hard. So hard it nearly shattered in his hand. He knew his position all right, and it wasn't for some pompous little prick hiding behind a bed sheet to tell him otherwise. But he needed this. Just for a bit. The bit that he assumed was about to come up.

"Yes, sir," he spat through gritted teeth. "Of course, your shop. So, you mentioned, briefly, the next part of the transaction?"

"Of course, how rude of me. So the way it works, as I am sure you already knew from the rather unsubtle hints that we dropped along the way, is that not only do we offer a product for you to buy, but we also offer a very useful service. Something that a man in your position would probably appreciate a great deal. Think of it a bit like a Tesco Clubcard. As a valued customer, or more to the point, our single best customer on any particular night, we like to reward you with the honour of providing us with our next guinea pigs. It could be a rogue dealer of yours, gone off with your stash. A customer who failed to pay their last instalment. A weird uncle who molested you as a child, causing you to have the anger issues you so clearly demonstrate. Your choice."

Terence's attention perked up. He realised what Slater was up to. The drugs were a bonus, no doubt that Slater would make the most of his financial investment. But this was what he was really after.

"Okay, so say I have someone who I want to kill, but rather than simply kill them, I decided to go through your 'service', then what?"

"I am assuming you are capable of taking this person, how shall we say, into your possession. And have adequate means of transporting them under the radar. We will then designate a drop-off point, lock-up, storage, that sort of thing for your convenience. You will then drop said person off at the precise date and time set by us and immediately leave the area. Should you not vacate the area at once, we will kill you. Consider it us metaphorically cutting our palms and clasping them together."

Strangely, given that one of them had just threatened to kill him, Slater was starting to like these people. They talked a lot of sense, the way he liked to do business. Get in, get the job done, and get the fuck out.

"I can live with that," said Slater. "Now I seem to remember you mentioning something about a nominating privilege."

"Yes," said the Smart Man excitedly, "I almost forgot. As you have seen, you were the latest addition to our little group, the Majestic 12. But because those stuffy old traditionalists from Sicily, or as they officially like to be called, the 'Cosa Nostra', decided that our new Brainfood was a touch radical for them, they have to leave. Being bound by god-knows how many vows of honour, or whatever they call them, we don't have to worry too much about what they may or may not do. So, it leaves a space in our little line-up. As the rather hefty winner of the bidding war tonight, you therefore have the option to nominate a replacement organisation that you wish to partake. We also nominate one and whichever completes the trial the quicker will win a seat at the table. The more the merrier remember. A full house the merrier, if you see what I mean."

"So, we beat someone during all that shit then, did we?"

"By the skin of your teeth."

"Presumably I can recommend someone from my own country?"

"Anywhere in the world, Mr Slater," replied the Smart Man. "Although I wouldn't have thought that you would want to share your local market with anyone else?"

"Perhaps. Although the people I have in mind could be of huge benefit. Where are you based? Or is that a pointless question?"

"Pointless."

"You speak with a proper Home Counties accent. We're obviously fellow countrymen then."

"How very cute. Be clear on one thing, Mr Slater. You and I will never meet in person. Ever. But not to worry, Majestic Road has branches everywhere."

"Ha, I'm sure you do," said Slater, placing his glass down and standing up from the chair. "I have no further questions, your honour. If there is anything else that you want to say before I go, I'd quite like to get down to the business of arranging your guest."

"There is just one more thing, Mr Slater," the Smart Man replied, pausing for a couple of seconds. "I love your daughter's pink car. We'll be in touch soon."

And with that, the video screen went blank. Slater felt slightly cold, an inkling of doubt creeping into his usually granite guts. He detested not being in one hundred percent control of everything and everyone. But he had come too far to give up. The trial to reach the site had taken its toll, and he was two million lighter than that morning. The means to the end. That's all it was.

"Terence, book a ferry to the Isle of Wight. We need this done quickly."

Chapter 9

The next morning, Grace awoke as the curtain was pulled open casting a warm ray of sunshine across her face. She opened her eyes to the silhouetted form of Pete at the window.

"Morning, sleepy-head," said Pete as Grace sat up straight, pulling the bed sheets up to cover her naked body. He jumped over her onto the empty side of the bed, and grabbed her hand, kissing it tenderly.

"How long have you been up?"

"About an hour and a half or so," he replied. "I had to make Randy and Petunia their ludicrously large breakfasts. They've pretty much eaten an entire pig in one form or another, the fat bastards. I'm going to have a shower. They should be checking out in about twenty minutes, said he had some business to attend to and something about armies marching on their stomachs. After that, how about we live a bit dangerously? I'll stick the 'no vacancies' sign up in the window and then we could take a tandem ride around the island."

"You wild man," she replied sarcastically. "You really know how to treat the ladies, don't you? Go on then, it sounds perfect. I'll go and get myself a glass of juice downstairs if that's all right. You can add it to my tab."

After his shower, Pete dressed and went downstairs.

"Grace?" he said, peering into the empty bar area. He went into the kitchen, then the reading room before finally heading out to the reception and the entrance hall.

"Grace?" he called again, a little louder this time. But again, no answer. He looked out of the front door to see Mr Babcock trying to heave a large suitcase into the back seat of his small hire car. "Can I help you with that, Mr Babcock? Why don't you put it in the boot? Sorry I mean trunk."

"Hers is in the trunk. You'd think we were coming away for a whole goddamn month the amount of crap she's bought. These stupid British cars, no idea how much goddamn room most normal people…"

"Fine, on behalf of all British car manufacturers, you have my apologies for the size of our trunks. You haven't seen Grace, have you, my friend who arrived just after you?"

"What? Oh yeah, the nice little tight body wandering around in just a shirt. Sure did, she went out onto the lawn with a glass of orange juice. You're one lucky guy!"

"Thanks," replied Pete, ignoring the rather heavy-handed fist that Mr Babcock playfully planted in his shoulder, and turned to go back inside.

"Actually, sunshine, any chance you could give me a quick hand with some map reading," said Mr Babcock, suddenly adopting a more friendly tone. He unfolded an Ordnance Survey map and spread it over the bonnet. Grabbing Pete by the arm, he thrust his finger into the opposite side of the map. "So we're here, right?"

"No. You're here."

"What? Get out of it! I could have sworn we were on the west coast of this rock. So, she wants to go here and here. Do you suggest we go this way and then this way, or is it better taking in the coast road?"

"I'd always suggest the coast road. But it only takes a few minutes to drive from one side to the other so—" replied Pete, before being interrupted, his attention grabbed by a slam coming from inside the house.

"Probably the wind, what with the windows and doors being open and all. Okay, thanks," said Mr Babcock as he begun to haphazardly fold away the map. "By the way, I wasn't sure if you'd be back down, if you know what I mean. Petunia here was desperate to get to this stinking garlic farm, so I left the key and two hundred and fifty pounds on your reception desk. It's more than this place is worth but, frankly, if I ever come back to this goddamn country, it'll be about fifty years too soon."

"It's part of Britain, you fucking idiot," Pete muttered as he walked back inside. He turned right, through the bar and out into the garden via the open bi-fold doors. He stood on the patio and scanned across the lawn, shielding his eyes from the mid-morning sun.

"Grace!" he shouted, to no response. "Grace, where are you?"

He jogged to the end of the lawn, but finding nothing, turned around and made his way back into the house.

After double-checking the downstairs rooms and calling out a few more times, he walked upstairs, checked a few of the shared bathrooms and empty guest-rooms before ending up back at his room. Still nothing.

He raced back downstairs, double-checking each room as he went. And then he saw it. The expensive vodka bottle on the side next to its lid. The two smashed tumblers on the floor. The pool of blood.

As he stared, his mind racing and the dread spreading through his body, he barely noticed the phone at reception ringing. He inhaled heavily through his nose and out through his mouth in an attempt to control his breathing. Eventually, the ringing overtook his attention and he ran downstairs.

"What?" he shouted impatiently down into the handset.

"Mr Harris. I need you to remain calm and listen carefully. We have Miss Brooks. She is our special guest and is needed for a matter that does not concern you. It didn't have to be this way, but she gave us no choice. If she had co-operated then we could have avoided this unpleasantness and you need not be concerned. But she didn't. No harm will come to her provided you do not contact the police. It would be so very unfortunate for me to ruin Olivia's school trip. Especially as she seems to be having so much fun. Her friends all love that reversible emoji T-shirt that she's got on. She's somewhere in the Blackgang Chine maze, but I'm sure she'll be out soon."

Pete stood cemented to the spot, blood running cold through his veins. His face felt as though it was about to burst and tears ran down his cheeks. "You fuckers, don't touch her. She's all I've got left."

"Just our little insurance policy. Know, though, that we are watching her. And we are watching you."

A click and the line went dead.

Chapter 10

A huge bang rang out through the lower east wing hallway at Clifton Manor, followed by another and another. Gilbert followed the sound, carefully balancing a vintage sterling silver tray on his arm. He reached the entrance to the indoor squash court, went inside and dutifully stood in the viewing area and watched the game proceed through the back wall one-way mirror. The first player, his boss Alistair Goodfellow, made minimal movements across the court, his expert returns making his opponent cover much more area. The ball smashed into the back wall, and had it not been for the glass would have probably taken Gilbert's eye out. He watched as Alistair's opponent ran and stretched in vain, before their momentum carried them crashing into the wall.

Gilbert raised an amused smile, and entered onto the court as Alistair helped his opponent to her feet.

"Not bad, Daisy," said Gilbert, handing her a chilled bottle of some luminous blue isotonic sport drink, "but Alistair always was a bit of a bandit when it came to squash."

"You are getting better though, that's for certain," said Alistair. "Even over those three games, I saw a marked improvement."

"Piss off, that's a lie and you know it!" replied Daisy, after downing two thirds of the drink and placing the bottle back on the tray.

"No, seriously. I mean I only won that game by eleven points to one. The two before it, I won eleven nil. So, like I say, a huge improvement."

"She took a point off you?" asked Gilbert sarcastically, as Daisy rolled her eyes at the immaturity of these two grown, middle-aged men.

"Yes, she absolutely did. I remember it very well. I played a regular shot about waist height, she swiped wildly at it, catching the ball on the frame of the racquet. It had just about enough speed to reach the wall and the spin made it plummet to earth like a fat man falling out of a tree. It was a cracking shot. I had no chance!"

"Very funny," said Daisy collecting a towel. "I'm going for a shower and then I've got revision to do. It would be quite nice if you didn't bother me with your hilarious banter. I don't think I could take much more."

Daisy put her racquet against the wall and left the room. It had been over a year since Alistair Goodfellow had taken her under his wing. He had provided her security, food, health and an education far beyond the reach of most ordinary people. After seventeen years of both physical and emotional abuse, being shunted from one foster home to another, she finally felt settled. Even given the harrowing circumstances of their introduction all those months earlier as she witnessed a boiler-suited assailant in a clown mask ram a knife into a man's chest as he sat tied to a chair in the warehouse where she was squatting, she had come to see Alistair and his associates as family. It had been just over that same year since the last episode of The Red Room was broadcast. One that she had helped to set up. Her previous abuser, Saeed Anwar, had finally met his maker. She often fell asleep with the memory of watching the broadcast from the limousine still as fresh in her mind as the day it happened. A step that she had never imagined she would ever have to take was taken that night, and once it had happened there was no turning back. She had entered their world, a dark, hidden world where justice was meted out to the worst scum walking the planet.

And it remained a demon sitting on her shoulder, that she had led this man to his death. Not at her hand. At the hand of her captors, as a direct result of her actions. At times it was difficult to accept. But then the memories began and everything reconciled itself in her brain. The beatings, the forced drug abuse, they were the relatively pleasant parts. This man, Saeed Anwar, whom she had met at random, who had charmed his way into her life and into her trust, who had showered her with dinners out, mobile phones and as much alcohol as she could manage. This same man who then made her do things. With him it was bad enough, she still had the physical and mental scars to prove it. But it was the other men he brought to the house. Who paid a pittance to force themselves into her, to use her, to treat her worse than a sewer rat. It was that which disgusted her the most and it was those feelings that created the rival demon sat on her opposite shoulder, the antimatter that balanced her feelings.

In the past year, she had learned a great deal. Alistair had introduced her to learning for a purpose, to listening to music in order to appreciate depth and meaning, to physical exercise as a means to invigorate the mind and meditation as a means to clear it of clutter. She had a wealth of tutors and facilities at her disposal but the lessons she enjoyed most were the ones spent with Alistair in his dojo, learning Shotokan karate. It gave her a purpose, an endless journey where she would never stop learning and every step along the way would make her feel stronger and more invincible.

Apart from the first night she'd spent at Clifton Manor, where she opened up to Alistair and he to her, she had never tried to pry more information out of him as to why he chose to do what he did. Although he had never admitted it, and there was no way that she could ever prove it, she was convinced that he was the Host and the perpetrator of the violence that she had witnessed in that warehouse. But from living the hell that she had, she understood. And that helped her to fit the jumbled array of emotions — the fear, the hatred, the self-loathing, the confusion, the last shreds of childhood innocence — into a single coherent acceptance of her life. But more than that, an almost overwhelming need to better herself, to become the person that not only she would never have dreamed of becoming but also one which all the bastards who had hurt her along the way would have sneered at the possibility of every coming true.

The thing that frightened her the most was not the Host, not the possibility that this Brotherhood whom she had become part of would decide to start up their little show for the baying audience. It was her maths A-level exam the following week. Alistair had spent numerous evenings attempting to make her see the beauty in maths. The elegance of a Fibonacci sequence and its appearance in nature, the golden ratio, the wonder of pi. It was during these sessions that she used think she actually preferred him when he had a clown mask on and was making someone's hand explode with a crowbar. She had yet to come across a use in real life for logarithms but this exam was one she wanted, and if she had to know about them for just a few days before emptying her brain of all knowledge of them, then that's what was going to happen.

As she walked up through the main entrance hall, she caught sight of a large four-wheel drive Audi in one of the many giant ornate gold mirrors that hung in the cavernous room. It was a fair way down the long winding driveway that left the main building and practically reached the horizon before hitting the gates to the estate. She watched out of the window as she slowly climbed the huge wooden staircase to her room on the first floor.

After a few seconds, she realised that it was travelling at a speed usually reserved for rally cross, rather than the carefully manicured lawn-edged driveway of a country estate. The engine roar became louder, the cloud of gravel kicking up behind it grew larger.

She turned and made her way back down to the front door.

Just as she unbolted the final chain from the large oak door, the car screeched to a halt, spraying up a hail of tiny stones as it swung around in the main courtyard, an urgent evasive manoeuvre to stop it smashing through the front wall. Daisy pushed the door closer shut to shield her as the spray, like hundreds of tiny bullets, struck the other side. Before she could open to see what all the commotion was, she was sent reeling backwards as the door was forced open from the outside.

"Where's Alistair?" shouted the sweaty, bright red figure of Jarvis carrying a small cardboard box in his hand as he raced through the entrance hall.

"A hello would have been nice," replied Daisy as she pulled herself up by a small side table next to the door.

"Where… the fuck… is Alistair?" he shouted back, decidedly unimpressed by her response. "Now! Where?"

Daisy stood up straight, taken aback by Jarvis' unusually aggressive tone. "I don't know."

"Bollocks, I've got to find him," said Jarvis brandishing the box in front of him.

"Er, well, I've just come from the squash court," she just about managed. "He was there a minute ago with Gilbert, but I don't know where he was going after. Ring his phone or something. What's so important about that box?"

Jarvis stopped, slowly walked over to Daisy while removing the strip of brown tape from the lid, and then opened the box right in front of her eyes.

Daisy went white as she looked inside, inhaled deeply as she attempted to gather her composure. "I see," she gulped, "Yeah, he'd probably want to see this."

Chapter 11

The glass shattered into a thousand pieces against the patio doors. It had been twelve hours and half a bottle of Scotch since the worst phone call of Pete Harris's life. The frustration had become too much, he needed to do something. He was no longer Detective Sergeant Pete Harris of the Metropolitan Police Cyber Crime Unit. Civilian life suited him, but he longed for his old desk and access. This was like pissing in the dark. Assuming whoever had tapped his phone was probably also monitoring his Internet and even doing things the old fashioned way; just watching him. Each time he peered out through the slatted blind, the same small hatchback was parked across the road. It always had someone in it, although he couldn't be certain if it was the same person the whole time.

Earlier, he had spoken to his daughter's teacher, Mrs May, by telephone, a sort of pre-requisite of residential school trips that the parents have an emergency route to the teachers. He had needed to be doubly careful to neither cause any concern for Mrs May or Olivia or to raise any suspicion from whichever asshole currently had him by the bollocks. He had used the excuse that she was a little nervous at staying away from home for such a long time, especially since her grandmother had passed away. He thought he had sounded rather convincing, but as Mrs May pointed out, like the other phone calls she had already received from other parents, that it was actually he who had the problem. She assured him that Olivia was okay and that they would be heading back to their hostel for some quiet time after all the excitement of the theme park.

Pete was happier at least that she was surrounded by lots of people and some adults whose lives more or less depended on returning with the same amount of children as they went away with. He was also comforted by the fact that even the most ruthless, battle-hardened would-be assassin would be no match for the primary school red tape involved when trying to take a child out of a school trip early.

But there was Grace as well. He had always fought against his feelings for her since his wife died, for what reason he couldn't really fathom, other than he thought it too soon, both for him and for Olivia. Not that Grace wasn't practically perfect, he liked everything about her. She had looked after him during the time he was on sabbatical and on his return to work, almost to the point of mothering. But he appreciated it more than she realised, and the previous night he let himself bow to the inevitable. And she was missing, and presumably in grave danger.

His mind didn't know whether to concentrate on Olivia or do something about Grace. She was a detective. It's not beyond the imagination that someone with a grudge was behind this. There were more than enough people that she had pissed off in the past with the means to track her down and take her. But she was tough, she knew exactly how to look after herself. Provided she was still alive of course. And why did they need to involve him? Or was this just an insurance policy, to give them sufficient time to get far enough away that even if he did phone the police, the window of opportunity had passed? He didn't even have contact details for any of her family and the more he thought about it, the more he realised he actually knew very little about her, other than she had a brother, and that her father was still alive somewhere.

Pete stood on the patio outside the bar area and let the refreshing sea breeze wash over him. It helped to blow away the cobwebs, make him think more like his old self. The old self that happily tried to single-handedly storm desolate farm buildings in the hunt for the Brotherhood of the Righteous. Pete, who had stared deep into the eyes of his wife's killer and managed to keep his deep-seated sense of right and wrong, who had uncovered a web of corruption in his force. Perhaps his failure to bring them to account was the final nail in the coffin of him losing his edge. His ability to function in the most challenging of worlds that had begun to diminish after the loss of his childhood sweetheart and unborn son.

He desperately needed that edge back. Not to nail some hideous paedophile, murderer or rapist, but simply to protect his little girl. He slapped himself hard around both cheeks.

Think. Obviously they were after Grace. So technically it's her fault that I've been dragged into this. But how did they know she was here? And if they knew she was coming here, why wait until she got here and risk having to take her from a public guest house? Why not just intercept her en-route? Also, if they were really bothered about me, why are they watching from a distance and why am I not bound and gagged, tied to a radiator in my cellar? Or dead? 'A matter that doesn't concern you,' they said. Probably explains why I'm not dead, no need to draw any more unwanted attention than is needed. Also, they don't seem to believe I'm that much of a threat to them. Which is a good thing. Isn't it? Come to think of it, those Americans did leave in slightly odd circumstances.

He paced around the terrace, desperately trying to formulate a plan. The best he could come up with was to hope that his hunch about not being seen as a threat by these people was correct. Act as though they had gotten to him enough that he would bow down, act intimidated. He waved his index finger at no one in particular as something resembling a plan of action came to him.

Running back through the house, he decided to act as normally as he could, hopefully make the people watching him from the car think that he was resigned to the situation and just waiting for them to leave as soon as possible. Pulling the bulging liner from the kitchen bin, he made his way outside to the front of the house, trying as hard as possible not to look at the small car, and threw the bag in the wheelie bin.

He went back inside and locked the front door. No need to worry about anyone coming or going, it was fairly usual to find himself the only person in this guest house. Every front window needed closing and locking and then the downstairs lights were turned off.

Upstairs, a light blue glow cast through the thin roller blind pulled down over the window as the shadow of movement periodically moved across it. Then all the movement stopped. After half an hour, the final light in the house went out.

Chapter 12

Alistair Goodfellow sat at the head of the enormous oak table in the banqueting hall at Clifton Manor, staring silently at the open box in front of him. Daisy, Gilbert and Jarvis sat along the sides, waiting patiently for him to say something, anything.

Inside the box, resting gently on a luxurious pillow of crushed velvet specked with dried dark blood, sat a finger. The bright red varnish was chipped where the nail had broken, and there were small cuts along its length. Alistair carefully reached into the box, trying hard to control his breathing and gently lifted the finger from it. The large golden ring, with its enormous sapphire, seemed as though it had it been rammed onto the end as if to seal it shut. He recognised it. Slowly, he twisted it off, not towards the nail end as a ring would normally be removed but over the blood-encrusted joint. As he freed it from the dried blood, he revealed the small faded blue outline of a heart with an arrow piercing through the middle, confirming what he already knew.

"It's Grace's," he said, not making eye contact with anyone else in the room.

"Are you sure?" asked Jarvis.

"Of course I'm sure," replied Alistair curtly, knowing that Jarvis' knee-jerk response was more in hope than expectation. "This was the tattoo that she had done when she was shacked up with that waster. The one who put her in the hospital. That eventually led to my mother's death. And this ring. This was my mother's. She gave it to Grace just before she died in the hope that it would make Grace realise who was truly important."

The others bowed their heads as he spoke. Alistair rarely ever showed any emotion, whether in business or in his home. But clearly this was affecting him. As a businessman so used to being in control of everything he surveyed, it was difficult to see this knowing that his sister was in danger and he was not able to protect her. Or, worse, had already failed to protect her.

He placed the finger back in the box, gently as if laying a child's dead pet hamster into a shoebox filled with tissue paper for burial. Daisy watched in silence, waiting for him to speak. Jarvis and Gilbert did likewise. They had known Alistair a lot longer and knew better than anyone that whoever had sent this either had no idea who they were dealing with, or knew precisely and were trying to make the mother of all statements.

It wasn't strange for a man of Alistair's well-documented financial status to receive threats of blackmail, extortion, even physical violence against himself. But that was purely because of his level of wealth. Also, most were simply the laughably poor attempts from loner nut-jobs who had seen one too many episodes of CSI and gotten a little too over-zealous with their newspaper cuttings and glue-stick. But for someone to have gone to the trouble of sending him his sister's amputated finger? That was a different matter entirely.

Alistair continued to stare into the box, his usually razor-sharp mind spinning. He bought his hands up to his head, and rubbed his temples with the heels of his palms before clenching them tightly and slamming his fists down on the heavy wooden table, shattering the silence with thundering echoing thud.

"Someone is going to pay for this," he said softly. "Seriously pay."

"Any ideas who would do this?" asked Jarvis.

"It could be anyone," offered Gilbert. "She was a copper after all. Of course, she was a useful asset for us, but there's no doubt that she would have upset a great deal of people during the more legitimate side of her work."

"Doesn't seem right though," replied Alistair. "She was well behind the scenes of the CCU's work. Anonymity was of the utmost importance. It makes no sense that anyone would be able to follow any trails to her. They were good at what they did. They nearly nailed us after all."

"Unless it is someone from the inside," said Daisy.

"I agree," said Alistair. "I think that is almost certainly the most likely. So who does that give us?"

"Not many," replied Jarvis. "Grace's team was very small as we know. But we are looking at either Smith or Harris. Who was that technician that also worked alongside them?"

"Ah yes, young Danny Fowler," said Alistair. "But I can't see it being him. From what Grace told me, he was very good at his job, but was one hundred percent a computer nerd. So much so that he would practically make you seem normal, Jarvis. Had an almost robotic approach to the job. Very little emotion about the people he dealt with, just saw them as symbols in an equation to be either solved or moved or rearranged."

"But would he know who Grace was?"

"Probably not. Plus I understand that he left some time ago, presumably having found more profitable outlets for his ability."

"So, it must be Smith then?" asked Gilbert. "He had clear motive to want to get back at us. And he would have likely had the means, certainly the inclination, to do whatever he could to find out who the insider was and who they were working for."

"You're correct, my friend," said Alistair. "We had Smith exactly where we wanted him, but let's not forget that he was head of the Metropolitan Police Force's specialist team that dealt with cyber crime in all its forms. He would almost certainly have had access to resources to monitor everyone in his team. Grace was good, but there was always the chance that she might slip up. Fail to cover her tracks completely."

Gilbert nodded enthusiastically.

"But it's not him," said Alistair, motioning to Jarvis to show Gilbert his tablet. "Firstly, he retired a few weeks ago. It was too risky to make any big plays against him once he was out of the office, risk drawing unnecessary attention to ourselves. Keep an eye on him, of course, but from a distance."

"Yes, I remember," replied Gilbert slightly annoyed. "I was there when we discussed how to deal with him once he had retired but I still think…"

"Secondly, he's dead," said Jarvis as he spun the tablet around and slid it across the table to Gilbert.

Former Metropolitan Police detective found dead in car accident.

Gilbert muttered the article to himself under his breath. "*The former head of the Metropolitan Police Cyber Crime Unit, Detective Chief Inspector Robert Smith, was found amongst the burnt-out wreckage of his Toyota Prius by a dog walker on the evening of Tuesday 26 September. Fire crews attended, but Mr Smith was pronounced dead at the scene. The exact cause of the accident is not currently known but will be subject to an ongoing investigation.* Shit almighty. This cannot be a coincidence, can it?"

Alistair tapped his lips with his index finger in thought. "It does seem a little convenient, doesn't it?"

"So really, that just leaves our friend Pete Harris," said Jarvis.

"I don't believe it would be him," said Daisy sharply, causing the other three to glance at her inquiringly.

"Oh? And why not?" asked Alistair.

"He didn't seem the sort. You saw how he acted in the warehouse with Anwar. He has a huge sense of duty, of right and wrong. It was more important to him to bring Anwar to justice than take revenge for his wife. Plus, didn't he have something of a soft spot for your sister?"

Alistair smiled proudly. He had known from the first time he had met Daisy that she was a whole lot more than the wretched, broken, abused little urchin that they had found squatting in the warehouse. He always considered intelligence a far greater weapon than any amount of physical strength, and had made it a priority in her education to develop and sharpen the analytical side of her mind. But she was still young, still naïve.

"Yes, you're correct. But sometimes appearances can be deceptive. Just look at us. If all those people that I have to schmooze with at charity functions, business dinners and so on, if they all knew. You can imagine, can't you? Somebody has done this to Grace, and I will not stop until I find out who it is."

"Wasn't she going to see him at some point this week?" asked Jarvis.

"Shit, yes, you're right," said Alistair, leaping up from his chair and pacing around the hall to find his phone. He scrolled through his messages until he found the one she had sent him at the weekend.

Going to see Pete on Tuesday. Please don't make it difficult for me. I need happiness in my life as well. G xx.

"That bastard," Alistair spat through gritted teeth. "She would have been there yesterday and today. It must be him. Or he almost certainly knows what the hell is going on."

"We know where he lives," said Jarvis. "Shouldn't be too difficult to find him."

"Still doesn't make sense," said Daisy shaking her head.

Alistair ignored the comment as he sat back down, focusing on the box. He carefully picked up the finger again. At least he had his mother's ring, the bastard hadn't denied him that. He continued where he had left off, having found the tattoo.

As he removed the ring, he noticed something strange. The others stared at him oddly as he manipulated the finger, squeezing it along its length between his thumb and index finger. He picked up a piece of the velvet from the box and wiped the wound end. Daisy grimaced, covered her face with her hands, and peered through two fingers as Alistair reached into the opening of the amputated digit. A few specks of blood dropped onto the table as he pulled out a small black plastic item. He wiped the blood and tissue from it and examined it closely. Raising his gaze, he focussed on Daisy before throwing it across the table towards her.

"These things just get smaller and smaller don't they? Still don't think it's him?" Alistair asked.

Daisy sunk into her chair, as Gilbert and Jarvis joined in the staring contest, with her in the middle. Covering her hand in a paper napkin, she picked up the object to examine it closer. With her other hand, she pulled one end to reveal a branded USB memory stick, the type handed out at trade fairs to prospective guests or wedding planners. She looked at the lid that she had just removed and sighed a deep breath as she read the tiny gold embossed letters: *The Outlook Guest House.*

"But why would he send one of his own memory sticks? Surely that's just laying the blame right at his doorstep," she protested.

"Presumably he has found out from Grace who she really is," replied Alistair. "Grace was always a bit flaky when it came to Harris. There was always that risk that she would open up to him a little too much. I don't doubt that if he found out who ran The Red Room, who it was that captured him and very nearly made him a volunteer, he would want some sort of retribution. And anyway, as far as I am aware, it was always Grace chasing him. In fact it was a constant source of frustration to her that he never reciprocated. We have to assume the possibility that she said too much."

"But why would he do this to her, just to get back at you? He has a daughter. He left for the Isle of Wight to get her away from this sort of thing."

"Daisy, it's him, it has to be," replied Alistair. He had never felt at ease with the need that he might ever have to discipline Daisy. She wasn't his child and so far, he was not her guardian, legal or otherwise. But he found himself stopping short of sending her to her room without any tea. "In the morning, get Cornelius over to the Isle of Wight to obtain our friend Mr Harris. And as for the why, Daisy? I have a feeling it's on this."

With that, Alistair collected the memory stick and walked out of the dining room, slamming the door behind him.

Chapter 13

The sound of a shotgun echoed through the huge cavernous barn waking Grace with a start. Rays of morning sunlight shone through the misty glass high up in amongst the rafters, casting lanes of eerie white through the clouds of dust hanging in the air. She tried to sit up, but her body ached all over, especially her ribs, and she screamed in pain as the hay bale underneath her rocked and she rolled off onto the hard straw-covered floor.

As she put her hand down to push herself up, a bolt of pain shot through her arm. It was then that she noticed the unfamiliar, unstable sensation in her hand coupled with the large, padded, blood stained bandage. She sunk back down and sat upright against the bale, clutching one arm across her midriff to ease the pain thumping through her rib cage. The other one slowly raised in front of her face, as quickly as the shooting pain in her shoulder would allow. Her index finger and ring fingers protruded either side of the puffy white fabric that encased the gap where her middle finger used to be.

Desperately, she tried to quell the rising panic, the merest increase in her breathing sending large jolts of pain through her entire body. She sobbed and let out a muted scream. As one lot of pain fought against another she hadn't noticed the large iron manacle around her wrist, until the buckle dug into the side of her chest. She pulled against it, uncovering a long iron chain from underneath the bed of straw until it reached the wall. Again, she tried pulling as hard as she could on the chain despite knowing full well that it would be pointless.

More guns shots rang out. In her panic, she missed the fact that there were two shots, one after another, or the loud voice shouting 'pull' that preceded them. Gritting her teeth, she dragged herself up onto the bale, an almost inhuman feat of strength in her current state and sat down to catch her breath. Oddly, the amputated finger seemed to be the least painful of her injuries, and somehow she was able to put pressure on it.

After resting a few more seconds, she gathered all her strength and rose to her feet. One knee buckled slightly and she noticed the circle of blood seeping through her jeans. She tried walking forward but was held back by the chain around her wrist, restricting her to the small area of hay bales where she had been sleeping. In the middle of the barn, she could see two streaks of blood carving their way through the covering of straw and out through the large wooden doors. And then she saw it in her mind, the man being dragged by his ankles across the floor before they turned their attentions to her. Her legs suddenly gave way and she dropped down onto the bale as the last twenty-four hours came flooding back to her.

*

The morning before...

Grace had awoken in the manner that she had always dreamed about, in Pete's bed with him making lovey-dovey boyfriend-type comments about how long she had slept in for. As he busied himself with his guest house chores, she had sat up in bed and watched, thinking of how the previous night it had finally happened.

As Pete was in the shower, she dressed in his shirt from the night before. Perhaps a little early on to be wandering around his place of work in a negligée, maybe one of the times when he didn't have guests. She walked downstairs to fix a glass of orange juice, feeling the bannisters as she went, as though caressing a newly purchased house on moving-in day. She imagined living here, the little shit out at school. Just him and her, walking through their house, dressed in hardly anything, she could tempt him into a quick knee-trembler behind the bar or outdoors even. In fact the less guests the better. Then she saw the photo that reminded her of her place. Pete's wife, hugging Pete's daughter. Hugging Pete. The woman was beautiful, radiant as she caressed her burgeoning bump. That would have to go. Plus she was fairly certain she saw a sign for an all-girls boarding school as the taxi drove her across the island.

She stood staring, until she was snapped back to reality by the very loud, very obnoxious, very recognisable voice of Pete's guest demanding that someone "come and sort them out a couple of goddamn Bloody Marys before they hit the road."

"Hey? Did you hear me?" barked the voice again.

Grace turned and moved into the bar area, turning on her fake air hostess smile and most English voice she could muster. "Sorry, sir, but Mr Harris is taking a shower. It seems that the simple act of making your breakfast has left him sweating like a five-pound hooker."

Mr Babcock stared at her, one eye closing slightly, and smiled out of one side of his mouth. "Perfect. Now if you wouldn't mind, my wife and I would like two Bloody Marys."

"What, two each?"

"I noticed he has a bottle of Grey Goose up there in that cabinet. Must be saving it for a special occasion. We'll have them with that."

"Okaaaay," replied Grace sarcastically, raising her eyebrows. She'd ordered enough drinks from bars before to work out how 'being a barmaid' worked and grabbed a large brass shot measure from underneath the top. She turned around, taking the vodka bottle out of the cabinet so helpfully pointed out to her by Mr Babcock, and placed two tall tumblers on the small towel at the back of the bar.

"So, how long have you and Mr Harris been together?" asked Mrs Babcock.

"Oh, a couple of years," replied Grace, diligently pouring the rather expensive vodka into the measure. "We used to work together, but then a relative of his died and he had to move out here to look after this place."

"So, has he popped the question yet?" asked Mrs Babcock, again in a slightly childish, giggly manner.

"Petunia, don't embarrass the poor girl," said Mr Babcock.

"Oh it's okay," replied Grace. "Not yet. We've spoken about it, a lot. He's a widower, see, and he has a little girl."

"I haven't seen any children around here."

"No, she's on a school trip this week, residential. I think they're at the Blackgang Chine today or something."

"Thank you, Ms Brooks, you have been most helpful," said Mr Babcock, suddenly gaining a distinctly un-American and very English accent.

"What the—"

Before Grace could finish, or fully turn round, everything went dark as she felt a sickening thud across the back of her head. The two tumblers fell from her hand, shattering on the floor, sending glass and sticky red liquid across the bar. The glass crunched as she fell to the ground. She could feel it cutting her skin as they dragged her from the room. The lights were all that she could make out through her spinning vision, the sounds of their voices as muffled as her eyesight.

As they dragged her past the bottom of the stairs, she could just about hear the sound of Pete's shower stop and the glass door to the cubicle creak open. She opened her mouth and attempted to scream, but nothing would come out. With the last gasp of energy she could muster she grabbed at the bottom bannister and opened her mouth to shout 'Pete', but before she'd even gotten the first letter out she saw a large fist heading straight for her face and it went dark again.

*

She came to, with no idea where she was, how she got there, or how much time had passed. Her head throbbed along with the tiny cuts that stung like wasp stings across her back. A bottle of water was thrust into her mouth and as her mouth filled with ice-cold liquid, she tasted the metallic tinge of blood inside. She gagged, spilling most of it down her front and half-swallowing, half-choking on the rest of it. As she opened her eyes, her neck ached as she tried to look around, but was met by the powerful blinding glow of industrial warehouse LED lights that burned into her retinas. She was laid on a cold, damp piece of chipboard, her hands and ankle secured to the base by endless pieces of gaffer tape.

"Welcome, Ms Brooks. I trust you had a pleasant journey," came a voice behind her.

"Where am I?" replied Grace, her eyes slowly acclimatising to the glare.

"Come on, Grace, can't you come up with something a little more original than that? You must have interviewed loads of criminals in your time, surely you can think of a slightly ballsier opening gambit than 'Where am I'? Anyway, sorry I can't really tell you exactly where you are, for obvious reasons, other than you are in a place that you will very soon wish would just disappear off the face of the planet and transport you back to lover boy."

"Pete…"

"Yes. Pete indeed."

Grace turned her head away as the face of Curtis Slater appeared a few inches from her eyes.

"We've been in contact with Pete about you. And his daughter actually. It was incredibly useful of you to tell my associates of her whereabouts, especially when we had already been to her school to find the place largely devoid of human life."

"What day is it?" she asked, trying to piece together anything.

"It's still today," he replied gripping her jaw and moving in closer. "It's still the same day that you woke up in your happy little existence ready for the joys of the day ahead."

"So…" she gasped, "I'm still on the Isle of Wight then."

"Don't be fucking ridiculous," laughed Slater. "Why on earth would I want to spend any more time on that shithole? When I got there I forgot to turn my watch back thirty years, threw my brain right out. No, luckily they have ferries every half an hour to cater for all the people desperate to get the fuck off it. We got back to civilisation within a few hours, thank God. Anyway, now you're here, I need some information off you."

"Who are you?"

Slater landed a hard fist against the side of her face and then shouted into her ear, "I'm asking the fucking questions, okay?"

He stood up, allowing her a couple of seconds to regain her thoughts, trying to keep her a carefully balanced combination of utterly scared shitless and reasonably coherent. Adopting a calmer tone, he continued, "My name is Curtis Slater. You may remember me from such investigations as—"

"I know who you are, Slater," Grace interrupted, the adrenaline finally kicking in and endowing her with a little more fight.

"Good, I hate long-winded introductions."

"If you've bought me here because of Cramer McAllister, I can't help you. We don't know who killed him, but it wasn't us."

"Nope, wrong again," replied Slater. "Why on earth would we bother going to this much effort for a pointless, washed-up ex-copper?"

"What?" asked Grace.

"Oh we know, Grace. We know that you don't work for the CCU any more. We know that you couldn't cut it once your colleagues, who let's be honest pretty much carried your useless fat arse through most of your career, had left. So, as I said, why would we bother wasting time on someone like you?"

"Fine, I don't fucking know. Like you said, I don't work there any more, so I am of no use to you."

"Not according to your Detective Chief Inspector Smith. Now he was one pointless, washed-up ex-copper that it *was* worth our while bothering with. Because he put us in contact with you."

"What? Why? If he says I'm as useless as you seem to believe, so what if I've left the force. I can't help you with anything. Like I said, I don't know anything about McAllister's death."

"Are you thick in the head? We know that Cramer's death was never properly solved."

"So, why am I here?"

Slater stopped and leant over Grace, putting his hands either side of her head. "The Brotherhood."

Grace's blood ran cold, and she made the mistake of pausing long enough for Slater to realise that he had hit a nerve.

"Who?" she stuttered nervously, as Slater stood up waving his arms around as he also mouth the word 'Who' in unison.

Grace screamed as Slater turned around, slammed his hands back down by her head, and shoved his face to within inches of hers.

"The Brotherhood," he spat, specking her face with drops of saliva. "The Brotherhood of the Righteous. You know who they are and you're going to lead them to me."

His booming voice echoed through the hollow rafters of the barn. Grace closed her eyes and turned her head away. She tried to gather her thoughts. *Okay, okay. So, he hasn't kidnapped me because we couldn't save McAllister. He must think that I know who the Brotherhood are from the investigation.*

"They were all killed at the end, in that barn," she said, desperately trying to sound convincing. "Smith did the press conference. It was the Eastern Europeans—"

"Yeah, yeah," said Slater, mockingly, as she carried on speaking.

"I swear. I don't know what more I can give you…"

"Oh okay, whatever."

"Please…"

"No!" shouted Slater again. "That is all bullshit and you know it! Smith admitted as much yesterday—"

"Smith was the pawn, that proves it," she protested. "He was in charge of the entire investigation. If he covered it all up, how were any of us to know?"

Slater clicked open a file on his tablet and held it in front of her face. "Sorry, let me just make that a little louder for you."

Grace watched out of one eye as the silent grainy video footage played on the screen, instantly recognising herself and remembering clearly the phone call that she had to make to Alistair after CCU broke through the Brotherhood's firewall during the McAllister episode. Smith had known, and he had followed her and recorded her without her knowing it.

"That could be anyone that I'm talking to."

"Of course, how about this one?" replied Slater, as he flicked through a montage of video clips, all showing Grace in the midst of seemingly covert telephone conversations.

"I was ringing my mum."

"Do you think I'm a fucking moron? We know from Smith that he lied at the press conference. It was nothing to do with that pair of Borat look-a-likes or the tabloid fodder 'rogue ex-Secret Service agent gone bad.' Smith was just a puppet, and not a very fucking good one at that. He knew that the Brotherhood had someone else on the inside. He just couldn't prove it was you. But he was convinced enough to film you and I doubt very much it was so he could jerk off to them. So I will ask you again. Who. Are. They?"

"I don't know," replied Grace, desperately trying to work out the best way to play this. "Apparently Smith was receiving money from them. That was the rumour going round after the whole Anwar episode. But he would have had the means to cover his tracks…"

"As would you…"

"But what tracks? He's already admitted his part in it. Get him back in here and strap him to this fucking board. Interrogate him instead."

"Er, yeah, that might be a bit tricky," replied Slater, nodding to Terence who was stood nearby. "See, after Smith left here he had an unfortunate, how shall we say, mishap."

Terence stepped forward and placed the black charred arm, cut off at the elbow, down on Grace's chest. She pressed her chin into her chest as she strained to see. Once she had realised what it was, she groaned in disgust and threw her head back against the board, closing her eyes.

"So, that just leaves you, sweetheart, and I will ask you one more time. Who is the Brotherhood?"

"No, please. I don't know…" But before she could finish her sentence, Grace screamed in pain as Slater thrust his elbow hard into her ribs. The sound of Grace gasping as she tried to regain her breath was broken by the sound of footsteps and the whistled theme tune of *Beverly Hills Cop* as Slater walked around to the other side. This time he didn't even bother asking again before raising his right arm up high, staring at her with a wry smile and a little wink, before bringing his elbow down once again into her ribcage.

She cried hard, wincing in agony with every breath, feeling as though someone had stuck a knife in her side. All she could do was concentrate on controlling her breathing through the pain, which was far easier said than done.

"Come on, Grace. I know this hurts. Just tell me what I need to know and it'll all be over."

"I… don't… believe… you," she gasped. "I… think… you… are… enjoying… this…, you… pathetic… little… prick…"

Slater and Terence burst into floods of laughter, before Slater stopped abruptly and grabbed Grace's face and pointed it to the far wall. "You see that, I'll show you just how much I fucking enjoy it."

Grace watched as Slater walked away over to the other man who was manacled to the barn wall. Without even breaking stride, he thrust his foot into the man's groin. As he doubled over in pain, Slater continued to rain down boot after boot onto the man's head. The man fought in vain to cover himself, prevented by the chains from protecting his head and face. As he shook his head in an attempt to avoid the blows, Slater moved to his legs, stamping on his kneecaps and ankles. Grace could hear the cracks from her chipboard bed, even above the sound of her own sobs. After a few more blows, the man eventually ran out of energy and his head slumped forward, a small waterfall of blood running out of his mouth. Slater grabbed the man by the hair and pulled his head back. Slater reached into his trouser pocket and pulled out a small handgun, placing it in the man's mouth.

"Grace? Oh, Grace. Don't close your eyes, sweet cheeks, you'll miss the best bit."

Grace winced as her body shuddered, the loud gunshot thundering through the barn. Slater came back over, once more grabbing her jaw and forcing her to look at the man. She had to restrain herself from vomiting as the man's limp body still swung on the chains, the wall behind splattered with blood, bone and tissue.

"Do you know what he did, Grace? Do you?" he shouted in her ear.

Grace squeezed her eyes closed, and weakly shook her head.

"He accidentally knocked the door of my McLaren with his trolley in the Tesco car park on Monday. He was coming here to give me his insurance details."

Terence unshackled him from the wall and then together with another associate, dragged him across the barn floor by his mangled legs.

"So, I would strongly suggest that you give me the information I am very nicely asking for. This will be the last time that I give you the opportunity to freely volunteer said information otherwise you can kiss goodbye to this middle digit."

He took a large pair of bolt cutters out from under the board and placed it around her finger.

"Three."

"No please," she spat, shaking her head defiantly.

"Two."

"I can't." She felt the pressure tighten around her knuckle.

"One."

"Okay, okay, okay," she sobbed, the tears flowing like rivers, and she felt the cutters loosen off just slightly.

"Excellent, you know it makes sense. Now, who are they?"

"The Brotherhood. It's a group led by Alistair Goodfellow, he runs it all."

"Goodfellow? What, the bloke who founded Phone Giant? Bollocks."

"It is, I swear. But they don't exist any more," she said, trying to appease her sense of betrayal. "They quit after the Anwar episode."

"Why the fuck should I believe you?"

"Apart from the fact that you've just used all the methods at your disposal to get me to tell you and now I finally have, you don't believe me?"

"Answer the question."

"He's my brother."

"So you have a little Luke Skywalker/Princess Leia thing going on do you. That is very interesting. Very interesting indeed. And we will be able to find him how?"

"Do you actually need me to answer that? You really are a fucking idiot," replied Grace, not really caring any longer if she pissed this man off much more. "Everyone knows he lives at Clifton Manor. But I should warn you, when he finds out that you have me, and rest assured he will find out, he will come for you and he will make sure that you experience pain the likes of which even you could never imagine possible."

"Ha, as if I'm scared of a bunch of I.T. nerds just because they've got a bit of cash. Anyway, he will very shortly find out that we do have you. Whether he can work out in time exactly who *we* are remains to be seen. But *I* should warn *you* that I am very careful. And how is he going to find out that we have you? We are going to send him a little present."

Grace screamed as the bolt cutters sliced through her finger. Terence came back to the board and set about stemming the flow of blood from her hand with wads of bandage.

"Can't have you bleeding to death, can we? Where would our leverage go?" said Slater as he bent down to pick up the finger. "So, if you'll excuse me, I've got some wrapping to do."

*

The last thing that Grace remembered was Terence jabbing her in the leg with a vial of morphine and then shortly after passing out. The morphine had long before worn off, most of her pain had returned. As she sat down on the hay bale, the old rusty hinges of the barn door creaked as they opened, flooding the room with light. In walked Slater and Terence, dressed in their best country gentlemen tweeds.

"Good morning, sweet cheeks," said Slater, an open shotgun cradled under his arm. "Hope you slept well. Just to fill you in. You're going to be our very special guest for a while. I imagine that your brother, having had time to receive our gift and process its meaning, will be frantically trying to pass the test that has been set. It is more important to him that he does exactly what he has been instructed to do, than try to be the superhero and track us down to rescue his fair maiden little scrubber of a sister."

"You really think you can win, don't you? I will enjoy watching you beg for my brother's forgiveness."

"Ha, well, don't hold your breath. Like I said, you will be our special guest for a while, probably a few days minimum. So, in the meantime I suggest you make yourself at home and save your energy for the big surprise at the end. Oh and if you try anything stupid then…"

He closed up the shotgun and placed it against her temple. She closed her eyes instinctively as he pulled the trigger, flinching as the loud click reverberated against her bones. She let out her breath and opened her eyes, staring him straight in his as he held the gun in place, smirking with contempt.

"Even if he doesn't follow the trail, which he will, we have more than enough on him to bring his world crashing down around his head. And it's all thanks to you."

Chapter 14

Pete was on the fourth cup of his bottom-less pot of coffee and had just polished off the last of his gut-buster breakfast. He wasn't in the mood for eating but his overnight dash across two thirds of the Isle of Wight had taken its toll on his energy reserves. After making a big show of closing up his guest house for the night, he had waited long enough for the watching car to assume he was probably asleep before slipping out the back and down onto the craggy rocks behind the property. He knew this small stretch of coastline like the back of his hand having spent many weekends teaching his daughter how to scramble across the rocks searching for shellfish and fossils.

He was a good kilometre away from the guest house when he eventually ventured further inland, safely out of sight of his watchers. Like everywhere on the island, the hostel where Olivia was staying was not far away and so he decided to walk across, keeping cover in the fields that he knew so well from his triathlon training runs. Also, he figured that if these people were keeping surveillance on the hostel, the worst thing he could do would be to get dropped off right outside by a taxi. This way he could maintain a safe distance while monitoring for anyone looking suspiciously like they were out to get him.

Luckily the greasy spoon opened at a reasonably early 7am and he tucked himself away at a corner table behind a copy of *The Sun* waiting for the kids to finish their breakfast in the hostel; 8.30am according to the itinerary the school provided. He collected his phone and sunglasses, and put on his zip-up hoodie, pulling the hood up over his head. Folding the newspaper under his arm, he figured, would make him appear more like any regular passer-by rather than a man intent on rescuing his daughter from potential kidnappers.

Finally 8.30 arrived and he made his way to the hostel, telephoning his daughter's teacher as he walked.

"Good morning, Mr Harris," answered the teacher before Pete had the chance to speak.

"Er, yes good morning, Mrs May, it's Pete Harris, Olivia's dad. Again. Oh, you knew, sorry. I've got a bit of a family crisis so I am going to have to take Olivia home, if that is all right."

"Okay, sorry to hear that, Mr Harris," said Mrs May. "We are here for another three days, so if Olivia would like to—"

"No!" shouted Pete abruptly, before calming himself, given that Mrs May was probably doubly suspicious given the nature of the previous night's phone conversation. "Sorry, I mean no it's fine, thank you. I have to go back to the mainland for a bit and I don't really want to leave Olivia on the island, if that's okay. If you could ask her to pack her things that would be great."

"Right, fine, but I'm not happy about it. I'll need you to sign the release documents. It'll take me a couple of minutes to write one out. What time will you be here?"

"About two minutes."

"Oh, I see. We'll get on it right away."

Pete ended the call and scrolled along his phone to the Uber app. He punched in a booking for the hostel before going inside to sort the paperwork.

A few minutes later, he emerged from the hostel, largely dragging a thoroughly hacked off and protesting Olivia by her arms.

"It's not fair. Why do I have to leave? I was having fun."

Pete stopped and knelt down, pointing a finger in her face while hoping not to draw too much attention to themselves.

"Sorry, look, I really need you to just come with me. I'll make it up to you I promise, but please stop with the tantrum. Right, the taxi's arrived — we need to get in."

A taxi pulled up opposite and, as they crossed the street, Pete noticed a car parked a few yards down the road. He made eye contact with the two people sat in the front and as soon as he saw one of them put a phone to his ear, ushered Olivia quicker into the back of the cab. He jumped in after and shouted "the guest house" at the driver, before slamming the door. As he looked out of the back window, he felt a small touch of relief to see that the other car hadn't moved, and sunk back into his seat.

"Everything okay, sir?" asked the driver.

"Yes, it's absolutely fine, thank you. So are you busy today?" Pete asked trying to make the usual taxi small-talk.

"You're my first," he replied.

Pete smiled and sat back until a message notification chimed on his phone. *Your driver will arrive at the pick-up location in one minute.*

His heart pounded and he tried at all costs to remain calm. "Sorry, mate. I put the booking on in a bit of a hurry. Where did you have our destination as being?"

"The Lookout Guest House, sir."

"Okay, I think I typed it in wrong. In fact, any chance you could drop us off here, I think we'll walk."

"But Dad, it's miles away to the Lookout," protested Olivia.

"Shh, darling," he said, through gritted teeth. "It's fine, isn't it? We'd rather walk, wouldn't we?"

"Sorry, sir," said the driver calmly as he activated the door lock. "I can't stop, not until I get you home to the Lookout. There are matters to discuss. I suggest you sit quietly and remain calm and everything will be fine."

Pete grabbed Olivia's hand and squeezed it. Thankfully, she seemed to be more grateful at not being made to walk home rather than having any sort of understanding about what was happening.

Eventually, the car arrived back at the hotel and swung around the gravel driveway, stopping almost on the front door step. The driver got out and walked round to the passenger door. He pressed unlock on his key fob, opened the door and ushered Pete straight into the house. Olivia followed and ran after her father, holding him tightly by the hand.

As they walked through the hallway into the corridor, a hand grabbed Olivia by the arm, pulling her away from Pete. A large hand smothered her mouth, stifling the high-pitched scream. Pete shouted after her as she was dragged away up the stairs, but his attempts to follow her were blocked by two burly arms grabbing him under the armpits and around the back of his neck in a full nelson. He was easily lifted into the air, legs kicking, and carried into the bar area. The arms slowly increased their pressure, squeezing his chin into his chest and almost dislocating his shoulders. As the wind slowly left his lungs, and the pain increased, he gave in struggling before being dumped onto the sofa and a gun pointed at his head by the cab driver.

"You fuckers, who are you? What have you done with my daughter?" Pete shouted, trying to get back up from the sofa.

The driver hit Pete around the side of the head with the butt of the pistol and he fell back onto the chair. His fear for Olivia and need to protect her had sent adrenaline flooding through his body and he barely noticed the pain. He tried again, this time aiming a wild haymaker at the driver who dodged easily, sending Pete sprawling on the floor. The larger man then slowly knelt in the small of Pete's back, grabbed an arm and bent it down and up so he was nearly touching the back of his own head.

"Mr Harris, please calm down. Your daughter is fine, we just need her out the way for a little while to give us time to discuss matters," said the driver, kneeling down close to Pete's head which was being squashed into the rug. "How long she stays fine, however, is up to you, clear?"

Chapter 15

After a few seconds of silence, while everyone collected their thoughts, the large man pulled Pete to his feet and threw him onto a leather armchair, as the driver cocked his weapon and pointed it directly at Pete's head.

"Now, Mr Harris, you asked who we were," said the driver. "Unfortunately I cannot tell you that. My boss believes that you may be party to some very important information. You were a detective in the CCU working on The Red Room webcast and indeed supposedly foiled the Brotherhood of the Righteous, the group in charge. And it is very important to us that we find them, there are issues that need to be addressed. We do know, however, that while you were present at the final broadcasting of this show, you in no way foiled anything to do with the Brotherhood. The true Brotherhood, that is. But I think you already knew that, am I right?"

"So fucking what? I was just doing my job. It happens to be that the force was sick on the inside and I was going to be forever pissing into the wind trying to bring bastards like you to justice. But I don't know anything about the real Brotherhood. You need to ask Smith."

"We did," replied the driver, "and shortly before he ran into complications, he suggested that we speak to you and your girlfriend."

Pete thought about it for a moment. Why would Smith implicate him? Smith knew that he resented him for what he'd done, but Pete had left it all well alone, started a new life.

"I assume Smith thought there was something in it for him? Giving you this information," Pete asked.

"Yes, but you know, these ex-coppers who sell out their ex-colleagues for a bit of spending money… That's a bit low, isn't it?"

Pete laughed. "If *you* say it's low, it must be pretty low. Presumably you've taken Grace as well?"

"She is currently enjoying our boss's hospitality, yes. Unfortunately that darling little cherub upstairs did somewhat complicate matters. A fine balance between getting what we want, and also being sensible about what is going to draw the most attention. We decided it better to suggest you played by the rules and only make contact if absolutely necessary. Your little collection this morning was just a touch too risky for us to sit back and do nothing."

"I must say it's incredibly brave of you lot to come after a child and her dad. I mean, you'd have to be *double fuckin' 'ard*. Look at you, you utter fucking pussies, a six-foot-four psycho with 'roid rage and a spineless little shit hiding behind a gun. And using an eleven-year-old girl as leverage. Well done you. Well. Fucking. Done."

He was stopped short by a sharp blow around his face from the driver who then knelt on Pete's groin, grabbed him by the throat and pressed his head against the back of the chair.

"Okay, you want to play the smart guy, we'll play it that way," spat the driver. "Tell me everything you know, this instant, about the Brotherhood of the Righteous or I will, very slowly, shoot you in various parts of your body."

"I don't know anything about them, I told you," answered Pete, gasping for breath as the driver let go of his throat.

The driver held the gun up, aiming it at Pete's shin, and cocked it.

"I don't, I really don't…" he pleaded. The driver fired. The bullet skimmed the edge of Pete's calf, ripping through his jeans, and embedded itself in the chair. Instinctively he reached down to grab his leg, feeling the warm, sticky wetness of the blood that was pouring from the wound. "Please I don't know what you want me to say. Search this place from top to bottom, go through my laptop if you want. You won't find anything that will tell you I am lying."

"Your old boss seems to think that you and Grace Brooks know precisely who they are," replied the driver calmly.

"Grace? How the fuck would Grace know anything? She was lower down the pecking order than I was."

"Funny you should say that. She's actually been very compliant. So now we just need you to provide us with what *you* know and we'll be on our way."

"Bollocks, she didn't know anything."

"Oh, very well," sighed the driver. He pulled his mobile out of his pocket and typed in a text. "Won't be a minute."

He put the mobile back in his pocket and folded his arms, all the while maintaining aim with the gun. A few moments of silence followed. Pete checked his leg; the wound didn't seem too bad. He certainly couldn't feel it. The amount of adrenaline his overactive heart was pumping around his body saw to that. He looked at the driver, who shot him back a condescending smile until the silence was broken by the sound of footsteps, and a minor struggle, coming down the stairs.

Another burly henchman appeared around the corner, his arm across a squirming Olivia, who was dwarfed by his enormous frame. The huge forearm held her tight and he controlled her head with his other hand.

"Daddy!"

"Livie!" shouted Pete, jumping up from his seat, only to be grabbed by the hood and slammed firmly back into the chair. "It's okay, sweetheart. I promise."

He smiled at her. Even with three strange men in her house, one holding her in a bear hug, the other two treating her father with utter contempt, her dad's gesture reassured her and she smiled back. Thankfully so as well, as she couldn't see her captor reach into his back pocket and pull out a small pistol which he hovered over her head.

Pete's heart felt lower and more rotten than it had ever felt before. His eyes moved from hers, up slightly to the gun, and back to hers. It took every ounce of strength to keep smiling at her.

"Now, Mr Harris," said the driver, shielding the view of his own gun from the young girl, "let's call this a day now shall we, and you just tell us what we want to know."

"For the love of God, I... don't... know," he pleaded again. "Don't you think I would tell you now?"

"Sorry, Pete. That's just not good enough," replied the driver, cocking his gun once again. "Game over."

Pete closed his eyes waiting for the inevitable. The sound that came wasn't from a gunshot, but was a mobile phone ringing. The driver lowered the gun and took out his phone.

"Yes... right. Okay, we'll bring them back. No problem... yes, separate cars... Okay, no problem. See you later."

He hung up, lowered the pistol, and replaced both the phone and gun into his pockets.

"Slight change of plan, Mr Harris. Our boss wants to speak to you, so we will be taking you and your daughter back. We have a private plane waiting at Bembridge Airport."

He nodded to the associate holding Olivia, who nodded back and dragged her out of the room.

"Daddy!" she called out.

Pete shouted back, "Olivia!"

"It's all fine, Mr Harris. She'll be quite safe, as will you."

"He just held a fucking gun to her head, and you expect me to believe that?"

"Yes. In fact, it is now in my interest to ensure that you both remain unharmed. Well, at least until I get you back to our place. So I suggest that you don't do anything stupid and you will see your daughter at the plane. Of course, if you do try anything en route, a simple phone call is all that it will require and my associate will slit her from ear to ear. Do you understand?"

Pete sat with his head in his hands. "You fuckers. I *will* make sure that you pay for this."

"Okay, Pete, whatever. Here wrap your leg in this," said the driver, throwing him a tea towel from behind the bar.

Pete limped forward and picked up the towel. He looked through the door, down the hall and out into the front yard where he saw the burly associate open the car door and Olivia, disconcertingly compliant, climb into the back seat and put on her belt. She seemed about as okay as could be. At least that was how it appeared, and he decided just to do what they said. Very few criminals, apart from the obvious ones, that he ever came across would knowingly hurt children. It just wasn't worth the extra aggravation. He watched as the car pulled away, briefly catching a glimpse of Olivia as she turned to look out of the window, with what even appeared to be a smile on her face.

Maybe they never intended to kill her, just shit me up a little. Maybe the arsehole she is with is now under orders to be extra nice to her. Maybe all these people are just here for the money, the usual 'it's not personal it's just business.'

"Okay, I'll make this as easy for you as I can. But can I at least make sure everything is locked up before we go?"

"Fine, but hurry up. The plane leaves in twenty minutes."

Pete walked around the house, checking all the windows and doors. He knew they should all still be locked since he hadn't exactly had time to make himself at home since they arrived back. He walked up stairs and was followed by the burly associate.

As they got to the landing, a large black people carrier pulled into the driveway.

Pete caught sight out of the window of three men climbing out of the car, two running around the side of the building. "Either some more of your lot have arrived or I've got some guests."

"What?" said the man, barging Pete out the way to get to the window, just in time to see the last man knocking on the front door. "Fuck. There aren't any more of us. We're it."

"I think he wants to come in," Pete said sarcastically.

The burly henchman grabbed him and pulled him back down the stairs, where the driver was stood, gun at the ready.

"Fucking get rid of them. Now."

Pete opened the door. But before he could speak, the man barged in, easily knocking Pete, with his injured leg, off balance.

"Stay the fuck where you are," said the driver, aiming his gun at the first man. "Who the fuck are you?"

"That kind of welcome isn't going to earn this place a very good rating on Trip Advisor now, is it?" replied the man calmly. "I was hoping to have a quick word with Mr Harris."

"We were just leaving actually," replied the driver. "So, if you wouldn't mind stepping to one side. I really don't want to have to shoot your brains out."

"Come now, there's no need for that. I'm sure there's plenty of Mr Harris to go around," he said, watching as Pete stood up clutching his leg wound. He caught sight of the bloodstains on Pete's trousers and then Pete staring straight at him. Pete had no idea who this man was but he was the best hope he had. He stared at the man wide-eyed, as if saying help. The man looked at the driver and his associates, and then past them. He nodded.

Before the driver could turn to face the two men who had snuck in through the side door, he was knocked out cold by a straight right punch to the back of his skull. The burly associate was slow in reacting and caught a vicious roundhouse kick straight into his face, knocking him against the wall. Another roundhouse connected square with his chin, cracking his head backwards against the wall, and he collapsed in a heap on the floor.

The man grabbed Pete by the arm. "Come with me. These gentlemen will clear up and lock up. My name is Cornelius. We have some business that needs discussing."

"You as well?" asked Pete, grabbing his rucksack. "I'm guessing that if you had wanted to kill me, you would have done so already. But they took my daughter and quite frankly there is no business that you could want to discuss that is more important right about now."

Cornelius motioned for Pete to climb into the people carrier parked outside, and locked the door as he got in. He stood on the gravel driveway making a telephone call.

After five minutes or so, the man climbed into the front seat. "Okay, Mr Harris. It would appear that there has been some sort of mistake. I have orders to take you to the airport and we will do our best to retrieve your daughter, but if we are too late then you're coming home with me."

"*Retrieve my daughter.* Who in the fuck speaks like that? But I think you might be underestimating these people and what they're capable of. We can't just rock up at the airport and ask for her back."

"Says who?"

*

The people carrier arrived at the airport. It was an airport in the loosest sense of the word, little more than a strip of tarmac in the middle of a glorified farm. They pulled into the car park, next to the sign offering 'pleasure flights'. Pete and Cornelius got out of the car. Pete ran over to the nearest person who looked like an employee.

"I'm trying to find a man who arrived here with a young girl. They were catching a plane from here," he said, shaking the man by the arms.

"All right calm down," said the man, pushing Pete's grip away. "You just missed them. They're on that Islander there, just starting its take-off."

He pointed at a white twin propeller aircraft accelerating along the tarmac.

"Fucking hell. Olivia!" shouted Pete, running over to the fence. But as soon as the nose of the plane lifted, he knew it was pointless. He watched, helpless and desperate, as the single most important thing in his life sped towards the clouds. "Whose plane is that?"

"No idea. A lot of the people who fly in and out of here use company names or aliases. It's the way with these private planes."

Cornelius pulled Pete away and walked him back to their car. "I suggest you come with me, Mr Harris. They almost certainly know that their associates have been compromised so it is now more vital that you don't return home."

"What about Olivia?" replied Pete, wrenching his arm away from Cornelius.

"I don't know at the moment. We have a helicopter waiting. We'll be back at our group's headquarters within the hour. I suggest you do as we say."

Chapter 16

"That was Cornelius," said Alistair, hanging up his phone. "They'll be here in about fifteen minutes. Just enough time to discuss how we're going to play this with Mr Harris. And finish lunch of course."

He took another spoonful of Moroccan couscous and two more large langoustines from a huge silver serving bowl in the middle of the table.

"Daisy, you've not touched your lunch," he said, snapping the head off one of the prawns. "Need to get a wriggle on; our guest will be here soon."

Daisy sat staring at the solitary bread roll in the middle of an empty plate. She looked up at him and shook her head. "You're quite right. Our guest will be here soon. On his own. Without his daughter, who has presumably been taken by the same people who cut off your sister's finger and stuffed a memory card into it. But no, it's more important that I eat some sodding prawns before he gets here."

Jarvis and Gilbert laughed, mopping the sweet orange juice from their mouths and hands with their pristine white napkins.

"Enough," replied Alistair. "Fine, Daisy, you were absolutely right. It would now appear that Mr Harris is in no way connected to Grace's disappearance, other than the fact that she was visiting him when she was taken. If you must know, my intention had always been to just talk to him about Grace. As it turns out, I took what you said on board and instructed Cornelius to be open-minded. It would appear that, given when they arrived at Harris' house to find him apparently under a serious amount of duress, Cornelius has made an 'executive decision' that perhaps the real threat came from the uninvited guests."

"But why did you have to bring Mr Harris here? He didn't do anything to us."

"Oh really? You seem to be forgetting that he was the officer in charge of the investigation into The Red Room. And he very nearly caught us. And we would have gone down for a very, very long time. Just because he has a kid doesn't mean he isn't a threat to us."

"He was just doing his job," Daisy shouted back. "Just because it happened to inconvenience the great Alistair Goodfellow—"

"Stop this now!" shouted Alistair, slamming his fists down on the table. "You need to start showing a little more respect. What would have happened if we hadn't gone, Daisy? Eh?"

He watched Daisy as she held back from responding. He could tell she had realised that, as ever, he was correct. But it wouldn't hurt to hammer it home anyway.

"If we hadn't have gone in," he continued, as she tried to interrupt as if telling him not to bother, she knew it already. Which he decided to ignore. "Then firstly we would not have known that he wasn't responsible for Grace's disappearance, but also we would not have been able to stop him from being taken as well. Which means that he is now available to assist us in the search for Grace, which then follows on that, together, we will be able to find his daughter."

"So you'll help him?"

"By finding Grace, it should lead him to his daughter."

"But you said he is going to assist us. Why do we need him to help us to find Grace?"

Jarvis decided that this was the right time for someone of his technical expertise to stick their two pennies into the conversation. "We've analysed the memory card that was in the finger. There's very little to go on. It just has a single JPEG file with a slightly cryptic message on it."

"Aren't you the I.T. guru around here?" asked Daisy, to much amusement from Alistair and Gilbert.

"I.T. guru, yes. Cryptic puzzle solver, no," replied Jarvis, his geek-ego slightly bruised. "At first thought, it's some sort of trial, or indeed trail. To what, we don't know at the moment. But Mr Harris will almost certainly be able to add some value to us with his past investigating the dark net. He almost solved us remember?"

The sound of the approaching EC155 helicopter prompted Alistair to wrap up the conversation.

"Look, Daisy, it's not ideal. But it is what it is. Just so we are all clear, when Mr Harris arrives we must make him welcome. He'll be more compliant that way. We must not let him realise that we initially suspected him as Grace's kidnapper which is why we were at his house. As far as he is concerned, I sent my security team to check everything was okay, because we hadn't heard from Grace and the tracker on her phone indicated that someone had destroyed it."

"And of course," added Gilbert, "it goes without saying, that under no circumstances must he find out who we are. We have to assume that Grace was taken because of the Brotherhood, but we can't let on to him that is the reason we are involved."

They all nodded in agreement and stood up to leave the room. As Gilbert and Jarvis left, Alistair put his arm around Daisy. "Once again, your integrity shines through, Daisy. You know I've always admired that quality in you. But for now, we have a situation that requires both tact and a modicum of subterfuge. Of course I will make sure Mr Harris bends to my will in order to meet our ends, but I once promised Grace that I would leave him alone, and I will. Okay?"

Daisy nodded and they left the room, her arm linked in his.

Chapter 17

The helicopter touched down on the large white H painted into the grass, linked to the main house by a small gravel pathway. Alistair ran towards the helicopter, head down and arm in front of his eyes to block the debris being thrown up by the still rapidly spinning rotor blades. He wanted to begin the Clifton Manor hospitality immediately and thought it only right that he should be the first to welcome Pete.

"Mr Harris, welcome to Clifton Manor," Alistair said as he opened the side door. Pete took off his headphones and seat belt and suspiciously shook Alistair's extended hand. Olivia hung heavy in his brain and, as nice as his journey had been, and as opulent as the surroundings in which he found himself were, he was in no mood for pleasantries.

Alistair waited until they had cleared the whirlwind of the rotors before introducing himself.

"Mr Harris, I'm Alistair Goodfellow. Welcome to my home."

"Spare me," Pete shouted back, as he followed Alistair along the pathway towards the large bifold doors that led into the orangery. "I want some fucking answers. Some arsehole has taken my daughter and I think you know who."

"Please, Mr Harris…"

"Just call me Pete. Right about now I couldn't care less for formalities."

"Of course, Pete. Firstly, please understand that I deeply regret having to meet under these circumstances. It is beyond acceptable what happened to your daughter and I can imagine what you're going through."

"With the greatest of respect, I don't think you have even the slightest inkling of what I am going through, actually. Do you have children?" he asked, glancing over his shoulder at his captors who were following them in.

As they entered the house, the two men walked through the small guard of honour consisting of Gilbert, Jarvis and Daisy.

Alistair stopped and faced him with a look of indignant injustice.

"Yes, Pete, I do," he said, surprising the others with just how convincing his first lie sounded. Quite how he was going to back it up they weren't sure, and were even more surprised, especially Daisy, when he put his arm around her shoulders. "Daisy, please hello to Aunty Grace's friend, Pete."

"Er, yeah, hi," said Daisy, in her usual bored-sounding-teenager tone.

She held out her hand, looking anywhere to avoid eye contact. A pang of guilt hit her as he shook her hand, as she touched his clammy palm, his stress radiating through the handshake. Their lives were inextricably linked. But he knew nothing of it, and if ever he was to realise the extent that their fates had been intertwined, it would blow this whole thing apart.

As she caught sight of his eyes, a whole flood of emotions rushed through her and she fought to maintain a degree of nonchalance. What she would have given to have had a father who cared as much about her as Pete did for his daughter. Or even a mother who gave the slightest shit. She knew what Pete had been through at the hands of the same man who had caused her such pain. Not only that, she had watched him give a display of humanity, the likes of which she had not witnessed before. She had barely been able to control herself when she was faced with the same demon, so how he had managed to was beyond her understanding. While she stared at him, the conflict stirred within her. On the one hand, she was party to this group that had put him in the situation in the first place. On the other hand, they had both been victims of the same man. If a third hand existed, she would also want him to understand that part of the reason he is still alive was because of her and her alone. Had she not contacted Janusz then Pete may well have been killed. And she hoped that at some point she would be able to explain it all to him. But for now she needed to pretend to be Alistair's daughter.

"Nice to meet you," she managed.

"Right yes fine, nice to meet you too," replied Pete, becoming impatient at what he saw as nothing but a waste of time when they should be looking for Olivia.

But as he gently shook her hand and they made eye contact, he felt something. He wasn't sure what, but something.

"Come, Pete," said Alistair hurrying him along, "we have a lot of very important matters to discuss."

Pete followed him through the endless hallways of the ridiculously large house. It reminded him once of visiting the Vatican museum and the long walk through the hall adorned with frescos and tapestries on the way to the Sistine Chapel. Not that it made him feel any more serene.

Eventually they arrived at two huge oak panel doors, which Alistair held open for him to walk inside.

"This is one of my favourite rooms in the house," he said, as he walked around gesturing with his arms. "Please take a seat. You might recognise this room, it's been in Downton—"

"Please, Alistair, I don't mean to be rude but I really couldn't care less about your house. It's big. I get it. And I can see you're obviously an incredibly rich man, but I need to know exactly who you are and why, in the name of fuck, I'm here."

Alistair smiled and stopped to sit down. "You're right, Pete. My sincere apologies. I needed you here, and I am fully understanding, if not knowing, of how you must be feeling at the moment. Forgive me, I was simply trying to be a gracious host, without bombarding you with a whole load of heavy stuff the minute you landed."

Pete didn't say anything, but nodded a slight appreciation of the gesture.

Gilbert brought in a tray of sandwiches and a decanter of iced water.

"Please you must be hungry."

"Not really, I had a massive fry-up earlier."

"Excellent. The breakfast of champions," laughed Alistair. "The reason I brought you here is because I believe your life to be in grave danger."

"Why me? It's my daughter who is in danger. And Grace," he said, realising that in the midst of all the shit that was hammering around inside his head, he had missed something fairly important. "Hang on a minute, you referred to her as Aunty Grace earlier, does that mean…"

"Yes," replied Alistair. "Grace is my sister."

"She never said anything about you."

"No. Grace had a somewhat troubled youth. But she pulled herself out of the hole that she had dug, turned her life around, with a little help from me but mostly by herself, and built herself a career. It was very important to her that she remain her own person and that people didn't judge her for being my sister and think that she only got where she was thanks to my influence. She was funny like that."

Pete started to feel slightly more comfortable. "But why do you think my life is in danger?" he asked before realising it was a slightly stupid question.

"I would have said this morning's events demonstrated that?" replied Alistair, never one to shy away from pointing out the obvious. "I am sorry for what you have been through, I really am, and in a way it was lucky my men came to your house when they did.

"Grace has a tracking app installed on her phone. My colleague Jarvis over there developed it specifically for her. She liked her independence but also took comfort in the fact that we had her back. It's probably just like any other tracking app out there, but Jarvis added a little extra which pinged me a warning if anyone tampered with her phone. She had messaged me to say she was coming to see you, but then I received the message that her phone had basically been destroyed. We then received a very strange parcel at the front gates which contained nothing but a memory stick. Of course, what am I to think about a bizarre coincidence like this? So I sent my security team to check she was okay. Both of you, I mean."

Pete's head was pounding as he tried to assimilate this bombardment of information and something just wasn't stacking up. "Do you know who those other people are, the ones who took my daughter?"

"No. We're hoping that you might be able to tell us."

"I don't know. But they obviously know of my previous employment. How much did Grace ever tell you about what we worked on together?"

"Not a great deal. But one thing I do know, Pete, is that she thought the world of you. She had nothing but the utmost respect, both as a fine policeman and also as a friend. In fact, if I didn't know better, I'd say she was probably in love."

Pete shifted uncomfortably in his chair. This news didn't come as a surprise to him, he had just been in a state of semi-denial about it as some sort of appeasement of the guilt he would feel pursuing it. And hearing it from someone he had never met before made it all the more real.

Jarvis and Gilbert glanced at each other. Smart move by Alistair. Give this guy two reasons to want to help them.

"The men who were at the house when your friends arrived are definitely the same ones who took Grace. They kept referring to the Brotherhood of the Righteous and insisted that I knew who they were. And that Grace knew and had told them."

"The Brotherhood of the Righteous?" asked Alistair with as much inquisitive inflection as he could muster without sounding sarcastic. "Grace did mention something about them last year. You two were working on it, I believe. Didn't it end with that shoot out in the warehouse somewhere in the country?"

"The farm building, you mean."

"Yes, that's it. I remember seeing the detective addressing the press about it. They had smashed the international crime syndicate operating some sort of show on the deep web if I remember rightly. In fact, I believe that same poor detective was found dead only yesterday. Very nasty car accident."

Alistair scanned the room and then found the newspaper with the story in it. He folded it over at the right page and slid it across the table to Pete, who picked it up and skim read the article.

"Bugger me. Smith had only just retired, he no longer had anything to do with the force. This can't be a coincidence. I need to try to get hold of Danny."

"Danny?"

"He was the analyst who worked on the Brotherhood case with me. A little young and naïve, but he was a blinding computer technician. There was very little he couldn't solve when it came to computer problems. The last I heard he had packed it all in to trade Bitcoins and other crypto-currencies. During the couple of weeks the investigation lasted, he told me he had made more than fifteen grand just by buying up Bitcoins and doing nothing, their value was increasing at such a rate."

Pete got up from the table, took his mobile phone from his pocket and walked out of the room.

The others looked at each other and Alistair gave them both a 'so far, so good' wink. They said nothing until Pete returned a few moments later.

"I can't get hold of him. He might have changed his number. This doesn't make sense though. The group who are holding Liv were insistent that I knew information about who the actual Brotherhood of the Righteous are. Apparently before Smith died he had told them that the press conference at the barn was all a sham. While he didn't offer any solid proof who the leak was inside CCU, he was nearly a hundred percent certain Grace had something to do with it."

"So it seems," interjected Alistair, "that this group is going after the CCU team who investigated this 'Brotherhood' in order to track down the Brotherhood. Rather than it being the Brotherhood themselves who are behind this, going after the team in retribution for ending their activities."

"Perhaps."

"So, like I said," replied Alistair a little more forcefully, "it's a good job that we got to you when we did. If what little I read in the press about this Brotherhood's activities and their dark web show is true, they don't seem to be the type of people you want to get on the wrong side of."

The doors to the dining hall opened and Daisy entered, carrying a large mug of cappuccino. She sat down at the table next to Pete and took a sandwich from the tray. "So what's the plan of action?"

Pete shifted slightly uncomfortably in his chair. "Is this really the sort of thing that we should be discussing in front of your daughter, Mr Goodfellow?"

"Of course, it's fine," replied Alistair. "Daisy here works for my organisation and is technically, if nothing else, an adult. She has a very mature head on her shoulders, although at times does have a tendency to think she's right about everything. Don't you, dear?"

Alistair looked at her with a large smile. Daisy forced a half smile, half disgruntled teenage pout back at him. "Yes, *Daaaad*."

"But why do you think they involved you in this? Like I said, I knew Grace very well and had no idea that she had a brother."

"It's not a total secret, Pete," replied Alistair. "There are people out there who know. And while I tend to avoid publicity as much as I can nowadays, there was a time when I couldn't walk into a shop without seeing my mug shot splattered across every cheap tabloid with some fake scandal or other. Problem is that the press, especially the more left leaning, don't like it when someone, such as me, sells a business like Phone Giant to foreigners. Not only have I made a fortune but I also risked UK jobs, that sort of thing. Oddly, the worst slating I received was for turning down Dragon's Den. But that was a long time ago."

It all clicked into place with Pete. He remembered the press coverage Alistair was talking about, the scandal when he sold up.

But for Grace not to mention that she happened to be the sister of a man sitting in the top two hundred of the Times Rich List was a little strange. And true, Pete hadn't heard anything of him of late. The last time he remembered seeing Alistair on anything he was a lot more heavy set and clean shaven, rather than the lean, muscular, goatee-bearded man sat opposite.

"Presumably they want money then," said Pete, more as a statement than question.

"We don't know. We were hoping that you would be able to help us with the memory card that we received. I imagine that once we solve that, it will lead us to both Grace and your daughter."

"Can't we just call the police?" asked Pete, feeling like he was simply stating the obvious and wondering why no one had suggested it.

"You were in the police, Pete," replied Alistair, "you know how they work. I think that the type of people we are dealing with here will almost certainly have moles somewhere inside and the first whiff on being investigated could spook them into doing something drastic. I know it's hard to sit back and be patient, but I think that what's we have to do for now. If you could work together with Jarvis on the memory card, I think that we'll make some very quick progress."

Pete looked around at the faces staring back and resigned himself to the inevitable. "Fine," he sighed. "I suppose we should get on with it."

Chapter 18

"Will you sodding well hurry up with that thing!" shouted Slater, spinning a bespoke Scotty Cameron putter around his fingers, before addressing a golf ball lying on the carpet. "They'll be back any minute."

The putting machine a few yards away whirred as it returned the ball back in Slater's direction.

"I'm nearly done," came the reply from the figure hunched over the office desk, tapping away at the laptop connected to a phone. "You can't just swipe left to unlock these new iPhones, they're a tad more sophisticated than that."

"I know that, you tart, but just exactly what is it I pay you for?"

Slater was about to take another putt when he the saw the black Discovery turn into the property at the end of the driveway. "They're here. Hurry up."

He walked out of the office, through the hallway, stopping at the living room where his daughter lay on her back on the sofa, her face reflecting the mess of colours from the screen of the massive tablet she was holding in the air above her.

"Right, Paris, stop with that now and come and make yourself useful. I need you to do something."

"What? Can't you see I'm FaceTiming Mum?" replied Paris.

Slater walked over to the sofa, grabbed the tablet from her hands and took over the conversation. "She's busy, she'll call you later."

"Put her back on, Curtis," came the rather drunk-sounding reply. "She wants to come and see me. I said you'd sort her out some plane tickets."

"Listen, you pointless little pissed-up scrubber. Until you get your shit together, Paris isn't coming anywhere near you and that bunch of other losers that you hang out with. She really doesn't need you teaching her the best ways to sunbathe topless, get pissed up on cheap sangria before midday, and how to get gang-fucked by greasy Spanish waiters to avoid paying your tab."

The 'fuck you' that followed was cut off by Slater ending the call and flinging the tablet down onto a large cushion.

Paris huffed and reluctantly dragged herself off the sofa. Slater couldn't care less how inconvenient his little errands were to her whirlwind life of selfies, tweeting pictures of stacks of Chanel shopping bags, Instagramming herself on sunbeds and so on. She lived rent free with nothing more inconvenient than the Vietnamese nail artist turning up ten minutes late to ever have to worry about. This was her earning her pocket money.

Slater walked out of the house, closely followed by Paris, just as the Discovery pulled up in the middle of the courtyard. The driver got out and went around to the back door to let Olivia out.

"Who's that?" whispered Paris leaning closely into his ear.

"Can't remember her name, Lucy or something," he whispered back. "She's the daughter of someone I had invited here to complete a business deal, but would you believe he went AWOL en route. This little one was already on the plane, which of course had to take off immediately so that it didn't lose its slot, and so she is going to stay with us for a little while. I need you to babysit her. Make her feel, erm, not shit scared shall we say. I don't want her going off on one trying to do a runner."

"Bloody hell. Why have I got to do it?"

"Because you're a bird. You're not as threatening. What, do you think I should get Terence to look after her or something? It'll be fine, what I mean is that you're better at this sort of stuff than I am. She's going to stay in the annexe. Where we can keep an eye on her, but she can't go anywhere. And whatever you do, *do not* let her go in the barn."

"Fine," replied Paris, "but I want a holiday to Marbella afterwards."

She walked over to the car where Olivia was very slowly stepping out of the back door. Olivia held onto the inside of the door and turned her back towards the strangers who were there to meet her. She glanced over her shoulder as Paris approached and clung tighter to the handle.

"Hey," said Paris, bending down slightly — although only eleven, Olivia was nearly as tall as she was — and placed a sisterly hand on her shoulder. "I'm Paris. What's your name?"

"Olivia."

"Hello, Olivia. Would you like to come and say hello to my dad. He's a friend of your dad's."

"No, he isn't. You're lying. He hurt my dad. And he took me away from him. I'm scared. I want to go home."

"Er, yes, I'm sure you are," replied Paris, trying her best to comfort Olivia who had turned away again and buried her head in her arms. "So, Olivia. Do you like One Direction?"

Olivia shook her head in her arms.

"Er, right. What about Little Mix?"

"No."

"Lady Gaga?"

"No."

"Come on, Olivia, you must like some music."

"I like Ash."

"Who?"

"Ash. My dad plays it in the car all the time. Kung Fu, Girl From Mars, they're my favourite songs. And Guns N' Roses."

"Really? Er, I'm sure we can probably find you some of them. Do you like Xbox?" Paris sensed a small break-through in her defences.

Slowly Olivia turned her head. "No, I don't. My dad says that Xboxes are for losers who don't know how to play computer games. I like PlayStation 4."

"What's your favourite game?"

"Overwatch."

"Okay, have you ever played Overwatch on a cinema screen?"

"No."

"Would you like to?"

Olivia turned around, and clocked the friendly smile beaming back at her. She didn't know who this girl was, but she was certainly a lot nicer than all the big burly aggressive men she had met so far that morning since leaving the hostel.

"That. Would. Be. Epic."

"How about I order a PS4, with Overwatch, to arrive here later today?"

"Okay," replied Olivia, now decidedly more comfortable in her strange new surroundings.

Paris took her over to meet her dad. Slater knelt down on one knee and held out his hand, which Olivia took and shook like she had been taught to do at school.

"Hello, Olivia. My name is Curtis, but you can call me CS," he said in the friendliest tone he could manage. "I'm a friend of your dad's. We are working on a little business arrangement at the moment and I have offered to take care of you for a while. Paris will see to it that you have everything that you need."

Paris placed her arm around Olivia. "You'll need some stuff to wear. I know an awesome website that sells absolutely lush clothes. How about you and me go in and spend some of 'CS's' money?"

Olivia giggled and nodded. As the two of them walked past, Slater leant over and whispered in Paris's ear, "One holiday to Marbella coming up."

Just then, the quiet calm that had descended over the courtyard was shattered as the ridiculously loud roar of a souped-up, over-sized exhaust came thundering down the country lane.

Paris jumped up and down like an excited kid in a sweet shop, clapping her hands as the blue Subaru Impreza II with its drainpipe-sized exhaust and a spoiler as big as Belgium, performed a handbreak turn through the gates and came skidding to a halt in front of Slater and the others.

"Roach!" she shouted, letting go of Olivia's hand and running around to the driver's side.

"Great, that's all I f—" muttered Slater to himself, before realising he was alone with Olivia and exercising some enormous self-restraint continued, "f... flipping well need."

"Who's he?" asked Olivia. "He's got a stupid car."

Slater patted her head. "You're not wrong, little girl."

As Roach got out of the car, Paris was clinging around his neck like a baby baboon before he could even stand up straight. Fighting against the smothering kisses that peppered his face like machine gunfire, he finally got up, shut the door, and joined in the embrace, planting two massive hands onto her backside with a loud slap.

"Ah-hem." Slater coughed loudly, causing the two to break a cuddle that wouldn't have seemed out of place in a Greco-Roman wrestling match.

Ignoring his girlfriend's dad's obvious annoyance, Roach slid across the bonnet of his car, adjusted his sagging jeans closer to in line with the top of his arse crack rather than the bottom of it and went over to shake Slater's hand.

Slater held out his hand, boredom etched across his face, wondering why in the hell his daughter had ended up with this comical wannabe gangster.

William Roachford, nineteen years old, the son of two very respectable parents, one an insurance broker in the City, the other a local GP. By day, William stacked shelves in the local Lidl for eight pounds an hour — he called it 'the legitimate side to his business' — and by night he became 'Roach' — a convenient nickname chosen because it sounded like the small piece of card ripped from a packet of cigarette papers and rolled up to form a make-shift filter in joints — boy-racer extraordinaire and aspiring marijuana baron with the Twitter handle *@ganjamonster*. Roach's hand began its journey somewhere around his right ear, took a huge circular arc before slapping loudly into Slater's solid palm.

"Alri', Curt, was happ'nin', bruh," he said in his best 'street' voice.

"Bra?"

"Yeah, bruh, man. Like my bruh, innit. You know, like, brother."

Olivia giggled as she stood holding Paris's hand, who had now come to join them.

"Please don't call me 'bra', William," replied Slater.

"Nah, man, no one calls me William, Curt. Except for my mum. It'd mean a tonne, man, if you called me Roach. That's what my homeboys call me."

Slater pulled his hand and wrapped his other arm around Roach's shoulder, yanking the boy close so he could whisper in his ear. "Listen, you little two bit piece of shit, by *homeboys* I assume you mean the supervisor, and all the other pus-faced losers, in the frozen food section at Lidl. If you ever call me Curt or Bra again, I will rip that poxy bumper off your car and ram it up your arse. You call me Mr Slater. There are two reasons why I am not, at this moment in time, slapping *yo' bitch ass* around the courtyard and it's those two girls over there. Just because you have run a few little errands for me, does not, and I'll repeat slower so that you can understand it, does *not* make you my right-hand man. And it does not mean that I massively approve of you dating my daughter. Clear?"

"Yes, Mr Slater," replied Roach. "Sorry, Mr Slater."

Slater released his hold and turned back towards Paris and Olivia. "William, this is our guest Olivia. She'll be staying with us for a while. Paris is looking after her for me, which means that you're looking after her for me. Got it?"

"Yes, Mr Slater."

"Okay, good. Now, Olivia, do you know your daddy's mobile number? I think it would be nice to send him a little text message, just say that you're doing fine and having such a nice time."

Olivia read out Pete's mobile number. He had bored her senseless with forcing her to remember it in case of an emergency. Not that she saw this as an emergency, but it seemed okay to give it to this man.

Terence pulled a nondescript, slightly old mobile from his pocket and handed it over. Slater bent down to show her the text, saying it out loud as he typed it in.

Hi Pete, it's Curtis. Just to say Olivia arrived safely. She is going to have fish and chips for her tea. We've set the PS4 up in the cinema room for her. If I am able to drag her away from it, I will have her call you. Love you, Daddy (that bit was from Olivia).

Olivia giggled and nodded.

"Okay, great. So you go inside with Paris and make yourself at home."

Paris led Olivia by the hand over the front door of the annexe on the side of the main building, with Roach following whispering something in her ear about 'fucking babysitting.' Slater waved as they went inside and promptly deleted the unsent text from the phone and typed: *Pete. We have your daughter. She's fine for now. If I get wind of you trying anything stupid I will gut her like a fish and post you the contents.*

Chapter 19

After a few hours, the stark white walls, ceiling and floor of the clean room would begin to cause levels of sensory deprivation effects akin to military torture rooms. The glass bottles and flasks bubbled away on the metal laboratory table along one side of the room, their lurid-coloured contents, resembling soft drink syrups, breaking up the dull monotony.

Every now and again a single drip from one of the distillation columns would almost shatter the silence in the room. The three people sat on the other side of the tinted glass partition were spared from this double combination of Chinese water and white room torture. It was hugely important to the trials that their brain functions were not altered by such psychological disturbances.

A signal sounded. Once the preparation had completed the required number of stages of purification and reached the necessary level of potency and quantity, the trials could begin. As the door to the room opened, a triangle of light cast over the three figures slumped in their chairs, stirring them from their various levels of awareness. Around each one's neck was a piece of paper, dangling from rough pieces of string, upon which were written their names in large black marker pen: Anjem, Lewis and Miles. They each clenched and blinked their eyes, moving their heads to avoid the glare. They would have covered their faces with their hands, had their arms not been strapped tightly to their chairs.

Footsteps filled the room as the Professor walked through the holding area and into the clean room without saying a word. Like a conductor preparing his orchestra, he stood and admired the complex array of shiny glass tubes, Bunsen burners and Erlenmeyer flasks, held together with silver metal clamps and constructed with the childish glee of boy with a Meccano set on Christmas morning. He took the final flask from the end of the apparatus, held it up to the bright white light in the centre of the ceiling and swirled the faint blue liquid around the container. He held a card up against the flask, and compared the liquid's hue against six small similarly coloured squares. It was perfect, the same levels as the lightest blue on the swatch. The purity was increasing and with it the potency. It was his mastery of these chemicals, these reagents, these processes that he would be remembered for.

His employers knew what they were signing up for when they took him on. Sometimes, when you want a genius of his levels, you have to accept his less desirable personality traits. It was not his usual way of working, to be bound by other people's requirements, 'proper' — albeit under-the-counter — business transactions. But this was the opportunity he craved. Practically unlimited resources to buy the equipment he needed. Sophisticated, secluded premises to perform his experiments. And best of all, an almost endless stream of test subjects. Willing or unwilling, he wasn't really sure, but quite frankly, he couldn't care less. This was his work of art, his legacy to the world. His legend was already spreading amongst the world of clandestine chemistry, but some small rolling meth lab this was not. The culmination of his work would soon be unleashed, and while he would forever remain in the shadows — an unfortunate necessity in his line of work — his name would live on in both infamy and glory.

He took two pristine glass syringes and a rubber pipette from the sterile tray. The clean room allowed him to measure the purest results of his creations. Not contaminated by the usual filth that would surround a regular user. This way he could control everything and be sure that the effects he was watching were the effects that he had created.

Slowly the glass chambers filled with the blue liquid and he watched like a proud father, hypnotised by the wavy blurred image of his apparatus through the glass. The guinea pigs were waiting.

He placed the syringes and pipette in a small metal kidney bowl and walked back into the holding room.

"Good morning, my darling little piggies," he said cheerfully, before placing the bowl on a small table in front of the row of chairs.

Two of the three lifted their slumped heads to see who was talking to them, squinting as the shiny silver tray in front of them intensified the light shining from the clean room. The third remained stuck in position, a semi-constant river of saliva dribbled from the corner of his mouth and on to his chest, as his eyes darted from side-to-side, attempting to see what was going on. His head was braced forward in position by a metal bracket, protecting the cannula protruding from the base of his skull.

The silence in the room was being broken by the sound of increasingly heavy breathing as the realisation of the impending abuse became ever clearer for the three subjects. Heavy breathing and the cheerful whistling of *It's A Small World After All* came from the Professor as he walked over to the end subject.

"You, my little darling, are so lucky. *So* lucky. Yes you are. Because you, my friend, are trying my new, super-improved Brainfood directly through the gateway to your very soul."

The gaffer tape over the subject's mouth muffled his protests as the Professor jerked the man's head back by his hair. Placing a large wrinkled palm firmly on his forehead, the Professor reached down with his index finger and pulled the top eyelid back as far as it would go. The subject's body jolted, his other eye blinking instinctively, the acidic blue liquid burning slightly as it coated his iris. The Professor carefully controlled the man's head to prevent the involuntary need to close the eye.

"We can't have any spilling out now can we, dear boy?"

He placed another two drops onto the iris and waited a few seconds before adjusting his hand to repeat the process in the other eye. Lowering his head, he placed his eyes directly in line with the subject's, barely a couple of inches away and whispered,

"Your days of preaching are done my friend, your hatred now will see,

That as you near the bitter end, there's no one worse than me.

For when this Food doth hit your brain, my genius will show,

A most delightful type of pain that only you will know."

He waited a moment longer and then lifted his hand from the subject's head; the cue for the subject to start shaking his head and blinking furiously to temper the irritation.

The Professor took a large wooden old-fashioned egg timer from behind the chair, turned it upright on the table in front and then moved on to the middle chair. The man in it raised his eyes and kept a steely poise as the large strip of tape was ripped from his face in one fell swoop, like a mother removing an anxious child's plaster before they could protest. The men locked stares for a brief moment, before the man in the chair spat as much gob as he could muster as hard as he could. The large green mass hit the Professor in the middle of his blue surgeon gown. He pulled a cloth from a pocket and wiped it across himself before quietly smearing it back across the face of the subject.

"Now now, my dear..." he said, bending down to take an exaggerated look at the sign around the man's neck, "... Lewis. There is no need for such unpleasantness. I can see by the words 'Fuck All Muslims' tattooed across your forehead, and the swastika-shaped scars on your chubby rosy cheeks that you're clearly a man of high moral standing and behaviour like that is most unbecoming. Why, what would your neighbour Anjem here say? I think he would be most appalled."

"Fuck you, you little—" he started but was muffled by the same cloth being rammed so far into his mouth that he nearly choked.

"And you, my darling little boy, have the pleasure of taking my creation how nature intended. I always considered the use of delivery implements such as these a vulgar, but unfortunately necessary, burdens that hamper the true experience I am striving to create. I'm sure I don't need to educate a highly intelligent,

Neo-Nazi sophisticate as yourself in the ways of the epicure. But just as the finest Almas caviar should be served on mother-of-pearl from a chilled crystal glass, my Brainfood should be consumed neat. And then one revels in the intoxicating ecstasy as the warm, tart liquid engulfs the throat on the way down. A brief moment as the wonder of nature that is the human stomach works its magic before, BOOM, it begins."

He picked up the second syringe from the tray, a larger syringe with a much wider longer needle, clearly not intended to pierce the skin. More for the precision aiming and firing of the liquid as far down the back of his victim's throat as possible.

"You have an unrivalled potential, a marvellous demonstration,

For showing just how it's essential, to keep healthy circulation.

Bottom's up! Chin-chin! And the rest! The excitement has started to swell!

Along with your friend, you truly are blessed. It's one for the road…"

He paused and pulled the cloth from the subject's mouth, quickly squeezing the blue liquid past the man's epiglottis, before slamming his jaw shut and forcing him to swallow. Once he felt the gag reflex, he let go and whispered into the man's ear.

"…into Hell."

Upending another egg timer up and placing it in front of the chair, he moved on to the final subject.

"Miles, Miles, paedophile, cannibal and more.

Now every child you did defile, can rest in peace for sure."

Miles's head was held stock-still. He tried as much as he could to move his head but not only was the bracket which curved around his skull a very snug fit, the Professor also tightened two bolts positioned at either temple as a last safety check before the test began. As the Professor picked up the last syringe, his continued whistling was interrupted by the start of Anjem and Lewis's incessant bullshit talking. He placed the syringe back down in the bowl and walked over to the tables in front of the chairs.

"Forgive me, dear boy," he said to Miles. "I simply must check the timings on this. They're faster than even I predicted."

He picked up the egg timers and held them up to the light, closing one eye to read the graduations etched into the glass.

"Quite splendid," he said to himself, replacing the egg timers and making some notes on a small piece of paper taken from his overall pocket.

"My sincerest apologies, dear Miles," he said, returning to the final subject. "How very, very rude of me. Now where were we? Yes, yes, yes of course."

He checked the cannula at the back, causing Miles's head to twitch and another torrent of drool to flood from his mouth as he tried to protest through the semi-anaesthetised numbness of his face. The Professor patted him on the head and collected the last syringe from the bowl.

"And finally we've come to you, for all of us to treasure,

My eau de vie as it travels to, your brain's H.Q. of pleasure.

A fine line exists within the soul, where joy blurs into pain,

Dear boy, you've done it, you're on a roll. Let's look inside your brain."

Miles squeezed his eyes shut tightly as the Professor gently flipped the end cap off the cannula and inserted the syringe, letting out a small excited squeal as he watched the blue liquid slowly disappear into the skull. Once all the liquid had left, he closed off the cannula again and taped it to the back of Miles's head. He then loosened the bolts and removed the head brace from the chair. The minute he became free, Miles laughed and swung his head around. He fought against the restraints, swinging his shoulders from side-to-side. His laughter became more and more maniacal, arching his back away from the chair as if struggling to release enough noise.

The Professor stood in front of the three of them, watching in glee, clapping his hands together in celebration at his creations. Miles writhed within the confines of the chair. A huge scream accompanied increasing spasms, a large wet patch emerging on the front of Miles's gown as he ejaculated spontaneously.

"Absolutely splendid," said the Professor, going back to Anjem, who was hyperventilating through clenched teeth, his eyes wild and black.

"What's the matter, Anjem? Don't you like Daddy's Brainfood?" he asked, cupping a hand under the man's chin like a puppy, before moving it out of the way swiftly to avoid the attempted biting. "Oh, perhaps you like it a little *too* much, my dear? Don't worry, I will let you all go forthwith. I'm sure you're itching to get to know Lewis here a little better. How about you Lewis, my dear? Same I'd imagine! Oh, something seems to be the matter."

Lewis was so drenched in sweat that his gown had turned a good few shades darker. His breathing was slower, more laboured than the others, as if taking his time to make sure every breath inhaled as much air as possible. A demented smile crossed his face, green snot from his nose mixed with the torrents of sweat running over his inked forehead, bridging the gap in his permanently open mouth.

The Professor bent over, hands on knees, and looked upwards at Lewis's face and into his mouth like a mechanic examining the underside of a car. "Hmm, a little strange, methinks," he said scrunching his nose up and peering over his spectacles. "Not as much glorious pleasure as I had hoped. Perchance the increased purity has reacted too violently with the stomach acid, eh, Lewis? What do you think?"

A short gargling sound was followed by Lewis's head jerking violently as he retched up a mouthful of frothy blood which fell onto the front of his gown.

"Yes, that seems to be the problem," said the Professor rising to his feet. He took the notepad out of his pocket and scribbled down his observations. "We live and learn, dear boy, live and learn. Good job you're here, isn't it? Anyway, enough of the formalities. I think it's time that I let you fine young gentlemen enjoy yourselves. But don't worry, I'll only be in the next room. And once you have finished each other off, it'll be time to examine your brains. Okay?"

With that, the Professor loosened the buckles on all of their legs.

"Legs first, dear boy. Always legs first. We don't want you getting over-excited, falling over and hurting yourselves now, do we?"

He loosened the wrists straps just enough for them to remove their hands, collected his belongings and headed for the door. The three subjects thrashed more wildly, their impending freedom seemingly registering through the drug-induced haze. Just as the Professor reached the door, he felt a cold, sweaty hand on his shoulder. It pulled, twisting him around back into the room. He stared face-to-face with the soulless glare of Miles who clamped his hands around the Professor's neck and threw him onto the ground.

At the other side of the room, Anjem and Lewis had freed themselves from their own restraints. They rose from their seats and Lewis, by far the larger of the two, leaped at Anjem, digging his fingernails deep into Anjem's eyes. Miles looked up briefly, but was far more interested in his prize. The Professor strained for breath, his weak arms failing helplessly. Miles's eyes burned with fire and the intense strength in his grip forced the Professor's windpipe almost to the point of rupturing.

The door to the holding room swung open, distracting Miles, forcing him to look up just enough for the bullet to strike him between the eyes. His body jolted off the Professor, who scrambled backwards on his hands and knees through the open door, before it was locked shut behind him. A hand reached down, picking him from underneath his armpits and helped him to his feet.

"Are you okay, Professor?" asked the Smart Man.

"Yes, my dear boy. Thank you. Quick, no time to dwell. I must observe the remaining pigs. Come, watch with me."

The pair stood by the two-way mirror and watched as Lewis ran around the room repeatedly smashing his head into the wall. Meanwhile, Anjem crouched over the still body of Miles, ripping large chunks of flesh from the man's face with his mouth.

"Interesting selection of pigs," said the Professor, simultaneously writing copious notes on his pad.

"We thought you would enjoy them," replied the Smart Man. "Anjem Al Massani, hate preacher. He was supposed to be in custody pending an extradition order to Pakistan. And his very good friend, Lewis Johnson, head of the up-and-coming Fascist Protectors Of England right-wing Neo-Nazi group. He was supposed to have gone underground following his arrest warrant for inciting racial hatred. Finally, you had—"

"Yes, I know who he was."

"Indeed. Miles Blackmore, everyone's favourite child killer, satanist, cannibal. You name it, he probably ate it or fucked it, or both."

"Yes, he was an interesting one. Put me in something of a quandary though. Actually, look, I think they're done now."

Anjem stood over Miles's body, shards of flesh hanging from his fingernails. Before he could see it coming, he turned around straight into the frothy, saliva filled mouth of Lewis bearing down over the centre of his face. The two fought like rival lions fighting over a pride, before eventually Anjem pinned him down, clamped a vice-like grip around his windpipe and squeezed so hard that his fingers nearly met around the back. As he began more mutilation, the Smart Man took his cue from the Professor's nod, opened the door and shot Anjem through the back of his head.

The Professor entered the room, and wandered around examining the carnage closely.

"Yes, very interesting. You see, my dear boy, this batch was very carefully engineered to reduce the level of keto oxygen, which renders our Brainfood relatively hydrophilic, thus making it able to cross the blood-brain barrier much more efficiently so maximising the amount of good stuff reaching their grey matter."

The Smart Man stared at him blankly. "I'll take your word for it, Professor."

"So, by essentially injecting the Brainfood into Anjem's eyes it had a much more direct transportation to the brain than with poor Lewis here. And with Miles, well do you know what we did?"

"Surprise me," replied the Smart Man, sarcastically. He didn't really care how this stuff worked as long as it did.

"We injected it directly into the nucleus accumbens," said the Professor excitedly. He stared quietly at the Smart Man's blank expression, waiting for the enormity of what he had just said to dawn.

"Oh."

"Oh? Is that all you can say, dear boy! Why the nucleus accumbens is the very pleasure centre of the brain. By injecting it straight there, the blood-brain barrier was rendered irrelevant and he basically received a hundred percent proof, or is it two hundred percent — I can never remember — shot of Brainfood right into the centre of his head. His dopamine and serotonin production would have gone through the roof. Then when you mix in my little secret ingredient…"

"Which is?"

"Aah, now, one has to keep some secrets to oneself, doesn't one? Right on cue, if not a little quicker than anticipated, hence my close shave, the primeval part of his brain would have gone into meltdown. Not only his thalamus and hypothalamus, but the pons, amygdala…"

"Aren't they all places in Greece?"

"Don't be flippant," said the Professor, slightly exasperated at the Smart Man's lack of understanding the sheer beauty of what he had achieved. "His primeval instincts kicked in. Fight or flight. In this case, and in any case going forward thanks to me, of course, it will always be fight. I just need to open him up so I can get a clear measure on the precise nature of the chemical reaction going on—"

"Professor," interrupted the Smart Man, trying his best to hide his impatience and general lack of giving a shit about the technicalities of it all, while still retaining the necessary levels of respect. "I'll ask my question as simply as I can muster. Can we go into production with this new batch and ship it off to our new best friend Mr Slater?"

"Oh, yes, of course, dear boy. It would be rude not to. With the improvements we have just witnessed, the cleansing of society which Mr Slater is about to help us with will be even more… majestic."

Chapter 20

"I'm sorry, Pete," said Jarvis, sitting down at the dining room table next to Pete. "It's a pay as you go number, could have come from anywhere. We've got no chance of tracing who sent it or where it was sent from."

Pete just about managed a resigned nod of acknowledgement, but it wasn't anything that he didn't already know. No one in their right mind holding an ex-police officer's daughter hostage would do anything to give even the slightest chance of being traced, especially by something as obvious as a mobile number. He slumped in the chair, spinning the phone between his finger and the table, the words flashing in front of his eyes with every rotation. How had he managed to allow this to happen?

His mind wandered back a few years to sitting at his desk in CCU, a quiet day by anyone standards, flicking through photographs from his holiday to Ibiza. Olivia was three and Caroline was proudly caressing her seven-month baby bump that protruded between the two parts of her bikini. Pete had his arm around them both as the sun broke through the palm tree behind them. They all had the biggest smiles that they could manage. If anything summed up their happiness, their love, their hopes for the future it was this photo. He'd only been back at work a couple of days but already the holiday felt like a lifetime ago as they prepared for the impending arrival of their little boy, the one who would make their life and family complete.

Pete remembered the precise photo that he was looking at when the call was put through. It burned its image into his brain as the lady on the other end of the phone told him that his wife had been in a serious accident and he had to get to the hospital as soon as he could. Between the few seconds of opening the file, receiving the phone call, and slamming his phone back down on the receiver before sprinting from the office, his whole world came crashing down around him.

The second he arrived at the hospital and saw the doctor coming out of the resuscitation room, beckoning him into a nearby office, he knew she hadn't made it. As his whole life shattered into pieces, he wandered from the hospital to collect Olivia from her nursery. He pondered a thousand different ways of how to explain that not only was she not going to get the little brother she had longed for, that the little stuffed donkey she had made with Grandma would now remain unhugged, that the room she had decorated with her hand prints would lay empty, but that also her mummy would never be coming home again. He considered it a tiny blessing that perhaps Olivia was still a little too young to comprehend the full extent of what had happened, but she was clearly upset and he made it his sworn responsibility to see her come through it unscarred.

And now he found himself here. He had let her down, and he couldn't feel any more of a failure of a father if he tried.

"Pete," said Jarvis, trying his best to sound sympathetic. "I'll admit, straight up, that I have no idea what you're going through. Never had kids, never cared for them. But for what it's worth, I'd say that the best thing you can do now is help me solve this."

He waved the memory stick in front of Pete's face.

"I don't know what help I can be. The image of her petrified face as she was dragged upstairs... She seemed fine when she got in the car. It's just messing with my head. And now I get this text."

Jarvis sat and thought for a moment. As an only child, never having had anything approaching a serious girlfriend, the idea of being a father never even occurring to him, the whole idea of family was a slightly alien concept. The Brotherhood was his family and he had enough experience dealing with the wrong side of the moral compass to at least offer a small piece of reassurance.

"In my opinion, I would say that most hardened criminals, organised criminal especially, can't be dealing with children. Unless of course they're some sort of trafficking outfit. Er, I mean…"

Pete cut him a death stare that would slice through concrete as he struggled to scramble out of the hole he suddenly found himself digging.

"No, what I mean is," he floundered. "Sorry, that came out wrong. What I mean is that for a criminal organisation dealing with, er non-child, er based activities, a kid is going to be a major inconvenience. Most that I've ever dealt, well no, not dealt with, I mean read about, accept the risks and moral dubiousness of their activities but consider the abuse and killing and trafficking of children to be utterly abhorrent. Even for them. So, what I am trying to say is that, firstly, I doubt you would have even gotten a text if they were some sort of nonce brigade and it certainly wouldn't be threatening. And secondly, based on what I tried to explain earlier, I would imagine that your daughter is simply leverage and that really they could do without the hassle of dealing with a dead child."

Pete thought about it and tried to make sense of Jarvis's jumbled attempt at making him feel better, and with his ex-policeman hat on knew that he was probably talking a ray of sense in amongst the gibberish. If they had wanted to kill her, they would probably have done it by now. And something the driver of the car had said stuck with Pete. *It's in my interest to make sure you remain unharmed.* Even if they never intended to return her alive, there would be no benefit to them to cause her harm.

"Fucking hell!" Pete shouted. "There's no way I can look at this and be happy with it, the whole situation stinks."

"So while you can't go out there and do anything about it," replied Jarvis, gesticulating wildly with both hands in the direction of the window, "you should put all your energy and effort into helping me with the memory stick. I won't lie to you, we're at something of a dead end and we've only seen the jpeg file on the stick."

"Yes, you're quite right," said Pete as Jarvis opened the laptop and slid it in front of him.

Pete stared at the image. It was a photo file, a black ground with white, plain Arial text.

Hello. We are seeking highly intelligent, highly enlighteNed individuals to join us. To find them, we have devised a test. There is a message hidden in this image. Find it and it will lead you on the road to Enlightenment. Few peopple will make it. We look forward to meeting you. The Professor.

Pete whizzed the mouse around the screen, trying to highlight bits of the texts.

"So, it's not text then. It's a single photo," he said, as the whole image moved with his mouse.

"Yes exactly, very little to go on."

"What have you tried?"

Jarvis puffed out his cheeks and exhaled a tired breath. "We're fairly certain that the clue is hidden within the words themselves. We punched the whole text verbatim into Google but nothing comes up. Some similar sounding phrases showed up in various message boards on 4Chan and Reddit and so on, but nothing to give any clues. So we tried opening in programmes such as RAR in the hope of extracting anything of use from the image. We also used several filters in Photoshop, you know, increase the brightness, decrease the brightness to see if anything showed up in the image noise, but nothing."

"Why don't you go and get me a cup of tea while I have a little play around with this, Jarvis," said Pete.

"Well, usually that's Gilbert's job," he replied. "But I will make an exception on this occasion. Tea is almost as important as Pro-Plus when it comes to long winded I.T. projects."

After a few minutes, he returned with a cup of tea and placed it on the table. As soon as he sat down, Pete turned the laptop around with a huge grin on his face. Jarvis looked at the screen to see a Notepad file open with the usual streams of computer code and jargon that most non-computer people either ignore or never even see.

"Bugger me backwards." Jarvis scrolled down the file. "Of course. Why in the hell didn't I think of that?"

"You wouldn't probably. Most people hardly ever use Notepad. But look at the image; the capital N in 'enlightened' and the extra P in 'people'. NP. Notepad."

There, hidden amongst the seemingly random string of letters, numbers and symbols was something slightly more clear.

CLAVDIVS CEASAR says lxxt ##jvieoc[]wyfpmqi*9!1#4\7£ntk

"What do we have so far?" asked Alistair, pushing open the large double oak doors into the dining room, closely followed by Daisy.

"It appears to be a trail," replied Jarvis.

"And a trial," added Pete. "Some sort of recruitment drive, but only people who are capable of solving their little puzzles. I came across a couple of instances like this during my time in CCU. Organisations like GCHQ would put out job adverts for coders, cryptographers that sort of thing. And the best way to find the most talented people? Make the recruitment poster the start of the test, that only the very best will even spot it's a test, let alone be able to decipher it. The first image indicates that they, whoever *they* are, want people to find them, but not just any people. I would say this has either come from some Government agency with a strong bent in cryptography—"

"Which doesn't make sense," interrupted Alistair. "It's far too out in the open. And I wouldn't imagine a Government recruitment campaign would involve kidnapping innocent citizens."

"No quite. Most likely this is some very sophisticated organisation, with ideas above their station, who like to think of themselves as some sort of Holy Grail of the Internet. Look at the language they have used; enlightened, intelligent. It's all very poetic. But to what end? I guess we won't know until we get there. One thing I am fairly certain of is that they will be careful, they will be difficult to track down, but I am yet to find someone who does it perfectly. Without wanting to give too much away, when we were investigating the Brotherhood of the Righteous and their Red Room, in a way their arrogance was their weakness."

The other four looked at each other with raised eyebrows.

"They were good, of course. Very good. It was some of the most sophisticated firewalls we had ever encountered..." Jarvis nodded smugly, as Pete and the others stared at him. "You've, er..." he stumbled, "got to appreciate the craftsmanship of a well-designed firewall, right?"

"But we still got in," said Pete abruptly. "You're not aware of what happened that night, but during one of their broadcasts some sort of security breach knocked out one of their servers just long enough for us to gain access. And that was all we needed. I would imagine that whichever of their group was responsible for all their I.T. must have got the bollocking to end all bollockings afterwards, the amount he nearly fucked up their entire operation."

"Poor chap," said Gilbert.

"Yes, he sounds like a bit of a tosser," added Daisy, much to everyone except Jarvis's amusement.

"Okay, if we could get back to the matter of your missing daughter and my missing sister. Where are we up to?" asked Alistair.

"We've cracked the photo file, which has thrown up another small encoded message. But this seems fairly straight forward," replied Pete.

"Yes indeed," said Jarvis, trying to regain some credibility. "At first glance, it's a fairly simple Caesar cipher."

"Quite right," replied Pete, with a slight air of condescension.

"I *was* in charge of Phone Giant's website and e-commerce. I designed the security systems for that, so I am reasonably au-fey with encryption methods and this is one for even the most inexperienced of code-breakers."

"You'll have to enlighten us," said Alistair.

"A Caesar cipher is a very simple way of coding a message in which the standard alphabet is written out. Each letter is then transposed a set number of places to either side and written again underneath. So, for a one place cipher A becomes B, B becomes C and so."

"And this one?"

"The first four characters are *lxxt*, so we could comfortably assume that these are *http* which means that each character has moved along four spaces," said Jarvis.

"Okay, and the weird characters, the question marks, brackets, colons? How are they mapped?" Alistair asked.

"That'll probably be a bit of trial and error. Different keyboards configure their keys differently. Shouldn't take too long though."

After a few minutes of playing around with the coded URL, trying different configurations of characters, they found the one that worked; http://freaky#\sublime=9%1/4!7.jpg.

"Bollocks," said Jarvis as he clicked the link. "It's a dead end."

They transferred the laptop to the main bank of monitors on the wall of the dining room so everyone could see it. A large stationary picture of a cartoon rabbit appeared, with a large 'whoops' written across the top. Underneath appeared the words 'This way not right. Looks like you can't guess how to get the message out.'

"What the hell does that mean?" asked Alistair. "Are you sure this is the right file? Perhaps it's another one of the character configurations if this one is not right."

"Nope, I don't think it is," said Pete with a large smug grin. "I think this is a not-so-subtle piece of steganography."

"Isn't that a dinosaur?" asked Daisy.

"Nearly," Pete explained. "Where cryptography is the art of making a message unreadable by the use of secret codes and so on, steganography is the art of *hiding* information within an innocuous file, or so on, that someone at the other end can extract. A secret code is fairly easy to spot, right? You might not know what it says but you can tell it probably is a coded message because it just looks like a load of garbage. But if you can hide a message within, say, a standard JPEG file like our fluffy friend here, within the very code for that file, then it is far less likely to be discovered."

Alistair nodded in appreciation. This man certainly knows his stuff and between Pete and Jarvis, and with his resources, they would make a very powerful alliance. "So what message is hidden here?"

Pete circled the cursor around the words 'guess' and 'out' in the picture, accentuating their rather clunky usage. "I briefly flirted with a programme called OutGuess at CCU. We used it every now and again during covert operations to blend in with the hacker community."

Pete spoke as he worked, downloading the programme as seamlessly as if he were making a sandwich while helping Olivia with her homework.

Jarvis looked on, equally impressed as Pete opened OutGuess, opened the bunny file and watched it spit out a brand new web address. He clicked on it and it opened another image. The others all stared blankly as the screen displayed it's new clue.

Here is a book code. To find the book, and more information, go to http://www.reddit.com/r/a2G3F0Gmd2sg

It was then followed by a list of sixty-two numbers resembling graph co-ordinates, each line consisting of two numbers separated by a colon.

"So, it's more numbers that mean nothing," said Daisy.

"Not quite," replied Pete, pointing the cursor to the top of the image. "It's a book code. Or rather this list of numbers is the code. It's very simple actually. Once we have the book, that is."

"Presumably that link there will give us the book."

"Only one way to find out," said Pete, clicking on the link.

Alistair stared at the Reddit thread. He had used Reddit a lot. It was a sort of online Reader's Digest, aggregating news stories, website content ratings and generating discussions. Somewhere deep within the sub-Reddits, the surface web blended with his more familiar surroundings of the Enter The Dark message board that he made such great use of down on the dark web. There was some very disturbing content on this site, masquerading as innocent discussions.

The sub-Reddit was unlike anything he had seen on the site before. A long list of more than 170 posts, nothing but jumbles of letters and numbers. Even the name of the sub-Reddit, *a2G3F0Gmd2sg,* meant nothing.

"Gentlemen, I have some business to attend to," said Alistair standing up from the table. "I think I had better leave you to play."

The three of them stared at each other. It was going to be a long night.

Chapter 21

"Right, Fanny, we're off," said Slater, collecting his keys from the desk. "If you could please try to not fuck anything up while we're gone it would be much appreciated. We've got the call coming in about an hour, so this had better be fixed or you can kiss goodbye to one and or the other of your bollocks. We might even have a little pop in on Frank on the way, see how your old dears are doing."

While Slater went off on his business errands, 'Fanny' was usually left with some sort of problem to fix on Slater's computer system. In most cases they were caused by Slater thinking he actually knew how to use a computer, deleting some entire programme or file then blaming it on 'fucking Bill Gates.' He watched out of the window as the ludicrous motorcade of blacked-out expensive vehicles, with the respective number plates *5LATER, SL4TER and SLAT3R,* trundled out of the courtyard as though they were escorting the President of the United States through central Fallujah.

The main computer in the office was shut down. No one, but no one, knew the password to get in apart from Slater. Which made the job of fixing his little cock-ups difficult, so he logged it on and in one of his other little control freak tricks, set the sleep function to kick in after nine minutes precisely. 'Just enough time for a fag and a dump' was his theory, and he expected gratitude for even being that gracious.

'Fanny' set the virus checker running on the computer. Slater had a habit of believing spam emails that were addressed to him were actually meant for him personally. Always best to run a virus scan first just in case he had inadvertently installed some Trojan or other such malware.

The progress bar slowly turned green, ticking up to 1%, 2%, and after five minutes had only reached 6%. He sighed. He neither smoked nor needed a dump, but some fresh air would probably do him good.

Outside, he pulled out his phone and dialled his parents' house. This was his secret phone. When Slater had hired him for this job, he removed any and all forms of private communication with the outside world. 'It was important to remain discreet' apparently. But this phone had made its way in, hidden amongst the lining of his suitcase.

"Mum, it's me," he said, as he backed into the door at the side of barn, double-checking there was still no one else around. "Yes, yes, please, just stop talking, I've got to be quick… Remember, you need to pretend that you're not talking to me, okay? Just answer my questions as if I'm some sort of cold caller claiming to be from Microsoft and I'm here to fix your computer problem… No, I know you don't have a computer problem…"

He peered through the gap in the door, ever vigilant for Slater or his cronies.

"Okay, just give one word answers and don't refer to me by name… How are you doing?… Good, and Dad?… Is he still taking his medicine?… I don't know when I'll be home, don't ask me questions like that… No, I know you didn't refer to me by name, but—"

Before he could finish the sentence, he felt a hand over his mouth pulling him backwards. He dropped the phone in the straw as he stumbled. Quickly realising that his assailant was in no way over-powering, he swung an arm back knocking them away from him and onto a bale.

"Daniel? Daniel, are you still there?" the voice came faintly from his phone.

He turned to face his attacker, dropped down and gripped the front of their top, raising his clenched fist in readiness to knock them into the middle of next week.

"Danny?"

"Grace?"

He released his grip and held out his hand to help her up. "What the hell are you doing here? What happened to you? You look like shit."

"I could say the exact same things to you," she said, pulling herself up with his assistance.

"But your hand, what happened?"

"How long have you got?"

Danny checked his watch. "Bollocks, hang on. I'll be back in a minute."

She watched slightly confused as he ran out of the barn, stopping to pick up his phone and hang up on his mother. He never was great at multitasking.

A few moments later, he returned back in through the same door.

"What was that all about?" Grace asked.

"Never mind. Right, I've not got long. What are you doing here?" he said, examining the chain attached to her hand, and giving it a test tug against the wall bracket.

"They're holding me hostage. They brought me back here, kicked several bells of shit out of me, oh and relieved me of my middle digit. I've been here since, not sure how long precisely. No idea what they're waiting for. To be fair, since the beating, I've been treated all right. I get nice food, warm blankets. I saw Slater kick another man to death, so I've tried to be as courteous as I can. And you? You seem to be here more out of actual choice. How on God's green fucking earth did you end up here?"

He sat down on the bale next to Grace. "After I left CCU, I did a bit of freelance, how shall we say, 'specialist' I.T. work for various organisations."

"Specialist?"

"Yeah, you know, the sort of thing that we were trained to catch people doing back at CCU. Not dodgy, with kids or anything like that, I hasten to add. And never face-to-face. But then the work started to dry up. My mum was beginning to struggle with my dad's dementia. And it didn't help that my pointless waster of a sister had finished university and refused to get a job. I answered a job advert, an I.T. expert to join a small, family-run haulage firm on a short term contract. The pay was amazing. Hundred and fifty grand for three months' work. I came along here, not realising precisely who it was for, had an interview in which they asked me whether I knew anything about the dark web and 'Internet trials' as they put it. I never said I worked for CCU, but was able to demonstrate how easily I found myself around the dark net. He signed me on the spot."

"What's he having you do?"

"He was invited to join a shadow organisation, the one that presumably ran that Majestic Road website. But in order to do it, he had to pass their test. To prove he was 'enlightened' enough to be offered a seat at their table."

"I thought Majestic Road was closed down by the FBI?"

"It was. Or at least the public-facing dark net site was seized. I don't know the full ins and outs of it, but I'm guessing that the organisation still exists in an even deeper, encrypted form and the test they set was to establish the person's credentials for operating on the dark web undetected."

"Why don't you just leave?"

"Bollocks," he said again, before running back out of the barn and across the courtyard.

After another few minutes, he returned and sat back down as if nothing had happened.

"Why do you keep doing that?"

"I'm trying to fix his PC for some important call later this afternoon. I can't do it until the virus checker finishes and I have to make sure his computer doesn't go into sleep mode because I don't know his password. And I can't change the settings on the sleep mode because he'd notice so—"

"But did you realise what it was he wanted you for?"

"Not initially. I didn't realise it was Slater either. I dealt with one of his meat-head associates at first. They sold the job to me as their rich boss, with nothing better to spend his money on, had come across this mysterious puzzle online looking for 'highly intelligent' and 'enlightened' individuals. He wanted it solved but being a fuckwit, my word by the way not theirs, decided he would just pay someone to do it. And it was an utter ball-ache. I've never seen anything like it in anything we ever did at CCU. It was full of riddles, logic puzzles, advanced encryption methods."

"When did Slater introduce himself?"

"I investigated the puzzle further and happened to find a thread on our old friends, the Enter The Dark message boards, saying that Majestic Road was alive and well and searching for very select people to join its Members' Area. Once I put two and two together, it became clear that this was the end goal of this trial, but naturally I assumed that this guy didn't realise what he was getting himself into. When I brought it to their attention, Slater appeared and very calmly explained to me that I would still get my money, in fact he would double it, if I carried on and that he would trust me to be discreet and not leave his premises until the trail was solved."

"Why didn't you just escape, like now, when he's not here?"

"Because after telling me that he trusted me to be discreet, he then told me that, in return for not betraying his trust, he would not hurt my family who he took great pleasure in displaying on the TV screen going about their daily business unaware of the covert CCTV cameras he had installed in our house. Turns out that while he himself is a bit of an imbecile when it comes to regular computers, he does have some fairly clued-up people in the world of covert surveillance who work for him. They're just shit at solving riddles and so on."

"Do they know you worked at CCU?"

"No. Why?"

"I'm fairly certain that the reason I'm here is because of the Brotherhood of the Righteous investigation. In fact this missing finger here proves it," she said holding up her bandaged hand. "You've got to help get me out of here."

"No chance. I just want to do what I need to do, not piss him off, take my money and get the hell out of here. I'm sorry for what he's done, truly I am, but I have to think of my family. Anyway why do you think it's because of the Brotherhood investigations?"

"Because he wouldn't stop all this until I told him who it was."

"But we never knew. I mean, we knew it was all bullshit what was officially leaked, but who they actually were was never revealed. Didn't you tell him that?"

"Of course, but he seemed to think it was some bloke call Alistair Goodfellow and that somehow I could lead him to him."

"What? The phone guy? Why would you be able to lead him to him?"

"If I tell you, you have to promise not to say a word to anyone. Especially not the police… no one, you understand?"

"I'm not exactly in any great hurry to go to the police about anything at the moment."

"Danny!"

"Yes, fine, I promise."

"He's my brother."

"What? *He's* your *brother*? Okay, so if you forego the fact that someone I worked with for years and I thought was my friend has been keeping a secret billionaire brother, does Slater have any justification for thinking it's him?"

Grace kept quiet and made a deep sigh as she hung her head in semi-shame.

"Get the fuck out of here! As if," laughed Danny, before taking the cue from the fact that Grace still stared at the floor, rubbing her bandaged hand. "Bloody hell. Really?"

Grace nodded.

Danny paced around the barn, rubbing his forehead while trying to think of something to say.

"You can't say anything about this to anyone you hear?" she said eventually.

"You've got to be kidding. This could be my way out of here."

"Danny, no. You promised," she pleaded.

"I need to think about this," he said, checking his watch. In all the intense conversation he had lost track of time. And to make matters worse, he saw numerous pairs of headlights pull into the track from the main road. "Bollocks, bollocks, fuck, shit, bollocks. I've got to go. He's going to kill me."

"Danny," she shouted after him as he barged through the door. "Please, don't do anything stupid."

Danny ran back into the main house, through the hallway and into Slater's office. He shot around the other side of the desk and thumped his fist on the chair as the black screen, very clearly in sleep mode, stared back at him. "Shit, shit, think," he whispered to himself, peering through the blinds as the cars pulled up and the headlights went off.

Slater got out of his Land Rover and went inside. A few yards from his office he shouted to announce his arrival. "Fanny! I hope you've fixed my little problem you little pussy. Fanny?"

He peered in through the door and, seeing it empty, walked around to check his monitor. "Fanny!" he shouted louder, "where the fuck are you? When I find you I'm going to very slowly remove your testicles and shove them down your gob."

He left the office to search the house. A few yards down the corridor he heard a noise. It was coming from one of the downstairs lavatories. He pressed his ear against the door. Inside he heard the sound of heaving and splashing and banged on the door. The toilet flushed and he stepped back as the door opened and Danny staggered out, dripping in sweat.

"What in the fuck happened to you? My computer's off. You were supposed to fix it for later."

"I know, I must have eaten something dodgy. I couldn't keep it down. Didn't think you'd want me spraying it all over your nice office. Why's it such a big deal if it goes into sleep mode anyway. I've only been gone a few minutes."

"Because I like to know what you're doing when I'm not here. If I set it for a few minutes, you have to stay here working. Like I say enough time for a smoke and dump. I did not say enough time to go and puke your guts out. Let's go and see what you've been doing shall we?"

Slater led Danny back into the office, stopping him in front of the desk.

"Stand there, there's a good boy. Can't have you seeing the magic words, can we?"

Slater punched his password in and hit the enter key. "Scan completed, no problems found. What the fuck does that mean?"

"I had to run a virus scan first before I fix the main problem you caused," he replied, correcting himself as Slater threw him a stare. "I mean, that appeared on your PC for no reason. It'll take me a couple of minutes to sort. Then if it's all right with you, I'd like to go and lie down."

"What do you think this is, a fucking holiday camp? I suppose, you're no good to me firing from both ends," he replied, slapping Danny around the cheeks as he passed him. "Get to it then sunshine, there's work to be done, deals to be had, total and utter mother-fucking-carnage to create."

Danny sighed a huge sigh as he sat down in the chair, his conversation with Grace whirring around his head. He would sort Slater, then he would begin his plan to escape.

Chapter 22

"Yes, I suppose I am a genius, but then I guess you all knew that already," announced Jarvis triumphantly.

"I'm the only one here," replied Pete, staring at his laptop.

"Yes, unfortunately it has been a recurring theme in my life that the only people usually around to celebrate my most important accomplishments are me, me and, er, me."

"Is he moaning again about how under-appreciated he is?" asked Alistair, walking into the room carrying a cut glass tumbler of whisky, closely followed by Daisy.

"To be fair, this was quite impressive," said Pete, taking a sip from the glass that Daisy had placed next to him.

"Go on then," said Alistair. "Tell me about the boy-wonder's fantastic achievement. And don't hold back on the brilliance."

"Would you like to tell it or shall I," said Pete, before continuing from the smug prompt from Jarvis. "Okay, well, the Reddit post had the rather catchy title a 2G3F0Gmd2sgGmg32a0Fsm2 and was set up by a user called BoxThrottleMe. There were 170 posts on the sub-Reddit, all seemingly random letters. Jarvis here then noticed some symbols at the top."

Pete pointed his cursor at the row of hieroglyphic style symbols along in the header of the post.

"Egyptian?" asked Alistair.

"No, Mayan. A single line represents five, a dot one. So one line and three dots is eight, two lines and four dots is fourteen and so on. And what do we get when we write these all out as numbers? This..."

Pete typed the numbers out on a blank spreadsheet.

14 2 6 3 4 0 9 22 16 2 10 6

"And what we noticed was that this bears a similarity to the original sub-Reddit, which is then further expanded in the main full title. If you put it underneath the numbers from the Mayan numerals, you can continue decrypting the whole string of numbers. Like so."

14 2 6 3 4 0 9 22 16 2 10 6
a 2 G 3 F 0 G m d 2 s g G m g 3 2 a 0 F s m 2
6 22 6 3 2 14 0 4 10 22 2

"Which gives us our final code of 14 2 6 3 4 0 9 22 16 2 10 6 6 22 6 3 2 14 0 4 10 22 2."

"That was always one of my favourite codes," replied Alistair. "And it means…?"

"Ha ha, well," said Jarvis, pushing his spectacles back up to the bridge of his nose with his index finger; a sure sign to Alistair that he was about to enter ultra-geek mode. "This was the really clever part. See these threads of seemingly random numbers? What we realised was that we needed to copy them into a Word document in exactly the format they appear, and remove any funny formatting, URLs, that kind of thing, so we were left with just the letters. Then, you remember the Caesar cipher? This is a more advanced version, in which you take the first letter in the jumble and move fourteen places one way. Thankfully we chose the correct way first off. In this case backwards. Then the second letter you move back two places, the third letter six places as so on."

Daisy and Alistair stared at them blankly.

"I'm not entirely sure what you're talking about, Jarvis, but if you say it worked then I am inclined to agree with—"

"It's very simple," Jarvis interrupted, eager to educate his more simple boss. "Take the following letters:

Ongvxarn yu k joyq

"Now the first letter is 'o' and the first number in the sequence is fourteen, so you go back fourteen places and you get 'a'. The second letter is 'n' and the second number in the sequence is two, so counting back two you get 'l', 'g' go back six you get 'a' and so on. Until you get 'Alistair is a—"

"Okay, I think we've got it, Poindexter," It was Alistair's turn to interrupt. "That's what I love about geeks. Even in the face of my kidnapped, mutilated sister and his kidnapped daughter, they somehow manage to forget what it is they're supposed to be doing and start showing off how clever they all are. So, you've converted this ream of letters into legible text. Then?"

"This is where it becomes a bit more regular code breaking," replied Pete, trying to return a bit of gravitas to the proceedings. "We go back to the previous web page that had the book code on it. Remember, the list of seventy-two pairs of numbers? The first number in the pair is simply the line and the second number after the colon is the number of spaces along that line. We punch in all the co-ordinates and take the letter that each one falls on. And we got this message:

"Call us at us tele fone number two one five six four nine three three zero one."

"Have you rung it?" asked Daisy.

"Of course. Once we realised that it was in the US format of 215-649-3301."

"What did you get?"

"Listen." Jarvis clicked the play button on the wav file recording they had taken of the message that played when they dialled the number. A synthesised American male voice spoke out from the screen.

You are doing well. There is one prime associated with this telephone number and two associated with the original jpeg. Once you have found them, multiply them together and add a .com to the end to find the next clue. Good luck. Goodbye.

"By primes, I assume he means prime numbers?" asked Daisy.

"Yes, the phone number one is easy. In the US format, the last four digits are 3301. So that's the first one."

"And the other two?"

"The only thing we could think of were the actual dimensions of the image. And conveniently, the original image was 503 pixels high and 509 pixels across."

"And they're primes, I suppose."

"Bingo. Multiply the whole lot together and we get… drum roll please… 845145127.com."

Alistair rubbed his temples. "I realise that this is all vital, but it is seriously starting to drain my will to live," he sighed.

"To be honest," replied Jarvis, "I'm surprised that you have made it this far and are still even paying attention, congratulations. But it's the nature of the beast, isn't it? Whoever has set this is clearly very intellectual, very advanced, and like Pete here said, extraordinarily up their own arseholes. They consider that only the truly enlightened will have the qualities required to complete the mission, the qualities that they believe rank you alongside them. Of course, we never made it particularly difficult, you just had to demonstrate that you had the cold hard cash to be able to compete."

Alistair's loud, not-so-subtle cough alerted him to what he had just said and he stopped.

"Compete with what?" asked Pete, looking at them both.

"Well…" stammered Alistair. "Not a lot of people knew this, so I'm kind of letting you in on a fairly big secret of ours."

Jarvis stared at him, wondering precisely what he was going to say.

"In the not-so-distant past, we had a fairly exclusive section of our website dedicated to particularly high spending corporate customers. The Phone Giant one I mean, and, er, what Jarvis is alluding to is that it wasn't necessarily difficult to join. It wasn't like the AMEX Centurion card or anything. You just had to spend a lot with us and then you got exclusive access to top-of-the-range smartphones, deals, that sort of thing."

"Oh I see," replied Pete, disinterestedly.

"Anyway, getting back to this thoroughly interesting number website thing, to where does it lead, captain?" asked Alistair.

"There's only one way to find out," said Pete, typing the address in the search bar at the top of the browser.

An image of a highly stylised 'M' appeared on the screen along with a list of fifteen GPS co-ordinates, down the side of the browser window sat the usual array of adverts, mostly suggested websites with titles such as *Leftover iPad Stocks Selling for $50, 20 Unexplained Mysteries, Weight Loss Professionals Hate This Woman's Secret Technique.*

"Sooo, any ideas, gentlemen?" asked Alistair.

"They're GPS co-ordinates, easy enough to find out where they point. But in terms of what we do with them, not sure," replied Pete. "First thing, I suppose, this image of the M, let's do what we did with the rabbit and open it in Out Guess."

He right-clicked on the file and saved the image as file. After opening it in Out Guess, a new message appeared.

"This is all becoming fairly predictable," sighed Alistair. "See something, don't know what it is, open it in some programme or another, get new cryptic clue. Etcetera. Etcetera."

"Yes, it does appear that way," agreed Pete. "They're nothing if not thorough, and creatures of habit. Let's see what they're not saying this time... *You have done well to get this far. Patience is a virtue. This isn't the search for the Holy Grail, don't make it harder than it is.* Hmm, okay, not really sure that helps."

"There's more," continued Jarvis, "*The answer you seek, to lead to your prize, is hiding in plain sight, in front of your eyes. Before upon rocks the wanderer slams, the last wretched call, a surgeon damns.*"

Underneath this was written another series of numbers.

3,43,55,25 **75,57,28,12** *29,30,50,96,40* **16,79,65,31,19** *23,2,9,25* **59,57** *24,19*

P.S. no spaces

"For fuck's sake!" shouted Pete, throwing his pen down onto the table. "This is ridiculous, Grace and Olivia could already be dead for all we know. There must be another way of finding them."

"I don't think there is," replied Alistair. "I think we've been given this for a very clear reason. It's intended to lead us somewhere.

I don't know where, and chances are we won't like it once we get there, but I am almost certain that this is, at the moment, the only chance we have to save them. We've got to stick with it. It's getting late, why don't we get some sleep. This isn't the sort of task we can approach with fuzzy thinking. We need to be sharp. Go to bed, we can crack on with it with clear heads early doors."

"Fine," replied Pete, "No, it's not fine, but my brain feels like it's about to explode so perhaps you're right."

"Good. Think about it, of course, you know, see if you can come up with some solutions. If it helps, I'm pretty certain that the girls will be safe until we have solved this."

Pete and Jarvis stood up and left the room. Alistair also got up to leave, pausing behind Daisy as she pulled one of the laptops around towards herself and begin clicking.

"Are you really sure you should be doing that?"

"I want to help," she said. "I'm not really tired anyway. I just want to have a little play around, see if I can come up with anything that they might be missing."

"Okay, but don't be too late."

Chapter 23

"How much longer are you two going to be?" asked Paris, holding her hand up to the light, fingers straight and pressed against each other as she examined the sparkly spots on the bright pink background of her nails. "We've been in here for hours. I've done my nails twice. I'm bored. I want to do something else."

"Hmm?" replied Roach.

"Hmm?" said Paris, in mock imitation. "Is that all you can say? Drag your eyes away from that stupid game for just a second."

"What?" he said, increasingly agitated. He swung the controller around in front of him, as though it were a real steering wheel and that leaning his body from one side to the next somehow made his imaginary car on the screen turn better.

"Ha ha!" laughed Olivia, as her car overtook his on the bottom half of the screen. "You lose. Again."

"For crap's sake," replied Roach as he threw the controller down onto an empty recliner.

The three of them had been holed up in the home cinema room of Slater's guest quarters for what seemed like an eternity. Paris's promise of a PlayStation 4 had materialised along with a whole raft of games to keep her new eleven-year-old charge occupied and quiet. Unfortunately it also had the same effect on Paris's nineteen-year-old boyfriend, who seemed to have regressed ten years in age to a level of childlike delight at being able to play video games on a cinema screen that she found quite shocking. At least it was keeping the kid quiet so that Paris could concentrate on the important things. Updating social media with fish-pout selfies, nails, updating social media with more selfies, and reading *OK!* magazine.

"You play by yourself," said Roach, moving to the back of the theatre to join Paris. "You're way better than me anyway."

He climbed over the two rows of plush red leather recliners and slumped into the empty one next to his girlfriend.

"I'm bored. Can't we go next door for a little bit," he whispered, placing an arm across her front underneath the magazine, before sliding his hand up the front of her tight white vest top.

"Piss off, Roach," she replied, grabbing his wrist from under her top and planting it hard back down in his groin. "Not while we've got the brat."

"Ugh," sighed Roach flinging his head over the back of the chair, spreading his arms and legs wide and closing his eyes. "I'm so bored. Why won't your dad give me more jobs to do? I think he likes me. Just imagine how much my cred would go through the roof, it'd be fucking sweet as. I could tell my supervisor that he can shove his frozen pizzas up his arse and there would be nothing he could do about it. It'd be like *Goodfellas*. Look at me, I'm a fucking wise guy."

"Watch the language, will you," said Paris, slapping him on the thigh and silently pointing over the chairs at Olivia.

"Don't worry," said Olivia, without averting her eyes from the screen. "My daddy says those words all the time. Mainly when he's watching England play football. Can we go outside for a bit?"

"No, we can't," replied Paris, before turning her attention back to Roach. "Babe, I'm sure he'll come round to it. First, you need to prove to him that you're not a twat. He's very careful about who he lets into his *orbit of trust* as he calls it. Secondly, you need to be useful to him."

"But that's what I'm saying, I just want him to give me a chance."

"Can we go outside now?"

"I said no," replied Paris.

"Just imagine how cool it would be. Cruising around town in the Impreza, doing what we want, people eyeballing us. Just knowing who we were. And then shitting their kecks."

Paris turned and placed a hand around his opposite cheek, pulling his face towards hers. "Don't worry, soon he will see you're as amazing as I said."

As they locked in a kiss, Paris felt a sturdy index finger jab on the top of her thigh.

"Please can we go outside?"

"Fine," said Paris, reluctantly releasing Roach from their kiss.

"Great, I could do with some fresh air," replied Roach excitedly.

"Do you know how to play 'sardines'?" asked Olivia. "I'll hide first, and you two count to twenty and then have to come and find me."

"No, wait," said Paris, watching her run off. "Shit. Go and find her."

"She could be gone a while. I reckon I could give you a fairly large portion in that time," replied Roach, running his hand up the inside of Paris's thigh.

"Roach! Fuck off!" she shouted back at him. "Go and find her!"

"Ugh, fine," replied Roach, pulling himself out of the seat and slowly walking out.

"Go!"

Roach didn't need telling a third time and ran off through the guest quarters and out into the back garden.

Olivia peered out from behind a large upended beer barrel at the far edge of the huge terrace. On a few-hundred-acre farm such as this, the area of grass, trees and paved terrace had been designated as the 'formal gardens.' It overlooked the vast empty landscape that stretched into the distance, a patchwork of green and brown shapes of different size squares and rectangles. Not one single human dwelling in any direction, as far as the eyes could see. And it remained hidden from the main courtyard by the guest area. As soon as Roach looked the other way, she ran.

Turning back, he just about caught sight of her disappearing around the side of the house and sloped after her in no particular hurry.

Olivia arrived at the corner of the house and scanned around the courtyard. The guest quarters panned away to her left and then joined perpendicular to the main house. She watched the row of lights downstairs that seemed to go on forever. Directly opposite it, and in front of her, a huge wooden building stretched up into the hazy orange sky. She checked again behind her and then ran across the gravel to the door on the side wall of the barn. It took all her weight leaning against it to nudge the door ajar enough for her to slip inside.

The bottom of the door scraped a clump of straw along with it which helped to wedge it open a little. The last vestiges of sunlight cast eerie streaks through the gaps in the beams, crossing the barn like dusty vapour trails. She inched further in and looked all around, up and down the huge piles of hay bales that sat like skyscrapers in the void. She peered around the corner of the wall of hay and then saw it, stopping dead. The chain on the wall. She followed it with her eyes until it arrived at the body lying on a makeshift bed of loose straw. The body lay in a foetal position, not moving. Olivia stood and stared. She thought it strange that someone would already be asleep since it was barely teatime. Not so much why there was even someone asleep in here in the first place.

She turned to walk away, hoping not to disturb this person.

"What is it?" the body jerked around, glancing over its shoulder.

Their eyes locked for no more than a second. Olivia inhaled sharply. But she was dragged away by a yank on her arm. Groggily, Grace stood up, still hampered by her injuries, her attempt to follow them thwarted by the chain.

"I told you before, you don't go in that barn!" shouted Paris as she dragged Olivia across the corner of the courtyard towards the gardens.

"I know her though. It was Aunty Grace, my dad's friend," Olivia protested. "I need to see her. She looked hurt."

"Don't be stupid," replied Paris, struggling as Olivia pulled in the opposite direction. Eventually she let go and grabbed Olivia by the shoulders, holding her square on to emphasise the point. "That was Susan, one of our farm workers. She'll get a roasting from my dad if he finds her asleep on the job again."

"No it wasn't, I know it wasn't. She was tied to the wall."

"Don't be ridiculous. Why would we have someone chained to the wall in our barn?"

"I don't know, but it looked like—"

"It wasn't, I promise you."

"I want to go home now. I want to speak to my dad."

"It's fine, honest," replied Paris through gritted teeth, trying hard not to become too aggressive. "I promise you that was just one of our farm workers. I'll try to call your dad later, but I'm sure he'll still be away on business. So, why don't we just go back inside and what's say I make you the biggest bowl of nachos and cheese and we watch the entire Harry Potter box set back-to-back? You ever done that before?"

"Er, no, I don't think…"

"Excellent, so that's settled then. And please don't worry about Susan, she falls asleep in there all the time."

"Okay, I suppose."

"Great," replied Paris, taking Olivia's hand and leading her around to the garden.

As they reached the corner, Olivia glanced back over towards the barn to see a face staring at her through a window half way up the wall. The face registered for a brief moment before she was led around the corner and out of view.

In the barn, Grace tried her best to balance on the rickety pile of bales that she had managed to throw against the wall. The chain didn't reach all the way so she had to pull herself up with her good arm, while the other stretched out beneath her. It just about allowed her to climb enough to peer out of the small smoky plastic window to watch the young girl be led out of sight.

"Olivia," she whispered to herself.

Chapter 24

S later reclined in the leather armchair that had now found almost permanent residence directly opposite the huge television screen, currently doubling as a computer monitor. His beverage of choice for tonight's entertainment was Foster's lager, 2018 vintage, straight from the can. The first time he watched it he was, not that he would admit to anyone listening, a little bit nervous. Drinking the expensive cognac from a suitably expensive tumbler helped remember who he was. Or rather how important he was and how these fuckers would have no choice but to stand up and listen to him. Now, five cans down, he might as well have been watching the four o'clock kick-off on a Sunday afternoon such was his ease with viewing the demonstrations on the Majestic Road members' area.

He watched as the sinister form of Professor Black, in usual demonstration uniform of full on seventeenth century plague doctor, skipped across his screen, stopping briefly to grip the throat of the single subject bound to his chair. The subject opened his mouth to gasp for air. As he did so, the Professor held a small white tube which popped as he pressed the tip and fired a tablet to the back of his throat. He then poured a small cup of water in, let go of the throat and pushed the subject's bottom jaw shut. The liquid forced him to swallow, and happy that the pill had disappeared the Professor walked away.

"I've always enjoyed a good movie. The best? Where the zombies all play.
And Carlos, right here, needs to prove he, has what it takes to repay,

150

the treachery paid to his bosses, who have now brought him
here for my pleasure.
Let's watch as his sub-conscious crosses, new boundaries from
my drug of leisure.
The zombies of folklore do call me, the secrets of death have
they shown!
But what could be better than watching TV? Why, an undead
of my very own!"

Slater clapped in appreciation. At first the whole spectacle and
showbiz thing annoyed him, but he had fully decided why not
just enjoy it? This was his exclusive country club of choice. A place
where he could kick back with like-minded businessmen, chew
the fat over the current state of the illegal drugs market, relax,
have a beer, watch an anonymous young girl have drugs injected
into her eyeball shortly before having her throat ripped out by a
whacked-off-his-tits junkie. What wasn't to like about this place?

On the screen, the camera zoomed in on the Professor's plague
mask, whistling as he went about his business. Slater tapped the
side of his can in rhythm to the sound of 'The Blue Danube'
playing softly over his sound system. He squinted, concentrating
hard, as the subject's face, contorting in a mixture of pain and fear,
reflected out from the glass eyepiece. This was Slater's favourite bit.
He hoped beyond hope that they had saved the most incredible,
most destructive, most innovative of the Professor's creations for
when it was finally his honours to provide the pig. She deserved
to die special after all.

The camera panned out and the Professor untied the subject
from his chair. His head rocked forward and rolled around his
chest. He stood up and stumbled forward, raising his head to the
ceiling lights, mouth agape, before his head flopped downwards
again. His arms hung limp at his side, swinging forwards and
backwards gently as he walked towards the Professor, who stood
a few yards in front of him, arms outstretched as if welcoming a
returning child into a warm embrace.

"My friends," said the Smart Man from behind the white screen, "you have almost certainly all read the press coverage of the 'zombie drug' *Spice*…"

"Read about it? I fucking caused it," laughed Slater out loud to himself.

"Indeed some of you probably caused the last epidemic, especially in the UK. Am I right? Looking, metaphorically speaking, at you, Slater Associates!"

"Ha, ha, you bet, yer fuckin' ass boi," he replied at no one in particular, and for no reason other than he found himself hilarious, in his best deep Texan imitation.

"Here we have the Professor demonstrating our latest, greatest, most up-to-datest strain of this which we like to call… wait for it… *Super Spice*. I know, I know, it must have been one hell of a super genius to have thought that one up. Many of you are probably aware of the mechanics of *Spice* so I don't really want to teach you lot how to suck eggs. However, whereas your common-or-garden synthetic cannabinoids amplify the effects of Tetrahydrocannabinol, that's the good stuff in regular marijuana to you and me, by its total, rather than partial agonist activity at the cannabinoid receptors CB1 and CB2. Stop me if this is getting too technical and/or too dull by the way. *Super Spice*, well now that's another story. It works by… Fuck it, who cares. It just does all right. So, if *Spice* totally agonists… is *agonists* even a verb? I don't know, but if it's not it is now. If *Spice* totally agonists the nervous system receptors, then our *Super Spice* takes them out for dinner, back to their place, before fucking them senseless on the sofa and then going upstairs and doing their mum. It. Fucking. Rocks. Just watch this."

Slater sat mesmerised as the subject edged towards the Professor, his feet scraping along the floor, head swinging backwards and forwards, saliva spraying from his mouth. His fingers curled up into claws, swinging as much as his semi-paralysed arms would allow. Then, just as he reached within a few inches from the Professor, he stopped. His arms hung even more lifeless than before, his head dropped into his chest and he simply stood as if his feet had become stuck in quick drying cement.

"See? How quick was that?" said the Smart Man. "If we were to let Abdul here just be, he'd probably come around in a couple of hours, not have the slightest fucking clue where he is or how he got there. But simply itching beyond words for another hit. That's if we were to let him be of course. Which we're not. Firstly, Professor if you would."

The Professor pulled out a razor-sharp scalpel from his chest pocket. Very methodically he pulled the loose skin from around the subject's elbow into an elongated cone which he then sliced through as easily as a hot knife through butter. Nothing, not even the slightest flinch. He then held the subject's hand up for the camera to zoom in, before proceeding to slice, one by one, through the first tendons of each finger. Again nothing.

"As you can see, ladies and gentlemen, our friend's brain has switched off to such an extreme level of unconsciousness, he might as well have been watching a three hour documentary about the history of bricks."

"Fucking brilliant!" shouted Slater at the screen. "I've got just the town in mind to unleash this into. York. Never liked York, poxy up-its-own-arse shithole."

"There will be the usual purchasing opportunity at the end of the show. But first, we thought that you would like to see how our batch of Brainfood is coming along. Especially you, Slater Associates. We are very excited to bring you a sneak preview of your purchase."

Two orderlies appeared from the side of the stage. Between them, thrashing around as they tried to control him by two heavy chains manacled to his wrists, was another subject, dressed only in a white T-shirt and white underpants. At the same time, a cage descended from the ceiling, covering the zombie-like form of the first subject.

The two orderlies dragged the new subject to the door being held open by the Professor, who stopped them suddenly, dragged the thrashing head of the subject by the jaw as if to have one last examination of his creation before setting it free. The subject, wide-eyed and laughing hysterically, stopped for a brief second as he slammed his mouth shut. He then opened it again and spat the tip of his own tongue at the Professor's face. The Professor pulled him, one-armed, by the chin into the cage along with a helpful shove from the orderlies.

"Get ready, our most distinguished guests," spoke the Smart Man. "I am sure you're absolutely going to—"

Silence. The screen went black and the words 'connection lost' appeared in the middle.

Slater held his hands out, questioning exactly what had just happened. He jabbed at the tablet resting on the arm of his chair. "What the fuck? Fanny! Fanny! Get in here now."

He stood up, trying the tablet again, before crushing his can and throwing it against the mirror hanging behind the chair, sending dregs of beer spraying over the wall.

"Fanny!" he shouted again. "Fanny! Get the bastard hell in here, you useless piece of turd."

He heard the footsteps approaching down the hallway.

As soon as Danny appeared at the door, Slater grabbed him by his T-shirt, and pulled him to the monitor screen.

"What the hell's going on, Poindexter?" he asked. "It was just getting to the good bit and then this happened."

"Okay, Curtis," replied Danny, swiping Slater's hand away from his chest. "I could probably work better if you didn't insist on cuddling me while I did it. It's just your rubbish broadband again. I realise you have your reasons for being this far out in the sticks, but even with a dedicated fibre-optic line, it still only takes a cow to dump in the wrong part of the field and you're screwed. And that's not my fault by the way."

"Fine. Just sort it out. I'm going for a piss and I think I'm out of beers. This had better be fixed before I get back."

"I need to log on though."

Slater grabbed the tablet, held it up in front of his face and punched in his password. Danny watched intently as he drunkenly poked at the screen, before finally handing the tablet over.

"Get it back on, and then get the hell out."

Danny didn't bother responding and set to checking all the network settings, turned the router off and on, all the usual tricks. After a couple of minutes he breathed a sigh of relief as the light flashed green on the router.

"Poxy farm broadband," he muttered to himself.

He pressed the refresh button on the Tor browser address bar. He heard the toilet flush and Slater stumble out into the kitchen. The screen finally connected to Slater's previous viewing. Danny stared at it and smiled. It was nothing worse than what he had seen before in his time at CCU, but had half-expected to find some grotty porn site rather than the current footage. He watched as the figure sat astride its victim, fleshy lumps stuck to his face, flailing huge strips of skin from its victim's chest with his bare hands.

"Okay, so that was a fairly conclusive demonstration, I'd say," spoke the Smart Man. "Sorry, we appear to have lost Slater Associates. It would have been nice for them to see how their next delivery is coming along. And also to give them a sneak preview of the amazing hospitality that their chosen subject can expect here at Majestic Road."

Danny heard the fridge door slam and ran out of the room, meeting Slater in the corridor.

"I got your connection back up and running, Curtis. It should be on the screen by the time you get there."

"It had fucking better be," replied Slater, barging past him.

"You're welcome."

Slater returned to the room and picked up the tablet from the table. He punched in a message apologising for the I.T. trouble, but assured them that he was here now very much in the market for some *Super Spice*.

"Okay, Slater Associates, but you go to the back of the classroom and you wait while the good children whose daddies have upgraded their dial-up get first dibs."

"Fucking hell," Slater said under his breath, before angrily punching a new message on to the tablet.

I think you'll find that I am still waiting for two million quid's worth of your gear so how about you treat me with a bit more respect?

"Of course, how very, very rude of me, my friend," replied the Smart Man.

As he spoke a message popped up on Slater's screen: *We will discuss this properly in private. Important not to let standards slip in front of our other friends.*

Slater sat back in his chair, a big, smug pissed grin of self-importance plastered across his face as the Smart Man continued on the screen.

"Roll up, roll up, ladies and gentlemen. This *Super Spice* won't be around for long. So place your orders."

The can fizzed as Slater opened it. He necked close to half the contents and waited for the call.

After a few minutes of bidding and some more theatrics from the Smart Man and the Professor, the lights went off and the show finished.

Almost instantly, a call box opened in the bottom corner of the screen. In his half-cut state, Slater found it tricky holding the tablet steady but he answered the call anyway.

"Good evening, Mr Slater," said the Smart Man.

"All right. Now what was it I was supposed to call you?" replied Slater. "Something like Shirley, or Sheriff of Nottingham. No wait. Sir. That's it. Good evening, sir."

"Mr Slater," said the Smart Man, ignoring the rubbish attempt at a salute from the other end of the call, "any chance you could move to somewhere not so moving? You're making me feel a little sea-sick."

Slater pulled the small table in front of the chair and propped up the tablet.

"Thank you. Now, it was very unfortunate that you missed the demonstration. We would have loved for you to have seen our 'gear', as you put it, in action. It is vital to us that our customers, especially ones as important as you, can buy with confidence safe in the knowledge that you will be receiving a first-class product. Now, as you're a relatively new customer who has already become one of our best, I thought it prudent to process this transaction with you in person. We saw how you made the most of the regular Spice and I think that we can do an amazing deal for you. It is very much our organisation's tactic to strike while the iron is hot, so to speak, and make sure our product hits the market place while everyone is still talking about it. So, what would you say if I told you that we could send you a kilo of this for the bargain price of five thousand?"

"I'd say thank you very much."

"Of course you would. So how about we—"

"We what?" asked Slater as the conversation box froze, the image of the Smart Man flickered beneath the slowly rotating circle in the middle of the screen. "Bloody bollocks. Not again. Fanny, get your fat arse back in here now. Fanny!"

After a few minutes of more ranting, eventually Danny appeared at the door.

"It's gone again," said Slater, flinging the tablet at Danny like a Frisbee. "I was just about to close the deal of the century."

"I can't do anything about it, Curtis," Danny replied.

Before he had a chance to not do anything about it, Slater lunged forward, grabbing him in a headlock and dragging him towards the router.

"I know it's something to do with that box thing. Make it work."

He knelt down, dragging Danny down with him, keeping the pressure on his neck. Danny tried his best to reset the router one handed, using his other to try to ease some of the pressure around his throat.

After a minute or so, the light on the front of the router blinked orange.

"There's… no… Internet… coming… through…, Curtis… Please… let… me…" Danny strained.

"No fucking way!" shouted Slater. "What kind of useless fucking piece of shit are you? I'm paying you an absolute sodding fortune to not bloody well screw shit like this up."

He pulled Danny to his feet, still gripping his head in his right hand and laid short sharp uppercuts to his face with his other hand.

Danny shouted for him to stop.

"Stop! You want me to stop punching you, do you? Okay fine, I'll stop."

He pulled Danny up straight and, holding him by the collarbone, head butted him once, twice and then again.

"What's the matter, Fanny? I stopped punching you like you asked."

Danny slumped to the floor holding his face as blood poured from his nose. Slater grabbed the glass tumblers from his sideboard and threw them from point blank range at Danny's head. One by one, the glasses shattered on Danny's skull.

"Come, you stupid little skunk pussy, get up."

He pulled the back of Danny's T-shirt until Danny was almost sitting up, the front of his top now sodden with blood.

"Why is it that I have to rely on pointless little nerds like you to get anything done nowadays?"

Slater took aim before planting his knee square in Danny's face. Danny fell backwards, slumped in a heap against the front of the armchair.

As Slater knelt down he grabbed Danny's swollen, red face and squeezed his cheeks hard. "Let's just call this the one chance that you're going to get. Next time you fuck up so monstrously, it won't be you I treat to a little Slater-time, it'll be that darling little sister of yours. Clear?"

As his head throbbed, and the blood pooled at the back of his throat, Danny tried his hardest to tolerate the pain. But sensing he could pass out at any minute, a single thought raced through his brain. *The reflection in the mirror. Just remember his password…*

Chapter 25

*P*ete stared down the craggy rock face, the stormy sky thundering overhead. Behind him, the bright lights of the bar illuminated the guest house against the darkness. He was cold and alone. Inside, the people were laughing and joking. Each had a drink, and there was a man almost identical to himself wandering around topping up their glasses. Next to him, Olivia sat on the jagged edge, throwing stones into the foamy swash which smashed against the rocks before ebbing away. He touched her hair but she didn't notice.

After a while, she ran out of stones, and spotted a large rock a couple of feet beneath her legs. She changed from sitting to kneeling, reaching down over the ledge. The rock sat tantalisingly out of reach. Pete watched as she strained, adjusting her position to gain precious inches.

"Olivia, I think you should come away now!" he shouted. "Olivia, it's not safe."

But as she ignored him, the noise from inside became louder and louder. His brain became a tangled cacophony of shouting, laughter, thunder, crashing waves and quiet giggling. From behind, he heard the sound of smashing glass, and as he turned around, he heard a scrabbling sound followed by a scream that turned his blood cold. He watched as her body fell into the darkness, her shouting disappearing in amongst the turbulence. Suddenly he felt a tap on his back. He turned around to see all the guests stood feet away from him, each one staring at him with a sinister, demented smile. Slowly they edged towards him, one step at a time. You failed her, came the chant. He looked at them, rooted to the spot. As they came closer, he shuffled back until his foot slipped over the edge. You couldn't save her, they continued. He regained his balance just in time. Then they stopped.

One man in the front turned around and grabbed something. He spun around, and held out the limp, lifeless, body of Olivia, bones broken, skin bleeding, limbs contorted at impossible angles. YOU… KILLED … HER, *they all shouted as the man threw the body at Pete. As the body hit him, he stumbled backwards, falling over the edge into the abyss below. The words echoed as he looked up to see faces leant over the edge.* YOU… KILLED … HER.

"Pete, get up. I've got something."

Startled, Pete opened his eyes. He was dripping in sweat as his eyes grew accustomed to the light suddenly flooding into them.

"Pete," said Daisy again. "You need to come and see this, it's urgent."

"What? What is it?" he asked groggily. Waking up in the middle of a dream was always the worst.

"I was playing around with the last web page and I've found the solution to the next clue."

"Okay, that's fairly important." He leapt out of bed, still wearing the same clothes from the day before. Or was it still actually the same day? He had no idea. "What time is it?"

"Two am," replied Daisy as she left his bedroom, almost breaking out into a slight jog.

"And you've been sat at the computer all this time?"

"Yes," she answered, hurrying him along as they marched through the hallways. "I didn't have as much of a stressful day as you. Plus, I felt it was important to help. I can't imagine what you're going through. It must tear you up inside having a family member, especially a young daughter, caught up in something like this and you can only watch from afar."

Pete said nothing. She was right, she couldn't imagine. No one could. The dream still raced around inside his mind, her lifeless body flying towards him. The helplessness as he fell. He'd heard that if you dream of falling and you don't wake up before you hit the ground, it's a premonition of your own impending death. Luckily, Daisy may have stopped him just in time.

They arrived back in the dining hall where the two laptops still sat, the main sources of light in the huge dark room until Daisy turned on the main lights.

"Okay, so what did you get?"

Daisy took the laptop out of sleep mode. "Putting the image into Out Guess didn't give any hard and fast instructions like the first time you used it, right?"

"No. I guess that would have been too easy," Pete replied, settling into the chair next to her.

"But from watching you and Jarvis solve all the other clues, I figured there must be something. And then I saw this, kind of stumbled across it by accident." She clicked on the web browser to refresh the page. The same image of the M, the same co-ordinates, the same adverts.

"I don't see it."

"Look again."

She clicked the refresh button one more time, and pointed to the column of adverts down the right-hand side. "There. See, that one advert isn't changing."

"Hiding in plain sight, in front of your eyes," he whispered, quoting the clue.

She pointed at the advert titled *20 Unexplained Mysteries*.

"Okay, go on."

"Clicking on it throws up one of those media-type sites full of adverts for useless shit and in the middle is this picture box that you can scroll along."

"The type you click through a couple of the top twenty whatever it is you're reading about until you get fed up with how deathly slow the whole thing is and click out of it?"

"Precisely, just like this one."

She clicked the right arrow on the picture box, slowly scrolling past various articles of unexplained mysteries; *The Dyatlov Pass Incident, The Babushka Lady, The Solway Firth Spaceman, The Hinterkaifeck Massacre, SS Ourang Medan.*

"This is it. The *SS Ourang Medan*. I quite like the stories in this page actually, some of them are spooky as shit. But this one is particularly interesting."

Pete read the article aloud. "*In 1947, two American ships received a Morse code distress call from a vessel called the SS Ourang Medan. When the rescue ships arrived and boarded the Ourang Medan, they found the entire crew dead, sprawled on their backs, with their faces contorted in agonising death faces. Before the rescuers were able to assess the situation, a fire broke out, forcing them to abandon ship just as it exploded and sunk without trace, taking all evidence with it.* Okay, well this seems to fit with the boat theme from the poem, but it doesn't say that it crashed onto the rocks. It says it exploded and sunk."

"Yes, I know. It's probably just a red herring. But, it talks about a *last wretched call*. Like this one, right?"

Pete watched as she copied and pasted the supposed distress call from the middle of the article into a Word document. "*We float. All officers including the Captain, dead in chartroom and on the bridge. Probably whole of crew dead. I die.*"

"Spooky. But what about the 'a surgeon damns' part? There's no mention in this article of any sort of ship's doctor. Could be the 'Professor' mentioned in the very first message from the memory stick, I suppose?"

"Nope," replied Daisy with a huge grin of self-satisfaction beaming across her face. "Watch."

Pete watched, oblivious to his mouth dropping as she highlighted the individual letters from 'a surgeon damns', cut and dragged them onto a new line one letter at a time until they spelled out 'SS Ourang Medan'.

"Fucking hell, that's brilliant," he exclaimed, "oh shit, er sorry, excuse my French, Daisy. I keep forgetting you're of tender years."

"Tender years? You sound like a pensioner. I am eighteen, you know," she replied. "Plus I've probably seen and heard far worse things that would make a squaddie blush."

"Okay, so this must be the last wretched call. And I am guessing that numbers in the last message are another sort of book code. I think if we—"

"Already did it," she said, clicking onto an Excel spreadsheet. "Take out all the spaces, give each letter a number from 1 to 96 and then simply take each number from the sequence in the message, find its corresponding letter, and bingo."

"And bingo you get…?"

"*Find logo. Three codes will lead to us,*" she replied. "I think that at each of these GPS co-ordinates there is this M logo, presumably with a code, QR perhaps. We scan them and once we find three different ones, we get our next clue."

Pete was somewhat taken aback. When he'd first met Daisy, he'd just assumed that she was nothing more than a privileged little rich girl, probably being groomed at some expensive finishing school to marry a rich banker or thirtieth-in-line-to-the-throne minor royal. But he found himself brimming with respect. "Daisy, I won't lie. My initial impression of you was so far off the mark that I'm ashamed to admit it. Here's me thinking that you were simply a rich daddy's girl, probably more concerned with where her next pair of Louboutins was coming from than school work. And yet, some of the detectives I worked with at CCU wouldn't have been able to solve what you've just done."

It didn't surprise Daisy; it was the natural thing for him to think. She so wanted to tell him the truth. To tell him about how she grew up being abused by whatever chav pisshead her mother brought back to their squalid little council house. About how she had tried to do well at school, when she was taken, but that her mother preferred Daisy doing all the housework for her while she serviced her clients upstairs. Or how she ended up in the clutches of Saeed Anwar, forced to prostitute herself to the most disgusting, the most vile of fat slobbering, stinking-of-shit old men. Or how she saved Pete's life.

She hoped that one day she would be able to explain it all to him. Just the thought of what he had been through, how his world revolved around his daughter, how he spoke to her and made her want to help him. She had longed her whole life to have a dad, someone who cared as much about her as he did for his own daughter.

"That's quite understandable," she mustered. "I am very lucky to live in such a fantastic house and have such a successful and doting father. But I do strive to be much more than simply the daughter of a multi-millionaire. He wouldn't want me to settle for that."

"I think you're wise beyond your years. And you're a credit to him," replied Pete, before a thought occurred to him. "But it's strange, I always assumed Alistair was unmarried. The press always painted him as the serial bachelor type, rich playboy, that kind of thing. I never knew that he had a daughter."

"Thank you," she replied, flashing a gentle smile at him. "Alistair, I mean Dad, always insisted on the utmost privacy for me when I was growing up. Even the people at school weren't allowed to give interviews to the local press when I started there."

"What about your mum?"

"I don't really want to talk about that," Daisy replied curtly.

"Of course, my apologies."

"We should get back to this."

Daisy turned from him and stared back at the screen. She punched the GPS co-ordinates from the list in the clue into her spreadsheet. Pete took a deep breath. She was somewhat of an enigma and there was something about her that didn't quite fit. But with the intense cloudiness that currently weighed on his ability to think, he was unable to put his finger on it.

"So, this is the list as it appears on the image. This way we can just copy and paste them straight into Google. Let's see where they point to."

She copied the first one into Google Earth. "52.25153 and 21.0641 takes us to... Zupnicza, Warsaw. I've always wanted to go to Warsaw. Next 48.85900 and 2.4068. Ooh Paris."

After a few minutes of punching in the co-ordinates and writing down the quite specific addresses, a fairly exhaustive list covering the vast majority of the globe had begun to appear. Denver, Barcelona, Okinawa, Sao Paolo, every continent was covered.

"Are we going to have to visit all those places to find these codes?" asked Pete. "That would take an absolute bloody eternity, and it's not time I believe we have."

"No, I'm sure that Dad has associates there. He seems to know someone, or have someone who owes him a favour, in pretty much any place on earth you could name. Anyway, I think it's time to go to bed."

Pete nodded and yawned simultaneously, before standing up and walking out of the dining hall. He stopped just short of the doors, and turned around, scratching his head.

"Why did only you come and wake me up, Daisy? Why not Jarvis or your dad?" Pete asked.

Daisy laughed a slightly uncomfortable laugh. "I didn't think it needed everyone to be woken up. Plus, the way I see it, you have by far the most to lose here. I know Aunty Grace is in danger, but that is nothing compared to what you must be going through. I was pleased that I had cracked at least a part of the puzzle and it was very important to me that I had contributed a small part to help you. But I wanted to share that with you, so you knew. We can go through it with Jarvis and Alistair in the morning."

"It is the morning," joked Pete. "Okay, well, thank you. I appreciate the sentiment and I can confirm that your fairly amazing contribution has been well noted. Goodnight."

"Goodnight, Pete."

Pete left and walked back to his room with one thought bothering him more than any other. *Maybe it's just kids nowadays, but why does she keep referring to him as Alistair? He doesn't seem like the type who would accept such a lack of respect.*

Chapter 26

Danny stared into the mirror in his room, slowly dabbing the warm flannel across his face, faint pink streaks ran down his cheeks as the damp cloth loosened clumps of dried blood that had accumulated at the corners of his mouth and eyes.

He winced as the warmth pressed against the tender swelling over his partially closed right eye. Even wincing hurt, as the one or two cracked ribs stabbed when he moved too sharply. He placed the flannel in the bowl of reddish water, supported himself with both hands on the side of the basin and looked in the mirror.

Through the thick thudding that pounded his brain, he slowly tried to open his mouth. Thankfully, that one part of his head had somehow remained intact. Except for the chipped tooth that he had no recollection of receiving.

His staring and daydreaming was cut short by a bang at the door.

"Danny, Curtis wants to see you."

Danny closed his eyes, his head drooped and he let out a huge sigh. The door opened and in walked Terence. He stared at the shirtless Danny hunched over the sink, a huge purple patch down almost the whole of his left-hand side. An immediate sense of sympathy swept over him, this wasn't a new thing to him either. Thankfully, so far, he had managed to avoid one of Slater's kickings, but he knew that they were potentially always just around the corner.

Danny collected his shirt from the rickety wooden chair, sweeping his good right arm through the sleeve and grabbing around the back of his head so he didn't have to bend his left arm backwards into the sleeve.

"He's in the kitchen," said Terence. He left before Danny could reply, or his pang of consciousness kicked in to make himself do more to help.

Danny slowly followed him out of the room, pulling the shirt across his body and buttoning it one-handed as he walked down the corridor to the kitchen.

He was met by the noise of extractor fans, a room full of smoke, and the strangely welcoming sound and smell of bacon.

Across the central island, Danny could see Slater stood in his grey sweat pants and matching hoody, busy juggling fry pans across the huge Aga.

"Daniel, top of the morning to you," he shouted enthusiastically. "Take a seat."

Danny eyed him suspiciously, and slowly walked across the kitchen to the enormous wooden dining table. Slater stopped his frying and held out Danny's chair.

"Coffee?" he said, pouring him a large mug from the glass jug, whether he wanted it or not.

"Do you know what, Danny? There are very few pleasures in life that come close to a colossal fry-up paired with a gallon of strong coffee to blast away the cobwebs after a night on the beers. Don't you agree?"

Danny stared at the steam rising from the dark pool of turbo-charged liquid spinning hypnotically in the mug. He pushed the coffee away. "Absolutely, Curtis, I couldn't agree more. There's just something about ropey meat products that makes them the only thing a good hangover needs. The only thing is, I'm pretty certain that I didn't have any beers last night. Plus, whether or not a fry-up has the same effect on cuts, black eyes and cracked ribs after taking a massive fucking kicking from someone you're trying to help, I couldn't possibly say. Although I guess I am shortly about to find out."

"Ha ha, that's the spirit, old boy," replied Slater, ignoring the sarcasm, as he slid a huge plate of fried breakfast in front of Danny. "Can't say my guts agreed this morning though. My first trip to the bog was a bit like trying to shit out a McFlurry. But anyway, this is a Curtis special. And you're honoured to have it cooked for you personally by the head chef."

"So, is this pig?" Danny stuck his fork into a disc of black pudding and held it up in front of his face. "Or is it the last person who couldn't get your poxy Internet to work?"

"Danny, Danny, don't be like that," replied Slater. "Okay, fine. I'm… I'm sorry. There, does that make it better?"

Danny scoffed. He imagined sorry was not a word that had found itself coming out of Slater's gob too much.

"Was it entirely necessary, Curtis? I mean, you really had to knee me repeatedly in the ribs? Punch me in the face?"

Slater gave Danny a matey slap on the shoulder, forgetting the pain he had inflicted until Danny's loud profanity made it obvious. "Oh, shit, sorry I forgot. Okay, I went over the top, but I do pay you to do a job, do I not?"

"You had one job to do…" muttered Danny sarcastically.

"Precisely," replied Slater. "And, you know, the beers. I just saw the mist, mate. But I do need to be absolutely clear about this. I'm in the middle of some business transactions at the moment. Serious transactions. We're not just talking about a few hundred Latvian DVD players from Del Boy here. We're talking millions and millions of pounds. These deals will put my organisation at the top of the tree. I cannot, and will not, put up with incompetence. Everyone has to be focussed. There's too much at stake."

"Is that right? So, presumably killing the one person in his place who actually knows anything about the deep web is a slightly fuck-witted thing to do?"

"Okay, fine," replied Slater, as he grabbed a laptop from the table and spun it to show Danny. On the screen was a bank transfer instruction. "To show you there's no hard feelings, take a butcher's at this."

Danny looked at the screen. "Is that to say sorry for kicking the shit out of me or to stop me reporting you to the police for GBH?"

"It's whatever you want it to be," replied Slater, with a fake reconciliatory tone. Although Danny wasn't going anywhere it wouldn't hurt to grease the wheels a little. "I think it shows a level of understanding between us. Just think of the difference it could make to your dad's treatment. One click of that button and a hundred grand will be winging its merry way into your mum's bank account. That was where you wanted it, right?"

Danny stared at the screen a little while. His mum was used to random payments dropping into her account. He had told her that he had hit a healthy vein of useless and very rich clients who would pay him just about anything to do their 'I.T.' stuff, as he put it. It was too much money to turn down, even considering the amount Slater was paying him by way of a regular 'salary.' But he knew that by clicking the button himself, he was essentially embedding his life deeper into Slater's pocket.

"Good boy, you know it makes sense," said Slater, smiling his usual, and very common, self-satisfied smile as he watched Danny click the *Proceed* icon. "Now, let's eat."

Slater sat opposite him, flashing an over-exaggerated grin in his direction. They sat in silence for a few moments, eating their breakfasts.

"I saw what was on that show," replied Danny bluntly, taking Slater aback slightly.

"Right," he said, stumbling a little as though caught on the hop. "That show was…"

"It was some sort of off-shoot of Majestic Road, wasn't it?"

"Majestic Road? I don't know what…"

"I've seen enough dark web shit to know that just because the news reports a site being shut down, it rarely ever is. Especially one making as much money as it was."

"But how the hell could you tell it was Majestic Road from what little you saw?"

"So it was then?"

"Ha, you fucking little tart," replied Slater, grinning through gritted teeth. He wasn't used to having anyone get one over on him, even while hungover. "So, you know all about Majestic Road?"

"I know enough," he replied, chewing on a mouthful of the greasy pile of meat, which even though it would have pained him to admit, was actually very tasty even if of slightly dubious origin. "There's the stuff that was made public: the online drug dealer market place, the ability to order whatever drugs you want anonymously and have them shipped to your house. In fact, without realising it, Her Majesty's Royal Mail, along with all its foreign equivalents, had inadvertently turned itself into one of the biggest drugs traffickers in the entire country. Then there was the triumphant announcement by the CIA and Interpol that they had closed the site down, seized a pile of computers and arrested a few armchair dealers. Cue lots of Daily Mail headlines with the screenshot of the front page that was replaced with a CIA badge and their defiant message, along with a whole bunch of scaremongering about the 'Dark Web.' The reality, to those in the know, was, of course, far more interesting."

"Oh yes," said Slater leaning forward, resting his chin on his interlocked fingers, adopting a slightly sinister scowl. "And what is 'the reality'?"

"I think you already know," replied Danny, holding his arm across his torso as he tried to catch his breath after a particularly loud belch. "The word from dark net sources was that the people who the CIA had seized were nothing more than shills. Decoys. Extradition fodder. Simply someone for the yanks to parade in front of their media to show just how much they were winning the war on drugs."

"Yeah, stupid fucking Yanks," laughed Slater. "No doubt some chisel-jawed jock with a flat-top standing in front of God knows how many eagles and star-spangled banners."

"But in actual fact, they had stopped nothing. Various message boards pointed to the fact that Majestic Road was still operating. An invitation-only site. Presumably they realised that they could make a lot more money going to the organ grinders instead of the monkeys."

"Is that right? What else did it say?"

"Just that they ran shows, where they demoed the drugs and the big wigs around the world that they invited could order direct. Most of them must presumably own the opium farms or whatever, that their merchandise comes from, so quite why they needed to use this type of site, I don't know. Perhaps you could enlighten me?"

Slater was slowly warming to this nerd. He had taken a proper kicking, had just weaselled a hundred grand from him, and was now even starting to question. There was something about him that he couldn't quite place. Obviously he knew his stuff when it came to computers, but he had a certain swagger that Slater hadn't seen before. Perhaps he'd taken a blow too many to the cranium the previous night. Or perhaps he now felt like he had nothing to lose. But either way, he could be a useful asset. As someone so at home on the deep web it meant that, not only was he comfortable on the shadier side of the law, but also that Slater didn't have to spend too much time somewhere he didn't really understand. *Sorry your honour, I didn't mean to stumble across that kiddie porn site. I was trying to find my experimental drug laboratory-cum-supermarket. Honest.* No, much better to keep him on side. For a bit. Then he could be dealt with in the usual way.

"Okay, okay," said Slater, holding his hands up in mock surrender. "You got me. I was invited to join this Majestic 12 thing. Not sure how. But I'm sure you have guessed what a large portion of my business involves."

Danny thought about this. *Do I know what your business involves? A few years ago I sat and watched one of your henchmen have his knee cap smashed with an angle grinder before nearly having his heart ripped out by a clown-masked dark net celebrity. I'm pretty certain I know more than you realise about your business.*

"I could probably hazard a guess at, er, recreational drugs?"

"Exactly," replied Slater. "Although I prefer the term lifestyle enhancement supplements. This site gave me the opportunity to conduct my business even more under the radar. No more need for any of that Escobar-style smuggling, you know speed boats out in the Azores, helicopters deep into the Columbian jungle, condoms full of cocaine bursting in some poor student's guts on the plane back from Thailand. You know what I mean. Think of it a little bit like porn sites. The ease of watching hard-core porn nowadays has pretty much put an end to the embarrassment of standing in some grotty corner shop, pretending to read the angling magazines while scanning the top shelf, before having to pick one, pay for it and walk out as the turbaned shopkeeper gives you the smile and nod that says, 'I know you're going home to have a wank.' This is the same thing; you end up with the same result without the risk of bumping into someone you know's mum. Sort of."

"I see," said Danny, finishing up the last of his fry-up. "And the girl with no face? What was she?"

"For fuck's sake, you saw that as well?" sighed Slater. "They do what you said. They demo the drugs. They've got some weird professor that does it all. He wears one of them plague doctor suits, you know, that look like a pelican. Talks in rhyme as well for some reason. Anyway, they peddle some really serious shit on this site. And you know what the most important thing is for a supplier of my level?"

"A gun?"

"No, it's—"

"Ten guns?"

"No, shut up. It's reputation. I've built my reputation up over many years, very carefully making sure that the people who work for me are the best through a carefully controlled mixture of paying them exorbitant amounts of money while dangling the risk of losing everything they hold dear directly above their heads. It's a potent formula. So, when the opportunity to be behind beautiful headlines like *Zombie Drugs Take Over Town Centre* and *Flesh-eating Drug Krokodil Wastes Junkies* comes along it cements you as the biggest baddest most untouchable son of a bitch in the industry. That and the nice warm fuzzy feeling I get from knowing I'm doing my bit for society."

"I see. I only saw a couple of seconds of it, but it reminded me of this other show on the dark web that I watched once called The Red Room," replied Danny, deciding it was time to test the water a little. The words hit Slater, just as he was shovelling an entire yolk, careful trimmed of all its white into his mouth. He stopped still and cocked his head like a terrier trying to work out what the hell its master was saying to it.

"It was run by some group who called themselves the Brotherhood of the Righteous. I mean, can you think of a more wank name?"

"No I can't. Perhaps they meant it, what's the word, ironically," replied Slater.

"Anyway," Danny continued swiftly. "They ran this show, right, where they had a volunteer, basically some old criminal that they had deemed to have gotten away with their crimes lightly, and people could bid to punish them. Actually live, there and then. And then this bloke in a clown mask would perform whatever the winning bidder asked for. After a few token trial-type questions. But really everyone just watched to see these scummers be sliced and diced in the most inventive ways I've certainly ever seen. Do you remember that couple that were all over the news for killing their two-year-old son? They did them on the episode I watched. It was utterly brutal, yet strangely satisfying. I certainly wouldn't like to get on the wrong side of them, that's for sure."

"And how did a little scrote like you come to access a show like The Red Room?"

Danny itched to tell him precisely how. But not yet.

"You hired me as your dark web guru, why would it be a surprise to you that I knew all about it? As long as you paid your Bitcoins you were in. Nothing like that trial that you had me solve so you could join Majestic Road. So you know about it then?"

"Not really," replied Slater. "I mean I heard that it existed. In my line of work you hear of these things. But some things you take with a pinch of salt and other things you take a little more seriously."

"Like Majestic Road?"

"Exactly. Much more my cup of tea."

The two men sat in silence for a few uncomfortable seconds. Despite the aches that throbbed his body, Danny was suddenly feeling a little less vulnerable.

"Okay, Danny, it's like this," started Slater, adopting possibly the friendliest tone he has since Danny had met him. "I'm always on the look-out for good people to join my party, and I'll be honest, they're few and far between. I've met some total and utter fuckwits in my time and it's taught me that when an opportunity arises, you've got to go for it. And I had a good feeling about you, Danny, the first time we met. And that's precisely why I had to test you."

"And hold my family hostage without them even knowing it."

"Insurance, Danny. But you aced it. So, how about I make you an offer?"

"Go on."

"How about I pay you the two hundred and fifty that I originally offered, you've already got the extra tonne this morning, so that's three fifty. Next, you come and work with me. Obviously we don't have contracts as such, but clearly you can see I'm a man of means who rewards loyalty and performance bloody well."

Danny sat and pondered, the whole situation spinning around his head. Here he was face-to-face with a criminal underworld kingpin, someone who he had spent a good few years in a previous life trying to arrest, offering him a very well paid job. The same person who also happened to be holding one of his ex-colleagues hostage. The same ex-colleague who had announce that not only was she the sister of one of the richest men in the country, but that said man was the brains behind The Red Room he had also spent so much time trying to close down. But so what, he didn't have anything to lose.

"Okay, I'm in. But I really can't take another shit kicking like last night. And I want my mobile back and to be able to come and go as I please."

"No chance," Slater snapped back. "The phone I mean, I can't see me giving you another shit-kicking. Not in the near future at least. I just need to finish this current project that I'm on, so I need you to stay where you are and focus on the job in hand. Once it's all done, then I am happy for you to have your freedom so to speak. But just so that we can trust each other, I'll do this for you."

Slater pulled his mobile phone out and dialled a number while simultaneously logging onto the CCTV camera of Danny's house.

"It's me," he said into the phone. "Stand down. Next chance you get remove the cameras, they're no longer any use to me."

He hung up the phone after a few more words of small talk and turned his attention back to Danny. "Okay? See, I can be reasonable. Not very often, obviously."

Danny stared into space. He wasn't quite sure how to react. It would take some time on his own to pull all the strands of this situation together in his head, but for now he was at least on Slater's good side. Danny's parents appeared to be in the clear, and he had tapped into a cash cow that he could keep happy simply by connecting to websites he was too fuck-witted to find himself.

"Okay, done," he replied eventually, holding out his hand, which Slater took and shook firmly.

"Shit. Sorry. Again. Keep forgetting about that. So, what we need to do now is—"

"Curtis," Danny interrupted. "Is it all right if I go and have a quick fag and then go for a lie down? That fry-up was blinding, but my head's pounding away like an Afghan immigrant in a brothel."

"Ha ha. What the fuck? I must be going soft. You'll be wanting maternity pay next. No wait, that's just the birds, isn't it. Thank fuck I don't employ any of them! Fine, you go rest your pretty little head and we'll talk later."

Danny stood up slowly, his muscles stiffening up from sitting in the uncomfortable kitchen chair. He walked out into the courtyard and took a cigarette from his pocket.

As he wandered around the gravelled area, he stared at the barn. The one with Grace in it. And he thought. As he pondered, he was snapped back to attention by a red plastic disc hitting him on the shin. He bent down to pick it up and looked around.

"Sorry," came a young voice from around the corner. "Can I have my Aerobie back please?"

Olivia ran over and held her hand out.

"Hello," said Danny. "What's your name?"

"Olivia," she replied.

As he returned the Frisbee, he stared at the young girl and something niggled in his brain.

"Thank you," she said, after waiting a while for him to say something, before running off around the corner.

Danny stubbed his cigarette out on the floor and walked back into the house, before returning to his room.

As he lay down on his bed, he wracked his brain trying to think of why this girl was significant. Then it hit him, adding another string to his already complicated and generally messed up bow, one that on any other occasion he would happily dismiss as being just too improbable. He convinced himself that he had just seen Pete Harris's daughter.

Chapter 27

Pete stretched, letting out a massive grunt of a yawn as he climbed out of the huge super-king size bed and pile of expensive silk bedding. He picked his phone up from the bedside table and swiped his finger across the screen, tracing a big O through the array of nine white dots to unlock it.

His mind clicked back to the hunt for Olivia. The opulent surroundings were beginning to make his stay feel more like a weekend at a health spa, taking his focus away from the job in hand. He stared at the text at the top of his list, scared to open it, although its message was seared into his consciousness. The trial, he felt, must be nearing its conclusion. At least he prayed it was. In a way, he was hugely grateful that fate had somehow landed him in the lap of Alistair Goodfellow, and now Pete found himself in a life or death race against time to find his daughter, he was glad he was on the same team as someone who had as much to lose and an endless supply of resources to prevent it.

He walked over to the large bay window and opened the heavy red curtains, bright morning sunlight flooded the room. Across the carefully manicured lawn, as a thin layer of mist hung just above, he watched Alistair and Daisy going through a series of slow precise movements. Alistair wore a pair of black karate trousers with a red belt tied loosely around his waist and nothing on top. Apart from the fact that he looked freezing, Pete couldn't help but be impressed by his chiselled physique. Tai chi, he thought. He had heard about its restorative and calming qualities. Daisy followed his lead, watching intently every subtle move, until suddenly Alistair exploded into a series of lightning fast punches and kicks as Daisy struggled to keep up. Tai chi this was not, Pete thought. More like traditional karate from the style of the movements.

Pete carried on watching, mesmerised by Alistair's precision, his energy, the startling way he moved so fluidly. It reminded Pete of something. Of what, he wasn't quite sure. As Alistair leapt in the air towards a large oak tree, Daisy threw a basketball into the air in front of him. He landed cleanly, before side-stepping and thrusting his leg out to the side, almost snatching the ball in mid-air and pinning it to the trunk of the tree level with his face. He held it there for a few seconds, perfectly balanced, fists raised in guard in front of his face, before spinning on the spot and kicking the ball away with his previously standing foot.

Pete wondered whether this was a regular morning routine or for his benefit. He stood at the window applauding as Alistair turned to see him and gave a pretend bow. If it was a regular morning thing, it was obviously hugely important as not to let a trifling matter like his kidnapped and mutilated sister get in the way.

Alistair walked inside and motioned to Pete to come downstairs. Pete replied back with a mimed 'taking a shower' which was met with a thumbs up from Alistair.

After the shower, Pete joined the others back in the dining hall. Alistair still wore his karate trousers, but had covered up his top with a sports hoodie.

"Good morning, Pete," said Alistair, gesturing to the huge spread of fruit and pastries laid out on the table in front. "A little continental breakfast? I took an educated guess that since you had a massive fry-up yesterday, you probably wouldn't want one today. Personally I usually only have a full English on special occasions, and even then I can rarely manage it two days in a row."

"No, I imagine it's not good for your physique or your, what was that, karate?"

"Indeed. Shotokan. It keeps my mind as sharp as my body."

"Very impressive little trick with the basketball. The way you held it there, it reminded me of something. Can't think what at the moment, probably some kung fu movie I watched once."

Alistair looked at him, wondering. He remembered finishing off Mark Rankin using a similar technique, but he was fairly certain from Grace that CCU hadn't been party to that particular episode of The Red Room. Probably best to not jog his memory if he could help it.

"Anyway, good news," Alistair said enthusiastically, punching some keys on his laptop. "Daisy filled me in on what she found last night."

"Yes, she's full of surprises. I must say, I was hugely impressed. You must be very proud."

"Of course. She's a chip off the old block. So anyway, she gave me the list of co-ordinates first thing this morning which I passed on to a few of my associates around the globe to check out these locations. It soon became apparent that this group had placed some fairly piss-poor posters in some pretty nondescript places."

He displayed the photographs up on the large bank of monitors. The first showed a scrappy piece of white A4 sized paper sellotaped to the inside of a bus shelter in Tokyo. The second was another similar piece of paper taped around a lamppost in Barcelona. Each piece of paper had the large 'M' logo at the top with a QR code beneath.

"That's it?" asked Pete. "All that effort just to find some scrappy bits of paper? I'm assuming then that the QR codes are what throws up our clue?"

"Quite right," said Jarvis, as he strolled into the dining room, cradling another laptop on his forearm as he picked up a small Danish pastry and shoved the whole thing in his mouth. "It turns out that although there were fifteen different locations, in the end there were only three QR codes to find."

"It said that in the clue actually, three codes will lead you to us," added Pete. "And what do the three codes give us?"

"Each one of them is another set of new images, but luckily we don't need to decode or unencrypt them. They're just pictures that make up this clue. Or rather two of them do. The third one is presumably another book code."

He put the two images on the screen, one above the other. Pete went and stood in front of the screens and read the clue out loud.

"*Named for a king, a poem where death doth fade,*" he said, before moving the second image. "*Meant to be read just once and vanish, alas could be seen no longer.* Any ideas on this one?"

"Yeah, it was a piece of piss compared to the others. I just typed the whole verbatim into a Google search, and there were enough words to give a relevant result. It seems to have picked out 'king', 'poem' and 'vanish' mainly, which gives us the work it is referring to. Then all it needed was a quick check on everyone's favourite online resource, Wikipedia, just to confirm."

Pete carried on reading as the article appeared on the screen.

"*Agrippa (A Book of the Dead). Agrippa is a work by science fiction novelist William Gibson...*" he mumbled the parts he assumed were of little relevance. "*300 lines... semi-autobiographical... embedded in an artist's book.* Ah okay, *its principal notoriety came from the fact that the poem, stored on a three-and-a-half inch floppy, was programmed to encrypt itself after a single use. Similarly the pages of the artist's book were treated with a photosensitive chemical, effecting the gradual fading of the words and images from the book's first exposure to light.* That's got to be it right. Seems to fit the clue. Fairly certain Agrippa is the name of a whole bunch of Roman emperors."

"Indeed, not only that but William Gibson was kind enough to stick the whole poem up on his website. Non-fading, and non-encrypted of course."

"So, do I need to do a drum roll for the next part?" asked Pete.

"Not really. That was as far as we had got. We're were just about to go through the book code when you walked in."

"Okay, you read them out and I'll find them."

Jarvis read out the line numbers followed by the second digit indicating the particular character as Pete scanned his finger along the screen, calling the character that he landed on.

"So, what have we got?" asked Alistair, mopping some pastry crumbs from his mouth with a serviette.

Jarvis typed the numbers which appeared on the screen.

pg9jf3wpv6ndi.onion

"Another web page?" said Alistair again. "Seriously, I've had enough. This had better be the last one."

"It's a Tor URL," said Pete. "I assume you know all about Tor, Jarvis?"

Jarvis and Alistair stared at each other briefly. "Yes, Pete, of course."

"Go on it much?" Pete asked.

"I know my way around." Jarvis opened up the Tor browser from his desktop and copied the link into the address bar. The three of them watched as the screen went black and another nondescript message in plain white writing appeared on the screen.

Congratulations. You have done well. Create a new email address with a public, free, web-based service. Paste it below. We will email you a number. The number is the product of two primes. Once you have found them, choose one. Come back to this page, add a / and then the number to the end of the URL. If you chose correctly, the trial is finished and you have won. If you chose erroneously, the trial will end and your computer will be infected with a virus. Good luck.

"Jesus H Fucking Christ!" shouted Pete. "What is it with these people and prime numbers?"

"It's a geek thing, presumably," replied Alistair. "Jarvis? That's right, isn't it?"

"Whatever. I wouldn't expect either of you to appreciate the beauty of a prime number. Anyway this shouldn't be too hard."

Jarvis spoke as he typed, setting up the new email account and copying it into the space provided on the website.

"There. Let's see what this brings. One number. Two primes. Shouldn't be too difficult to work out."

They watched on the screen as an untitled email dropped into the inbox almost instantly.

Jarvis's jaw nearly hit the floor as he opened the email and stared at the monstrous number sitting on the screen in front of him.

7467492769579356967270197440403790283193525917787433197231759008957255433116469460882489015469125000179524189783

"Come on, Jarvis, get to it," said Alistair.

"What? Hang on," he replied. "I was expecting a six or seven digit number, not… a hundred-plus sodding digits."

"Now you can find two of those beautiful numbers, can't you?"

Jarvis still sat open-mouthed. "*I'm* not going to. But I know a little programme that can. It may take a while though."

He opened a programme called Python. A box appeared at the top of the screen with the words 'Enter your product here.' He copied the large number into the box and pressed another button called 'calculate.'"This is basically what Jarvis does in his spare time," Alistair explained. "He sits there, farting around with Python trying to find prime numbers. Or he takes prime numbers and tries to crowbar them into real life. If he sees two buses go by, one after another, and both their route numbers are prime, he practically gets a semi."

Pete chuckled and he watched as the small circle in the middle of the screen rotated. He doubted that this little programme, available on the Internet for anyone to use, had ever had to contend with a number this large. And it was probably crashing the host's server as they spoke.

After a good half an hour, during which Alistair had gone for a shower and come back, Pete had helped himself to more pastries than he cared to think about, Daisy had come into watch proceedings, and Jarvis had played numerous games of Minesweeper, finally the programme came up with a result.

Two equally intimidating numbers showed up in the results box.

7908462205224226484423868349572769166324734025186 7615781

9442408113990137188346916654240709551757626004869 7655243

The four of them stared at the screen for what seemed like an age before finally Alistair broke the silence. "So, which one is it, Jarvis?"

"How the hell should I know? We've got a fifty-fifty chance of being right. Why don't we just pick one, punch it in and hope for the best?"

"No chance," said Alistair. "I don't do playing the percentages. I like the odds firmly stacked in my favour. You know that. There must be something about these numbers that makes one the correct one. We just need to find it."

For another hour, the four of them sat and discussed every permutation and combination of the two numbers. They counted the number of times each number appeared, gave each number a corresponding letter to see if any word spelled out, ordered the numbers to see if there were patterns. Nothing.

Eventually, Daisy piped up.

"This may be nothing, but if you add up all the individual numbers in each, you get 251 for the one starting 790 and 253 for the other; 251 is a prime and 253 isn't. Just saying."

The other three sat in silence. They knew she was probably right and were just waiting for one of the others to acknowledge it.

"It would seem to fit," said Pete. "They do appear to have an unhealthy obsession with primes."

"Agreed," replied Alistair. "I can't think of another way of choosing between the two. The prime thing seems as good a way as any. And anyway, if it all goes horribly wrong we can just blame Daisy. And ground her for a year."

"Ground me for a year? Seriously? At least I managed to come up with a sensible suggestion, unlike you three. And anyway…"

"Jarvis, put in the number Daisy said."

"Okay, here we go," he replied, carefully double-checking the number again in the address bar. The whole room took an almost audible intake of breath and watched as Jarvis hit the 'enter' key.

"Shit or bust time."

Chapter 28

Danny awoke from his midday sleep, the cocktail of painkillers mercifully taking effect. His head felt clearer despite the fact that sleeping during the day usually made him worse. The bruising had stopped throbbing quite so much and just left him with a background level of discomfort that he could happily contend with.

He stood up and dressed himself, then double-checked the door was closed. Reaching under the fitted sheet, he slid his hand through a slit in the mattress and pulled out the mobile phone. Listening with his ear to the door as he dialled, he was happy that the coast was clear.

"It's me," he whispered after a few rings. "I'm in with Slater. I had to take a bit of a shit kicking but I think he trusts me now... No, oddly, there's been something of a strange turn of events... A previous colleague of mine is being held hostage... Yes I think that's exactly why she's here... But also, there's a kid I've seen around the place that I think Slater is also keeping hostage... No, agreed, a child is a major liability we don't need... I think there might be a link but I can't be a hundred percent... I can't talk long in case someone comes, but I'll sort the situation... Okay, I'll be in contact when there's more to report."

He hung up, tidied the bedding and left his room.

Walking across the courtyard, his attention was drawn to the shouting and laughing coming from around the back of the outhouse. Peering around the corner of the building he saw the young girl smashing the swing-ball as hard as she could and laughing as her male opponent stood there allowing it to hit him in the face before falling to the floor in the most over-the-top manner he could muster.

Danny pondered. He was sure the daughter was eighteen, so that must be the dopey boyfriend he had heard Slater slagging off. As far as Danny was aware, Slater had no other children.

"Sorry," he said, raising a hand as Roach made eye contact. He had turned on the floor, prompted by Olivia looking past at the stranger stood behind.

"Wrong turn," Danny said again, quickly wheeling away back towards the barn. He opened the barn door and went inside to find Grace pacing up and down, the pain slowly subsiding allowing the intense boredom to kick in.

"Danny, fancy seeing you in here," she said. "Are you going to have to keep running back inside to fix Slater's computer again?"

"Nope, not this time."

"Where is Slater?"

"No idea actually. He's always running off on some sort of business. You know, to kneecap someone, or smash someone's face in with a baseball bat. Those petty street dealers won't kick their own heads in you know."

"Is that how you ended up looking like you'd gone ten rounds with Floyd Mayweather? Drop a crisp on his desk, did you? Forget to put a sugar in his coffee?"

"Very funny."

"So how come you can just walk around his house. He must have CCTV cameras all over the place, doesn't he?"

"Yes, but only on the perimeter pointing out. He figures that anyone who makes it inside has either been invited or forced. Also, the fewer cameras there are recording what actually goes on in this place, the better for him. There's always the chance that they might catch something incriminating. Even if the police investigated and saw lots of people coming in but never going back out again, there wouldn't be any proof of anything untoward happening within the property. At least, not on camera."

"So what do you want, Danny? Have you worked out how to get me out of here yet?"

"Not really. It's become a little bit more complicated now. Slater's taken me on—"

"You are shitting me?" she interrupted, a very obvious disapproving tone hanging on her words.

"Kind of like his I.T. guru. I'm getting paid an absolute shit load of money to basically surf the Internet for him. The boring stuff's been done. Solving that Majestic Road trial was only the beginning, my foot in the door. But now I'm on the inside pissing out."

"Danny, please, you've got to help me," she said, her voice taking on a much more brown-nosing tone given his revelation. "Whatever he is paying you, my brother will pay you double. Triple even. You could pretty much name your price."

Danny thought about this for a moment. He suddenly found himself holding all the cards. Perhaps having the crap beaten out of him was the best thing that could have happened. On the one hand he could play Slater for as much money as he could. On the other, he could shop Slater to the multi-millionaire leader of the Brotherhood of the Righteous for even more money. It was win-win as far as he was concerned and making his assignment a great deal easier. "Well there's one very easy way of getting you out of here."

"Really?" she asked, with a sudden shot of optimism.

"Yeah, we just let Slater do whatever he's going to do."

"What! Are you mental? Surely whatever he's got planned for me isn't going to involve tea at the Ritz or a weekend away in a five-star hotel?"

"No, I'm fairly certain that what he has got planned is to hand you over to the shadow organisation that runs the Majestic Road website, in exchange for about two million quid's worth of the most potent recreational drug ever produced. He is then going to flood the market with said drug, sit back and enjoy the carnage as his reputation as the single most feared drug baron in the country is cemented. As a way of celebrating his little triumph, he's then going to hunker down for the evening and watch as you're paraded on the Majestic Road members' site and used to test their latest drug-based creation on."

"Please, Danny, you've got to help me," she said, her voice cracking as the enormity of what he said begun to hit home. "Why's he doing this to me? I never did anything to him."

"Isn't it obvious?"

"No it fucking isn't? Why doesn't he just hold me here and keep cutting various parts off until Alistair pays him a tonne of money?"

"It's not about the money. It's payback for the Brotherhood daring to take on his organisation, call him out during the McAllister episode. You were there, you watched your brother do it. You can't be surprised. This is nothing more than a little recreational sport to him."

"Why not simply out Alistair as the real perpetrator of The Red Room site? Surely that would do more damage to him?"

"That's not how Slater works. Anyway, why would anyone believe a suspected underworld gangland boss suddenly pointing the finger at a fine upstanding pillar of society like your brother? Slater knows full well that Alistair would have painstakingly covered his tracks and Slater would just end up looking like a moron. This is much more fun."

Grace appeared to be coming around to the realisation that she was nothing more than an expendable pawn in Slater's revenge game.

"Please, you've got to do something. Danny, we were friends, colleagues, doesn't that mean anything to you?" she asked, starting to sound desperate.

"I can't, can I? Like I said, at the moment your best option is just to go with it and hope that your brother cracks the trail and can somehow reason with the Majestic Road people. But given that they take great pleasure in creating the most mind-expanding, destructive drugs known to man, they're unlikely to be particularly compassionate, are they?"

"Okay, if you don't want to call my brother, call Pete. I was with him on the Isle of Wight when they took me. He's bound to be trying to find me. Tell him where Slater's going to take me. He can come and rescue me."

"Aah yes, Pete. So, you were with him when Slater kidnapped you. That explains why Slater also has his daughter."

Grace froze. "What, that little girl running around outside? Don't be ridiculous."

"Yes, it makes sense, doesn't it? He's taken you while you were with Pete and presumably taken Pete's daughter as a little insurance policy. And she said her name was Olivia, and that I do remember."

"So? There are millions of girls named Olivia; it's been the most popular girls name for like the last four years. It's not her, trust me. I'd know, right. I'm the one she called Aunty Grace. You only saw the photograph on his desk from a few years ago. I'm telling you, it's not her. You need to call Pete, tell him when and where they are going to drop me, and then he can sort it all out."

"But if it is his kid, and Slater realises that Pete has even attempted to rescue you, he'll more than likely kill the girl."

"Precisely. But it's not her is it, so he won't. Pete's my only hope, you need to get him."

"I'll think about it," replied Danny, watching out of the window for any signs of Slater returning. "What's his number?"

Grace read out Pete's new mobile number and placed a gentle hand on Danny's arm coupled with a warm smile and flutter of her eyelids. "Thank you, Danny, I'll make sure that once we're out the other side of this, that my brother makes it all worth your while."

Danny stared at her. "I'm not promising anything. Remember, I'm in with Slater now."

"Just tell Pete where to find me as soon as you know."

Chapter 29

"Gaze, dear boy. Gaze in wonderment at this work of art that we have created. See how its ethereal majesty shines through. It shimmers like fireflies dancing in the twilight. How something so exquisitely beautiful can hide such devastation is something the likes of you and I will never be able to comprehend."

The Professor held a small clear plastic bag of his creation up to the bulb, staring as the light flickered off the luminescent specks of blue powder.

"Yes, Professor, it's very nice. Reminds me of the powder you get in dishwasher tablets. But not as blue," replied the Smart Man.

"God speed, my child," said the Professor quietly as he gently laid the bag into the final cardboard box. "Go forth. Spread your delights. Such levity awaits, dear boy. Such levity."

The Professor's moment of contemplation as he bade farewell to the last of his batch was shattered by the screeching sound of an orderly running the tape gun across the top of the box, sealing it shut. "When do we make the handover, dear boy?"

"I will be contacting Mr Slater later on this afternoon. The others will be contacted shortly after by the local associates. It'll take a day or two for this shipment to arrive at its various destinations around the globe, but I would expect our customers to begin unleashing it very, very quickly."

"And how do we think Mr Slater will perform?"

"It's his first drop-off. But it's not like we're teaching him anything new. That's why we chose him. He can hit the ground running. And with his most admirable distribution channels, I think it will be very quick that we start to see a result."

"Is he providing a guinea pig for our delectation?"

"Of course. I imagine for a man of his temperament his list of potential candidates would be quite sizeable."

"I do hope there's an interesting backstory. You know how much I love a good back story."

"You sure do," said the Smart Man, trying to avoid the inevitable lecture he could sense was about to appear.

"You see, my dear boy, the thing is…"

The Smart Man sighed and smiled politely, waiting for the Professor to say his piece.

"… that I have dedicated my life to understanding the single greatest creation on this green earth. The human brain. Ever since I cut open my pet cat's skull when I was but a boy and watched, mesmerised, as the pulsating grey mass of cells throbbed before my eyes I yearned to know its secrets. The brain is the ultimate gestalt entity, the perfect example of the whole being greater than the sum of its parts. It consists merely of cells and blood vessels; pathways, channels, locks and keys, but from it arises something so much more. You can perform your Turing Tests all you like, *appear* conscious as though living. The simple fact of the matter is that consciousness arises. You don't flick a switch and electricity causes a small wire to heat and produce light. Computers will never, repeat never, attain the same levels of consciousness as a sentient being. The voice in your head when you think, where is the sound coming from? It is arising from your consciousness. And what bridges the physical chemical processes taking place in amongst the matter, the cells, and the thoughts that emanate thence forth? Who knows?"

"Professor, this is all—"

"But there in lie the two sides of the puzzle. The chemistry and the result. The chemistry is simple. Create a compound that mimics the natural, very complex, chemical already in the brain and you can predict to a certain extent. Key fits in the lock, but won't turn. But the resultant effects that *arise*? That is far more exploratory and easily the majority of the fun, wouldn't you say? But the physical effects of a compound are measurable. What I like, when it comes to our customer-provided guinea pigs, are the *reasons*. The psychology. What makes one who is a provider of our narcotic delights tick? There is so much more to understand about the human psyche than I will ever be able to, at least in my lifetime."

"Hopefully you will soon get some of your answers."

The two men stood and watched as the final box was stacked in the back of the van and it left the facility up the service ramp and out onto the bustling street above. They followed and left through a side door, stepping out into the light drizzle.

"I don't know about you but I make that time for afternoon tea?"

"Shall I hail a cab?"

"No, I think we should walk, for 'tis but a short stroll down Piccadilly to the Ritz. The fresh air will do us good. And there we can wait."

Chapter 30

"You'll wear a hole in my dining room table if you keep doing that, Pete," said Alistair from across the dining hall, as Pete stared at his mobile phone, drumming his fingers on the hard mahogany.

It had been around three hours since they'd hit send on what they assumed was the final part of the puzzle. Three... long... punishing hours. At least for Pete anyway. Every minute felt like an eternity; yet more time that he was unable to do anything constructive for Olivia. At least during the last couple of days he had maintained a vague sense of fatherly worth, that he had very little choice other than attempt to solve this puzzle and was therefore doing *something*. He had slipped back into the despairingly depressing feeling of failure, no further forward.

"Pete," Alistair snapped again.

"What?" Pete snapped back. "Sorry, I just can't deal with all this waiting around. It's messing with my head."

"We need to be patient. I know it's hard, but—"

"Do you? Do you really? It's all right for you. With your... your... massive house, your fuck-tonne of money, your lackeys at your beck and call twenty fours a day—"

"Er, we're not exactly lackeys," injected Jarvis, stopping when he saw Alistair put his finger to his lips from behind Pete.

"Your daughter," continued Pete. "I mean, does all this shit make you happy? Does having a house that you can fit Wembley Stadium into make you feel complete?"

"It does actually, yes."

"Really? But if you had to give it all up and it just be you and Daisy, could you do it?"

"For a long time that wasn't going to be an issue, was it? It was just me and what else was I to do. Until Daisy came along, this place was just going to be, I don't know, a National Trust place or a wedding venue or something."

"Hang on. Daisy's, what, eighteen? You didn't sell Phone Giant until five years ago. What do you mean 'until Daisy came along'?"

Jarvis stared at Alistair, berating him as much as he could with by the movement of his eyebrows for what was a rare slip in Alistair's almost steel-like consistency.

"Metaphorically speaking. You know. The issues with her mother, it meant that only recently…"

A new email pinged into the inbox being displayed on the large monitor on the hall wall.

"Finally!" shouted Jarvis, standing up and moving over to the laptop. "And with such exquisite timing."

The email sat in bold at the top of the list, the subject *Enlightenment Awaits* sat enigmatically next to a blank sender column. Jarvis double-clicked the mail with a level of impatience matched only by children on Christmas Day.

"Don't you want to savour the moment, Jarvis?" asked Alistair. "The anticipation? You know, the chase is always better than the catch. This could be a massive let down."

Jarvis ignored him and read the mail.

Congratulations. You have done well and proven yourselves to be worthy. Our playground is now yours. A gateway to the furthest, unexplored reaches of the most powerful machine on earth. The human brain. Welcome to the edge of sanity. Welcome…
To Majestic Road.

"Is that it? Majestic fucking Road?" shouted Pete. "We've gone through all of this just to find a poxy online drug dealing site that doesn't even fucking exist any more. Someone is messing with us and wasting our time."

"I don't think they are, Pete," replied Jarvis, scanning around the email for more clues.

"Of course they are," said Pete. "We knew all about Majestic Road back at CCU. It was just a bunch of hippies who happened to know a, how to make a website, b, how to run it on the dark web and c… there wasn't even a c — it was that bloody amateurish. The other agencies didn't even bother to ask for our involvement it was that easy to nail the pot-heads behind it."

"I think we still need to be wary, treat this email as part of the game," said Jarvis, scanning over the email with his cursor until it changed from an arrow to a pointing finger, indicating a web link. He clicked on it, to bring up a plain, black screen with a list of meaningless, random numbers and letters followed by *.onion*.

"Obviously," he said, switching to the Tor browser on his desktop, and copying the URL into the address bar at the top.

The huge flat screen on the wall went momentarily black, before the room shook to the instantaneous hypnotic synthesiser sound of the intro to 'Baba O'Reilly' by The Who.

"For God's sake, Jarvis, will you turn it down," said Alistair, covering his ears.

"Sorry, I forgot I even had the sound up." Jarvis muted the television with the remote.

As the first note had rung through the room, the screen flashed psychedelic colours blending into fractals in time with the music and in the middle of it all a black box appeared, first with the word *Welcome,* then *To,* before finishing with *Majestic Road.* Underneath the words *Enlightenment Awaits* materialised, and apart from the swirling background colours, the screen eventually stayed still.

"It reminds me of my old ZX Spectrum," said Pete, to much sniggering from Jarvis. "What?"

"Don't worry, Pete," explained Alistair, "Jarvis has gone into über-geek mode. He was very much a Commodore 64… 'man' I suppose, although that doesn't feel like the right word. A Commodore 64 'dweeb', shall we say. Anyone who had any other home computer in the mid-eighties just wasn't a proper Poindexter, were they, Jarvis?"

"No, Alistair, they weren't," Jarvis replied sarcastically. "Anyway I don't remember you complaining too much about my computer skills when you needed them. And where did those skills come from? I tell you where they came from—"

"Can we please get back to the matter in hand?" Pete cut him off impatiently. "Any ideas on what we do now?"

As the last strains of music faded, the screen switched to more of a message board with instructions on when the next show would take place, along with a link requesting the download of encryption software.

"This reminds me of The Red Room, except they don't seem to be requiring payment," said Pete, studying the screen. "Still doesn't make sense. Why would a defunct website send us a memory stick with one of the most bizarre trails I've ever come across, even trawling through the endless mire of the dark net?"

"Come on, Pete, use your head. I would have thought with your famously analytical CCU brain, you wouldn't have been so quick to dismiss it."

"What? Why?"

"If I know the mind of the average cyber criminal," replied Alistair, "and believe me I came across quite a few attempts on the Phones Giant I.T. systems, then I would say that this is the most obvious place for it to be."

"Where what would be?"

"Quite," added Jarvis. "It's hiding in plain sight. Pure and simple."

"For fuck's sake. What is?" asked Pete.

"Well, er, whatever is going on behind this big charade," replied Jarvis, sounding somewhat stumped by what he did actually mean with his initial statement. He looked to Alistair for some assistance as Pete pushed his chair back sharply from the table and stood up, rubbing his eyes in frustration at their seeming lack of progress.

"I had heard…" began Alistair slowly, stroking his fine goatee beard as he paced around the table, "rumours… shall we say. Nothing more than murmurs, urban legends, I suppose.

I had hoped, once it dawned on me what this could be, of course, that it wasn't. But I think that events have taken a rather sinister turn."

"Will you just spit it out."

"Okay. According to some, there is a site on the dark web where they test drugs. On people."

Pete was now starting to regret being out of the game for so long. Back at CCU, he would have known about this kind of site in an instant, had links to the dark underworld who could have provided a wealth of information on not just who was running the site but from where; in return for his turning a blind eye to their activities, feeding them information. Nothing illegal, just titbits that helped them avoid any unnecessary law enforcement entanglements. And now his chances of using this as an avenue for progress were significantly diminished.

"What sort of drugs?"

"Don't know," replied Alistair. "But you hear of these so-called designer drugs turning people into walking zombies all the time. One can only assume that it would be along those lines."

"That's just fucking marvellous," he shouted, smashing the back of his chair with his fist, a loud crash echoed through the room as it fell backwards hitting the floor. "I'm going to get my laptop."

With that, he stormed out of the dining hall, nearly knocking the incoming Gilbert and a heavily laden tray of refreshments over with the door.

Jarvis grabbed one of the crystal glasses and downed the fizzy contents in one go.

"So, what do we do now?" he asked, wiping the froth moustache from his lip. "Is he really useful to us any more? He's running around like a headless chicken. I realise that his kid is involved in this, but he's being too emotional."

"Let's see what he's got for us when he comes back," replied Alistair, collecting a glass and taking a much more refined sip. "But agreed, if we are going to investigate this, it would be easier with him out of the way. Don't want him learning the tricks of our trade now do we?"

"What tricks?" asked Pete as he hurried back into the hall, before taking a seat and slamming his laptop down, already opened, on the table.

"Oh nothing," replied Alistair. "Just talking about one of our old competitors who's just been in contact, ironically about cyber security. Please… do your thing."

"Okay, it's a long shot but worth a try."

The others sat and watched as Pete tapped furiously at his keyboard, each keystroke resounding with the sound of a desperate parent searching for their child.

After a couple of minutes, he opened up the chat window and started the conversation, hoping that the recipient would pick up.

Lostboy: Spang…?

He sat back, rapping his fingers on the desk either side of the laptop. The others stared at each other, maintaining a respectful silence while Pete did his thing.

Lostboy: Hey Spang. Pick up.

Pete stared at the screen without blinking. His eyes concentrated on the text area next to the name *Mr$pangle* with such intensity they could have set fire to his laptop.

"Come on, arsehole, I know you're there. You're always there," he whispered to himself, before finally the flashing sequence of one, two then three points appeared, indicating the contact was typing something.

"Get in. I knew it!" shouted Pete triumphantly.

The others gathered around, intrigued.

"Who is this guy?" asked Alistair.

"No idea," replied Pete, to much eyebrow raising from the others. "He's one of your regular gutter-crawling denizens of the deep web. From what I gather, he runs 'alternative lifestyle seminars' at some woodland retreat somewhere in Europe. Basically, he's a massive sex pest who runs swingers' parties, probably in Germany somewhere, they love that kind of thing, in the woods. But what he doesn't know about the goings-on of the deep web isn't worth knowing."

Mr$pangle: What the fuck do you want?

Lostboy: Is that anyway to talk to your best buddy.

Mr$pangle: Ha! Word is you're no longer a pig. Why should I even be talking to you?

Lostboy: Because I'm no longer a pig! I need your help.

Mr$pangle: If you're no longer a pig, then you are of no use to me.

Lostboy: What do you know about Majestic Road?

Mr$pangle: …

"He knows doesn't he?" asked Jarvis.

"He always tends to go a little silent when I hit on something he knows that he probably shouldn't be telling me about."

Mr$pangle: I know a lot. Why do you want to know about it? I never had you down as a junkie.

Lostboy: I'm not. Just interested.

Mr$pangle: You're 'just interested' in Majestic Road? It's shut down, so nothing to tell.

Lostboy: What about the members' area?

Mr$pangle: …

"See," said Pete, "he's done it again. He knows what I'm talking about."

Mr$pangle: I know quite a lot actually. But since you have nothing to offer me, you get nothing.

Lostboy: I still have contacts. I could make a lot of trouble for a man in your line of work.

Pete knew he was starting to sound a little desperate, something that hadn't gone unnoticed by the lengthy message that seemed to take ages to appear.

Mr$pangle: Ha. I'm shitting my pants, I really am. You DO NOT get to come on here asking for MY help and then start making pathetic threats. Especially after I gave you the Brotherhood of the pissing Righteous on a fucking plate. If you have something to offer me, I might, MIGHT, help. Until then, fuck off.

And with that his name turned red showing he had disconnected.

"Fucking bollocks!" shouted Pete, slamming the lid of his laptop shut and pushing it into the middle of the table.

A few moments of tense silence followed, a general sense of realisation that their entire operation had more or less been brought down thanks to an anonymous sex guru that sounded like a Japanese washing powder.

"Okay," said Jarvis eventually, "while you have been having not much luck with your weird friend, I have been downloading this encryption software and analysing it for any holes, back-doors etcetera…"

"And…"

"None. It's water-tight, better even than our very own firewalls on the… Phone Giant website," he corrected himself quickly after a loud and not-so-subtle cough from Alistair, taking the lead.

"Okay, Pete, I think it would be best to, how shall we say, split up on this. Jarvis and I need to work on this Majestic Road site, see if there's anything we can glean from it. Jarvis is something of an expert at following electronic trails, even through mass onion routers like Tor. So, while we do that, why don't you head back to your suite and work on finding anything you can about the alternative side to Majestic Road."

"Okay, but why can't I just do that here with you?"

"I get that you know your way around the Internet and the dark web, but do you know how to find your way around the sub-levels workings of deep web traffic, the connection nodes, the multiple routes a single bit of information might take?"

"No, Danny used to do all that."

"Exactly. If you could do it you would be welcome to stay. Plus, our methods are... not secret so much... more proprietary intellectual property, if that makes sense. And to put a finer point on it, we don't want you to see it, okay?"

"What?" replied Pete, struggling to keep calm. "What about my *proprietary intellectual property* that you were more than happy to make use of over the last couple of days since neither of you two fuckwits were capable of solving the riddles?"

"And we're extremely grateful, we really are. Remember that we are doing this for you as much as for me. But this is how this next part has to work. It's not up for discussion."

Pete stared at Alistair and then at Jarvis. He shook his head and reluctantly grabbed the laptop from the table and stood up to walk off.

As he walked towards the door, numerous niggles that had started to eat at his conscience came together and he stopped. In the midst and haze of the frenetic last hour or so, none of it had seemed to register. But a brief moment of clarity had given him just enough reason to ask a few questions of his own.

He turned around to see Alistair taking a seat and the others all watching him leave like partygoers all secretly glad that the one they didn't really want to invite was finally going.

"I was just wondering, Alistair," he said slowly, "why a regular e-commerce site like Phone Giant needed such an extensive and advanced firewall system?"

Alistair sat still and smiled a broad smile. The one that Jarvis knew was his 'buy time while I think of a response' smile.

"Well, Pete," he replied, "since you ask, we didn't. We, or rather Jarvis using my vast resources, developed what we saw as the ultimate firewall for another one of our many ventures. The reason that we installed it on the Phone Giant website was nothing more than a flexing of muscles. To show our competitors that they could never even get close to being the type of company that we were. That, and the fact that it added in the region of one hundred million pounds to the valuation of the company. Is that explanation satisfactory enough for you?"

"Yes, thank you," replied Pete, who again made to walk out of the room before turning around. "Just one more thing. Does it bother you that your daughter keeps referring to you as Alistair and not Dad? I mean, it's a bit Bart Simpsonesque, isn't it? And I would have thought that a man of your strong moral standing wouldn't appreciate such a lack of formality from your own child?"

The smile again. "No, Pete, it doesn't. Now if you can refrain from grilling me on my daughter, we have work to do trying to find yours. So, if you'll excuse us."

The two locked stares for an uncomfortable few seconds, neither one's forced smile convincing the other that whatever trust there had been, still remained as strong.

A few metres down the corridor, Pete heard the doors to the dining room close and lock shut.

"Right, he's out of the way," started Alistair. "Jarvis go and get all The Red Room hardware, we'll need the routers, servers, the lot."

"Okay, I'm on it," replied Jarvis. "What do we do about PC Pete? I knew it was only a matter of time before his old detective instincts kicked back in and he stuck his nose in where it's not wanted."

Alistair said nothing and nodded to Gilbert, who said equally little, nodded knowingly and walked out of the room.

Back in his room, Pete lobbed the laptop down onto the soft pillow of his bed, before kicking a scatter cushion that had fallen on the floor across the room. More and more of this situation was starting to rankle him. He took his phone out and dialled Grace's number, for no other reason than to just reaffirm what he already knew. Still dead. He dialled the number for his guest house back on the Isle of Wight. He had forgotten allowing Olivia to record the answerphone message, and when the message started, he nearly burst into tears.

Thank you for calling the Outlook Guest House, the Isle of Wight's best hotel. Unfortunately we are completely full because we are so great. Only joking, we've got loads of room but for some reason Mr Harris is busy at the moment. So please, please, leave a message and contact phone number and my dad will call you back as soon as he can. Byeee!

The sound of her voice cut through Pete like thousands of razor blades. He hated himself for the situation they were now in, but hearing her gave him a new burst of strength, like the hysterical mothers who suddenly find themselves capable of superhuman feats of strengths and able to lift cars off of their trapped children.

He opened up the laptop again, a new resolve to find his daughter as he clicked open the Tor browser.

Page unavailable, please ensure you are connected to the Internet.

"What?" he said, noticing the small yellow triangle covering his Wi-Fi symbol. It was obviously connected just moments earlier, he was using it. He clicked again, trying to connect, but the same message appeared: *unable to connect*. It couldn't be. Unless they had changed the password in the couple of minutes since he left the dining room. "Bollocks."

He placed the laptop down on the desk and walked to his door. Locked. He turned the old-fashioned iron key that hung from the lock and heard it click in place. He turned it back and forth another couple of times, saying in his head *locked, unlocked* but even when he knew it wasn't, the door would not open.

Outside in the corridor, Gilbert quietly slid the small round room number panel that concealed the bolt that was embedded within the door frame, and walked off down the hall.

The shouts of *Gilbert! Alistair! Jarvis!* and the loud thumping on the heavy oak frame rung in his ears until he turned the corner and re-joined the others.

Chapter 31

"Good evening, Mr Slater. I trust that there will not be any issues during this conversation," said the Smart Man from behind the white screen on Slater's wall-hung TV.

"No, I can assure you that we are—"

"Because let me make this clear," the Smart Man interrupted, the white screen doing little to shield the very clear and obvious authority in his voice. "If anything happens as we are making these vitally important arrangements then you will leave us no choice but to cut all communications from your organisation and remove you of the privileges that we have bestowed upon you. Is that understood?"

Slater motioned to Danny, who was kneeling down by the side of the screen, double-checking all the incoming wiring, making certain that no plugs fell out, the power back-up was connected and the mobile data router acting as a safety net was fully functional.

"Hear that, Danny? Don't balls this up."

"Who is that?" asked the Smart Man. "Bring him out, I want to see him."

"What? It's no one, just my resident I.T. hamster. Why do you want to see him?"

The Smart Man didn't reply, and Slater stood staring at the silent screen, raising his arms out to the side, looking at Danny and then back at the screen. Eventually, without talking, he motioned for Danny, who duly, albeit reluctantly, obliged to stand up and show himself to the television.

"And what is your name? I am assuming that it is not Mr I.T. Hamster."

Danny stood and shook his head.

"Well, well, well," said the Smart Man. "Either your I.T. hamster is a tongue-less mute or he deems himself way too far above his station to tell me his name. It's not a difficult question, what is your name?"

Again Danny stared at the webcam and shook his head.

"Come on, Danny, don't be shy," said Slater.

"Thanks, Curtis," replied Danny, shaking his head. "As *he* said, my name is Danny Fowler."

"*Sir*," whispered Slater, leaning in closer to Danny's ear.

"Sorry, Danny Fowler, sir," he said again.

"Okay, Danny Fowler," said the Smart Man, "I think it is time for you to leave. The information I am about to share is for the ears of Mr Slater only. So off you trot."

"But I need to stay here and make sure that the connection doesn't go down," replied Danny.

"You will leave now!" bellowed the Smart Man, making the men jump slightly. "And you had better hope to God that your connection holds up because, like I said, if we lose connection again we cut off Slater's privileges, and then I dare say that Slater will cut off your bollocks."

"Yeah, and the rest," interjected Slater. "Go on, piss off. I'll deal with this."

Danny eyed over his set-up one last time, and then walked out of the office and down the corridor, hearing the door shut behind him. He pulled out a cigarette and walked into the courtyard.

As he wandered around the gravel drive, aimlessly drawing crescents in the small stones with his foot, he heard voices from the end building, the one where he had previously seen the small girl. He walked over, trying to avoid crunching his footsteps as much as he could and leant in to listen to the conversation.

"Roach, you really are useless at this game," came the youngster's rather teacher-like voice. "I told you it's circle, circle, cross, square and down twice for the Electric Wind Hookfist. Not circle, circle, square, square and left twice. That's for the Dashing Godfist."

"I was never any good at *Tekken*," replied the man that Danny had presumed was the boyfriend. "Can't we play *Call of Duty*?"

"Urrgh, my dad always used to play that. It was so dull."

"The sooner we get you back to your dad the better, as far as I'm concerned. I'm bored of this babysitting," came the third voice Danny recognised as Slater's daughter. He had been living in the same property as this girl for the last couple of weeks, but at no point had she ever even acknowledged his presence, as though he was just another one of her dad's hangers-on that she had put up with since being born.

"When do you think I'll see my dad again? I miss him."

"I don't know, Olivia. It's up to my dad."

Danny's suspicions seemed to become more and more valid and he leaned in closer to hear better.

"I don't see why Curtis is looking after you anyway. What does your dad do exactly? Is he some sort of bad-boy gangland enforcer on the run?" asked Roach, making big gun gestures with his fingers.

"No. We live on the Isle of Wight. My dad runs a guest house there, which no one ever comes and stays in. It's so boring."

Danny stood up straight. The facts were indisputable. Grace had lied to him. His head whirled as he tried to make sense of it all. He understood entirely why Slater would kidnap Grace. But what did he have to gain from kidnapping Pete's daughter? Slater knew Grace was with Pete at his hotel before she was taken, but surely Olivia was there as well. If he needed an insurance policy, why not take Pete instead? Slater didn't appear to want to hurt Olivia, so presumably she would go back once Slater had finished with Grace, but then Slater was notoriously unpredictable. But mainly, even though it had niggled away at Danny since the first time he bumped into the little girl, what bothered him the most was why Grace would want to convince him that she wasn't the daughter of the love of her life?

He needed time to assess his options. The last time he'd spoken with Grace, the situation changed in his favour, but this time, through Grace's indirect intervention, it had thrown one massive spanner in the works. As he turned to walk away, his arm knocked a stone owl sitting on a pedestal right behind him which fell off and smashed on the ground.

"Shit," he muttered, looking up as he saw the movement through the window, and decided just to walk away.

"Oi!" shouted Roach, coming out of the front door. He glanced down at the pile of broken stone and then up again as he saw Danny disappear into the main house.

"What was it?" asked Paris.

"Don't know, just that bloke that's always in the house fixing your dad's computers," replied Roach. "He was hanging around here the other day and I reckon he must have been stood right in this spot."

"Good work, Sherlock," said Paris sarcastically.

"Stop taking the piss. I reckon there's something dodgy about him."

"Forget about it, I'm sure my dad's got it sorted. Come back inside."

*

Danny walked back into the large farmhouse kitchen of the main house and leant on the huge oak table, his head sinking into his chest. So far this project had gone amazingly to plan, and then this. He had learnt, through an intensive training programme, to put his conscience aside for the good of the project. Even watching the surveillance of his family with the stark, cold acceptance that they were a collateral risk had shocked him, and he had seen it through, come out of the other side unscathed. He always considered Pete a good guy, his friend, and certainly the daughter had no need to be caught up in this game. This was for grown-ups, who could make their own decisions, be in the game out of choice. But not an eleven-year-old girl.

Danny shook his head a couple of times to try to clear the haze and then headed in the direction of his room.

"Ah, Danny, there you are. I wondered where the fuck you had got to!" shouted Slater.

Danny turned on the spot, as though he wasn't really going anywhere.

"Sorry, Curtis, I was just going to get something from my room."

"Later. I need you to come back to the office. The project is reaching the business end now so we need to start making plans."

"Right, yes of course," replied Danny, following him back to the office.

They walked in, and Slater continued around to the other side of his desk and sat down in the big leather chair. Sat in the chair on the other side of the desk was Terence.

"So, Danny, time to fill you in on some 'inner circle' business. As you very clearly guessed earlier, I have become a member of the Majestic Road's exclusive members' area. Part of my first involvement was to purchase a rather large amount of one of their designer lifestyle enhancers, a brilliant little concoction called Brainfood. This evening I have arranged with the Majestic Road people to make a business transaction. In the barn over the other side of the courtyard I have been keeping another guest, a young lady by the name of Grace Brooks. Later on I am going to transfer Ms Brooks to the place of their choosing in exchange for around about two million pounds' worth of this new drug."

"You're swapping a woman for drugs?" asked Danny, doing his best to sound like this was all new to him.

"No, don't be a knob. I've paid real money for the actual drugs. Well, not real money. One of those cryptic currencies."

"Crypto…"

"Yeah, them. Ms Brooks is just going along as part of my loyalty bonus. A bit like redeeming a massive Tesco Clubcard voucher you've been saving up all year to spend at Christmas."

"But what did she do to you?"

"Let's just say I need to make a very big point to a business rival who made rather specific threats against me, who also just happens to be a very close associate of Ms Brooks. Anyway the instructions for the exchange are very clear. These people are obviously pros, and very, very careful."

"And why are you telling me this?"

"Because you're onside now. In with the big boys. In the orbit of trust. There's going to be a lot of movement going on in the next couple of hours around here so it's best that you're up to speed. Okay?"

"Got it. Just one other thing, Curtis? When I was out having a fag, I bumped into a young girl. I didn't think you had any other children."

"I don't," he replied with a stern expression. "And that shouldn't concern you."

"No, of course. I just thought that since I'm living in your house, I should know who the other residents are so... so that I can treat them with the necessary levels of respect."

Slater tapped his fingers on the desk a couple of times before taking a large swig of whisky from the tumbler next to his keyboard. He stood up and walked around to Danny, placing a strong hand on his shoulder. "Nothing for you to worry about. Just being my usual friendly self and helping a mate. She'll be going off with my daughter later tonight anyway. Probably safer that they are all out of the way, you know, just in case."

"Okay, I see," said Danny, feeling Slater still staring at him without even the slightest hint of emotion.

"Anyway," said Slater, more upbeat, "I need you to stay here and man the fort, but in the meantime if you could just double-check the incoming connection one more time that would be much appreciated. I've got a final call with our erstwhile *Man Behind The White Sheet* friend, just to dot the Is and cross the Ts."

Chapter 32

It had been nearly two hours since he'd found himself locked in his room, suddenly a prisoner in the home of people who he had presumed were trying to help him. Pete tried his laptop once more, and again the Internet claimed to be disconnected. It had worked earlier, so the only explanation was that his hosts had changed the Wi-Fi key. He hadn't felt truly comfortable since the moment he arrived here. Outwardly, these people had seemed to have a common goal, finding Grace as a means to finding Olivia. But something had seemed to stick in his guts, their intentions seeming not entirely honourable. And now this.

His phone chimed. He rushed over to the dresser and pulled the USB cable from it, the charging complete. Swiping the screen to unlock, he hoped desperately for a message, an email, anything, from Olivia. Or even about her. Instead, a BBC news notice flashed up on his screen. *Labour Party leader resigns amidst infighting.* Usually, as staunch Conservative supporter, this sort of news would at least raise a smile, but on this occasion he couldn't give the slightest toss. And it took all of his self-restraint to not smash the phone against the wall, but it did remind him that while his laptop was no longer Internet-enabled, he did still have his mobile phone data. The last couple of days away from the guest house had somewhat rinsed his data allowance. But for now at least, it was better than nothing.

He paced around the room, the frustration at his inability to do anything for his daughter now tenfold that he wasn't even contributing to the search. Then, after seemingly hours, but in reality only a few minutes, the phone rang. A proper ring. Not a message chime or another pointless news update, but someone calling his phone to speak to him.

Falling over a couple of footstools and the coffee table, he ran to the dresser and grabbed the phone before the vibrations sent it falling to the floor. A random mobile number appeared on the screen, one he didn't recognise. He thought for a moment about not answering it. It wasn't as if he was in any sort of position to do anything about, well, anything. Alternatively, it could just be another pointless guest house enquiry. But he had to answer it, even if simply to pass a bit of time.

He swiped the green circle to the right and spoke. "Yes, how can I help?"

"Pete?" came the almost-whispered reply, a slight hint of surprise at the overriding boredom of Pete's welcome.

"Yes," he replied. "Who is this?"

"Pete, it's me, Danny."

All of sudden, Pete recognised the voice and became more animated than at any point in the last couple of days.

"Danny, what the fuck are you doing calling me? How did you get my number?"

Danny carried on whispering into the phone, although speaking at a thousand words per minute. "Pete, shut up a second. I need you to listen very carefully, but I have to make sure that no one hears me."

"Where are you? Do you know what's happened to Olivia? She's been taken and I've somehow ended up at Grace's brother's enormous house. And now I'm locked in my room. I think it's something to do with the Majestic Road website."

"Pete!" said Danny in a louder whisper. "Just shut up and listen."

Pete pulled the phone from his ear and looked at it indignantly before resuming the conversation. "Sorry, it's just that—"

"I know. I need to explain this in as much detail as quickly as I can. The long and short of it is that I took employment with Curtis Slater—"

"What! Are you out of your fucking mind?"

"I didn't know who it was at first. Basically I just answered an advert for an I.T. engineer, but it seemed to spiral, and I've ended up deeper and deeper in with him. Anyway, he's got Grace and I'm convinced that he's got your daughter."

Pete's blood ran colder than it ever had. He knew that the people holding his daughter weren't going to be peaceful Buddhist monks, but of all the people in this world, Curtis Slater was just unbearable. And to make matters worse, he then remembered the text, the threat to gut his daughter like a fish. Over the course of his police work, Pete had heard of Slater doing far worse and the urgency of the situation became extreme.

"You've seen Olivia? Is she okay?"

"Yes. She's absolutely fine, I promise. And for what it's worth I don't think Slater wants the hassle of dealing with her. In all honesty, if you hadn't tried to rescue her, or whatever the hell you thought you were doing, he almost certainly wouldn't have taken her. But he knows how good you are, and she is his leverage over you."

"Where is she?"

"Here for now, but whatever is about to go down will do in a few minutes. Slater's moving her to a safe house somewhere with his daughter and her dozy boyfriend."

Pete felt a mixture of fear and sheer anger that someone was using his daughter as nothing more than a pawn, but at the same time a wave of relief washed over him that she was being moved away from Slater's base. Never, at any point in his life, had he wished for his old CCU tracing software more than at that particular moment.

"Where are you? I'll let Alistair know and we'll come and get you. Once he unlocks me from my room that is."

"I'd rather not…"

"What! Are you some sort of dickhead?"

"I'd rather not *at this minute*. What's the point in you lot coming in, all guns blazing? Anyway, remember when you didn't want to go straight in and arrest Joe Henderson, but preferred to wait until a more opportune moment presented itself? It's a little like that. What, hang on, why are you locked in your room?"

"Not sure. He was sent a memory stick with a trail on it, a sort of cryptic quiz that he had me help him solve. Then, once we got to the end of it, I came back to my room to get something and they locked me in. And changed the Wi-Fi. So, anyway, where are you?"

Danny was desperate to tell him the truth. His mind whirred over whether Pete would actually benefit from this information given his current location and situation.

"What was the trail for?" he asked, trying for a brisk change of subject, hoping that Pete wouldn't notice.

"Not sure entirely. It ended up, apparently, at that Majestic Road website on the dark net. Remember, the one that was shut down?"

"Yes, I remember it," replied Danny rather robotically, glad that Pete couldn't actually see his face. "I don't know, maybe the enormous house of his is down to some vast drugs empire. Or perhaps it's all some elaborate test for you."

"A test? Why the fuck would he want to test someone whose daughter has been kidnapped and is clearly desperate to get her back?"

"I don't know," replied Danny, aware that tact never was one of his strong points. "Slater also has Grace."

"Okay, yeah, I pretty much assumed that whoever took Olivia was the same lot who took Grace. What are they planning on doing with her? Have you spoken to her?"

"Yes. She seems fine." He winced as he spoke it, knowing the full extent of the bullshit he was now spouting. "I'm guessing Slater has some sort of beef with Grace's brother. Again, maybe the multi-millionaire playboy Mr Goodfellow is caught up in some sort of underground world that we don't know about—"

His sentence was cut short by the sound of footsteps outside his room. "Shit…" He dropped the phone on his bed and covered it with the duvet.

"Danny?" Pete shouted down the phone. "Danny?"

Danny quickly opened his door, but there was no one there. Only the sound of footsteps disappearing off down the corridor.

"Bollocks," he whispered.

He went back in his room and removed the phone.

"Pete, I've got to go," he said, a slight panic washing over him. He hung up the call and replaced the phone under the fitted sheet and through the slice in the mattress.

"Danny, no wait!" shouted Pete desperately. He hung up his own phone and hit redial. *Your call cannot be connected at present.*

Pete threw the phone down onto the sofa as hard as he could in frustration, part wanting to smash it into smithereens but part making sure he didn't.

He sunk onto the sofa next to it. He had always said, back in his CCU days, that a little knowledge was a dangerous thing, and that by planting very carefully selected nuggets of information into someone's hands was a great way of controlling them without them realising it. Was Danny trying to help him, or reassure him in some way? Or was he fully in the Slater camp and trying to lure Pete into a false sense of security? Pete couldn't be sure, but he had no other choice than to take what Danny had said at face value and hope it was true. At least it offered Pete the slight glimmer of hope that his daughter was relatively safe, and if he could somehow get through to Slater he would happily shop Alistair in exchange for Olivia.

Chapter 33

Slater stood in the middle of his office, tapping away at the tablet. He reflected for a brief moment on how his situation had changed, moved with the times. Barely a few years back, his modus operandi would have consisted of breaking into his enemies' warehouses, lock-ups, actual houses or, on occasions, their children's nursery school, making various exceedingly violent threats until he got what he wanted and then leaving.

Sometimes he needed to break a few kneecaps, sometimes he needed to cut his business partners from ear to ear with a rusty scalpel. Other times, he let his employees have the pleasure. But the world had evolved at a pace beyond thinkable even a decade earlier. *Stay one step ahead of the competition.* He had heard it spouted on some television show where a bunch of jumped-up, cheap-suited tossers pretended to play at business in order to impress some equally jumped-up but actually successful expensive-suited tosser.

Even so, he had been smart enough to see its value. Especially when most of the old-school career criminals he knew were basically either thick-as-shit or wary of new technology. But, like many of the great minds of the silicon age, he had seen the value, the potential on offer to anyone open-minded enough to grasp it with both hands.

The best thing about it? Anonymity. Distance. Some sort of weird currency that no one understands. Not having to worry about the pigs turning up just as you're about to slice someone's ear off and stuff it in their mouth for forgetting to pay the three-thousand-pound interest on the five hundred pound loan they took out with you. Any of those will do. This was the future and actually required less effort to become more of a merciless bastard.

He could make a tonne more money with just a few clicks on his tablet, and a couple of drop offs of course, than he ever could doing it the old fashioned way.

And he had watched, over Danny's shoulder, and learned. *One step ahead.* That way, if he ever needed to dispatch Danny for some reason, he was sufficiently well versed in the ways of the computer nerd.

"Right," he whispered, scanning his finger over the array of icons on his tablet. "Pretty certain it's this purple onion thing."

He pressed it and watched with a sense of achievement as the Tor browser opened on the main screen on the wall. A few more clicks on the pre-saved links that Danny had set up and he was in.

The Majestic Road holding page.

"I. Fucking. Rock."

He clicked on the members' link, opening up a message screen by which he could request an audience with the administrators. He typed in the message box. One finger at a time, touch-typing even on a glass screen was some sort of black magic as far as he was concerned.

It's Slater. All ready for tonight. Hope you lot got your shit together.

He hit enter and waited.

"For crying out loud!" he shouted after a whole three seconds. "Anyone there, or am I talking to my fucking self?"

He watched as three full stops indicated a response was being typed.

Do not presume to question us, Mr Slater.

…

One important point you need to remember for tonight.

…

Slater waited for the response, the bobbing full stops seemingly telling him that he would wait until they are ready.

Growing impatient, he paced around the office. Suddenly the tablet was knocked from his hand as the door to his office swung open, quickly followed by a sweating, panting Roach.

"Curtis, Curtis," he struggled out between breaths. "I mean Mr Sla—"

The final word stuck in his throat as he found a strong, stumpy hand gripping his windpipe. The numerous sovereign rings dug into his neck as the overwhelming strength pressed him against the mantelpiece.

"You stupid little retard," Slater spat, inches from his face, as Roach's face quickly turned purple.

Roach's back repeatedly smashed against the hard wooden shelf that sat at the same height as the top of his spine, punctuating Slater's every word.

"You. Do. Not. Come. Anywhere. Near. My. Office. You. Fucking. Little. Piece. Of. Pointless. Shit."

Each word was accentuated by Roach's muted attempts to let out pained cries. As his eyes bulged and rolled back in their sockets, Slater relented and dropped him to the floor.

Roach sunk to his knees, gasping desperate lungfuls of air while massaging the red welts that had appeared on his neck.

"Mi…" he wheezed, his voice struggling through the pain and trauma his throat had endured. "Mi…"

"I've told you before, and I will tell you again, you are nothing. A pathetic, shelf-stacking fucktard. If it weren't for the fact that my daughter, for some reason that I will forever be unable to comprehend, likes you, you would currently be puking blood, pissing blood, shitting blood and fucking firing blood from your fucking nose."

"Please, Mi—" Roach managed before he saw Slater grab his cricket bat from the umbrella stand and effect a few air shots just in front of Roach's face.

As Slater made a large back swing with the bat. "There really is nothing like the sound of willow on skull, wouldn't you agree?"

Roach strained his last ounce of effort to shout, "It's your computer guy!"

"What?" replied Slater, taking the bat a little further back as though to make a forward leg drive down through mid-wicket.

"Wait! I heard your computer guy. Danny. On the phone."

Slater stopped mid-back swing. Ordinarily, a potential victim-to-be lying on the floor declaring he had heard someone on the phone would be nothing more than a further invitation to smash his brains around the floor. Instead, this prompted Slater to drop the bat and grab Roach by the hood of his sweater and drag him to his feet before planting him down in the armchair.

"Say that again," he said pointing the end of the bat at Roach's throat.

"Danny, that's his name, right?" replied Roach, a little easier now both the crushing of his windpipe and the threat of death had mostly passed. "I caught him sneaking around the out-house earlier today so I followed him back to his room. I stood outside and heard him talking."

Slater stood arms folded in front of him and let out an ironic laugh.

"Okay, Mr Undercover Spy," he said in the friendliest manner he could ever remember speaking to Roach in. "Tell me some more."

"Well," replied Roach, "he said he was working for you and—"

"Yeah, I'd always suspected he probably had a phone somewhere," said Slater, watching Roach's slightly confused expression that his revelation hadn't elicited a more congratulatory response. "I'm pretty certain he used it to call his old dears. But thanks for the info, now you can fuck off out of here."

"He was talking to some bloke called Pete," Roach added, much more to Slater's interest. "He was telling him about that girl that you had us babysit for the last couple of days. Is Pete Olivia's dad?"

Slater stoked his chin as he took in the information. Roach sat and watched as he deliberated.

"Are you going to sort him out, Mr Slater?"

"What?" replied Slater, snapping out of his thoughts. "No, sunshine. No, I'm not. Softly, softly, catchy monkey and all that."

He held out a hand to pull Roach up from the chair, a gesture of acceptance that Roach wasn't slow to grasp.

"Listen. We can't let on to our friend Danny that you have shared this information with me, okay, William?"

Roach's chest puffed at the sudden raise in status that came with Slater using his first name. "Absolutely, Mr Slater. You can trust me. I won't say a word."

"Glad to hear it," replied Slater, placing a heavy hand on Roach's shoulder before planting his other into Roach's groin. "Otherwise I'll rip these off and feed them to my koi. Got it?"

Roach nervously reciprocated Slater's over-the-top laughter, slightly unsure whether he was laughing because he didn't really mean it or laughing because he did.

"Good lad," he said, finishing with a not-so-gentle slap across the head. "Run along now."

Roach turned and made his way to the office door. His head spun with the temporary lack of oxygen and overwhelming gratitude that he had not only survived an encounter with Curtis Slater, but survived one in which he could justifiably claim to have been about to die before Slater saw his worth and made him part of his deepest inner circle.

"Anything else I can do for you, Mr Slater, just let me know," said Roach as he left the room.

"Actually, William, there is something else you could do for me," came the reply.

Roach let out a small air punch in the corridor and hurried back into the room with a swagger he usually saved for nightclubs or the pool in Ibiza. "Of course, Mr Slater."

"Well, Roach... It's okay if I call you Roach, right?"

"Of course it is, Curtis. It would be an honour."

"I didn't fucking say you could call me Curtis, did I? Anyway, I'm guessing Paris has already informed you that you and her will be taking our little guest later on this afternoon to another one of my properties..."

"A safe house, got it."

"Christ, your generation watch too much The Bill."

"The what?"

"Never mind. Yes, if you want to call it that. It's just another one of my properties that I use when I want certain people to be kept out of the way of the main important business that might be going down here. So, there's that obviously—"

"Yes," interrupted Roach. "No problem whatsoever. I'll drive us all there, it'll be safe as."

"Will you shut up before I shut you up," replied Slater impatiently, wishing slightly that he hadn't put his cricket bat away. "Christ, I doubt that even you could fuck up getting in your car at A and driving it to B. A little bit later on, I'll be taking delivery of some very special merchandise. Now, it's vital that this package finds its way safely to a business associate of mine called Klaus who owns the Blue Oyster nightclub. Do you know it?"

"Of course. I actually got thrown out of there once 'cos I got caught by the bouncers shagging some…"

Slater raised an eyebrow as Roach stopped abruptly, remembering that Slater wasn't his new best friend but the rather psychotic dad of his new girlfriend.

"Good, so you'll know exactly where it is then. To put it simply enough so that even you can understand, I just want you to take the package around to the tradesman's entrance and drop it off with Klaus. I need someone new for this. There tends to be a lot of spies watching my associates and I think you would make the perfect foil. You could just be some random Amazon driver or something. What do you say?"

"Not a problem, Mr Slater. I won't let you down," replied Roach. And with that, he swaggered out of the room flushed with his new gangster pride.

Slater waited until he saw Roach strutting across the courtyard and took out his mobile phone. He clasped it between his ear and shoulder as he retrieved the tablet from the floor. The message he was expecting when Roach had burst in sat waiting.

One important point you need to remember for tonight.

…

If you try anything stupid, or we even suspect that you are trying anything stupid, we will kill you and we will kill your daughter and we will kill your wife.

Slater sniggered to himself. This sort of posturing was nothing new to him and the fact that they offered to dispatch his wife was something of a bonus. He tossed the tablet onto the armchair just as his call picked up.

"Klaus, you big German twat, how's things? Got rid of that mullet yet…? Listen, I've a very important consignment arriving this evening… Correct, the one I told you about… If all goes to plan, it should be in your possession later tonight… No, a new boy… He's as thick as two extra thick short planks… No, the fact that he's fucking clueless means he'll draw less attention… If he gives you any problems…? Then you have my permission to break both his legs… Good, let me know how the new stuff goes down with your clients, I expect it to hit the Daily Mail headlines tomorrow… Okay, yep, yep, right, auf wiedersehen…"

Chapter 34

Grace raised herself upright on the hay bale. It seemed ages since the last morsel of food had passed her lips the previous evening and her stomach cramped with the emptiness. Since arriving a few days earlier, and the traumatic ordeal that Slater had subjected her to, her stay in this barn had been relatively uneventful. Maybe down to the fact that since he cut her finger off with bolt cutters, Slater had failed to put in any other appearance and the friends of his who did come in with her food and water had treated her with politeness and respect.

But the fact that no one had come to her recently with food seemed a little strange. Her conversation earlier with Danny played over and over in her mind. Majestic Road. Was she really going to be some sort of human guinea pig on an underground drugs site? What sort of sick human beings kidnap people and subject them to that kind of abuse for the delectation of the dark web viewing public? It can't really be a possibility.

But then she remembered her brother, his Brotherhood and their very popular show doing just that. At least he is the best person to find a way of sorting this. Use a thief to catch a thief. She just hoped that Danny had contacted him or, at the very least, Pete. Perhaps she should have told Danny that the little girl was his daughter instead of trying to persuade him to concentrate on rescuing her. Even if she did want the little shit out the way. At least that would have motivated him to want to find them both. Did Alistair even know she was in this predicament? Her head spun with the confusion, but there was very little she could do except hope and pray that Alistair was trying.

She stood up and walked as far as the shackle would allow, piqued by the sudden sound of multiple vehicles crunching over the gravel courtyard and the many voices that had accumulated there.

*

Slater hung up the call on his mobile and looked at Terence.

"Did that confirm it?" asked Terence.

"Hmm," replied Slater. "It certainly does. Seems that our new resident geek learnt to ply his trade alongside Pete Harris at our good friends the Cyber Crime Unit. I must admit, he did very, very well indeed to hide his previous life from me."

"Does seem strange that we couldn't find anything on him."

"Yes, but they tend to hide in the shadows though, don't they? The techie ones. A bit like MI5 workers. You probably pass a dozen of them without realising it when you walk down Kensington High Street."

"Does he still work for them?"

"No, that much is for sure. He left in no uncertain terms after the Brotherhood case. So what's he doing here then?" Slater pondered, tapping his index fingers together in front of his eyes.

"It could be a huge coincidence," replied Terence. "Don't forget that he had no idea you were behind the job being offered until we offered it to him. It's not beyond possible that someone of his talents answered a job advert looking for what was being advertised."

"True. I think it's time to see how he acts when we bring our little piece of bait out into the open."

*

A convoy of blacked out saloons and 4x4s lined up in a semi-circle around the edge of the courtyard. Proudly parked on the end of the line was Roach's Impreza. A number of people, dressed variously in sharp black suits, casual clothes or sports clothing, accumulated in the courtyard waiting for Slater.

Eventually, he walked out of the house carrying a steaming Darth Vader mug filled with coffee, followed by Terence. He greeted the various associates with serious, stout handshakes, a few backslaps and the odd jovial crotch grab.

"Evening, everyone," he said. "Now, I'm no Steve Jobs when it comes to motivational company speeches, but I assume that everyone is clear on what is going down tonight. We will be making an exchange for our guest currently residing in that barn over there. Danny, if you wouldn't mind going and getting her for me please."

Danny hadn't really been paying attention until now, just leaning against one of the monster Land Rovers and staring at the floor as he smoked. But the sudden instruction made him shift nervously, and the eyes of his new colleagues made him feel incredibly uncomfortable.

"Me? Er…" he stuttered.

"Yes, you, Danny," Slater replied frankly.

"Surely I'm the least qualified here to deal with a prisoner after last night's shit kicking. Even someone of Grace's stature could probably do me over at this moment. Perhaps one of these gentlemen would be better placed to do this bit?"

"Probably, Danny," replied Slater, not taking his eyes off Danny's. "But I want you to do it."

They locked stares for a few seconds, before Slater broke into laughter, closely followed by all the others.

"Danny," he continued, as Danny nervously laughed along with all the other men who clearly gave very little shit about who he was. "It's just a bit of hazing. A bit like a rite of passage. Consider us your future fraternity and this will make everyone comfortable that you have the balls and the strength of character for us to welcome you into our inner circle."

The laughter stopped as abruptly as it had started. Danny felt the harsh, battle-hardened eyes of the group of men burning into him and he stood up as straight as he could muster and made his way to the barn.

"Oh, Danny," said Slater as he walked past, "you'll probably need these."

He held out his hand and dangling between his finger and thumb was a set of keys. Danny stopped and walked over to Slater to take them from him.

"Whoops, sorry," said Slater as he dropped them on the floor before Danny could take them from him. Danny heard the laughter again as he bent down to pick the keys up from the gravel. He collected them and stood up as Slater leaned in and whispered in his ear.

"How did you know she is called Grace, Danny?"

Danny froze briefly. "I'm pretty certain I heard you talk about her to Terence."

Slater kept his head near Danny's and waited for a suitably uncomfortable length of time. "Oh okay, that's fine then. Right, off you go and get her."

He gave Danny a suitably heavy slap around his already swollen face and watched as he walked away towards the barn without making eye contact with anyone else.

Inside, Danny pulled the door as hard as he could, not noticing as it failed to stay in the latch and swung back open.

"Hello again, Danny," said Grace as he walked past her and over to the shackle on the wall. "Have you come to release me?"

"Shut up, just let me do this," replied Danny, looking around the chain for the padlock.

"It's here," said Grace holding up her arm. "You never were very good at the practical stuff, were you?"

"I said shut up."

"Ooh, don't go trying to be all gangster on me now, Danny. You do know what this means don't you?"

"It's just a test. I'm the new guy. He's testing me."

"Don't be a fucking idiot, Danny. He knows. He knows who you are," she said as he struggled with the steel padlock, trying his best to ignore her. "That's why he sent you in here to see how you do it. Whether you'll show any emotion. The usual method in any film I've watched is for him to hand you a gun and have you shoot me in the head, but unbeknownst to you, the gun is empty. Then, after much deliberating, when you eventually pull the trigger thinking you are shooting me in the head and realise it was all a test, you've proved your mettle and he welcomes you into his fold. But obviously he can't really shoot me, so this is his way. I could, of course, make this very easy for your or very difficult, but that depends on how much you have done to help me, doesn't it?"

Grace rubbed her wrist as Danny finally got the manacle off.

"How can he possibly know who I am? I'm just his I.T. geek that applied to his job advert. Anyway, you lied to me, and you betrayed the supposed love of your life. Why the fuck should I help you?"

"What?"

"I know that's Pete's daughter over there."

Danny noticed the colour drop from Grace's face and he could sense the cogs in her brain begin to work overtime. "So what if it's his little shit of a daughter. I just wanted you to concentrate on finding my brother and finding Pete. I knew they wouldn't hurt her, it's not worth their while, you know that. And if they found me, they would find her."

"That's some twisted way of looking at it, I suppose. Anyway, I spoke to Pete, he's with your brother."

"What, really? So presumably you told them where we are then?"

"Not quite, I …"

"You dozy wanker. You are in with Slater, aren't you? We'll see how long he takes before chopping you up and leaving you to rot in the woods. Slater! Slater!"

Danny wrestled her in an attempt to shut her up. She fought against the hand that was trying to cover her mouth. "Slater! Danny's a pig!"

"Grace, please shut up," Danny replied, trying to get her to see reason, as he heard footstep crunching across the yard. "I know what Slater is doing with you—"

"Slater, in here please!"

"And I know that they know as well. It wouldn't work if I told him where—"

"Slater! My brother's on to you. Danny told them where we are!"

"Grace, please!" shouted Danny, becoming more desperate.

Slater appeared at the door carrying a roll of duct tape.

"Ha ha, Slater. I said you were fucked. Thanks to Danny, my brother—"

Her words were cut off by the sharp blow to the back of her head. Danny stood over her, shaking slightly at possibly his first ever act of physical violence to another human. He turned and looked up at Slater who tossed the roll in his direction.

"You might need this," said Slater. "We could do with the stupid bint being a bit quieter, wouldn't you say?"

"Er, absolutely, Curtis," replied Danny, as he applied a thick layer of tape across the temporarily stunned Grace's mouth. "She's fucking deluded this one, really is. Where the hell did you find her?"

"Never you mind. Right let's get her bundled up. After you."

Danny pulled Grace to her feet and frog-marched her to the waiting 4x4. He bundled her into the boot as the door was held open for him by one of the larger of the assembled men. Slater walked up alongside Danny and placed a brotherly arm around him as they watched the 4x4 rumble across the courtyard and disappear up the driveway to the main road.

"Glad to see the back of that one," said Slater.

*

"Look at me, look at me," said Roach excitedly as he danced around the lounge area of the outhouse, making pistol shapes with his hands. "I'm a motherfucking gangster. No one messin' with me now I'm in the Slater Crew. Oh yeah, oh yeah."

"This is it big boy. Time for everyone to see how fantastic you are," replied Paris, grabbing his crotch as she walked past. "Olivia! Get the hell out here now. Olivia!"

Paris's shout was easily loud enough for Olivia to hear, but she remained silent in her room. She had heard Roach boasting and swearing, and even she could tell that Paris was becoming fed up and irritated with her. She sat on her bed with her arms folded as the door burst open. Paris grabbed her arm and dragged her out of the room.

"Ow! You're hurting me," protested Olivia.

"Just shut up and come with me," replied Paris, bending down to eye level and grabbing Olivia by both shoulders. "Quite frankly, I don't care. Days now I've had to babysit you, you little shit. One more night and then I'll be rid of you and off to Marbs."

"I'm scared."

Paris ignored her pleas and dragged her from the outhouse, shouting for Roach to hurry up.

Slater and Danny watched as the three of them made their way over to Roach's car. Olivia climbed in the back and Paris in the passenger seat. Roach slid across the bonnet and opened the driver side door.

"Everything set, sweetheart," Slater said, bending down to Paris's window.

Paris sat in the front seat, arms folded tightly across her chest and a wasp-chewing pout that told him in no uncertain terms that while everything may be set, she was less than happy about it. "Seriously? She's starting to piss me off. I'd better be getting first class seats to Marbella, and a private chef."

"Yes, fine. Just look after her a little while longer for me. One more night, I promise."

"Bollocks!" shouted Roach.

"What?"

"I've left my keys inside," replied Roach, climbing out of the car and sliding back over the bonnet.

"For fuck's sake!" shouted Slater, following him back towards the outhouse. Paris climbed out of the car and ran after them, thinking that she needed to offer a little personal protection to her boyfriend.

Danny watched as they disappeared inside, angry shouts of 'moron', 'better not fuck this up' and 'jibbering imbecile', echoed around the courtyard before disappearing into silence. He scanned around the couple of cars that were left, all occupied with the odd heavy checking their phones or tapping away on steering wheels waiting for the off. He ran over to Olivia and opened her door.

"Hello, it's Olivia, isn't it?" he asked as gently as he could, and she nodded back silently. "My name is Danny, I'm a friend of your dad's. I spoke to him earlier and told him you were okay, but I need you to not say anything to these two, do you understand?"

"I'm scared and I miss my dad."

"I know, but I think that Curtis is taking you somewhere away from here and I swear that no one wants to hurt you, or your dad. After you've gone I'll try your dad again and send him some more information, okay?"

She gazed at him blankly. Danny knew the fear that she must be feeling. He had watched from the window when she arrived, Paris taking Olivia under her wing and then dragging her out here, kicking and screaming, just a moment earlier. Olivia would have no reason to believe another strange person, just because he was being nice to her at this moment.

Danny noticed the iPhone sitting in the central console of the car. He looked back over his shoulder to check for the others, but the running bodies and failing arms of shadows behind the lace curtains indicated they were probably still frantically hunting for keys.

"Do you know how to unlock this phone?"

Olivia reached forward and grabbed it, scribing a capital 'R' among the nine white dots on the lock screen. "He used to let me play on it," she shrugged, handing the phone over to Danny.

Danny took it and quickly swiped through the various apps and then opened the camera. Double-checking that the other heavies were still dozing away in their cars he ran around the back of the Impreza and quickly took a photo of its rear. As he moved back around the car to the passenger seat, he opened another app, typed a few words, deleted the photo, and then locked the phone up before placing it back in the console.

Danny pressed his finger against his lips, before slipping a tiny USB memory stick into Olivia's cardigan pocket without her noticing. "Okay, shh, not a word to the other two about our conversation, okay?"

With that, he stood back outside the car and closed the door, just as Roach came bombing across the gravel shaking his bunch of keys, closely followed by Slater and Paris.

"Everything okay, Daniel?" asked Slater, watching as the other two climbed back into the car and started her up.

"Absolutely, Curtis," replied Danny, "just making sure our little guest didn't try to make a run for it, or something stupid."

"Excellent work," replied Slater, not entirely convincingly. "Muscling eleven-year-old girls is probably a bit more at your level, right?"

Danny winced as Slater dead-armed him, before heading off to the last remaining blacked out 4x4. "Okay, Danny, we'll be back shortly. You can probably go and have another one of your beauty sleeps if you need it."

He stood, rubbing his arm, as the black car disappeared up the lane and out of sight. For the first time he can remember, he was alone. Were it not for Slater's overtly intimidating behaviour in front of all his mates, Danny could have sworn he was well 'in' with Slater. A slight wave of doubt rumbled in his stomach. Did Slater know something? Was it him outside Danny's room during the phone call to Pete? Danny convinced himself that the hazing was just that, a bit of one-upmanship in front of his cronies. And anyway, not just Slater, but everyone here had left. Weirdly Slater hadn't left him with any I.T. jobs to do, which was a little odd given the enormity of the main event later that night. But the preparations for it had been thorough. Danny had left it so that, in theory, even Slater could just turn it on and go.

In any case, Slater was probably happy enough leaving him alone, given that he hadn't left the system on its usual nine-minute sleep mode. But, in amongst the haze from the previous night's beating, Danny recalled, one by one, the password that he saw reflected in the mirror.

Chapter 35

Pete paced around his room, staring at the phone sat charging on the dresser. Still no word from his supposed colleagues-turned-captors. He pressed the handful of toilet tissue harder against the back of his hand, a small dent in the plasterboard specked with blood marking his frustration. But at least he hadn't cut his head as well. He tried the door countless times, tried the window. Obviously this was somewhere that they were used to holding guests that they didn't really want wandering about their palace.

And then it rang. Not his regular ring tone but one he forgot he had on it. A video call was coming through. He had hoped it was Danny but the username that appeared was a little more sinister; *slaterthehater64*.

Pete wondered for a second whether to answer it. Coming face-to-face with the man who held his daughter, who had threatened to gut her. Face-to-face over the Internet, Slater's actual location of no importance.

The 'Answer with video call' flashed temptingly like the lure of the fruit machines. Eventually, he decided to answer it.

"Pete, it's me," came the voice, before Pete had time to process the fact that the face he was looking at wasn't the one he was expecting.

"Danny!" Pete replied with an overwhelming sense of relief. "What the hell are you doing? I thought that you had to keep a low profile. Can you keep your device still. It's like watching The Blair Witch Project."

"Sorry, I'll try," he replied, holding the tablet more steadily. "They've all gone, to do the drop off."

"What drop off?"

"Do you still not know what this is all about?"

"I assumed that Slater was out for revenge over Cramer McAllister and being threatened by the Brotherhood on The Red Room. He found out somehow that Grace was involved, presumably from Smith, given the coincidental timing of his death. So he's kidnapped her and is now trying to get information out of her on the Brotherhood and failing that, can just use her to extort some of her brother's vast fortune. That trial was his little way of prolonging the agony for Alistair."

"It's just a game, Pete. Slater's doing this for fun. Have you got any way of tracking this call?"

"No, it's all on my laptop. They've changed the Wi-Fi password or blocked it or whatever. I'm running purely on data. I doubt the signal from my phone is strong enough to use as a hotspot either."

"Ok. Thing is, I'm still not sure where I am exactly."

"Really? Why can't you trace your location through the IP addresses of all Slater's computers?"

"He had a dedicated fibre optic broadband line installed in the farm and it's behind a whole tonne of proxy servers and firewalls. Even with all my gear from CCU it would be a struggle to break through. Just a sec, I'll switch to the rear camera and walk and talk. That way you can at least see the layout here, if you do eventually manage to do something."

Danny held the tablet in front of him and wandered around Slater's house, pointing the camera at various points that might be useful to Pete; doors, room exits and entrances, guns hanging on the wall. Pete tried to scribble as much down as he could on an old receipt he found in his wallet.

"Tell me about the drop off," asked Pete.

"Slater's got in with the Majestic Road site. It's not shut down, far from it," he said as he moved outside. "Remember how The Red Room meted out its own brand of summary justice on the pretence of it being for the supposedly moral elite, for the righteous? Majestic Road exists as a dark net market place for brand new designer drugs. Hang on… you getting all this?"

Danny stopped talking as he stood near the barn and panned the camera around the courtyard, concentrating on the large gate and the entrance leading to the long winding drive way that snaked up the hill. He turned to show the main building, then the outhouse, before pointing at the barn. Taking the tablet in one hand, he opened the door and reached inside to turn on the light.

"Danny, I know you have to be quick but I need more information about Majestic Road," said Pete.

"Right, yes. I just wanted to show you in here. This was where Grace was held, manacled to the wall over there. Hang on a second, just switching the camera back so you can see my gorgeous, albeit slightly black and blue features. Shit, I forgot to say, about Olivia, what I've done is…"

Pete watched as the view on his screen changed from bales of hay back to Danny's face. "Danny!" Pete screamed as a figure appeared in the doorway just over Danny's shoulder. Before Danny could finish his sentence, Pete saw him turn in shock as something swung and connected with his head. A sickening thud accompanied by a grunt and then a moment of silence before the tablet fell into a pile of straw on the floor, the camera pointing at the timber rafters of the barn roof.

Pete turned up the volume. Figures moved across the view of the camera and a sound echoed around the barn, something being dragged across the floor, moving away from the tablet.

Suddenly a face appeared on Pete's screen. It picked up the tablet, switched viewfinder again and pointed it to one of the barn's walls. Pete saw Slater lifting a groggy Danny into a wooden chair near where the chain that had held Grace still hung. Slater wrapped the chain around Danny's body, pinning his arms to his side and pulled it tight. The chair and Danny slid a few inches as Slater pulled the chain back on itself until he could padlock it together.

"Good evening, Mr Harris," said Slater, facing the camera, his shoulders rising and falling heavily as sweat ran down his reddened face. "We're going to play a little game. It's not as sophisticated as those utter cunts, the Brotherhood of the Righteous, granted, but it should be sufficient. Except the difference is going to be that, instead of you paying for the right to question good ol' Fanny here and then have me dish out some sort of punishment of your choice, I'm just going to miss out all the dull shit and get straight down to the fun part."

"No, don't!" shouted Pete, vastly more in hope than in expectation.

Slater slid a toolbox out from under a nearby work bench and rooted around in it. Pulling out a pair of pliers, he gripped a large chunk of the top of Danny's left ear and planted a boot in the side of Danny's face.

Facing the camera with an almost joyful smile, Slater counted, "One… two… three…" before simultaneously pushing his leg out and pulling his hands into his chest.

Pete took a deep breath, shifting his gaze away to the side of the screen as the hellish scream filled his room.

"Bollocks," said Slater, dangling half of Danny's ear in front of the camera, "usually they come away in one piece."

"Slater, stop. What is it you want with my daughter, with Grace?"

"Well, Pete, it's like this," replied Slater pulling out a small stainless steel hacksaw and pulling Danny's head back by his hair. "Imagine that this hacksaw is me, and this beautiful face here isn't a pointless, traitorous geek but your lovely little daughter."

He held Danny's head and placed the blade of the saw against his eye.

"Please, Slater, don't."

"You weren't supposed to be involved. But now you are, your daughter has become less of an annoying little hindrance and more of a useful asset. I'm sure you'd hate for this to happen to her."

Without so much as a flinch, Slater ripped the hacksaw blade across Danny's eyelid, slicing through the skin and causing fluid to drip down onto his shirt.

"If there's one thing I hate, Pete, it's traitors. And Danny here has been feeding you information."

"What?" protested Pete. "No, he hasn't. This afternoon was the first time I spoke to him. As far as I could tell he was working for you, but for some reason wanted to tell me about my daughter."

"Aaah, how sweet," replied Slater, drenched in sweat and breathing heavily. "Warms the cockles of my fucking heart, Pete, it really does."

"I swear, that's all he said," said Pete desperately trying to distract Slater and keep him talking. "But why Grace?"

"Ha, Grace," replied Slater, reaching across the workbench and putting a plug in the wall socket. "I'm sure you remember it very clearly, the episode, the one where they kneecapped my trusted right-hand man Cramer. God that makes it sound like an episode of *Friends*; the one where etcetera, etcetera. The same one where they threatened to put me in that chair. No one fucking calls me out and gets away with it. Do you hear? I will not go in that fucking chair."

His maniacal face twisted as he fired up the angle-grinder. "You remember this one, don't you, Pete?"

Pete watched Danny's body convulse as Slater knelt down in front and pressed the spinning blade against his kneecap. Even on the less-than-perfect resolution of the video call, Pete could make out the blood, and bone and cartilage spraying forth from Danny's leg, until eventually he watched the bottom half drop to the floor under a torrent of blood from the remaining stump.

Pete's heart thumped in his chest so hard it felt like it would leave through his mouth as waves of sweat barrelled down his face. A small mercy, it seemed, that Danny had passed out, and his body sat still, with his face drooped in his chest.

"Slater, you won't find the Brotherhood, they were taken out. Everyone knows it, it was all across the news, remember? I was there."

"Do you think I'm fucking stupid?" replied Slater, tossing the angle-grinder into the wall of hay bales. "That was just a front. You want to know who the Brotherhood is?"

With that, Slater pulled out a gun, aimed it at Danny's head and fired, splattering the wall of the barn behind the chair.

"No!" screamed Pete.

Slater grabbed the tablet from his accomplice and held it in front of his face. Pete's blood froze as the words came through the tinny speakers on his phone.

"Alistair Goodfellow. It's *all* Alistair Goodfellow."

The call ended, and Pete found his face staring back at himself in the cold, black mirror of his smartphone.

Chapter 36

"What do you think he was watching?" asked Gilbert.

Alistair sat in his usual chair at the head of the enormous banqueting table in the dining room which had doubled as his operations hub for the last couple of days. He picked at the brass studs stuck in the green leather of the arm, his usual tick while pondering. On the large monitor on the wall, they watched through the hidden camera in Pete's room.

"We could have done with the volume being a little higher on his phone but what we could hear, well, it didn't sound great, did it?" added Jarvis. "Between Pete scrapping his chair and kicking the table at whatever it was he was watching and the shouting coming through the tinny little speaker, we've not got a lot to go on. I've run it through a few of our filters and I can definitely make out 'the Brotherhood of the Righteous', but not much else."

Alistair stood up and went over to the screen. "Play back that last bit."

Jarvis rolled the recording back to show Pete looking away from his phone as the screaming started.

"It's no good, he's holding it at the wrong angle," replied Jarvis. "We can't even slow it down, watch it a few times, before one of us notices it's reflected in the window or something."

"No, quite," said Alistair, still concentrating on the screen. "Unfortunately this isn't Hollywood. Anyway we need to get moving and he will almost certainly be able to help us with the information we have just uncovered. I think we're probably safe to bring him out now, yes?"

"Absolutely," replied Jarvis, "He can't see anything we don't want him to know."

"The Brotherhood thing is still bothering me," said Alistair. "What on earth could he have been watching that mentions us? It's not an old recording of one our episodes is it? I didn't recognise it."

"No, doesn't match any of them. The dialogue isn't like anything on our shows, it all happened too quickly. Plus there's no awesome, thumping soundtrack. And why watch it on a phone, it's much better on the big screen with surround sound."

"We could just ask him," added Gilbert. "You know, say, 'We watched you on the hidden camera watching something on your phone; what was it?' What's he going to do? He probably suspects he's being filmed anyway."

"No, it's too direct," replied Alistair. "We don't want to give anything away unless we absolutely have to. But either way I think that Pete knows something new and we need to find out what it is."

*

Pete stared out of the window, across the vast expanse of carefully manicured formal gardens. He traced his eyes around the maze of hedging, a mixture of straight lines and circles, appearing to him not unlike crop circles. He wondered how this man, with his public image carrying a Bruce Wayne-type aura that he seemed to revel in, the mega-generous acts of philanthropy that he 'didn't like to talk about' but still somehow made it into the national press, the shy unmarried recluse, could really be the brains behind the group that he nearly died trying to apprehend. The more he thought about it the more it seemed to make sense. Many successful business people had that narcissistic trait that they were better than everyone, that they could point out people's faults and judge everyone. It's probably what drove him to be so successful.

"Fuck it," whispered Pete to himself, as he opened up the same messenger app on his phone and clicked on his old friend Mr $pangle.

Lostboy: Spang, pick up. I've got that something for you that you wanted.

He watched with bated breath, just hoping the other end would respond. A few minutes passed and nothing.

Lostboy: I know who the Brotherhood of the Righteous is.

This, he figured, was bound to capture his attention. But still nothing. Last chance.

Lostboy: I mean it. I'm with them now.

After a few seconds, he received the response he wanted.

Mr $pangle: Go on.

Lostboy: Majestic Road. Tell me about it.

Mr $pangle: Fuck you. BR first.

Pete thought about it. Really, he was in no position to barter. And quite frankly, if Alistair and Jarvis really were behind The Red Room then they were probably well placed to track down Majestic Road. No shit was going to hit the fan so quickly that would prevent that.

Lostboy: Alistair Goodfellow. Although my source is decidedly dodgy.

Another pause. Right now he imagined Mr $pangle hastily scouring as many message boards and chat rooms as he could. Chances are, he might already know this information and, being of no real use to him, was just forcing Pete into a position where he could use this information as a blackmailing tool. Either way, Pete figured, desperate times called for desperate measures. But eventually, his enigmatic friend replied.

Mr $pangle: Interesting. I will need to confirm this.

Lostboy: Fuck off. Need information NOW.

Another pause.

Mr $pangle: Word is Majestic Road site was shut down to cover up its real activity. Designer drugs. Selling and demonstrating.

Lostboy:	Demonstrating?
Mr $pangle:	A little like your Red Room friends taking criminals they wanted to re-try, MR demonstrates its wares on human guinea pigs provided for them by their very select clientele.
Lostboy:	How do you get a seat at the table?
MR $pangle:	Existing members nominate. MR sets a trial, series of complex puzzles. If they prove that they can find their way around the dark net, they're in.
Lostboy:	Never saw Goodfellow as the sort to get involved in that.
Mr $pangle:	Maybe he doesn't know…

And then it all fell into place. Slater took Grace in revenge for McAllister and being called out on The Red Room, with the information being provided for him by Smith. Danny was right; this was just a game for Slater. Send Alistair the trail, make him sweat and fight for the privilege of then watching his sister become a guinea pig for a designer, and presumably very unpleasant, drug.

Lostboy:	I think Goodfellow was sent the trail because a man called Curtis Slater took his sister for the show.
Mr $pangle:	Never heard of him, sounds a dick.
Lostboy:	He also has my daughter.
Mr $pangle:	Oh.
Lostboy:	Is that it? "Oh?"
Mr $pangle:	Yes. Good luck.
Lostboy:	Wait.
Lostboy:	Anything else you can tell me about them?
Mr $pangle:	Yeah, try their champagne crack. It fucking rocks.

And with that, Mr $pangle disconnected. Pete was no closer to finding Olivia but at least a clear picture of motive and the series of events that had led to that point began to emerge. If Grace hadn't visited him when she did, he wouldn't be in this mess. But it wasn't her fault. Although, he thought, actually it was.

He thought back to the Red Room investigations, the times that Grace was alone with Olivia, dropping her off at his mother's house. And all along she not only knew exactly who the people committing these horrendous crimes were, but that it was her own brother. He knew she was a confused soul but she had never been anything but nice to him. If you took out the facts that he had learned about her, he would have considered her perfect to be a potential future partner and mother-figure for Olivia. Now, though, that had all gone out the window.

As he unplugged his phone and put it in his pocket, he heard the outside lock of his room undo and in walked Alistair with a huge grin on his face.

Pete ran at him, grabbed him by his jacket, and forced him against the wall. "You utter fucker," Pete spat, a few inches from his face.

Alistair remained ice calm and merely moved his face out of the way of any potential flying spit. "Yes, Pete, I am terribly sorry for locking you in your room. It was most unsporting of me."

"What? Not for that."

"Oh, the Wi-Fi. Sorry for that too," replied Alistair before reaching over both of Pete's arms with his right hand, grabbing a hand that held him against the wall, and calmly levered it off of his clothing, gently twisting it and forcing Pete to his knees with one arm bent at a most uncomfortable angle.

"Pete, I apologised for the lock-in. And the Wi-Fi. But now we need to be working together and there is information that I want to share with you. Remember, my sister and your daughter are still out there, and whatever anger you feel towards me at this point, you need to channel it into finding Olivia. I think we're close."

Pete thought about it from his ridiculous position with his face a few centimetres from the carpet. Not yet. He would wait. "Okay," he mustered, as another jolt of pain shot through his shoulder. "I apologise, it's just all getting a little bit much."

Alistair held his grip a few seconds longer before relinquishing it. He offered a hand to Pete, which he duly accepted and pulled himself to his feet. The two men locked eyes, as if a psychological game of chess were brewing in each of their minds, neither wanting to lay their cards.

Eventually, Pete held out his hand which Alistair graciously accepted.

"Great," said Alistair. "Like I said, I think we're close. I don't know exactly where Grace is, but we're fairly certain that we know where she's going. We came up against the Majestic Road firewalls but if there is one thing Jarvis is good at, and to be fair it might only be one thing, it's firewalls. As I said before, Jarvis developed the firewalls at Phone Giant and he sees it as some sort of sad hobby trying to crack others. Predictably he's managed to find a way in, only for a brief second, but long enough for us to gain vital information. He's just running a diagnostic to ascertain a location."

"I'll bring my things," replied Pete, and together they walked off back to the banqueting hall.

Chapter 37

Olivia curled up, feet on the back passenger seat, covering her ears to the thumping grime soundtrack that blasted through Roach's massive stereo. A thick smog of skunk smoke hung heavy in the air as Paris and him swapped a giant joint between them.

"Can we open a window please? It stinks." Olivia asked, trying hard not to choke on the thick, pungent air. Paris took a long, deep drag of the joint and turned around to face the back, blowing a thick plume of smoke straight into Olivia's face. She wafted her hands in front of her face, coughing as she tried to clear her throat.

"Did you hear something?" asked Paris.

"Nope. Don't think so."

"Please, this music's too loud and I can't breathe properly," Olivia protested, tears rolling down her cheeks.

The huge exhaust of the Impreza roared as Roach put his foot down, joining the dual carriageway and undertaking as many cars as possible who were simply not going quickly enough for his liking in the outside lane. He weaved in and out of the lanes, punching the car up to over a hundred miles an hour.

"There, there, little girl," said Roach. "Is this better for you?"

He pressed the control on his door, lowering Olivia's window. The speed of the car forced a cyclone of air directly into Olivia's face, and she curled up into a ball to shelter from it.

"Please," she cried.

"Oh shut the fuck up, you stupid little pain in the arse. He was only messing around with you. Christ, grow a pair, will you," came Paris's wholeheartedly unsympathetic response.

"Why are you being so horrible to me?" pleaded Olivia. "I don't want to be here either."

"Then I suggest you just shut up and do what we say. I've only got to deal with you for another couple of hours and then we're pissing off to Marbella. What happens to you after that? I don't give a fuck."

Roach broke heavily as the lights turned to red. Usually he would have ignored it and just jumped it. "Better not draw too much attention to us," he said, revelling in the new position Slater had bestowed upon him. "Don't want to fuck up this operation."

Paris laughed. "No you're right. I doubt we were already drawing any attention anyway. I suggest you drive *normally* from here on in."

One last revving of the engine as the lights changed to amber, before blasting off like a dragster once it turned green.

"Sorry," he said turning to Paris. "It's just that dick in the Audi next to me was giving me looks. So I burned him."

After a couple of miles of relatively careful driving through the more built-up residential area of town, they pulled off the main road and up a single track road before turning into the first driveway; a small flint bungalow. Worlds away from the main Slater residence they had left, but equally as inconspicuous, and more akin to a quaint retirement home.

Paris handed Roach the front door key. "Open up, the alarm code's 151199. I'll get her out."

As Roach did as he was told, Paris got out of the car and pulled open Olivia's door.

"Come on, out."

"No," Olivia replied petulantly, pulling her knees into her chest and curling into a ball.

"Fucking just get out!" shouted Paris, reaching across and unclipping the seatbelt before grabbing Olivia's arm and dragging her violently from the car. Olivia fell out onto the hard paved driveway. She yelped; first as she banged her knee on the ground and then after the sharp dig of a shoe in her ribs. As Paris pulled,

Olivia scrambled to get to her feet, continually losing balance and falling back to the floor. Paris just walked, unconcerned, dragging her along behind and ignoring the protests.

She carried on into the house.

"Should be one of these," she said, looking in each of the pokey little cubbyholes and cupboards that came off the cramped passageway, until eventually she found the empty one. Slater's special little 'cupboard under the stairs', reserved for only the most special of guests.

She opened the door and pushed Olivia inside. Olivia screamed in pain as she hit the back wall and slumped into a pile on the floor, rubbing the various parts of her body that were injured on her short journey from the car.

"Shut up. Stop being a little pussy. Here, I'll turn on the light."

And with that, Paris slammed the door and turned the large iron key in the lock. She walked back down the hallway to the lounge to where Roach sat rolling another joint.

The screams and crying slowly faded as Paris turned the music up on the Bluetooth speaker, before slamming the front door shut and sliding the chain across.

Chapter 38

After an hour or so, the car came to a halt. The low, hypnotic vibration of the engine that had penetrated through the deck of the boot, through the hessian sack over Grace's head and into her brain for the entire journey, finally stopped. With her hands cable-tied behind her back and her ankles bound the same, she had found it impossible to change position, other than where she was thrown into by the movement of the car.

In the blackness, she heard the two front doors open. The footsteps came around the back, and her heart raced as she waited for the sound of the boot opening. Instead, she heard the clattering sound of a metal roller shutter door opening and one of the passengers climbing back in the car. The engine started and slowly the car reversed a short time before stopping again. After the roller shutter clattered to the floor, there was a brief silence.

Grace heard the muffled sound of talking before eventually the boot's door opened and the darkness inside her hood changed from black to a bright red as light filled the car. She could now hear the voices clearly.

"Get her out."

She screamed as much as the gaffer tape still glued to her mouth would allow. Two stout arms dragged her out of the car and lifted her into a fireman's carry, easily fighting off her attempts to struggle free.

"Over there, in that cupboard."

She heard the tinny sound that she recognised as a metal filing cabinet door. Again, she tried to struggle as the man dropped her onto the cold hard floor of the cupboard, bent her legs in order to fit them in and slammed the door.

"Now what?" asked the man, leaning against the doors to keep them closed.

The other man scanned around the garage and spotted a small wooden box on the worktop. It was secured with a padlock.

"Where are the instructions that Slater gave us?" he asked. The man pulled a piece of paper from his pocket and handed it to him.

The paper had the address that they were at and a list of instructions.

1. *Place the pig in the green cabinet, secured with cable-ties around wrists and ankles, strong tape over the mouth and a hood, fastened around the neck.*
2. *Remove the chain from the box and secure it around the door handles with two loops and a figure eight.*
3. *Lock with the same padlock, combination 3301.*
4. *The box will contain an envelope with the details of the secure storage.*
5. *Turn off all lights, and lower the shutter door. It will lock automatically.*
6. *Leave the vicinity of the garage immediately, driving in a westerly direction to the A308.*
7. *If any of the above instructions are not followed in their entirety, you will die.*

"What the hell? And a partridge in a pear tree as well I suppose? Dickheads."

"Just do it. And let's get the fuck out of here."

Grace heard the sound of the chain being looped around the door handles and a lock click into place. The cupboard was darker and far more cramped than the boot. Until then she had managed to maintain a degree of calm. The years of abuse that she had suffered at the hands of her old partner had made her mentally tough, and taught her coping mechanisms. In the car she had always held out hope that Alistair would intercept and stage some dramatic rescue. But now, being sealed in this aluminium cage, her mental barriers had begun to crumble and she thrashed around as best she could.

"Shut up, you dozy old bint!" shouted one of the men as he hammered on the front of the cupboard with his fist. "You're not getting out so just deal with it."

As Grace continued to kick and scream and smash her shoulders against the doors, she didn't hear the car start up and the roller shutter door slide to the ground.

Eventually, she stopped and all she could hear was silence. She sobbed, waiting for the inevitable.

*

The car pulled away, following the instructions given in the envelope and drove towards the A308.

"Curtis, I've got it," said the passenger, speaking into his phone. Slater didn't like his people using the hands-free systems installed in the very expensive cars he provided them with in case 'the Feds were listening.'"Good," replied Slater. "Get the envelope over to my daughter's dipshit boyfriend. We'll let him take it from here."

"Do you want us to tail him? Make sure he's okay?"

"Probably a good idea. But only until he's within spitting distance of the club. The whole point of sending him is that he's new and unknown. If anyone is staking out the club, I don't want them seeing you. Him? I couldn't give a fuck. And if anything happens to him after? There's even less of a fuck that I could give."

"What about cops?"

"I doubt it. Klaus has that well covered."

"Okay, we'll keep you updated."

Chapter 39

Pete followed Alistair into the banqueting hall, a huge spread of cooked pheasant, roasted vegetables and jugs of ice-cold spring water adorned the table. The others were already helping themselves.

"An army marches on its stomach, Pete," said Alistair, guiding Pete to a chair along the middle of the table. "All this pheasant is from the estate, Jarvis shot them himself. By which I mean that he pointed at them and someone else a little less physically inept shot them. They've been hung for two weeks, and are absolutely delicious. It's important to keep up your energy."

Pete was more concerned about his daughter, about Danny's death, than eating. But as he hadn't had anything since breakfast, he thought he should probably follow Alistair's advice. Pete sat down and helped himself.

"Okay, great. Now, Pete, you sit there and enjoy your dinner while Jarvis brings you up to speed with what we have found out while you were away."

Pete laughed ironically at the statement. "While you locked me in my room, you mean?"

Jarvis, chewing on a mouthful of food, stabbed at the keyboard of his laptop with the bottom of his fork and pointed to the large screen on the wall.

"So... excuse me... right. So, once we received the log-on in the email we went on to the Majestic Road site. Now, we all know about Majestic Road that was in the press, but it would appear that the stories were all a smoke screen. We did a little more digging around the dark web and found a few people in the know. It would appear that Alistair's darling sister has been kidnapped in order to be a guinea pig. There is a members' area open to only the select few who are both nominated and pass the little trial that we spent the last few days trying to crack. We are now entitled to join in their next little demonstration under the pretence of being purchasers of their wares. But we believe that we have simply been invited to the party by whoever it is that kidnapped Grace so that Alistair can watch her be tested on."

"It took you that long to work it out?" replied Pete sarcastically.

The others all stared at each other in silence.

"How so, Pete?" asked Alistair. "Do you have some information that you would like to share with us?"

Pete decided it truly was shit-or-bust time. "Who invited you?"

"We're still not entirely sure," replied Jarvis. "We've done all manner of forensics, software and hardware, on the memory stick, but there's nothing. All we know from the brief chat that we were afforded by the site admins was that we were nominated by someone calling themselves the CSA and that they looked forward to seeing us later tonight."

"And you really have no idea who that is?" Pete asked again.

"No, Pete, we don't," said Jarvis, throwing his head back and rubbing his temples. "It's not a business we've dealt with or even recognise. There are a lot of people we know with the initials CA but—"

Pete interrupted by sliding his laptop across the table to Jarvis. "If you wouldn't mind putting the Wi-Fi back on and transferring it to the monitor please."

Pete continued eating his dinner as Jarvis poked around the keyboard before sliding the laptop back across the table. Pete logged on to his cloud account and clicked on a movie file called *RR1*.

As the room filled with the sound of a thumping techno soundtrack, Jarvis, Alistair and Gilbert all stared, stunned into silence as their work played on the screen. The clown-masked, boiler-suited figure speaking into his gold microphone.

"So, this is the Red Room that I was telling you about earlier. This guy is the host and calls himself 'the Host'," Pete said, making air quotes with his fingers and taking in the tension that he just created in the room. "The man tied to the chair is a gang-land enforcer by the name of Cramer McAllister. Wait, I need to get to the right bit."

He slid the scroll bar along the bottom of the video screen until he reached the point and played the video again. The figure tied to the chair screamed as the masked figure poked the corner of his clipboard into a huge open wound in his kneecap. "Oops, sorry, too far," said Pete.

The reality dawned on everyone else in the room, but no one could bring themselves to speak up.

"A-ha, here we go," said Pete as he turned up the volume.

We know precisely who you are and we know full well who you work for. In fact, we might send your good buddy Curtis Slater a little video of this. You never know, he might even be next to sit in the hot seat.

Pete rewound it and played it again.

"Okay," said Alistair. "So, Curtis Slater explains the C and the S, I suppose. What about the A?"

"Arsehole? Anti-Christ? How the fuck should I know? But it's him. *He* is who took Grace and, more importantly, and in no small part due to this fucked up freak show, my beautiful innocent daughter."

Pete's eyes burned into Alistair. The others watched Alistair's very uncharacteristic squirming.

"But it still doesn't—"

"It's him, Alistair!" shouted Pete. "I just watched him slice my good friend's eye with a hacksaw before copying this shit and cutting his leg off with an angle-grinder. He knows who I am, he knows who Danny was, and he knows who you are."

"Yes, yes," replied Alistair. "So he realised that Grace worked on the case and that she has a rich brother. It's fairly elementary-level extortion and blackmail..."

"But it isn't, is it?" said Pete calmly, before eventually breaking the awkward silence with his fist banging the table. He pointed at the screen, frozen with an image of the Host's maniacal clown face staring close up to the camera.

"That. Is. You."

Chapter 40

The bright white light flooded into Grace's eyes as the hood was removed. This, she assumed, was the final part of her journey. She would either be rescued or she would be killed. The journey there had been marginally more comfortable than the journey to the lock-up. The cable ties were still in place but at least she was allowed to sit upright. About forty-five minutes, she reckoned, although where in the country was beyond her. She'd entirely lost her bearings once she arrived at Slater's.

She found herself in a small windowless room, a variety of different sized pipes adorning the wall, to one of which she was chained. There was nothing but silence apart from the odd creaking pipe that followed the loud metallic clattering each time she tried to pull the pipe from the wall with the chain.

It had been around twenty minutes since the man who had marched her into this room had removed her hood and left. Finally, the door opened.

"It's about time," she said, standing up tall and defiant. "Do you know who I am?"

Her posturing and bravado waned as she watched the tall masked figure slowly emerge around the door. They stood in front of her, the pointy beak of the plague mask, the smoky glass eye covers, the thick black elbow-length gloves and the large black hat.

The figure walked over to her and gripped her jaw between its thumb and finger, turning her face from side-to-side as if examining her for lice. Grace's eyes widened and she maintained her eye contact with this person as her head moved. Not once did their eyes blink.

The figure stepped back and looked at her. They spotted her bandaged hand and reached forward, gently grabbing it in a thick rubber glove and cupping it between both hands, almost mother-like in an attempt to make the pain go away.

They locked eyes before the figure leant in closer.

Grace could see her reflection, in both the glass eye coverings and in the eyes of the person behind the mask.

Finally, the figure spoke.

"For you, my dear, I wish the best, as you're our very special guest.
The pain you feel is sure to fade, as soon your farewell will be bade.
When all is said and all is done, we are not many, we are but one.
My role on earth is heaven sent: provide it with… *Enlightenment.*"

Grace stared in a state of disbelief and the figure stroked the back of a gloved index finger down her cheek. It turned away before walking out of the room. Grace realised that she had been holding her breath and let out a long sigh, before sinking to her knees and starting to cry.

A few minutes later, another person entered the room. Not masked, or dressed like a plague doctor, but smart. A sharp, close fitting single-breasted suit, pressed blue shirt and pastel yellow tie. He carried a small stool which he dropped in front of Grace, and sat down.

"Good evening, Ms Brooks," the Smart Man said, causing Grace to lift her head from her hands at the sound of her name.

"How do you—?" she started before being cut off.

"I see you have met our Professor. Usually, the Professor doesn't like to meet with our guinea pigs before a show, but it seems that in your case, an exception was made. Have you had anything to eat today?"

"What? No."

"Okay, good. The Professor did request that but we were never really sure that Mr Slater would actually follow the instructions we gave. It is of the utmost importance for the demonstration that you haven't eaten for at least twelve hours. The… *effects…* will be a lot more profound on an empty stomach."

"What effects? Anyway, where am I? Do you have any fucking idea who my brother is, you stupid little tax accountant?"

"The effects, Ms Brooks, of the Professor's latest creation. It's been specially designed on the assumption that most of the gutter-crawling dregs of society who will be buying it up in their droves, really have no proper diet and so we wanted it to work its magic best on an empty stomach."

"Please, I don't know who you are, but my brother has more money than God. I've got no idea why Curtis Slater took me and brought me here, but whatever he's paying you, my brother—"

"Yes, yes, yes. He'll pay me treble or quadruple or quintuple or… what would actually come next in that little series? Not interested," the Smart Man replied as though this was a standard last-ditch attempt made by all of their special guests. "Mr Slater has the honours and it is important for our operation that protocol is followed, otherwise the whole thing will crumble down around itself. But in answer to your other question, yes, we are fully aware who your brother is. Telephone magnate Alistair Goodfellow, residing at the world famous Clifton Manor. I must admit to being somewhat surprised when Mr Slater nominated him, as we were not aware that the world of lifestyle enhancements such as ours was something that floated his boat. We were even more surprised when his darling little sister arrived to take part in our little show. But hey-ho. Ours is not to reason why as they say. It'll certainly make for an interesting show, that's for certain. Although I doubt very much that your brother will be partaking in our end-of-show purchasing spree. But we can deal with that another time."

Grace cried again as her fate became sealed. She thought back to waking up in Pete's bed, finally getting everything that she had ever wanted. That briefest moment of contentment instantly ripped away, first by Slater and now by these people, whoever they were. How she longed to be back there.

"Anyway, if you'll excuse me," said the Smart Man, patting her on the shoulder before standing up and walking towards the door. "I need to begin preparations for tonight's episode. I'll see you again in approximately an hour. And if you want some advice, since there is nothing you can do to change what's about to happen, when it comes to it, you might as well just enjoy what it does to you."

With that, the Smart Man left the room, slamming the heavy metal door behind him.

He walked on a little further down the corridor, until he reached the room where the Professor was changing out of the plague mask.

"Have we heard from him?" asked the Professor.

"Not for two hours."

"Try him again."

The Smart Man pulled out his phone and dialled a number. After a few seconds, he hung up. "Nothing."

"Something must have happened to him. Leave a message."

"It's pointless…"

"Just do it. Now!"

"Okay, okay," sighed the Smart Man redialling the last number. He waited for the voicemail message to finish.

"Fowler, it's me. Ring me as soon as you get this message."

Chapter 41

Alistair stood up and slowly walked over to the monitor. He stood fixed in front of the screen, and placed a hand on the face as if greeting an old friend.

"Well? Are you going to deny it?" asked Pete.

"No," replied Alistair without turning. "Ask yourself why, Pete."

"Why what?"

"Why we did it."

"You're a fucking psycho?"

"To cleanse society, Pete," replied Alistair, walking back to the table. "To right wrongs. Surely, it's no different to your reasons for joining the police force?"

"Don't tar me with your rather twisted brush. I tried to stop people like you doing things like this."

"But we were on your side, Pete. Where you hit brick walls because of *protocols*, and *due process*," spat Alistair, "we carried on your work. We sent a message out to the scum of this world that, yes, they may not have any reason to fear the justice system, but they sure as hell have every reason to fear us. Are you seriously telling me that when you heard that a grotesquely overweight, semi-retarded woman who tortured and beat the small human being that she was singularly responsible for protecting, causing him unimaginable suffering and fear, leaving him to die at the hands of her brutal thug of a boyfriend, that you felt no single shard of gratitude? No single thought that, hey, she *totally and utterly* deserved all of this? Nothing at all?"

Pete sat and pondered. He had always approached the investigation from a policeman's point-of-view. Like a doctor faced with saving the life of an attempted suicide bomber brought in by police, or of a child murderer attempting to commit suicide in their cell, it was not for him to decide to save the life or not based on his opinions, his calling made him. This was Pete's Hippocratic oath; stop what he was witnessing not what he felt. He couldn't help but feel a little empathy for Alistair. The frustration at the limits of police power, the bureaucracy, the corruption.

"It was wrong," said Pete, annoyed with himself that this was the best he could muster.

Alistair scoffed. "I know you think differently, I can see it in your eyes."

"So what? It's still illegal, and if anyone found out what you have done, you will go down for a very long time."

"No one can prove it's us though, can they. Plus, I'm pretty certain that more than a couple of chief constables, high court judges and city lawyers were amongst our most dedicated subscribers."

And then Pete remembered. He remembered being tied to the chair, the sack over his head, being face-to-face with the man who killed his wife. And he remembered the gun pointing at his head. The anger welled and very quickly spilled over into a rage.

He kicked his chair back and launched himself at Alistair. "You threatened to kill me! Did you really want to make my daughter a fucking orphan, or is your big fucking ego more important?"

Alistair deftly moved to the side, avoiding Pete's swinging haymaker, and before Pete could react further, grabbed him under the arm and around the back of his neck, before slowly lowering him to the ground in a headlock.

"We never had any intention of killing you," Alistair said, pressing a knee into Pete's back. "We offered you the chance to take vengeance. To exorcise the demon in your life that was Saeed Anwar. We knew that Smith was on the way and we knew that Anwar's associates were coming to kill him. And didn't my man look after you?"

"What?" Pete just about managed to force out. "*I* had to drag *him* out of harm's way after he managed to get himself shot."

"Yes, but he stopped you from playing the big hero and trying to save Anwar. It's very honourable and all, but that is what would have made your daughter an orphan, not us."

"That's the most twisted fucking logic I've ever heard."

Pete's phone vibrated on the table.

"Seems you've got a call, Pete," said Alistair, relinquishing his grip slightly.

Jarvis picked up the phone. "It's a message from your good friend Mr$pangle. Mind if I?"

Alistair grabbed Pete and picked him off the floor.

Jarvis unlocked Pete's phone as if it wasn't locked in the first place and clicked on the message. "Er, actually Alistair, you might want to see this."

He plugged the phone into the USB hanging from the TV screen, displaying the message.

Not that I owe you anything, you piece of shit, but during my search for the Brotherhood I found this. It should help. And it makes us quits. Don't ever contact me again.

Underneath was a screenshot of a Twitter post. It showed the back end, and number plate, of a Subaru Impreza with the caption *Rolling with the Slater Crew. Taking down the Brotherhood of the Righteous.*

"Who is this?" asked Alistair. "Pete, why would your underground friend have sent you this?"

"How the fuck should I know?" said Pete dusting himself down, before thinking about it a little longer. "Danny!"

"Jarvis, find out who *@ganjamonster* is."

"Are you going to lock me in my room while you go through your 'proprietary information' again?" asked Pete. "I think Danny took this on whoever @ganjamonster is phone because he knew we would be scouring the Internet searching for any sign of Slater and any link to the Brotherhood. He said they were taking Olivia to a safe house. This must be the car."

"Why didn't this Danny of yours just tell you where the farmhouse was?"

"He didn't know. But I think Slater must be using this joker as his drugs mule, so if we find him, we find Olivia and Slater."

"And Grace?" asked Alistair.

"The tracer is still doing its thing," replied Jarvis, referring to cracking through the Majestic Road firewall. "But give it a few more minutes and it'll at least give us a street."

Pete grabbed his laptop and phone from the TV and made his way to the door.

"Going somewhere, Pete?"

"I'm going to find Olivia. I've still got contacts in the force who can trace that car for me."

As he reached the door he heard the lock click; he tried to open it but it wouldn't budge. He shook the handle before hearing the familiar click of a gun cocking behind. He turned to find himself staring directly down the barrel of a pistol.

"Pete, don't," said Alistair, his arm unwavering as it aimed at Pete's head. "For what it's worth, I like you. Like I said, we're on the same side and over the last couple of days I've come to see what Grace loves about you. You're smart, honourable, a dedicated father. In many ways I wish I could be more like you. Still with my money obviously, but as a person. Now, I made a promise to Grace that I would never hurt you, so it is imperative that we work together. To show that there are no hard feelings, we'll provide you with an awesome car and some of my men to go and get your Olivia. Jarvis will start work on tracking this Impreza and he will guide you as you get there. He'll be Chloe O'Brian to your Jack Bauer."

He clicked the gun off cocked, placed it down on a side table, and held out his hand for Pete to shake. Pete stared at it. The last few days had been more of an emotional rollercoaster than at any other point in his life. Even the death of his wife seemed fairly easy to mentally pigeonhole compared to this. If he was to be brutally honest with himself, he had started to like Alistair as well. A charismatic, yet mildly psychotic, multi-millionaire was a useful asset. And unfortunately was Pete's only real help.

He took hold of Alistair's hand and shook it. Alistair pulled him closer and whispered, "Good man. I will do everything in my power to find your daughter. But be under no illusions of exactly what we are capable of, so seriously do... not... screw with me."

He let go of Pete's hand and gave him a huge, friendly smack on the back. "That's the spirit. Right, let's get to work!"

Chapter 42

Roach took a long, hard drag on the carrot-shaped spliff he had spent the last quarter of an hour lovingly rolling. He sunk into the deep cushions of the sofa, arms spread-eagle across the back, tilted his head towards the ceiling and blew a thick plume of smoke into the air. He looked down at the top of Paris's head as it bobbed up and down over his groin and afforded himself a huge grin. If only his colleagues in frozen produce, and especially his dickhead supervisor, could see him now. Not only working for one of the most feared gangland bosses in the country, but being sucked off by his daughter.

"Yeah, babe," he said, staring up at the ceiling. "I told you it was only a matter of time before your old man appreciated my skills."

Paris looked up at him, wiping her mouth with the back of her hand. "That's why I love ya! Wait 'til we're in Marbs…"

He placed his hand on top of her head and pushed it back down. The song that was playing stopped, and in the ensuing silence they heard the locked cupboard door being smacked with something from the inside.

"Shut up, you little shit!" shouted Roach. "You're putting me off my stroke."

But the slamming continued and then the screaming started. It made the house shudder.

"Fucking hell," said Roach, standing up and nearly choking Paris in the process. He pulled his trousers up, before fastening them and then pulling them back down a few inches.

"Leave her in there, baby."

"Nah, she's doing my fucking head in," he said, storming out of the room and down the corridor. He wrenched the door open just as the handle of a broom slammed into his genitals. Olivia stepped back with her hand over her mouth, giggling as he writhed around clasping his crotch.

"Get out here, you little shit," he said grabbing her from the cupboard and pulled her down the corridor to the lounge. Olivia fought but her futile struggle just made an already-pumped Roach even more hyper. He threw her down on the sofa, and she crawled to one end, huddling in a ball, as he stood over her. He tapped the end of his joint over her head, small grey specs of ash floating down and landing in her hair.

"Roach, that's enough," said Paris.

"Nah, it's not nearly enough," he replied, bending down and holding the joint upright in front of Olivia's face. "Do you want this in your eye, little girl? Do you?"

Olivia shook her head in fear, pressing herself against the back of the sofa.

"How about this then?" he said. He reached into his rucksack and pulled out a small pistol, which he twirled around his finger like a cowboy.

"Whoa," said Paris, running over and grabbing his arm. "Where the fuck did you get that?"

"Your old man's. Don't worry, I'll put it back."

"He'll kill you if he finds out."

"Chill out, sweet tits. I'll just say I borrowed it in case I got into any agro."

"Stop being a dick, Roach," said Paris, more sternly. "Seriously, my dad has just given you one job to do. You're not Vito Corleone all of a sudden."

The doorbell rang.

"Shit, it's my dad's mates. Hide it," said Paris.

Roach panicked. "Oh my god, oh my god. Where?"

"Just put it back in the pissing bag."

Roach put the gun back in the rucksack, and took a huge drag of the joint to calm himself down. He went and opened the front door.

"All right, gentlemen," he said, in the most confident manner he could muster.

The man at the door held out the envelope, which Roach took. He opened it and read the address.

"We'll be watching you," said the man sternly. "Do not fuck it up. Understand?"

"Yes, sir," Roach replied, but the man had already turned to walk away. Roach closed the door behind him and went back into the lounge, collecting his car keys from the coffee table.

"I'm off," he said. "You stay here and look after the shit."

"What? Why can't I chuck her in the cupboard again and come with you? She'll be all right here until we get back."

"Nah, look, I need to do this on my own. He wouldn't want you involved. It won't be long, the lock-up's nearby. I'll call."

She gave him a hug and big tongue-filled kiss. "And then I'll finish you off later, big boy."

He smiled at her and then gave her a big slap on the backside before leaving and getting into his car.

The headlights shone around the walls of the lounge as Paris watched him pull out of the driveway. She stamped her foot, before kicking the coffee table.

"This is all your fault," she screamed at Olivia, not sure exactly what was Olivia's fault. "If I hadn't had to be your sodding babysitter, I'd be in Marbs now."

"No you wouldn't," replied Olivia.

"Whatever. Just shut up," said Paris, grabbing Olivia by the wrist and bending her arm back towards her face. "Either way, I wish you were dead. Do you have any idea how many parties I've had to miss because of you?"

"Ow, you're hurting me."

"Yeah, well, just sit there and shut up until my dad comes. If you don't, I'll smash your head against the wall."

Olivia rested her head on the arm of the sofa and begun to cry.

*

Roach walked out of the huge Super Storage warehouse, right in the middle of a retail park, and got back into his car parked on double yellow lines out the front. Gently, he placed the small brown package on the passenger seat. He opened his phone, ignoring the endless Twitter notifications that appeared at the top of his screen. People liking some Tweet or other that he couldn't even remember sending. He'd check that later. He scrolled down his list of contacts to 'Curtis' and dialled.

"It's me, Mr Slater," he said when the voice answered at the other end. "I've got your package. What do you want me to do with it?"

"Good lad. Now, very carefully open the box. There should be smaller boxes inside. I want you to split them equally. Put half back in the big box and take it to Klaus. The other boxes you put under your seat or something and bring them back here after you've done the drop off. Is that clear?"

"What's in the boxes?"

"Is that clear?"

"Yes, sir. You can count on—" he said before the line went dead.

He followed Slater's instructions and separated the box accordingly. He started the engine, turned the stereo up as loud as he could stand and wound down the windows.

A few metres along the road, he crawled past a group of youths congregated on the corner. One of the lads made a hand gesture to him as the others watched him and laughed. As he edged past them, Roach leaned out the window and shouted, "You're lucky I don't come out there and fuck the lot of you up."

More laughter, and a few more 'wanker' signs, ensued. Roach returned with a hand-gesture of his own, before putting his foot down and loudly accelerating out of the retail estate in the direction of the Blue Oyster.

Chapter 43

Pete stared out of the passenger window as the enormous Mercedes 4x4 trundled through the quiet, post-rush hour town centre. Rows and rows of terraced houses flashed by, people going about their daily business; making supper, settling down in front of the television to watch a box-set, having a blazing row with a partner, tucking their children into bed. Any one of these houses could have Olivia in it. He might be staring through the window of a room where she was cowering in the corner from her captors, watching as his car speeds past, begging him to stop, and he wouldn't know it.

Then the phone resting on his lap vibrated. In years gone by, he would have objected to the slightly dubious methods by which he was now supported, thanks to Alistair and Jarvis. But there was nothing he wouldn't do to find his daughter.

"We've got him," said Jarvis before Pete even had a chance to greet him. He tapped his pen on the bank of monitors at the grainy greyish CCTV footage of the storage warehouse.

From his years in one of the more secretive departments of the Metropolitan Police, Pete knew the complexity of the ANPR network and their CCTVs and quite how someone like Jarvis could access it was beyond him. But his mood shot through the roof, the pain and tiredness from the last few days washed away.

"Where?"

"This kid's Impreza just left the storage facility on the edge of town and is heading away towards the Reading area."

"If you punch the number into the search field, you should be able to access all sightings from the last few hours."

"Way ahead of you. We're going to send someone to tail him, see where he goes. But we managed to track him backwards to a small, sleepy little village where we were then able to call on some of Alistair's more, how shall we say, official police friends for a list of Slater's suspected safe houses."

"And…"

"Sending you the address now."

Pete's phone pinged as a message arrived and he promptly punched the address into the car's satellite navigation system. Twenty minutes away.

"Thank you, Jarvis," he said, more out of mandatory politeness than actually being grateful.

He resumed his position, staring out of the window as Alistair's man drove them as fast as he could legally muster to their new destination. Pete felt a huge sense of déjà vu, another calm before the storm and he chuckled inwardly at the irony. The self-loathing he had felt since putting himself in the position of trying to take down the Brotherhood of the Righteous, storming the warehouse on his own, risking his life and making an orphan out of Olivia for his job. And now he was relying on the same Brotherhood to help him save his daughter's life. Neither was a great situation, but he knew which way around he preferred it.

Chapter 44

The Mercedes GLE turned into the country lane, its hybrid engine almost silent as it rolled to a stop a short distance from the driveway.

"Let me go," said Pete. "I have to do this. Just wait at the end of the lane and if I need anything, I'll shout. What's your name by the way?"

"Carl."

"Okay, Carl, I'll be back in a minute."

Before Carl could suggest an alternative, Pete jumped out of the car and gently closed the door. He walked as quietly as he could, keeping to grass verges, sidling along the rows of hedges and trees for cover.

As he approached the front bay window, he pressed himself against the flint wall of the bungalow and peered around into the lounge.

There she was. This was the first he had seen of his daughter for days. Even if none of this happened and she was still safely on her school trip, he would have had to have waited longer to see her. But it took all of his self-control not to just bang on the window shouting her name. His heart pounded, she was within touching distance. But she was clearly scared. His fears rose when he saw her cower back into the corner of the sofa as the other figure entered.

A girl, dressed like some uber-cool hipster in a super expensive tracksuit and sports gear that had obviously never seen any physical activity, walked into the room and grabbed her arm. The double glazing muffled her words, but he could sense the aggression and the fear in Olivia's eyes. Olivia struggled and he saw the older girl raise her hand as if to strike her. Olivia buried her head in her other arm as the girl pulled her off the sofa and onto the floor. She bent down, pointing an aggressive finger almost into Olivia's eye to hammer home whatever point she was trying to make.

He'd seen enough. He slid past the window to the front door and rang the bell. Nothing. He pressed it again, longer this time. A shadow moved across the small, blurry pane of glass at the top of the door and he heard a few locks and shackles being unfastened. He took a deep breath and composed himself.

"Yes," said Paris as she opened the door a few inches.

"Good evening, madam," replied Pete. "Sorry to bother you, but I'm collecting for the Lifeboat Association and I was wondering if you would care to donate."

"No thanks," said Paris, and she went to close the door.

"Please," said Pete immediately, placing his foot at the bottom of the door. "I just need a few more pounds. I'm on a commission, you see, and you're the last house to try in this village. If I don't get just two pounds I'll miss my target and not get paid."

"I don't care."

"Please," he said a little louder. "You'd be doing me a massive favour."

Pete smiled as he heard the chain being removed.

"Fine, just wait a minute."

Pete pushed past the door and stood in the hallway. "You don't mind do you? It's a little bit chilly in here."

Paris reached into her handbag to get her purse just as her phone rang. It was her dad.

"Jesus, can't people leave me alone."

Olivia peered around the doorframe. "Daddy!" she shouted running from the lounge towards them. "I knew you'd come!"

Paris, realising what was going on, pulled the pistol from her tracksuit pocket. She pointed it at Pete.

"Stop there, you little bastard," she shouted, as Pete's eyes switched from the gun to Olivia, to Paris and back to the gun. "Get in the lounge, both of you."

Pete had been in this position before although last time it was a lot more frightening knowing that the person holding probably knew how to actually use it. Olivia ran into the lounge, as Pete held his ground and stared at her, watching her quiver.

"I think you're in a little over your head darling, aren't you," said Pete calmly.

"Don't tell me what I am. Do you know who my dad is?"

"Absolutely, and to be honest, I'd be surprised if he's still alive this time tomorrow. Perhaps you should get away while you can."

She looked at him. Pete shrugged, hoping that she had no idea whether he was bluffing or serious. He doubted very much that she had ever heard any sort of threat to her dad, it just didn't happen.

"Whatever," she replied defiantly. "I'd be surprised if your daughter is still alive in ten minutes after I go and put a bullet in her head."

The two locked eyes. Pete knew the girl was petrified. Yes, she was Slater's daughter but she was probably more used to iPads, manicures, parties and free cars from Daddy than weapons.

Then Pete saw Olivia over her shoulder. He gave her a small nod, enough for Paris to realise there was someone behind her. She glanced over her shoulder, giving Pete the opportunity he needed to grab the hand holding of the gun. He spun Paris around, pulling her arm across her throat, and he squeezed down on the top of her head with his other hand. Slowly, Paris's legs gave way as she slipped gently into unconsciousness.

"Is she dead?" asked Olivia.

"No, just sleeping. She'll be fine in a few minutes or so." Pete knelt down and pulled Olivia towards him, embracing her in the biggest hug he could manage. "I am so sorry," he said cupping her cheeks, as tears rolled down his. "I am so sorry that you had to go through all this. I promise that I will never, *never*, let you go again. I love you so much."

"To the moon and back?"

"More."

They hugged again and then left the house.

Pete opened the driver side door for Olivia to climb into the back and then opened the front door.

"My apologies, Carl," Pete said as he pointed the pistol at Carl's head. "But I really need you to get out of the car. The Slater girl is in there, but I'm taking my daughter and getting the fuck out of here. Sorry, Olivia, excuse Daddy's language."

Carl put his hands up in front of him, and complied without arguing. Pete quickly jumped into the driver seat and started the engine. As Carl walked towards the house, dialling a number in his phone, Pete called out of the window.

"You might want to disconnect the CCTV cameras in there as you go. There are loads of them."

He drove off into the darkness of the country lane, leaving Carl on the driveway talking on his phone.

"Yeah he's gone… Send another car to get me… Yes, the Slater girl is secured. Pete mentioned about the CCTVs. I know Jarvis was going to hack into the property's security system and run some loop on it, I assume he did that before we arrived?… Perfect, then we're ready to rock."

On the other end of the phone, Alistair smiled a huge grin. "Well done, Pete," he whispered.

*

A few miles away from the house, Pete pulled into a large multi-story car park close to the centre of town.

"Okay, we'll leave the car here. The train station is just a few minutes away. We'll get to the coast and then take the first ferry back home."

"Dad," said Olivia reaching into her pocket. "When we were back at that last house, I found this memory stick in my hoodie pocket. I don't know how it got there."

Pete reached behind and took the stick from her. He turned on his laptop and plugged it into the USB slot. A Windows Explorer box popped up with three folders titled *Open Me First, Open Me Second, Open Me When Safe.*

Pete dutifully followed the instructions, opened the first folder and clicked on the Word document it contained. *Unit D, Yarmouth Place. London. Code 33155137.*

"Do you have any idea who gave you this? Anyone talk to you about me?"

"I don't know."

"Could it have been this man?" asked Pete, bringing up a picture of Slater on this phone.

"No, that's Paris's dad. I don't think it was him."

"This man?" asked Pete again, scrolling through his photos until he reached one of Danny.

"Yes! He talked to me when I got in Roach's car. I think he did something on Roach's phone as well."

"Daniel Fowler, you son of a bitch," said Pete, hastily calling Alistair's mobile. "Alistair, it's me. Firstly, sorry for stealing your car, but hey, perhaps you shouldn't have locked me in my room. Secondly, you might want to write this down."

He read out the address from Danny's file.

"Thank you, Pete. Just so you know, we've got your location so will be coming to retrieve my property very shortly."

"You should think about being a little more grateful. I've got no idea how he had this information but I'm pretty certain that Danny died to get it to us. You might be mister big bollocks with more money than I'll ever see in my lifetime, but don't forget that I know. I know all about you."

"Which is why we are coming to retrieve you. An agreement needs to be made."

"Screw you. I've got my daughter back. You go and get your sister. Then we agree to never have anything to do with each other ever again. That's the only agreement we need."

"Pete don't be—"

Pete hung up before Alistair could finish. "Come on, we're leaving."

He packed everything up in his rucksack and got out of the car. Olivia followed him as he walked over to a group of youths gathered in the car park, drinking a mixture of high strength cider and garishly coloured energy drinks, kicking an empty can around the floor.

"Guys," he said, as the group turned to stare at him, a slight mob mentality kicking in.

"The fuck you want?" asked the more cocky of the boys.

"Do you mind? My daughter can hear that. Anyway, I've got a hundred pounds here that you can have and all that you have to do is take that massive Mercedes over there for a drive. For as long as you want. As far away as you want. It's top of the range. It's absolutely stunning. And it's yours if you want it."

"You for real?"

"Uh-huh," he replied dangling the keys in front.

It didn't take long for the lads' low intelligence to kick in and their cider-induced bravado to fly into overdrive.

"Go on then," said another.

Pete took the wedge of one hundred pounds from his wallet and handed it to the boy before tossing the keys in the air.

"Enjoy," he said as Olivia and he walked away, arm in arm, the sounds of 'Oh my days' and 'That is tope' ringing in his ears. "Right, young lady, we've got a train to catch."

Chapter 45

Roach stood in the back alley behind the Blue Oyster club as the door slammed in his face with a heavy metallic bang, his raised fist hanging in the air as his attempted bump to Slater's associates had gone thoroughly ignored. Not that he cared. He'd completed his first job for Curtis Slater. Now, he *commanded* respect. He could probably walk down this alley and out onto the main street, start on anyone he wanted, just for the sake of it, safe in the knowledge that he had the backing of the Slater crew. Give it another hour or so, and he'd be back at the safe house balls deep in Curtis's daughter, now entirely unable to resist his *swag*.

Without realising how much he resembled a little girl, he jogged, almost skipping, back to his car and got in. The music began pumping and he lit another joint, when the phone rang. He pressed the answer button on the car's hands-free system.

"Sup, Roach speaking," he said, blowing out a huge cloud of smoke and pulling away.

"It's Curtis," came the response, as Roach killed the stereo. "You'd better not be driving around trying to sell my gear, you pointless little shit, otherwise I'll break both your fucking legs and post them to your parents. Ha, ha, ha."

"Ha, ha, er no of course not, Mr Slater," replied Roach. "I've just left the club. I've still got the other half of the package."

"I'm joking, of course," said Slater. "I've literally just got off the phone to Klaus actually."

"Really? How did he say I did?" replied Roach, sounding like a desperate school child.

"He didn't say you were a complete fucking bell-end, which is good for him, so consider it a job well done."

"Thank you, Mr Slater. You're welcome."

"I didn't say thank you, but as my expectations of you *not* totally cocking this up were already set very low, you can consider it a *well done*."

"Er, right, I think. Shall I go back to the house with Paris?" he asked, slightly more comfortable that he wasn't in any immediate danger of losing some body parts.

"No, no, I need you to come back to the farm first. You know, drop the merchandise off. Okay? Good."

"Not a problem, Mr…" replied Roach before realising that Slater had cut him off. He turned the music back up, and began the tedious drive back to Slater's farm.

*

Slater hung up the phone and looked at the large TV on the wall of his office. After the slight mishap that had befallen his most recent I.T. guru, he had hastily called in a favour from the company who handle all of his security and CCTV around his various properties. This was one of the few companies that he didn't own but had a lot of respect for. The owner and him went way back and the idea of using a security firm as the legitimate face of a protection racket always tickled Slater.

"So, make it fucking work… what's your name… Nigel?" he shouted at the man fiercely tapping away on a laptop.

"It's not easy," replied Nigel, taking a swig from a can of energy drink. "The people who did this are obviously good."

"Can they trace anything back to this location?"

"Don't be stupid. Even the roads don't trace back to this location. If there's a place in England that's harder to find than this, I'd be surprised. Probably because no one's found it yet."

Slater watched as the monitor showed up video footage of his empty house where he had expected to see his daughter. The CCTV programme was stopping him from rewinding the footage to see what had been going on.

"It would appear that your system has been compromised, so everything you have been watching didn't happen. I'm just trying to access the hard drive and override the Trojan they installed... shouldn't be too much... okay, there, we're in, but it may be a little patchy in places. Depends on how much their little hijacking messed up the recording facility."

Slater grabbed the laptop and begun putting earlier times into the search function. He found them arriving at the house and the little girl being thrown in the cupboard.

"Okay, that's them. Good girl, using the special cupboard like I said," he said, changing the time forward a few minutes to something he really didn't like to see. "Christ all fucking mighty! Unsee! Unsee! That dirty little shit."

Then he saw Roach leave. And then it happened, the man entering. He vaguely recognised him from the Skype call earlier, but it was always a little difficult to pay attention to people's faces when you're cutting someone's leg off with an angle-grinder. But given the reaction of the little girl, it was obviously the ubiquitous 'Pete.' Slater watched as Pete laid Paris on the floor and left.

"Get over to the safe house!" Slater shouted into his phone. "Ten minutes? Okay, just get there as quick as."

He dialled Paris again, but no response.

"How do you think those people found your daughter?" asked Nigel.

"Probably from this," replied Slater holding out his smartphone, Roach's car plain to see.

Chapter 46

The black Mercedes GLX turned off Piccadilly into the narrow one-way Brick Street, closely followed by a matching saloon. They pulled up opposite Yarmouth Place, in an empty taxi rank.

Gilbert and Jarvis got out of the saloon, and walked along to the even smaller dead-end road that Alistair had sent them to. As they walked past the 4x4, three more of Alistair's more burly security detail, his new batch of goons, emerged from it and followed closely behind.

"Here it is," said Jarvis. "Unit D."

They read the sign on the door reading *Libertas Research Laboratory*.

"Libertas, the Roman goddess, the embodiment of freedom. Libertas, the company, hawker of health supplements, vitamins and other crap," replied Gilbert.

"Indeed," said Jarvis, "let's see precisely what *other crap* they do here."

"So how do we get in?"

There were no obvious bells or entry system anywhere around the vicinity of the door. They searched around until eventually Jarvis spotted a small plastic door a metre or so to the side, seemingly just an ordinary electricity meter cabinet.

"Bit strange that being so high up, usually they're down nearer ground level," he said, taking a multi-tool out from his pocket and unlocking the door. "Bingo."

Behind it sat a control panel, with a standard number pad and an array of other biometric systems, retinal scanner, finger print pad, the usual things.

"Bollocks," said Gilbert, "Alistair never said anything about biometrics. We'll never get in now."

"Yes, it is a bit of a bugger," replied Jarvis. "But from the odd few times I went out on jobs with Stan and Eric, they taught me a fair amount about these systems. The regular people who go in and out of here all the time will use the biometrics, but there's always a back door in through the front door, so to speak. What I think Alistair has somehow got his hands on is the override key."

"Really?"

"There's only one way to find out. Read out the number."

"Three, three, one, one…"

Jarvis typed the number in as Gilbert read them out. As soon as he typed in the second *one* the keypad beeped and a message flashed up on the screen.

Incorrect code. Alarm activation in 10 seconds.

"Bollocks, what did you do?" asked Gilbert anxiously.

"Three, three, one, one, that's what you said," replied Jarvis as the screen counted down from ten.

10-9-8

"What? No, three, three, one, five I said."

7-6

"You bloody didn't. Look just read it out again quickly."

5-4

"Three, three, one, five…"

3-2

"…five, one, three, seven."

1-0

The whole street shook as the piercing alarm rung out.

"There," said Gilbert, pointing to a tick symbol that had appeared in the bottom corner. Jarvis pressed the touch screen and the alarm stopped.

"Bloody hell, I could do without this," said Jarvis. "I'm much more a desk-based expert than a field agent. Anyway, chances are they know we're here."

The door clicked loudly as the locking mechanism released and Jarvis pushed it open. He stood back as the three goons pulled their handguns from inside their jackets, held them at the ready and carefully entered the building. Once the last of them was inside, Jarvis and Gilbert followed, closing the door behind them.

*

"What's going on?" asked the Professor, walking into the office.

"Not sure," replied the Smart Man. "CCTV picked up two men tampering with the entry system. Nothing unusual there, there's always someone trying to find a way in here. But they somehow managed to override the alarm."

"The only person not here who would have been able to do that is young Daniel. Are you sure it wasn't him?"

"No, definitely not. But don't worry, Professor, security will be there in seconds. The show will still be able to go ahead later."

*

The three men edged through the darkness of the storage area, guided only by a small shard of light that came in through the skylight, brightening and fading as clouds passed in front of the moon. Suddenly, the second man stopped as a small red dot appeared on the head of his colleague two steps in front. Before he could react, a small airy pop came from behind, instantly blowing a huge hole in the man's head and he slumped to the floor in a heap. The others covered their heads, desperately trying to find shelter, just as the whole warehouse was flooded with light from the powerful industrial LEDs that hung from the roof. They turned to see four men stood on a metal stanchion above the roller shutter, each holding a powerful silenced semi-automatic machine gun, training their red sights on each of them.

"Throw your weapons to the side, and get down on the floor, hands behind your head," barked one of the men.

All four did as instructed. Another two armed guards dressed all in black entered the warehouse at ground level, training their guns on their prisoners.

"You two, up," they said, jabbing the goons in the back with their weapons. The two slowly stood up, keeping their hands behind their head.

Gilbert, who remained on the ground with Jarvis, looked over his shoulder to see that the four men who were on the stanchion had left, presumably to come and join their colleagues. Slowly, he stood up, keeping his hands raised.

"Gilbert," whispered Jarvis, grabbing Gilbert's trouser leg and knowing full well that the guards could probably hear him. "What in the name of all that is shit are you doing?"

One of the guards trained his gun on Gilbert's chest, who was walking towards them slowly, with his hands in his pockets.

"Get down on the fucking floor."

"Come, come, that simply is no way to speak to your guests. See, I'm really quite tired—"

"Take your hands out of your pockets. NOW!"

"…And I can't really be bothered to go through this amount of Hollywood bullshit. So, I suggest that *you* lay down your weapons, or even better, just give them to my associates here."

Jarvis stared in amazement at the size of the balls that Gilbert had seemingly, just this instant, grown.

"This is your last chance. Get on the fucking floor!"

"No, this is *your* last chance, before I really lose my temper."

The two guards looked at each other, unsure as to quite why their carefully trained techniques of shouting and gun pointing weren't making this person comply.

And that was enough. Jarvis leapt behind a pallet loaded with boxes as his heavies lunged for the guards, grabbing their guns and pointing them at the ceiling. The cavernous room filled with echoes of muffled gunfire, bullets ricocheting of the ceiling and bright muzzle flashes as the four men fought with each other.

Each of the goons disarmed their respective guard, one smashing the butt of the weapon into his assailant's face, the other kneeing his opponent in the groin before kicking him hard in the side of the head. As the first of the guard reinforcements came around the corner, he caught a bullet square in the shoulder, the force knocking him off his feet.

Jarvis remained on the floor, covering his head as the two minders took out another two guards. The final guard stopped, and placed his guns on the floor and knelt down with his hands on his head. The other three guards squirmed around on the floor as the goons collected their weapons.

Gilbert stood over Jarvis and held out his hand to lift him to his feet.

"It's okay, Jarvis, the nasty men with guns have gone. You can come out now."

"Piss off. What was that supposed to be? Some sort of Jedi mind trick?"

"I did read something once that in high stress, high pressure events, if you can throw someone off their stride by just being as normal as possible, it messes with their brains so much that they forget what they are doing. A friend of mine was walking home one night when a mugger accosted him with a knife, demanding his money. He just talked about the hedge of the house they were stood in front of, and how small the garden wall was. The mugger didn't really know to respond and ended up apologising, before bursting into tears and running off."

"Is that right?"

"Have you two quite finished?" shouted one of the goons. "The guards are secure. You need to follow us and, ideally, keep your mouths shut."

Chapter 47

Slater watched out the window as the Impreza pulled up in the courtyard. Even with the windows shut, he could hear the ludicrous thumping music and ridiculous exhaust. Roach climbed out of the car, did his usual stupid slide across the bonnet, and then grabbed a box from the passenger seat. Slater sat behind his desk and begun typing away just as Roach appeared around the door.

"Hey, hey, hey, Mr S," said Roach, spinning the box between his hands. "I've got a little present for you. First drop all delivered nice and safe. Second drop delivered to your door."

"Thanks," said Slater, without taking his eyes off the screen.

Roach waited, slightly uncomfortable at the distinct lack of a huge congratulatory man hug, or a crystal tumbler full of Scotch to toast their newly cemented business alliance.

"Soooo," he drawled, "I'll just leave this here for you and be off back to the house then."

He paused for another few seconds, waiting for something a little more, and when it never arrived, turned and made to go out of the office.

"William," said Slater, just as Roach made it to the door. "Before you leave, just take a quick gander at that screen there please."

Slater pointed the remote at the monitor and switched it on. He walked over and pointed to the live CCTV footage. Roach watched as the screen rotated between different cameras within the house. In none of them did he see Paris.

"Where is she?" asked Roach.

"Very good question," replied Slater, and he clicked on another file with the earlier footage of Pete entering the house and taking Olivia.

Roach's heart thumped and he could feel the sweat start dripping down his face.

"I… I… It wasn't my fault. Honestly, Mr Slater. I had already left to do your job for you."

"Uh-huh," nodded Slater, in an over-the-top mock agreement. "Quite right, you had no idea that this would happen, did you?"

"No, I swear. How could I? Please, I did everything you asked. I took Paris and the girl, I waited for your instructions, then when your man turned up I did everything he asked."

"Absolutely," replied Slater, clicking on another file. "You have nothing to do whatsoever…"

As he finished the sentence, Roach hyperventilated as he saw a screen dump of his Twitter feed, the photo of his number plate and the message about 'taking down the Brotherhood of the Righteous.' Roach froze, his eyes unable to move from the screen. He'd wondered what all those notifications were on his phone. He figured he was being more conscientious by ignoring them and concentrating on the job in hand. If only he'd checked it there and then. He would probably still have a death warrant on him, but at least he would have a head start.

"I swear, that wasn't—"

But he couldn't finish. His eyes had been so glued to the screen that he didn't see Slater's hand reach around his neck.

Effortlessly, Slater pulled him down to the ground and then placed a heavy size nine boot on the side of his face.

"I should crush your skull just for having to sit there and see my daughter noshing you off. You had to play the fucking big man, didn't you, you stupid little piss stain." Slater pressed harder on Roach's face; they boy's eyes rolling back in his head as he tried to protest his innocence. "Now, I put enough safety measures in place to make sure that you couldn't fuck up the very simple little task that I gave you, but somehow you still managed it."

Roach gasped for air as Slater released his foot, but the relief was short-lived as Slater planted his foot into Roach's gut, again and again and again. Slater leant down and grabbed Roach by the hood, pulling him upright to his feet, just enough so that he could wrap his arm around Roach's neck for the second time.

"Luckily, about an hour ago, this happened."

He angled Roach's head towards the screen as the footage showed Carl enter the house and pick Paris up off the floor. As he turned around, he was sent sprawling by Slater's men bursting through the front door. He fell backwards, Paris landing on his chest. As he tried to push her off, his head fell instantly still on the floor as the double-tap hit him square between the eyes.

"She's safe. Thanks to me. But your little stunt could've ended up a different story."

"My stunt?" gasped Roach. "I did everything you told me to do."

"The gun, you stupid little shit stain. Did you really think I wouldn't find out? Apart from possibly having a dead daughter, I could have had to deal with a dead girl as well. You seriously are the biggest, most fuck-witted waste of oxygen, aren't you?"

Slater squeezed harder, watching in the mirror as Roach's face grew darker and darker purple. It was a struggle letting him go. He knew that if Paris was found safe and well, and she discovered that he had killed her boyfriend, the ear bashing, tantrums and banshee-wailing, and just general years of grief, would simply be unbearable. But, he just couldn't bring himself to let go.

"So we're clear, you're dumped. If I ever see your stupid fucking chav-mobile anywhere near Paris again, I'll slowly remove whatever body parts of yours I can fit in my bolt cutters."

Just as he sensed Roach's body give one last shudder, his arm was wrenched away and a heavy fist landed right in the middle of his face, sending him sprawling backwards onto the armchair. As he tried to stand up, a foot pushed him back down.

"Good evening, Mr Slater. My apologies for the sudden intrusion. Allow me to introduce myself. My name is Alistair Goodfellow. This is my associate, Cornelius."

Slater cupped a hankie under his nose, sitting forward with his elbows on his knees. He shook his head and laughed. "That fucking little prick."

"Indeed," replied Alistair, "although if it makes you feel any better I don't think it was him who posted it. Now, we need to talk about my sister."

Alistair nodded at Cornelius who grabbed Slater under the arm and hoisted him to his feet. Slater shrugged him off and walked over to his desk. Alistair and Cornelius turned towards him as he casually perched on the edge of it.

"Do you two really think that, once I saw Roach's little message, I didn't think that you would follow him here? Do you honestly take me for some sort of fucking mug?"

Before the other two could react, he picked up a large knife that he used for opening letters from the desk tidy and threw it. The knife spun through the air and embedded in Cornelius's right shoulder, sending him back a few paces. He knelt down as he tried to pull it out.

"Damn, wrong side," said Slater. "I suggest you stay down, my friend."

Two of Slater's associates ran into the room and aimed Uzi sub-machine guns at Alistair and Cornelius. Alistair very calmly put his hands in the air as the two men frisked him, pulling out his wallet and mobile phone. Cornelius groaned through gritted teeth as they pulled him to his feet and did the same.

"Please take a seat," said Slater, pointing to the leather recliner and a smaller easy chair alongside. The two men did as they were told, and sat down opposite the giant TV screen, the guns never wavering from their aim.

Slater picked up the tablet from the desk. Alistair watched silently as the familiar log-on screen for the Majestic Road members' area appeared and Slater punched in his details.

"I was so, *so,* looking forward to tonight's episode, Al," said Slater, leaning into Alistair's ear. "Just me, a few beers, the rhyming maniac with the pointy nose and your sister having God only knows what kind of shit pumped into her veins. And as I watch, I can reflect. Reflect on how you, the most self-righteous, jumped up little turd I've ever met, took away my little brother. Oh, and threatened to do the same to me. But now, we can do it together."

"Your brother?" said Alistair. "But he was…"

"Yes, yes, yes," replied Slater, growing more excited, the adrenaline coursing through his body as the feeling of control and power grew. "He was McAllister, I'm Slater. Technically, we were half-brothers, but the half meant nothing. We grew up together, did everything together, looked out for each other, got bollocked together. Everything. Except the shagging blokes thing, that was purely his bag. I was happy enough just watching tonight, hoping that you would be there too to witness it. But if you weren't, hey ho, at least I could watch that scrubber of a sister of yours take one for your team."

Alistair took a deep breath. He wasn't going to rise to it, just sit, dignified as ever, and hope.

Just then, Slater's phone rang on his desk. He looked at the screen. *Paris (mobile).*

"Sweetheart, are you ok… You sound funny… You're still in shock? Yes, I understand, just try to relax, you're safe now. Yes, I saw Harris come and take the girl… No, of course it's not your fault. Okay, good girl… Ok… Yep… Love you too… Roach? Er, yeah he came back here… No, just get back here, you can see him then. Yes, I'll see you shortly… Love you."

He hung up and placed the phone back on the desk. Clapping his hands together, he paced around the room impatiently. It was so nearly time. All the strands of his plan had fallen into place and here, in the palm of his hand, he held the great Alistair Goodfellow. He was going to enjoy this.

"Right, it would seem that after your little stunt at my house, my colleagues tidied up the situation satisfactorily, including a nice little bullet or two to the brain of your boy. So, you're here, she's on her way back. I'd say that calls for a celebration. Cognac?"

Chapter 48

"Professor, we need to go," said the Smart Man, shutting down as many of the computers and monitors as he could.

"What about my dear Daniel? He meant a lot to me," said the Professor adopting a more solemn tone, a rare sign that any sort of human emotion existed beneath the mask.

"I'm sorry, Professor," replied the Smart Man. "I know that you were fond of him, that he looked after you when you first arrived, but I really do fear the worst. Unfortunately, Fowler also knew the game. Slater was a huge scalp. But the biggest rewards come from the biggest risks and Danny knew that Slater was a gamble. It was his choice. We will do everything we can to find him, hopefully gone to ground somewhere, but now we have to leave."

"But, my dear boy, we have a show to do," replied the Professor. "My newest creation is ready and that lady downstairs seems perfect."

"I don't care," replied the Smart Man. "Do you not understand, they're inside?"

"But the guards will see to them. You don't just walk into a building like this—"

"They did," he replied, cutting off the Professor. "It's a matter I'll be raising with HR, that's for sure."

The Smart Man collected the last of his portable gadgets and belongings, grabbed the Professor by the arm, and together they snuck out of the office into the corridor. They kept close to the wall, sliding along it until they reached the corner. The Smart Man stopped the Professor and peered around the corner.

"Okay, it's clear, follow me."

They darted across the corridor, trying to minimise the metallic echoes from their footsteps as they crossed the steel floor panels.

At the next junction, the Smart Man checked all directions then turned around to grab the Professor.

"Right, Professor, let's go," he said, heading for an illuminated exit sign above a door directly opposite. "Professor?"

He turned to see the Professor gone. The Smart Man retraced his steps and it wasn't long before he heard the faint whistling sound coming from one of the offices off the corridor. Peering around the door, he stopped dead as the two men, all dressed in black, held the Professor up against the wall with guns aimed. Before he could react, he felt a tap on his shoulder. He turned and found himself staring directly into the barrel of a gun that was barely millimetres away from his forehead.

"Peekaboo!" said the voice behind it. "I see you."

The Smart Man stared directly into the man's eye. He pursed his lips together and placed his finger against them.

"Ssh," he whispered and gave a wink, before smacking the gun out of the man's hand and elbowing him in the face in one fell swoop. As his assailant dropped to the ground clutching his face, the Smart Man planted a knee directly into his face, knocking him out cold onto the metal floor. The Smart Man bent down and collected the gun, just as the men inside the room released the Professor and trained their guns on him. The Professor cowered under a table as the three men pointed their weapons at each other in a two-on-one Mexican stand-off. After a few seconds, the silence was broken.

"Gentlemen, gentlemen," said Jarvis, strolling up behind the Smart Man and placing a friendly arm on his shoulder. "We're all grown-ups. Let's put the kettle on and talk about this like adults."

"Who the fuck are you?" asked the Smart Man.

"Well, my dapper friend, we are here to rescue our good friend Grace who I believe that you are holding somewhere in this facility."

"I don't know what you're talking about," replied the Smart Man, glancing over his shoulder while maintaining an unwavering aim with his gun.

"Come on. It's obvious that you are highly unlikely to make it out of this situation alive unless you start being reasonable.

So, why don't we just cut out the guff and then we'll be on our merry way. Now, we're going to lower our weapons so that we can all talk normally and we'd like you to do the same."

The two men in the office gently lowered their weapons, while the Smart Man did likewise, placing his gun softly on the floor beside him. Before he could react, Gilbert grabbed the Smart Man's gun, one of the goons grabbed the Professor from under the table, while the other goon jabbed the muzzle of his gun into the Professor's neck.

Jarvis's phone pinged up a message. Gilbert led the Smart Man into the office and sat him down on a chair next to the Professor.

"Okay, let's see who you really are, my good man," said Jarvis.

The Smart Man squinted as he stared at Jarvis, trying to evaluate him. They weren't what he expected them to look like, and he tried to work out quite how they had managed to make it this far. But what he did know was that this wasn't part of the deal he had signed up to.

"You see," said Jarvis. "My organisation has capabilities beyond even the reach of the secret security services in this country. During that last little scuffle, I was able to take a mug shot of your face and send it to my colleague for identification. See, we had a hunch all along that this operation was far too sophisticated to just be the work of common-or-garden drug pushers. We suspected higher forces at work. And it would appear that we were correct, wouldn't you say... Agent Xavier West, codename *Blackfriar*."

Agent West smiled as he stared at the screen of Jarvis's phone, his own security service personnel ID staring back at him. "That's an old picture you've got there."

"So, which are you... MI5, MI6?" asked Jarvis.

"Neither."

"Then I suggest you start talking," said Jarvis, as Gilbert leaned closer, placing his guns inches from West's head.

"Okay, we're not part of any Government department. Not officially anyway. Even if you were to expose us or kill us, or both, the Government would have a stance of total and utter deniability. It's not documented anywhere, although the funding is huge."

"To what end?"

"Have you heard of Project MK Ultra?"

"Yes, of course. It was the old CIA programme in the sixties, attempting to create methods of mind control using various means including drugs. Is that what Majestic Road is then? The British Government's stab at an MK Ultra."

"Sort of," West continued. "But it is so much more than that. It's about pushing the boundaries of human cognitive function. It's about social cleansing. It's about ridding the planet of some of the worst drug cartels in the world?"

"Ridding it? Surely you're providing them with the tools to become even more powerful?"

"Not so," retorted West. "We develop new substances, expanding our knowledge of the human psyche beyond the limits of regular medical ethics. But the work we do feeds back into mainstream medicine for the greater good."

"Christ, you sound like Josef Mengele," said Jarvis.

West shrugged. "Depending on the point of view, you could say that his work, along with others of the time such as Unit 731, was ground breaking. A shining example of what can be achieved when you are not hampered by morality. And anyway, I don't think you are one to lecture me on morals."

Jarvis looked at him quizzically.

"As I was saying," West continued. "We provide a platform to both demonstrate the new products that we produce and to sell them. This gives us means of covertly releasing these drugs into the community so that we can examine their effects en masse. The cartels not only take all the risk, but they also provide us with massive amounts of funding to help catch them. It's win-win as far as we are concerned."

"So, the cartels are unknowingly funding the fight against their activities by buying the drugs from the same people trying to stop them?"

"Basically, although we have to be careful to strike a happy balance. We don't want to scare them off. Which is why we offer the little sweetener that they can provide the guinea pigs."

"And where does this… thing… fit into the equation?" asked Jarvis pointing at the Professor. He reached forward, first grabbing the large leather hat and throwing it onto the floor before taking hold of the plague mask and ripping it off.

The Professor let out a small shout as the tight mask struggled to come off. Jarvis stared, stunned. The pointy, wizened features, the wrinkles, all in stark contrast to his on-screen persona. As if the costume made him come alive, his voice, his actions, all belying the true weakness hiding underneath. After a few seconds of awkward silence, he spoke.

"Nice to meet you, my dear," he said in a deep, gravelly voice, tinged with the remnants of an East Coast American accent, and every so often breaking into the high-pitched squeak more akin to a teenage boy starting the first stages of puberty.

"Gentlemen," said West. "We are lucky to have Professor Darius Black, one of the original scientists who worked on the MK Ultra project, on board and guiding our research."

"Yes," continued the Professor. "I was but a research graduate back then, responsible for synthesising the LSD being administered to the subjects. But I learned to appreciate the human brain for what it is. The single most exquisite miracle of nature on God's earth. I learnt to harness its power, to access its innermost secrets, to control it. But once Ultra finished and the political correctness brigade sunk their teeth into us, I was cast to the trash. For years I scraped around, dabbling in my own underground labs. Yes, I became something of a celebrity in the world of clandestine chemistry but I wanted more. And when a fellow visionary like West here contacted me, coupled with my advancing years… well, it was an offer too good to refuse."

"I can imagine," replied Jarvis. "Unlimited funding, unlimited human subjects, what's not to like. But there is the small matter of people being killed. On the show and in real life once your products hit the shops."

"Yes, absolutely," said West. "But firstly, the pigs we have on the show are criminals, they're the drug pushers and users, they're the sort of people that no one would give the slightest shit about going missing. And once our products hit the streets, that's where the social cleansing comes in. It's just another form of natural selection. The lioness will always target the weakest antelope from a herd and by doing so the average strength of the herd increases. In a way, the lioness is doing them a favour. And it's the same with us. Drugs such as ours will naturally filter to the most worthless of society, the most pointless. If we weren't providing them with their outlet, someone else would. But at least with us, they are adding value to society. We advance human understanding and they increase the average strength of society by removing themselves from it."

"Interesting logic," said Jarvis. "It's a bit like saying that drinking a lot of beer makes me overall more intelligent, because it only kills the weakest of my brain cells. But, Grace? She's not a criminal, how do you justify testing on an innocent person who just happens to have pissed off one of your members? Or do you consider it to be collateral damage every now and again?"

"Ha! Innocent?" snorted West, slamming the gun away from his head and standing up. The other two goons trained their guns on him as he walked towards Jarvis. "Don't think for one minute that you are the only ones with access to systems, with clever little gadgets for snooping on people. Don't think that we didn't do *our* research before you arrived. We know precisely who Grace Brooks is, and we know who her brother is."

"So what if you know she's Alistair Goodfellow's sister. That's of no use to—"

"And a knowing participant in the Brotherhood of the Righteous and their Red Room. So, before you start judging us and our operation perhaps you should point that very critical finger of yours at yourself. Is what we do so different to what you do?"

"How do you know all—"

"How do we know all this? Oh, grow up, how the fuck do you think? We know *everything*. The dark web isn't quite as free and anonymous as the stupid little fucktards that believe it represents their freedom like to think. The whole Tor project, Bitcoins, they're just one massive project. The conspiracy nuts would call it the New World Order, but really it's just one huge collaboration between all the secret services around the world. So, yes, we know who you are and what you do. But, I have to be perfectly honest, what you do is fucking brilliant. Hence why we hadn't come after you earlier."

Jarvis and Gilbert looked at each other. West held his arms out as if inviting a denial. He went and knelt down in front of the two goons, reached up to grab their weapons and pulled them down until they were both touching his head.

"So, come on chaps, why don't you shoot me? Because you know that your little secret is out, right? If I know, my organisation knows. If you kill me, if our little show doesn't go out tonight, what do you think will happen?"

Jarvis and Gilbert knew he was right and they couldn't risk it. If anything, they were starting to like this man. The two organisations, in a weird way, shared a level of synergy. To the outsider, questionable morals. To the insider, a fully justifiable cause. Gilbert dropped the magazine out of his gun and ordered the goons to do the same.

"So what happens now?" asked Gilbert.

"I suggest that you get the fuck out of here, before our backup arrives. And we are going to make ourselves ready for tonight's main event."

"Oh, you are going to love tonight's episode," said the Professor, excitedly. "My new creation is something I've been having a bit of fun with. I've been playing around with the *Psilocybe mexicana* and managed to alter the two effective components, psilocybin and psilocin, actually at a genetic level. It is my hypothesis that by refining it at such a level, it is possible to create a never-ending and permanent state of hallucination. And that is what we will see tonight."

"So gentlemen," continued West, "if you'll be so kind as to let us continue as we have work to do. Our guests will be coming online soon. But I think we have an agreement that we can mutually co-exist without stepping on each other's toes. Yes?"

"Not quite," replied Jarvis. "We can agree with staying out of your hair and you out of ours, but we can't leave here without Grace."

"Sorry, no can do," said West. "What good would the Professor's demonstration do if he didn't have a pig to test it on? If you have nothing to offer, then I'm afraid these discussions have all been for nought."

Jarvis sent out the goons, closely followed by Gilbert.

"I don't think you quite understand," said Jarvis. "We are not leaving here without Grace."

West sighed in frustration. Firstly, that these people had even walked in here and made demands and secondly, that they didn't appear to have understood the rules. He pulled back his suit jacket to reveal a holster over his shirt and took out the small revolver it held.

"Sorry, I think it is you that doesn't understand. If you have nothing to offer, then you get nothing in return. Clear? And unless my ears deceive me, I'd say that our backup has just arrived."

Chapter 49

Daisy hung up. It seemed strange telling a man like Slater that she loved him, even though the whole conversation was total fabrication. He seemed to buy it, and she hoped that it bought Alistair a little more time. She looked at the huge pink smartphone with its garish diamante protective cover and she wondered what this girl was like. It had always been a huge, empty black hole in Daisy's heart where the identity of her real father was concerned.

And here was a girl who seemingly had it all; as much money as she could spend, the latest smartphone, expensive cars and holidays. But could anyone really be happy having a father like Slater? Or like she had known no different when she was growing up, presumably this Paris did likewise. In any case, it was no longer Daisy's problem and she shut the phone down.

She stared out of the window of the black 4x4 waiting for Jarvis and the others to return. She had done what had been asked, but now there was something that she had to know.

Pulling out her own phone, she dialled the number for Pete Harris.

"Yes?"

Daisy hesitated.

"Hello?"

She took a deep breath. "Pete, it's Daisy. I just wanted to check that you and your daughter are safe."

"Really," replied Pete. "Presumably you're tracking the call."

"No, of course not," said Daisy, aware that her genuineness would be unconvincing.

"Triangulating the signal to find my location."

"No, I swear. This is just me on my own phone, I promise."

"I'm done listening to any attempts at promises from you and your family. Just leave us alone."

Daisy welled up. She knew he was right to be dismissive and her sense of loyalty to Alistair was strong, but she needed to explain. "Please, don't hang up. Please."

There was a pause of silence, but she could see that he hadn't disconnected the call.

"Please, I just wanted to explain. When Alistair took me in, I had nothing. Literally nothing—"

"I knew it," interrupted Pete. "I knew you weren't his daughter."

"No. I never had a father. I never really had a mum either. At the time Alistair found me, I had just spent the last two weeks living in a derelict caravan in the woods. Before that I had only just escaped from a house where Anwar kept me. He used to ply me with drugs and his friends would pay to do things to me."

"Anwar?" replied Pete.

"Yes. I know how much he hurt you," said Daisy, knowing his very name would be ripping open scars that Pete was desperately trying to heal. "He hurt me too. In a different way, but I am as much a victim of his evil as you were. I enjoyed watching him meet his end. It was me who called Aleksander. I couldn't stand by and watch you ruin you and your daughter's life by killing Anwar. Although I figured you would probably want him dead, so I decided to have someone else do it for you."

"You? You set all that up?"

"I couldn't let your daughter lose you as well."

"But how on earth did you even know what was going on? Surely Alistair doesn't involve you in his little project?"

"No. But I did see it first-hand. It took a long time for Alistair to convince me that he wasn't simply some crazy psycho who was going to do the same thing to me."

There was a silence again as the penny dropped.

"That was you, wasn't it? You caused the disruption during the McAllister episode."

The silence that followed confirmed Pete's assumption and he took a moment to take in all the information. He could see exactly why she would jump at the chance to live with a man like Goodfellow. Even after witnessing the same events that he had watched? But then her life seemed one long series of misfortune, a period she would be more than happy to put behind her. And having been in both hers and Alistair's company, he could see why she chose him. They were both charming, intelligent with a very strong, if debatable, sense of right and wrong. He had the power now to bring Alistair's empire crashing down around him. But that would affect her, and she had, in her own way, gone out of her way to help him. Taking down Alistair would mean that he would simply join the long list of people who had succeeded in making her short life an absolute misery. And he knew he would never be able to live with himself.

"Daisy," he said, "I meant what I said back at your house, that you are a very remarkable young lady. And I suppose I should say thank you for saving my life. Although I did actually nearly die. I have no argument with you, and I appreciate you setting the record straight. But I should warn you that if I ever feel the slightest inkling that myself or my daughter are under any threat *whatsoever* from Alistair, the whole truth will be plastered across social media quicker than you can say Clifton Manor. Is that clear?"

"Yes, Pete."

"Good, now if you'll excuse me, I need to return to my daughter. Have a nice life, Daisy, you deserve it."

"So do you, Pete."

And they hung up, both a little more fixed.

Chapter 50

"Well, Slater," said Alistair placing the tumbler down on the floor, "I'll say one thing, you do have great taste in Cognac."

"You haven't seen anything," replied Slater, snorting a long line of white powder from his desk. "Usually I don't indulge myself, but on a special occasion like this I thought I'd treat myself. Care for some?"

"No thanks," said Alistair, "drugs are for losers. Please, Slater, be reasonable, I'm sure we can come to some sort of deal. How much would it take for you to call them off? Two million?"

Slater put his head back, sniffing the powder down the back of his throat, and laughed. "Two million? What do you think I am, some sort of peasant? Try adding a zero on the end."

"Twenty million?"

"Impeccable multiplication. Yep, twenty million is the absolute bare minimum that I would even bother trying to call them off for."

Alistair rubbed his face with his hand. "Fine, twenty."

"Hang on," Slater said, running around the back of his desk, ignoring the huge offer that had just been presented. "Just you wait until you see my taste in designer lifestyle enhancements, then you'll really be impressed. Ah, talk of the devil."

The main phone sitting on Slater's desk rang. He placed it on speaker, turning the volume up as high as it went.

"Klaus, you Teutonic shitbiscuit, how's my latest delivery going down?"

"Curtis, you pasty fat English cock-sucker, have you been... how do you English say... living under a rock for the last hour? Try turning on the news."

Slater turned on the television and switched to the news channel. He punched the air triumphantly. Leaning closer to Alistair, he read out the bright red message scrolling across the bottom of the screen, as though reading a bedtime story to his child.

Breaking News: Nightclub Carnage. Multiple fatalities, dozens injured. Mysterious 'zombie' drug suspected.

The programme switched to the news reporter stood outside the nightclub, the blue flashing lights and screeching sirens of multiple ambulances semi-drowning him out. Behind him, trolleys were being wheeled out of the club, draped in blood-soaked white sheets, some still thrashing, fighting against the inhuman pain. The reporter grabbed a young girl running after a trolley.

"Excuse me. Can you describe what you saw in there?"

"It was horrific," said the girl, total fear etched into her face. "There were, like, bodies all over the floor. Other people were, like, sat on top of them, eating huge chunks out of their faces. It was, like, just like Walking Dead. Seriously."

"Fucking get in!" shouted Slater, going back over to the desk phone. "Do you see that, Goodfellow, do you? Klaus, good work my friend. There'll be an extra hundred Gs popping through your letterbox in the morning. Ciao."

Alistair shifted uneasily in his seat as Slater hung up the call. "They're innocent people, Slater. Innocent. People's sons, daughters, brothers…"

"Oh, spare me. You sound like a politician. Innocent? If they weren't taking drugs in the first fucking place then they wouldn't have turned into fucking zombies would they?"

"What about the people that they attacked?"

"Er, oh yeah, I suppose they were innocent. Serves them right for going to a shit club like Klaus's. Anyway, I can't sit around wallowing in my own glory all night. It's about to start."

Slater was running around like a birthday boy waiting for all the guests to turn up to his party, the mixture of alcohol and purest Columbian marching powder rendering it impossible for him to sit still. He tapped around the tablet, showing the Tor browser up on the monitor on the wall. The welcome screen to Majestic Road appeared and Slater typed in his log-on details.

"Slater," said Alistair again. "The twenty million?"

"Oh yes, of course," replied Slater, nodding. "Er, I'll tell them about it when we get to the bidding stage."

The psychedelic synthesiser intro to Baba O'Reilly thumped through the sound bar hanging directly under the television set. Slater turned the volume up to excruciating levels just in time for the first power chord.

"This is my favourite bit," said Slater, playing air guitar in front of Alistair.

The music died down and Slater lowered the volume as the silhouetted form of the Smart Man appeared.

"Good evening, my friends," he said. "Welcome once again to Majestic Road's members' area. We have a fantastic demonstration this evening, but before we get to that, I just want to say a little something. Our second newest knight of the round table, CS Associates, has already proved what a valuable asset they are to our organisation…"

Slater thumped his chest and then grabbed Alistair by the throat, forcing him back into his chair. "Hear that? I'm an *asset*. Unlike you."

"In case our other guests around the world haven't seen the news, our Brainfood is already doing its thing to a quite remarkable extent. But tonight, our product is a little different. It's something that the Professor has been experimenting with and represents the latest breakthrough in neural pathway customisation."

Slater typed into the message box; *Hopefully it's still going to fuck her up though, right?*

"Slater, we had a deal," protested Alistair. He made to stand up and go for Slater, but was promptly placed back in his seat by the muzzle of the machine gun.

"Nah, not for twenty million. I'll make way more shifting that little box of blue powder over there. Call it forty. No wait, fifty. Come on, Goodfellow, what's your sister's life worth?"

Cornelius looked at Alistair. He had his eyes closed, head slumped and was shaking his head. Cornelius smacked him on the arm, and gestured at the screen with his hand. "Come on, boss, think of something."

"I can't. I don't have that sort of cash free in one place to just transfer immediately."

"Good," replied Slater, "I think I'll stick with my original decision please, Monty, and take the demonstration."

The Smart Man continued. "Thank you for that lovely introduction, Mr Slater. Yes, I can assure you that it will *fuck her up*, although it won't kill her. Best if I let the Professor explain."

"Oooww," groaned Slater like a child being sent off to bed. "It had better be instant."

"Oh, it's instant all right," continued the Smart Man. "Unfortunately, we appear to be one member down. It is frighteningly rude of AG International not to put in an appearance, especially after being newly nominated by the man of the moment, Mr Slater."

Slater hastily typed a new message into the tablet; *Don't worry, they're watching it round my house.*

"Interesting. Okay, that's good, we'd hate for them to miss out, wouldn't we? Anyway, without further ado, let's get on to the demonstration."

The lights in the main warehouse came up revealing a single chair bolted to the floor right in the middle. Next to it was a small table with various glass receptacles, syringes and clothes. In the chair sat a slight figure, very obviously a female, with a hood over their head.

A door opened at the back of the set and out walked the Professor in full plague doctor outfit. He walked over to the chair and stood behind it with his arms out stretched.

"As heartbeat jumps and blood runs cold, I give to her my liquid gold.
Our pig is feeling such elation, as she tries my new creation,

Worlds she knows will cease to be, as she enters my reality.
The vivid colours, sounds and sights, all spinning their profound delights.
Every day a new surprise, until the minute that she dies.
The world is spinning round and round, the secrets of the brain are found.
When all is said and all is done, our pig has nowhere left to run."

Slater grabbed Alistair by the jaw and pointed his head at the screen. "Do you see, Goodfellow? Watch, man. Watch as that thing steals your sister's life away from her. Even if you make it out of here alive, which you won't, at least you know that your sister will be having the time of her life, wazzed off her tits in whatever permanent trip that freak up there is about to inject into her."

"Slater, please stop this, I'm begging you. Fifty million. Kill me after I transfer it. Anything. Just call them off."

Slater let go, and stroked his chin in mock contemplation. He watched as the Professor stirred the pale green solution with a glass rod, holding the flask up to the light, adding more powder and more liquid to achieve the perfect tone. "Okay, Goodfellow. It was fun seeing you beg. Fifty million, right?"

Alistair nodded.

"Okay."

Slater typed another message; *I have changed my mind about the pig.*

The Smart Man spoke, as the Professor sucked the solution up into a test tube. "Changed your mind? This is no time for a fit of conscience, Mr Slater."

The Professor continued, attaching the test tube to a cannula that hung from the back of the subject's neck. He paused awaiting further instructions.

"Mr Slater?"

Slater looked at Goodfellow and winked. *Double the dose, please Professor. Really fuck up that little scrubber.*

"No!" shouted Alistair again as he saw the message appear on the screen. "You bastard, we had a deal."

He watched as the Professor squeezed the entire contents of the test tube.

The Professor placed his apparatus back on the table, and placed a hand on the hood.

"Watch," Slater whispered into Alistair's ear, gripping him by the hair with one hand and wrapping a hand around his throat with the other.

The Professor gripped tightly on the loose flap of the hood with one hand, and pointed at the camera with the other.

"My drugs transport our pig to hell, I bow as their creator.

Before we bid a 'fare thee well'…"

He ripped off the hood.

"…to dear old Paris Slater."

Slater's grip weakened as his eyes froze on the screen. "Paris?" he cried.

He watch, transfixed, as his daughter's eyes rolled back in their sockets, as her head swung from side-to-side before stopping. The camera panned in on her eyes which darted as if following an imaginary butterfly. She laughed, looking around, followed by a guttural scream which cut through Slater like a knife.

"You fuckers!" he shouted, throwing the tablet against the wall. He turned to Alistair, grabbing the machine gun from one of his associates. As he aimed it at Alistair, Cornelius leapt from his chair, tackling Slater into the other associate, knocking him flying against the wall. Alistair leapt up, grabbed the machine gun from the floor and fired two well-placed shots in the centre of the man's thigh.

As the man howled and grabbed his leg, Alistair launched a snap kick at the other guard's head, smashing it between his foot and the door. Slater wrestled with Cornelius who easily overpowered him, pinning him to the ground on his front with his arms bent up around his back. Alistair finished off the remaining guard, who was still grasping his leg, with a vicious kick to the back of his head, knocking him out instantly.

Cornelius dragged Slater to his feet, his powerful grip keeping one arm pinned while his other trunk-like arm squeezed across Slater's chest.

On the screen, the camera panned away, leaving Paris tied to the chair as the Professor threw the hood into her lap and walked off.

"A short story, Mr Slater," began the Smart Man. "Back in the seventies, the rock band Van Halen used to make a demand on their backstage rider that there be a bowl of M&Ms in their dressing room with all the brown ones removed. To an outsider, this was simply the capricious demand of an egotistical rock band. In fact, the demand was listed in the band's technical requirements along with power availability and stage construction details. It was a test. If the bowl of M&Ms was present and the brown ones missing, the band could safely assume that the venue had read the rest of their requirements, and were taking their concerns seriously. If not, then the band could rightly doubt their credentials for hosting a safe concert."

Slater, his head forced to look directly at the screen, was silent. He simply huffed and spat as his heavy breathing strained against the iron grip that held him. "So?" he just about managed.

"Mr Slater, you really should select your associates a little more carefully," the Smart Man continued. "The rules at the drop-off were very clear. Follow every one of the instructions *exactly* or we would kill them. So if the people you select to do your work on our behalf can't follow a simple instruction like 'turn off the light' then it makes us doubtful of your ability to work with us. When we eventually caught up with them, and popped a couple of bullets in their foreheads, they had acquired a little extra baggage. Sorry, *baggage* is no way to describe your darling daughter. But when we heard what you had done to our colleague Danny, we were more than happy to exchange this utterly charming young lady for Mr Goodfellow's sister. We'll return her safe and sound. Well, safe at least. You can find her at the usual address in two days' time. For the rest of our esteemed viewers, my apologies for the slightly unorthodox events of tonight's show, but the good news is that the Professor's own personal recipe is available for your purchase, so start placing your orders."

Alistair switched off the television, retrieved his phone from the desk and called Jarvis. "Good work, my friend... Yes, we're ok... Slater's being... compliant... Yes, we just watched it... It's funny how fate deals its hand, isn't it? Anyway, need you to get here as soon as possible to go through all the security systems and remove any trace of us... See you back at the house."

The more Slater struggled, the tighter Cornelius gripped, until eventually Slater crashed. His eyes closed in resignation and his head slumped into his chest.

Alistair stood in front of him and gripped him by the face, forcing Slater to look him in the eyes. "Better luck next time, old chap."

Slater stared and mustering the final vestiges of aggression that he could manage, spat in Alistair's face, followed by a futile "Fuck you."

Alistair wiped the spit from his face with his hanky. "Indeed. Anyway, you're going to come with us. There's a very special friend of ours I want you to meet."

Chapter 51

*I*t has become a common sight in recent years, the 'Zombie drug' induced-victims stumbling around town centres, barely able to stand. But this new breed of recreational, if it can even be called that, narcotics is simply the stuff of nightmares. In the wake of this latest 'designer drug' atrocity, ministers are coming under increased pressure to clamp down on not only the clandestine chemists producing this filth, but also the dark web on which they ply their trade. If the regular drug war appears, at best, to be unwinnable, the market that exists even further beneath the parapet is probably feeling, right now, virtually untouchable. Robin Jones, BBC News, London.

Pete turned off the TV and tossed the remote onto the sofa. He had arrived back at the Lookout early that morning and was waiting for Olivia to pack some of her belongings in her suitcase. Despite his conversations with Alistair and Daisy, and his own confidence that he could bring down Alistair if he wanted to, he didn't feel safe coming home and the less time he could spend there, the better.

"Come on, sweetheart, hurry up," he shouted, before talking to himself. "Jeez, how many different clothes does she need?"

He scrolled down the endless news coverage on his laptop. Police had arrested a young teenager called William Roachford at a property of known underworld kingpin, Curtis Slater. They had also discovered a consignment of what they suspected was the drug responsible for the previous night's carnage. Most disturbing, they had finally found the body of Danny Fowler, horribly mutilated with a bullet wound to the head.

Curtis Slater himself was nowhere to be seen. Most of the reports hypothesised that he had simply underestimated the effect his new drug would have and had disappeared into hiding until the heat wore off. So desperate was he to save his own skin that he had left his psychologically disturbed daughter wandering aimless around the farm on her own. Apparently the mother was on her way back from the south of Spain. He recognised the farm and outbuildings from the Skype call with Danny, only now they were packed full of forensic investigators, uniformed police, and the press.

"I'm ready," came the voice from the hallway.

"Good," replied Pete, collecting his own suitcase and stowing his laptop under his arm. He went out to the front door to find Olivia there, coat on, shoes on, suitcase ready.

"Come on, Dad, I've been waiting ages."

Pete laughed and ruffled his hands through her hair. They walked out hand in hand to the waiting taxi parked in the forecourt and handed their bags to the driver.

He opened the door for Olivia and then, just as he was about to climb in and leave his entire life behind him, a car screeched across the driveway.

"Pete!" shouted Grace as she climbed out of the passenger seat before it had even stopped. She ran across the car park into his arms, and embraced him in the biggest hug she could manage. "I thought that I was never going to see you again."

"Grace," replied Pete, politely but slightly cold, "I'm glad you're okay. Your brother did well."

"What? I came back for you. Daisy told me that you said you were going away. I couldn't let you leave without me."

"You're not coming," said Pete.

"Please, Pete, why? What about the night before this all kicked off? We have something special, you know we do."

Pete unfolded his laptop, revealing the desktop screen. He opened the folder copied from Danny's memory stick and clicked on the file titled *Open Me Second*. The media player played a WAV file and he turned the volume up so that Grace could hear it.

Her heart sank as she heard herself talking, the conversation with Danny in the barn all of sudden coming flooding back.

There are millions of girls named Olivia; it's been the most popular girls name for like the last four years. It's not her, trust me. I'd know, right. I'm the one she called Aunty Grace. You only saw the photograph on his desk from a few years ago. I'm telling you, it's not her.

Followed by Danny speaking, and then Grace again.

But it's not her is it, so he won't. Pete's my only hope, you need to get him.

"Pete..." she stumbled.

"You knew she was with you at Slater's yet you tried to save your own sorry skin."

Grace panicked. She peered in through the rear window to see Olivia staring at her. Their eyes met and after a few seconds, Olivia turned away, her back to the window.

"Pete... I was confused, I didn't know what was going on. Slater had just cut off my goddam finger. I was scared and I just wanted you."

"Sorry, Grace. I think the fact that you would lie in order to save your own skin over Olivia speaks volumes. You and your brother are welcome to each other."

"Pete, please, I love you. We had something special and—"

"That was before I knew that you played me, Grace. I confided in you, trusted you with my most precious possession. During the Brotherhood investigation, I thought I was counting on you for your help when all along you knew exactly who it was we were searching for. You took advantage of my grief. How exactly do you expect me to ever be able to trust you again, or even look you in the eyes and see anything other than betrayal?"

Grace's demeanour changed from one of anguish to that of anger. She stepped back and pointed at Pete as she spoke. "I'll make sure my brother makes your life a living hell. You won't be able to hide. This guest house isn't worth shit. You've got nothing, no money. Nothing!"

Pete typed into the laptop and turned the screen so Grace could see it. He clicked on the final file in Danny's folder entitled *Open When You Are Safe.*

"That's not entirely true," he replied. "See, in this last file from Danny he very kindly pilfered Slater's entire wallet full of Bitcoins. Just over twelve hundred, to be precise. I've moved them all to my own wallet and converted eight hundred of them into regular cash. Even with the current volatility in their price, I still switched at a rate of around eight thousand pounds each. So, that means there's just under six and a half million pounds waiting for me in an offshore bank account, with another three million or so sitting in reserve for me should I need it. Okay, it's not as much money as Alistair has, but it's more than enough to ensure that you will never find us. Goodbye, Grace."

He closed the laptop and climbed into the car, pulling the door closed.

Grace banged on the bonnet as it drove away. The car carried on, barging Grace out of the way and the last thing she saw was the back of Pete's head as he pulled Olivia close for a hug.

Grace buried her face in her hands, sunk to her knees, and cried.

Chapter 52

"Ladies and gentlemen of the dark web. We! Are! Back!"

The Host strutted across the set, gold microphone in one hand, clipboard in the other, arms outstretched as if about to embrace a long lost relative. A thumping soundtrack echoed through the cavernous set, the pyrotechnic light display flashed around before stopping almost dead.

"I bid you welcome, my friends. Like I said, we are back for an extra special edition of the Red Room. The leader board is buzzing and already I can see a few familiar names. We've got SliderMonkey. We've got the gorgeous Housewife Superstar. We've got the equally gorgeous MafiaMama. Even UpsetDad has decided to show his face. I have a feeling that tonight will be one of the very best shows we have ever put on, and you, my friends, will be part of it. So let's not waste any more time and introduce our very special guest."

The double doors behind him parted and a plume of dry ice spread across the set. Two figures emerged in customary red retro tracksuits with white stripes. Between them a third figure wrestled for all he was worth, but he was no match. They dragged him down the front of the stage as the Host stood next to a large sheet. He grabbed the top of the sheet and, amidst a few more rockets and roman candles, dramatically whipped it away, revealing the sturdy wooden chair underneath. The two goons planted their prisoner down on the chair and strapped in his wrists and ankles with the leather straps and buckles.

"We promised, didn't we," said the Host calmly, looking into the camera and adjusting his tuxedo-patterned boiler suit, "that one day, *one day*, we would have this gentleman. We did his pet monkey a couple of years back in one of the most memorable episodes and now we have the organ grinder. Please welcome, Mr Big himself… it's… Curtis Slater."

Sounding like the master of ceremonies at a world championship boxing fight, the Host pulled the thick hessian sack, emblazoned with a large red 'V', to reveal Slater's bruised and bloodied face, a fat piece of duct tape covering his mouth. He blinked his eyes at the sudden influx of light and shook his head to remove the sticky blond tresses that were stuck to his head. The Host leant in and grabbed Curtis's face.

"This is where you learn about justice the Brotherhood way," he whispered before turning back towards the camera. "For those of you who may have been living under a rock and don't know who Curtis Slater is, he is nothing if not a total and utter shit."

Even through the tape, Slater clearly smirked as he listened to his unofficial biography and shook his head.

"One of the few people for who the term 'organ grinder' actually has a literal meaning. The sort of person who kidnaps small children, who unleashes frightening new narcotics on unsuspecting innocent people and generally hates everyone he ever comes into contact with. And do you want to know the best bit about it? He wanted to take revenge on us for killing his brother Cramer and for threatening to do the same to him. He even knows who we all are. Can't you tell he is just busting to shout it out? But you can't can you, Curt? In a break from tradition, we are not going to give Curtis the opportunity to justify his actions. We're just going to make absolutely sure that he regrets every single one of them. So, let's have the first bid."

The leader board flashed red and blue, a long list of names changing places as the bid values increased.

"Just a reminder that all proceeds from tonight's show will be going to a very worthy cause. The 'lifetime care for Curtis Slater's daughter, Paris, who is currently a delusional schizophrenic' fund."

Slater fought against the restraints at the sound of his daughter's name, the muffled scream only slightly audible over the sound of the Host.

Finally, the list of names stopped and a winner displayed on the screen.

"The winning bid seems an awfully small number compared to last time we did this," said the Host. "But I guess that's the nature of Bitcoins for you. And the first winner for tonight, with a bid of 1.3 Bitcoins is… Suspicious UniKorn. Hey, UniKorn, great to have you on board. Pick a punishment, any punishment, but make it a really nasty one."

Evening, Host, great to be here. Do you have the angle-grinder? I always loved that one.

"I'm afraid not," replied the Host, reaching behind the chair. "I've got a nail gun if that helps."

Perfect. Go with that.

"Okay, where do you want it?"

Go knee, bollocks, other knee and then a couple in the chest. Please.

Without hesitating, the Host fired a series of nails into the various body parts in exactly the order requested. Slater's body jolted violently against the restraints as each shot pierced deep into his soft tissue. The camera zoomed in on his eyes, clearly in pain, but now, and probably for the first time ever, mixed in with a lot of fear.

"Okay, next round of bidding please."

The names flashed, blinked and changed for another minute while the Host stepped off stage to take a drink and admire his new blood-soaked work of modern art.

"Wow, that's a fantastic bid right there; 2.3 Bitcoins. That'll go so far in helping young Paris fight her demons. Not her inner demons. The actual ones that she sees floating around the room every minute of the day. Anyway, the winner is our old friend DredHead. Awesome to have you back, Dred. What would you like to do to young Mr Slater?"

I think I speak on behalf of everyone here, Host, when I say that we've missed you and we want you back.

"Ah, Dred, I'm really touched. Never say never."

Excellent. To celebrate, I would like to go old school. Something with the clipboard.

"An excellent choice."

The Host carefully removed a strip of plastic from the bottom of his clipboard to reveal a pristine silver blade. He rested it over the top of Slater's hand, ruffled his hair, and then slammed the heel of his palm down, slicing Slater's hand off across the metacarpal bones. Slater's eyes widened in horror, frozen in shock at the sight of the wounds on his hands.

"And the other one?"

No I don't think so, thanks, Host. One's enough... Only joking. Of course!

The Host repeated it on his other hand, leaving Slater hyperventilating through his nose, spraying snot and sweat all over his legs.

"We've just about time for one more. It's the last one, make it a good one."

For the final time, the names on the leader board switched and changed as the Host counted down. "Five... four... three... two... one... And the winner is..."

He stopped, looked at the camera and then again at the leader board as the winning name flashed up. *Lostboy.*

"Ah-ha," said the Host, slightly nervously. "It would appear that we have a new viewer with us today, who just trumped everyone with that final bid. Welcome, Lostboy. What can the Brotherhood of the Righteous do for you today?"

Leave me alone. Forever.

"Right... okay. You're supposed to suggest a punishment for Curtis here. And I'm sure that it doesn't take an awful lot for you to imagine what you want doing to him, especially after what he put you through, right?"

I couldn't give a fuck about Slater.

"I see. Would you like to pick anyway? It's kind of why we're here."

Do what you want. Just leave me alone.

"We did come to an agreement, didn't we," he said, spotting Jarvis behind the control desk desperately making a 'cut' motion, which he ignored.

Yes, we did, and as long as you stick to your side of the bargain, so will I.

"Of course we will."

Good... I can't say the same for Mr$pangle though...

And with that, *Lostboy* disappeared from the leader board.

*

Pete hit 'enter' and then closed the laptop just as Olivia came running across the deck carrying two bottles of Coke and two ice-cream lollies. They sat down on the bench gazing across the sea back towards the mainland as the sun set over the Statue of Liberty.

"I think I'm going to like America, Dad."

"Me too, sweetheart," replied Pete. "Just one more thing to do."

They stood up to go back inside, and with no one looking, Pete dropped the laptop over the side into the choppy waters below, watching as it disappeared beneath the surface.

The End

CPSIA information can be obtained
at www.ICGtesting.com
Printed in the USA
LVHW111711010320
648615LV00003B/628